Untethered

A Magic iPhone Anthology

edited by Janine A. Southard

Contents

Acknowledgements from the Editor

I'd like to offer special thanks to editor Elise Mattheson, who kindly provided feedback on the one poetry submission to this anthology. While ultimately the poem didn't fit in the scope of this collection, I was very lucky that Mattheson made time in her schedule to read a multi-page epic (even consulting with another colleague who specializes in the type of poem!) for a relative stranger.

Plus, I learned a valuable lesson thanks to that one poetry writer: don't accept poetry submissions without a poetry-editing expert on hand.

Also, I have to thank my spouse, Jeremy Barton, who listened to my constant deliberations over the stories, who advised on software programming issues in a few of them, and who believed this anthology would be awesome even before the call to submissions went out.

This anthology might not have happened without every single person who read, reviewed, Kickstarted, and begged for more of *Cracked! A Magic iPhone Story*. Thank you all for reading and making these magical iPhones so popular.

Introduction

Our smartphones organize our lives, find our locations, and sync with all our other tech. We sleep with them beside our pillows. We check in with them first thing in the morning and last thing at night. They're everywhere, and though they come off the manufacturing lines seemingly identical, it takes almost no time for them to be easily distinguishable—whether based on apps and settings, or on cases and cracks.

Yet, for all we users know, they could be made out of magic.

I mean, how much do you know about how yours works? Could you take it apart and put it back together? And do you need to know these things in order to love it (or at least to respect its functions)?

Phones may have replaced the car as the "tool an average person could've built and fixed a mere generation ago, but now? Hah!" And, much like cars, we wouldn't want to do without them.

Ten years back, if you'd convinced me to toss out half the things in my purse or on my desk for a smartphone, I'd have kept all my stuff as a backup. Now I don't use a calendar or physical task list. Americans rarely grab a map from AAA before going on a road trip anymore, confident that their phones' GPS units are robust enough for anywhere they want to go. (Personal tip: this doesn't work so well if you cross a country border and don't have data turned on in, say, Canada.)

Are smartphones here to stay, or are they just another development on the road to something more permanent? Either way, this anthology looks at smartphones as they are...or, I suppose, as they would be in worlds with magic.

This volume includes twenty stories about the intersection of technology and magic in our smartphones. This necessarily means that the stories are very *now*. They record the fears and beliefs, the hopes and imaginations of this particular moment in time. Some pieces involve a hidden fantasy world, while others envision an alternate 2016 where magic is commonplace, and one bucks this trend to view our current world through the eyes of a magic-using outsider.

In choosing stories for this anthology, I wanted to find pieces that made smartphones even cooler than they already are. Face it; our phones are already something out of a science fiction novel. Technological and wonderful. Adding a "magic" lets these 21 authors play in the world of "sci fi device *plus*." *Untethered* isn't about the phones themselves; it's about going beyond the tech.

Many of these stories are very positive about their smartphones with extra magical oomph. You won't find the complaint that "people don't talk to each other" on their phones in this anthology. Instead, you'll read stories of greater communication. Here are the phones that play matchmaker and save lives. Here is the joy of taking the perfect selfie and starting your own magic app company with the help of a server demon.

I hope you'll enjoy all 20 stories of magic, technology, humor, and cleverness. (Sometimes all four.)

Swipe right to unlock.

Janine A. Southard
April 20, 2016

—Introduction, honest to goodness, written on my iPhone—

ERROR: KAPPA NOT FOUND

by Amanda Hackwith

———⊂⫘⊃———

The kappa was screwing with her IP authentication again. The server had failed its checks for the third time today.

Malora Clover gnawed on the frozen candy bar that constituted her lunch as she thumbed away another error notification on her phone. She'd just managed to return to her Zombie Match game when a new notice clogged her screen again. Mal swore and dropped her bar on the table with a *thunk*.

"Curse jar gets a dollar," Ronnie said. He didn't look up from his tablet.

"So dock it from my pay."

"We aren't making money yet."

"Then take it from my stock."

"At a tenth of a penny per that's…" Ronnie furrowed his brow, and Mal was immediately glad he didn't handle their financials.

Ronnie, Zapsumo's sales guy—"director of marketing!"— was more of a people person. Broad but chubby around the edges, like an affable footballer gone to seed, he was just approachable enough to maneuver his way around investor meetings and industry hackathons alike. Which was good, because neither Mal nor their cofounder, Bethany, could charm their way out of a paper bag.

Well, being a wizard, Bethany could *literally* charm her way out of a paper bag, but Mal didn't think that counted. Ronnie was the much-needed face of Zapsumo.

"Well." Ronnie gave up counting. "We'll just say another sprint or two of cursing, and you'll owe me the company."

Mal waved him off. She swapped her phone for her laptop and jabbed at the keys. She brought up a terminal window while she grumbled about temperamental server daemons under her breath.

Mal was what Ronnie introduced to potential investors as the "technical founder." As far as Mal could tell, that meant she evenly divided her time between keeping the app afloat and trying to plug holes in the marketing website's spaghetti code that Ronnie had thoughtfully outsourced when she wasn't looking.

"What's the fire this time?" Ronnie asked.

"Kappa."

"Again?"

"I told you, with the traffic we're starting to get, we need to upgrade to a full-on demigod core to handle the cantrip requests. A sylph, maybe. Or Beth and I had ideas about grafting an undine with the cooling and..."

Ronnie made a face. "You know we can't afford a new summon."

"So off to the server room I go. Again."

Mal heaved an extra-heavy sigh for Ronnie's benefit. She shoved the rest of the candy bar in her mouth and swept up her phone before heading to the door. She dug out her earbud, flicking the voice commands on. "Call Sparkles."

"Mal?" Bethany's voice chirped in her ear a second later.

"Your gremlin is fucking up my life, Beth."

Mal clomped down the stairwell. They technically only rented part of the workspace co-op. However, once Mal and Bethany had started filling the server room with franken-creatures like the Kappa deck—part hacked-together hardware, part shackled magical beastie—the rest of the renters had graciously given them their space. They were forced to host their own servers since the whole magic-as-a-service thing didn't exactly have ISPs lining up to take in stray daemons.

Uber for magic! Tap and summon up a spell! Cast from your phone and avoid guild fees. Disrupt the wizard elite! Ronnie pushed a bright, rosy vision to investors, but it came with a whole new set of problems.

"Kappa is technically a river guardian, not a..."

"What's the river *guardian* freaking out about this time? Because it sure as hell isn't hardware. That's a brand new rig," Mal gritted through her teeth.

"Hang on. I'm pulling together a scry in the living room."

Bethany was the only daughter of one of the oldest magical families in San Francisco. That led to a lot of friction with her relatives, who didn't appreciate the idea of "app-ifying" their field, but it meant her house was tricked out with every dusty monkeyclaw a wizard could require. Since Beth used a wheelchair, she found it easier to telecommute most days rather than deal with the hassle of the workloft's creaky elevator. And since her work as the company's arcane founder was not, per se, operating in the same physical plane as the workloft, it generally worked out okay.

Today was not being general.

Mal hit the bar on the server room door with her hip. "If this thing is just missing its mommy, you're going to have to get down here and—"

The server room was lit by auxiliary lights, accented by blue blinking LEDs. The door stopped abruptly as it hit something with a faint wet sound. Mal looked down.

A crumpled finger pointed neatly to the toe of her sneakers. The crumpled finger was attached to a mangled arm, which was attached to its body by only crushed flesh and a growing pool of blood that was black in the dim light.

The body was folded over against the door. The sight of familiar spiky orange hair hit her like a punch. Chocolate and bile revisited Mal's throat.

Zapsumo was too small to have much in the way of employees besides Ronnie, Beth, and Mal. Still, Ronnie had a younger cousin with a knack for running cables, and Ronnie had worn Mal down with the promise of help with the hardware.

"Anup." Mal meant it as a whisper, but it came out more as a squeak. The intern didn't move.

"Mal?" Beth asked in her ear.

"New plan. Tell everyone to go home and call the police or the sparkly police or—god, whatever your dad's guild uses for bad days? We need—"

Metal groaned as the nearest rack, burdened with a dozen blades of blinking lights, tilted toward her. Mal lost her grip on the door and tripped over Anup as she dove out of the way.

The server room was even dimmer with the door closed. She could just make out the racks that lined the walls and the dim glow of a Yoda lamp someone had left on the tiny folding table that served as Anup's desk most days. She fumbled for a flashlight in the table's mess.

Mal's throat clenched thinking about Anup, but then a slithering sound shot ice up her neck. Mal pivoted, searching the cramped basement. "Beth...?"

"I called my dad. Hold on, Mal. I don't get why my scry isn't picking up any..."

Mal swiveled her light, and a pair of navy saucers mirrored back at her through the dimness. The eyes were darker than the blue LEDs and were perfectly set into a slim shadow. A growl fluttered through the room.

And Mal forgot to breathe.

"Beth. Your gremlin is loose."

Beth took an audible breath. "That's... that's not possible. You must be—"

The eyes blinked out. A rack shuddered to her right. Mal jerked back until she found the wall. "Whatever you say. But 'not possible' is here, and sounds very angry. How do I make it not eat me?"

"Uh. You don't happen to have a cucumber on you?"

"Oh, sure. A cucumber. No problem. I'll just..."

Mal's throat constricted as a form swayed out from behind the racks. The silhouette was tiny, childlike. The shape of a girl with long hair in wet tangles against her head. But then it moved, and lamplight fell on its face.

Thick, glistening scales painted the kappa's body in muddy green and malice. Its face was vaguely human but with eyes too wide and a lipless mouth that pulled back to reveal razorblade teeth. Gills slit its throat, fluttering with each breath. It took another liquid step towards her, eyes narrowed.

Mal dimly decided it had seemed smaller when it was asleep and coiled around a hard drive.

A small window in the door cast light on the kappa as it approached. A faint chain pattern was permanently seared into the scales across its chest from where Beth had bound it.

They'd stumbled on the rather unorthodox technique for fusing arcane upgrades to mundane hardware while in college. Their early melds had been hacky, brute-force experimenting. Smashing one world against another. Like many magical creatures, kappas had a source of power they had to remain near. In the kappa's case, it was a pearl, kept in a home water source. Binding that pearl to a hard drive's liquid cooling system meshed the creature with the technology and made the magical storage and transfer of Zapsumo's service possible.

Bethany had placed simple magical bonds on top of that to keep the kappa drowsy and docile—important for a water creature in a room full of electronics. But those chains were gone, ripped away from raw flesh. The kappa was free of its limitations but still tethered to the server. Mal almost couldn't blame the thing for being pissed.

"Bow," Bethany hissed.

"You're kidding, right?" Mal slid her back along the rack, trying to maneuver around the kappa, but it twisted with her.

"Most supernatural creatures recognize manners. Bow, and make it a deep one. Lower your eyes."

Mal hadn't dared look away from the kappa since she entered the room, and she was not about to start now. "Fuck no."

"Dad says ABRA will be there in twenty. You really think you can dance around for that long?"

Mal made a feint and nearly twisted her ankle avoiding the kappa's claw. The creature may have still been tethered to the server by its pearl, but it had enough range to completely block her way to the door.

And she was close enough now that a hazy cloud of sour fish hit her nose. Mal swallowed hard before squeezing her eyes shut. "Bowing."

The growling trailed off. Mal opened her eyes with a wince. The kappa stopped just out of arm's reach, black eyes narrowed at her. The slits where its nose should have been twitched once. Then, with a liquid movement, it returned the gesture and bowed. A thin stream of water began to stream off its hair and puddle between its feet.

"Hey," Mal breathed, straightening. "I think we're in business. It—"

"Keep bowing!"

"What? You didn't say—" Mal jerked back as the kappa snapped up. The stream of water stopped. Its lips were pulled back from black peaks of sharp teeth. The wet growl in the air immediately grew louder. It made a flicking motion with its hands, and narrow surgical claws shot out between webbed fingers.

"You got to keep bowing until all the water runs out of its forehead."

Belatedly, Mal could see the small dimple where a steady stream of water flowed up and over its crown of hair.

"Too late." Mal toppled the rack of servers between them as the kappa lunged forward.

"ABRA will be there in just—"

"ABRA can eat me." Mal fled back along the wall. "You need to gimme something else."

There was a pause while Bethany considered. "Fire."

"Fire?" Mal verified the kappa was still pacing a tight circle around the server and pulled out her phone. "Keep talking."

"They used to hold fireworks festivals to ward off evil kappa. They were supposed to be scared of it. Explosives, fire. That might hold it off until ABRA gets there."

"Uh. Guys…" Ronnie's voice cut in, patched into the call. "Not that I add much when you two get going, but that server room has a Grade A fire suppression system, and our entire livelihood is on equipment in there. Equipment that doesn't react kindly to water. Or fire."

"A little cantrip might not trigger it."

Mal pulled the Zapsumo app up and flicked past the annoying logo animation. Their app was groundbreaking in that they'd figured out a way to deliver and store a spell in a smartphone, wirelessly, and without the usual fees, rituals, and hoopla the wizarding guild applied to that kind of service. Instead of having to bring an artifact to a wizard and have him fuss over it for a few days before a spell was attached, mundanes like Mal could press a button, pay a fee, and boom: instant magic wand in your pocket.

The problem was that phones weren't the best for holding a magical charge. Circuit boards and plastic were crap artifacts. As much as Bethany and Mal experimented, they could only seem to reliably transfer cantrips: cheap, weak spells with only mild utility. Fancy lights, finding your keys, stuff like that. And a phone could only hold a single-use spell at a time before you had to go back and buy a recharge. Their early users liked to grumble it was part of Zapsumo's sneaky business model, and Ronnie loved to promise investors the moon, but the embarrassing fact was they just couldn't figure out how to make it work yet.

Mal's phone still had a basic untangling spell loaded from when she and Anup had attacked the supply closet in a fit of spring cleaning. Mal's throat clenched, and she very carefully did not look at the intern's slumped form as she dismissed the spell.

The kappa was moving again, traceable by the methodical, wet drag-scratch of fish-like skin across the floor. Mal hunkered down lower behind the rack and muttered as she flipped through the Zapsumo store. It was a miracle it was even still up and running with the way the beast was thrashing through the room. "C'mon, c'mon..."

"Pocket Spark," Bethany prompted.

"Found it." Mal flew through the purchase window and hummed under her breath as it loaded. "Load, dammit."

"It's too small to hold off the kappa on its own."

"Already ahead of you." When the loading screen flipped to an illustration of a cheesy top hat and wand, Mal tightened her grip on the phone and ducked around the corner of the server rack. The amount of flammable material in the server room was minimal, but they'd just had to replace a backup drive. The box and sundry packing materials were still by Anup's desk. It was beyond the kappa's server, but if she could get past it to—

The center of the room was empty. The kappa was gone.

"Well, shi—"

Mal spun around just in time to catch a child-size blur before something sharp—several sharp somethings—sank into her knee. A shriek tore from her gut as she fell backward.

The kappa gurgled. It withdrew its webbed hand and flexed the claw tips before drawing back to strike again.

"Mal?!" her headset squawked, but Mal couldn't afford time to answer.

She just barely managed to avoid taking the server rack down with her. The kappa followed her to the floor and landed heavy on her chest. This time its claws sank into her shoulder. The kappa leaned forward, and a jagged, lipless grin filled her vision. A dark substance trickled out the side of its mouth, too dark for water.

Try as she might, Mal couldn't pry her eyes off those teeth. The phone was still in her hand, but it was wedged beneath the kappa. Mal inched her fingers around. She pointed the phone toward what she hoped was the kappa, rather than her own gut.

She swiped a thumb.

A muffled chirp sounded, and her phone grew hot in her hand. Something singed her fingers enough to make keeping a hold on it painful. The kappa's black eyes flew wide with a soggy screech. The smell of humid steam and the signature ozone smell of magic hit Mal's nose.

The kappa launched away, slicing more of Mal's chest as it went, but Mal didn't care. The minute the creature was off her, she scrambled to her feet and heaved a rack into the space created between her and the water beast.

"Mal?" Bethany was fully panicked by the time Mal slid far enough along the far wall to risk answering.

"Technical difficulties. I need to queue up another spell." Mal could hear the kappa moving around, but it didn't seem to be getting any closer for some reason. She flipped back to the app on her phone, and her thumb flew over the screen to load another spark spell.

The screen froze.

"Oh no..." Ronnie's mutter cut through her. Mal squeezed her eyes closed and cursed.

"Don't tell me. The shit took the server down."

"Yeah. I can spin it back up from our redundancies, but it's going—"

"—to take time. Yeah, I get it." Mal resisted the urge to chuck the phone across the room and instead shoved it in her pocket. She crept around the rack and saw the kappa trashing a rack near the door, just waiting for Mal to make her move.

Mal scanned the room for something, anything, to keep her from dying in her own server room. Her eyes were drawn to Anup's Yoda lamp, sitting on his desk. It was one of the few points of light in the room. An idea clicked into place. "All right. Let's try it my way."

"What?"

Mal ignored Bethany. "Ronnie, you still there?"

"Uh, yes?" Ronnie's voice wavered uncertainly.

Mal clambered between racks to reach Anup's desk, careful to keep out of the kappa's line of sight as long as possible. When she was nearly to the corner desk, she dropped the stealth and began dislodging and tipping any equipment in reach.

That got the kappa's attention. It glubbered its fury and launched itself on Mal's makeshift barricade.

Mal groaned and rubbed her shoulder as she snapped up Anup's keyboard. "I've got to start working out."

"Mal?" Bethany's voice rose a pitch.

"Ronnie, don't bother raising the servers. May want to tweet the users that we're about to go down for a prolonged round of maintenance." Mal took a hard breath as a familiar terminal window resolved on Anup's screen. The kappa roared again. "Or a press release announcing a sudden vacancy. Hey, if there's only three of us, does that count as a major downsize?"

"Not funny," Ronnie muttered.

"Just watch the servers. The slimy shit gave me an idea."

Mal fell silent as she typed three lines. Staccato taps interrupted the kappa's murky gurgles as it nearly cleared the trashed racks.

The kappa was connected to its server. And Mal was a programmer.

It was a stupid trick, what she was trying. Typically, the worst a technically minded malcontent could do to a server was to temporarily bring down software. But there were nasty, clever little scripts that could encourage a machine to commit suicide. Scripts that spin a server up with impossible tasks, overheating things, at least temporarily until the server shut down. And all Mal needed was a minute.

Any good server was protected against this kind of brute attack. For it to even have a chance, those scripts needed root-level access, terminal talking directly to the server with godlike permissions that escaped all the advanced security and self-preservation methods. Access that no one in their right mind gave anyone except the sys-admin.

So you needed administrative access. And a wasted youth learning all the malicious things you can do with a terminal window.

Mal had both.

She hit the Enter key just as metal shrieked behind her.

The path between Mal and the kappa was clear, though black blood dripped from its claws where it had torn against the server racks. It lurched toward her.

A grinding noise brought it up short. They both stopped and listened to the high-pitched squeal of a hard-drive fan working overtime. A low, grating *bzzt* kicked in as the hard drive began to struggle to execute the infinite tasks Mal had commanded.

It wasn't struggling fast enough. The kappa's clawed hand found her throat. Its skin wasn't as wet and clammy as it looked. The claws felt smooth and surprisingly warm, though not as warm as the blood that began to pool beneath as it flexed points into her skin.

The kappa hurled her across the floor. Her head bounced hard against metal. The impact on her spine sent gray fireflies flooding through her vision.

When Mal blinked, the Kappa's dainty scaled feet stopped in front of her. A furious, wet hiss floated somewhere above her ear, but Mal didn't look up. Her eyes were reserved for the server box still blinking in the center of the room. The lights flickered rapidly, a busy blue. Very busy.

The server was beaten, dented, but still working. Mal's heart dropped until she noted one more thing in the dim lights.

It was steaming. The liquid cooling was steaming.

The kappa lurched. A dull hiss squealed from the box as the processors continued to churn over unsolvable problems. The liquid cooling of the rig couldn't keep up with the heat the processor was throwing out. And, as Bethany had said, the kappa was a water creature. Connected to the server's liquid cooling by its pearl.

Mal was aiming for cooked kappa.

It lashed out one more time and caught its claws on Mal's shoulder, raking down. But there was little strength behind it. The kappa made a high-pitched wail that matched its machine's anguished sounds and fell forward.

A second later, there was a subdued beep as the server box overheated and died.

"Mal? ABRA is onsite and coming in."

"Of... course they are," Mal wheezed. She extracted the kappa's limp claws from her shoulder. "You know, I really shoulda thought of something clever to say."

"Huh?"

Mal gave the thing a kick for good measure, then fell back with a wince. The cold floor felt good beneath her throbbing head.

Such a comfy floor.

Good floor.

Mal closed her eyes.

———⬡⬡⬡———

Anup had made it to the operating table in time, if just.

After a few hours in the emergency room herself, Mal was patched up and folded into a cab headed to the workspace. ABRA, as useless as they were, had already cleaned up and gone. When Mal arrived in Zapsumo's break room, Bethany announced that the kappa had survived, and she'd contained it to a circle.

Mal decided she should have kicked the thing harder.

The kappa was changed, free of the server box. It crouched in the center of the circle, legs tucked neatly underneath it as it took careful, calculated bites of a cucumber. Bethany had even washed and bandaged the kappa's wounds and given it a set of purple sweats to wear. Mal tried to feel only slightly resentful.

Bethany brought the front wheels of her chair up to the thin line of black salt, but no farther. She'd given them stern orders to stay back, with which Mal was all too happy to comply. Let her arcane founder deal with the murderous critter. Mal had done her shift.

It wasn't as if she could have understood it anyway. Bethany and the creature spent the ensuing hour burbling at each other. The wet slurry of clicks and gurgles that came out of Bethany's mouth was impressive, but not nearly as impressive as the way the creature stilled and listened to her. The kappa held its head at a cant, pitiless navy eyes glinting at Bethany with near amusement.

Mal watched until her nerves couldn't take anymore. When she returned from the vending machine, Bethany and the kappa were engaged in even more animated conversation.

"C'mon, you little fucker..." Mal muttered under her breath as the Fritos bag slipped from her good hand again.

"Just give that here." Ronnie nipped the bag of chips from her lap and tugged the top open. He stole a handful before handing the bag back to her with a flourish. "Shouldn't you be eating healthier after what you went through? You just got out of the hospital."

Mal held up her bandaged arm. "It's not cancer, Mom. Some sutures and a fractured wrist."

"Maybe your bones are all paper-like from not enough vitamins."

"Maybe your head's all pudding-like from not enough minding your own business."

Ronnie looked abashed. "Come on. This thing scared me half to death. We got to get you and Bethany insured."

"No way..." The first human words from Bethany's mouth in an hour made Ronnie and Mal look up. Bethany raised a finger and gave the kappa a burble that seemed to mean "one moment" and turned toward them. "She wants to negotiate."

"We gathered that by the flying spittle," Mal said.

"She?" Ronnie echoed.

Bethany shrugged. "That's what the kappa prefers. She wants to negotiate for employment."

Ronnie stopped with a chip halfway to his mouth. "What?"

"The kappa doesn't want to get enslaved back to the server, for obvious reasons. We can't let her loose, for obvious reasons." Bethany waved her hand vaguely. "She wants to strike a deal to work for us. In exchange, she'll keep running our magical cores peacefully."

"It savaged Anup..." Ronnie reminded.

"Any magical creature can have geas put on it to render it docile. We didn't use them before because of cost. More expensive than the simple bonds we were using, but we can control her whether she's attached to a server or not."

"You're joking," Mal said.

Bethany shrugged. "If it helps, she said she would work for free. Well, free and cucumbers. I can whip up a Babel spell here if you'd like to talk to her yourself."

"That is a heart-felt 'fuck no.'"

"Free?" Ronnie brightened. "You know, if we can control it—er, her—we could use..."

"I said no!" That came out more strangled than Mal had intended. She grimaced into her Fritos. When she looked up, she noted that the kappa was watching them intently. Mal thought it was smirking. "That thing tore up the server room! And Anup! And me! It's lucky we don't put a bullet through its head."

Bethany hesitated. "Technically, bullets wouldn't—"

"Or whatever." Mal fixed a scowl on her. "Just chain it back up, and let's get back to work."

"I could." Bethany sighed. "But I'm still not sure how she broke free in the first place. Those chains were imbued to regulation, and she snapped them clean in half. She won't tell us, of course. Maybe it was a flaw with the liquid cooling. I can strengthen the bonds, but..."

The chips pickled in Mal's stomach. "So this could happen again?"

"Maybe. We're kind of operating outside of established arcane practices here. Disruptive tech and all."

"Too bad we can't get any investors to see it that way," Ronnie said dryly. "We can't take another outage and survive, financially. We're going to be blowing our profits for the next three months just to fix the trashed server room."

"Even so, I'll eat ramen if it means—"

"And don't forget the guild fees for ABRA showing up. They're going to fine us. No way we can afford to summon a new daemon on top of that," Bethany added.

Mal groaned and closed her eyes. "Fine. If it means no more problems. And only if you get Anup on board."

The words left a sour taste in Mal's mouth. She swore she saw the kappa form a lipless grin behind them. "But that thing doesn't leave the building. And tell it to stay the fuck away from me."

Bethany gave a grim nod and twisted her chair around to begin what was surely going to be a long, drawn-out arcane contract.

"Wizards. San Francisco was weird enough without freaking wizards." Mal fell back with a sigh. She crumpled the remaining chips in the bag. Suddenly, she didn't have an appetite.

Ronnie cuffed her shoulder. "I'll start working on the paperwork..." He paused. "Or creating the nonexistent paperwork for this kind of thing. Maybe Beth knows what the tax form is for magical creatures."

Mal snorted. "Somehow, I had envisioned our first employee would at least be human."

"Hey, at least she's free. And she didn't ask for stock."

"Ronnie. We've really got to get you away from the investors once in a while," Mal said as Bethany appeared to launch into an extended discussion of lanyards and smartphones, all in a bubbling language of dark water and hungry claws.

The Magic PalmPilot Pro

by Aaron Giddings, Sr.

Both times, it started with a box. Oh, certainly the second time it happened, the box with the smile on it, tucked under a welcome mat in an utterly futile attempt at concealment, was hardly an uncommon sight at any Seattle residence, but the first time, in 1997, it was a far more unusual sight, even if the owner of the door in question was an early employee of the company the box had originated from, an employee who was rarely, if ever, seen outside his door when the sun was up.

Charles "Chuck" Wilkins, as he preferred to go by during this period of time, opened the door of his overpriced Lower Queen Anne condo just after sundown one early fall afternoon in the mid-twenty-teens. Not that you could tell the sun had passed over the horizon, for, like most years in Seattle, the nigh-perpetual clouds had returned to the Pacific Northwest shortly after Labor Day, where they would, with rare exceptions, remain until sometime around the Fourth of July the next year.

Chuck groaned slightly when he saw the massive lump under his doormat. Not that he would have answered the doorbell anyway, had the postman rung it, but the point of hiding such an obvious package so poorly simply eluded him. Regardless, he twitched the rug off the top of the box.

He couldn't remember having ordered anything in the last few days, but then, if he was being honest, he didn't really remember much of his weekend either, so it was entirely possible that after he and last night's "dinner" companion had finished their fun, he'd ordered himself a present.

He returned the doormat to its customary, not lumpy position, and took the box back to the table. Slicing through the tape was a matter of moments with a convenient knife, and Chuck opened the box to find it staring back at him. Sleek and silver, it seemed to call out to him, begging to be touched, to replace the very expensive competition phone that rode on his hip.

Chuck picked the iPhone up, and an electric tingle, the likes of which he had only experienced on one extremely memorable day, jolted up his arm.

He dropped the phone back into the box. "Oh, not again. You're not doing that to me again. You can go back out on the porch and get rained on for all I care."

Now if we're honest, most of us have had conversations with the inanimate electronic devices that populate our lives at one point or another. Usually some variation of "Why are you doing that?" or "Why did you let me call him?" or some other question, to which our electronics invariably respond with utter stoicism.

Except that this one didn't. The iPhone vibrated, and Chuck could have sworn he heard a honeyed female voice quite different from the pre-equipped version respond through the speakers. "Oh, come on. Remember the fun we had? Look at me. I'm so much more capable now than I was then. Imagine what kinds of fun we could have, the people you could meet. You really missed out last time. Why pass up a second chance?"

"No way. I mean it. You got me in more trouble in a single day than I'd managed on my own in three centuries. Go find someone else. I don't even work for that company anymore. They got too corporate, and I had to move on. Go mess with a Microsoftie, or someone from Starbucks. Maybe do the city a favor and visit the mayor's office, why don't you?"

"Was it as bad as all that? I gave you the perfect feeding ground. You're the one who couldn't manage any self-control."

Images washed into Chuck's mind with an abruptness that sent him to sitting on his apartment's bamboo floor. He watched from a perfect cameraman's perspective as a single December day in 1997 played out in his head.

The late '90s version of Charlie, as he'd called himself then, looked almost identical to the Chuck of the mid-twenty-teens, though without the careful graying of the temples that Chuck had started adding around the turn of the decade. Charlie also wore some of the worst examples of late '90s tech fashion excess that Chuck could remember, and the less said about the music playing through his stereo system, the better.

Delivery drivers back then weren't any better at package concealment than their future cohorts were, but in this particular case, with the winter solstice just days away, it didn't matter anyway, since Charlie had been awake for almost an hour when the doorbell rang to announce a package.

Oddly enough, neither a telltale brown truck nor its driver was visible when Charlie opened the door, but the package was far more intriguing anyway. He didn't recall having ordered anything, but perhaps he'd fired up the old 56k modem over the weekend and gone shopping. He didn't remember much of the weekend, but no matter; it wasn't like he couldn't afford whatever it was he'd bought himself.

The box opened to the most beautiful sight Charlie could remember. The PalmPilot Professional was sleek black with a gray-green screen and a stylus tucked flush with the back. Nestled in the same box was even the optional 14.4k modem attachment and batteries, which Charlie happily dropped into the back of the organizer without a second thought.

It blinked to life, emitted a series of electronic beeps that could almost be considered musical, and displayed a grainy graphic of a heart, with the text "Grab a Bite" above it.

If Charlie had had more than a passing familiarity with top of the line PDAs at this point in time, he would have found that welcome a bit odd, to say the least. The Palm organizers normally started with a branded logo, and if the batteries had been out for more than thirty seconds, required the user to plug the device into to a computer-connected cradle to sync up all information.

This particular PalmPilot Pro did precisely none of that, preferring instead to grab the contact information from Charlie's computer all by itself, memorize the login details for his favorite UseNet groups and AOL chatrooms, then read his desktop rolodex and pocket little black book as well.

For this was, as should be no real surprise to anyone reading this far, a Magic PalmPilot.

Charlie, of course, knew none of this. He only knew that he hadn't had a drop for days and could use a drink. He extracted the stylus from the back of the PDA, and tapped inquisitively on the center of the heart.

Age/Gender/Blood Type appeared as the heart dissolved, with wheels underneath each bit of text. Below the wheels was a button labeled "Go," and below that, another button labeled simply "Whatever," which seemed to be the '90s equivalent of Google's "I'm feeling lucky" button.

Charlie really didn't have time for this. The holiday rush was killing the servers, and he needed to get some code written and out the door before a bunch of crazy last-minute shoppers dropped his fledgling employer's website into the dust. He tapped the "Whatever" button with the stylus, grabbed a rain jacket and hat, and headed out the door to catch the bus downtown. The slight tingle that ran up his arm when he hit "Whatever" didn't even register.

The dual-mode bus seemed like it was perpetually threatening to break down, and Charlie felt lucky to find an unoccupied pair of seats just behind the bend. Of course, only one stop later, a blond woman in her mid-twenties sat down next to him. Charlie ignored her, pulling out the PalmPilot Pro again and fiddling with the various numbers and range combinations.

"Bite me, why don't ya?"

He could have sworn the blonde was talking to him. He looked over, one eyebrow raised, hastily thinking through a reply and managing, "Excuse me?"

She shook her head, as if trying to clear out some cobwebs. "I... you tech jerks are all alike. Bite me." At which pronunciation, she stood and quickly exited the bus as it came to a halt.

Charlie shrugged and looked back at the PDA. This seemed like the perfect reason for the "Whatever" button again, so he tapped it, getting a *beep-ba-da-beep* for his efforts. The jolt as the bus bounced over a Seattle pothole made him totally miss the electric tingle up his arm once again.

At the next stop, Charlie barely registered the group of teenagers that hopped on, at least until they were occupying the seat and standing area around him. It was a group of six, four boys and two girls, all in black trench coats, and loudly gabbing about something or other. Charlie caught the words "LARP" and "Masquerade" a few times.

As he tapped the "Whatever" button on the PDA twice more, the surrounding conversation nearly drowned out the beeps, and an unintentional jostle of elbows totally concealed the tingle.

"Hey, I bet he's one of them!" said one of the teens. Charlie looked around. The group was looking at him with an intensity that was slightly alarming.

"Absolutely. He's got all the signs," said one teenage boy, pushing closer.

"I'm sorry, do I know you?" was all Charlie could think to say.

"The Masquerade! You're part of it, aren't you!" crowed the girl.

"The what now?"

"Oh, that's very good, pretending like you don't know." The girl's voice dropped to a near whisper. "It's okay, you're among friends. We're all vampires here. Well, except me, I'm supposed to be initiated tonight. Nightshade over there is supposed to be siring me, but you could do it instead."

Charlie blinked. "We're what now? You're what now?"

"I mean, you're in the game, aren't you? The quest said to look for a man with an electronic organizer who'd give me my next clue, and here you are."

It was a tempting offer, Charlie had to admit. Usually he had to put at least a little effort into these things. He decided to play along for the moment. "But what about... Nightshade over there?" he murmured back. "Won't she be jealous if her prize pupil gets turned by someone else? What if I'm not even in the same clan?" He winked at her, tangentially noting that her friend was starting to look a bit upset.

"Oh, I hadn't thought about that. Um... Nightshade?"

Nightshade looked at their leader. "I guess we could invite him to the ceremony. It's just a few stops from here, and I'm sure whatever clan you are won't be a problem. You're not speaking crazy rhymes or skulking in the sewers, at least."

Charlie was just about to agree when his pager buzzed. Which meant that his original reason for coming downtown had just turned into an emergency. "Sorry, maybe next time. It would seem I have other, more pressing duties. Farewell, kindred."

Charlie smirked as he got off the bus. "If they only knew the truth." There weren't too many people working at this time of day, and he was able to get things done in relative peace. Every now and again he'd tap the PDA, getting rewarded with the beep sequence. Tangentially he noticed the slight tingle up his arm but chalked it up to sitting in his chair too long.

His work night proceeded mostly as normally as emergency server maintenance on the last weekend before Christmas could be expected to go. By habit, Charlie left AIM and IRC windows up to keep him company while programming. Normally the conversations trended to the mundane, but today they were taking an odd direction. The first couple of chats were kind of cute, people from alt.rec.vampire.fans who had maybe seen a few of his snarky comments on Anne Rice novels and wanted to chat. Every one of them ended with, "So, if you were a vampire, I mean, really, really a vampire, would you bite me?"

That was a little weird, even for Charlie, especially given how his bus ride had gone. The next chat was even worse, a single opening line of "D00d, h34rd U g0tz f4ngz, bi73 m3 4 1337 n3\/\/ ski11z? Pl34z3!"

That one didn't warrant an answer. After two more similarly aggressive, if at least better spelled and punctuated offers, Charlie finally gave up. He'd gotten his check-in done; the servers were safe. All he wanted now was a drink, some conversation, and to go home for the night.

FinStorm's tavern on Capitol Hill was the kind of place most people walked right by without a second glance. It was Charlie's favorite bar, mostly because he could be himself. Fin, the owner, was a gnome who passed as a short human via stilts and a lot of practice, and made his place a safe haven for the varied non-human members of the Seattle community.

Charlie grabbed his usual seat and ordered a beer. While Fin poured, he pulled out the PalmPilot and tapped the "Whatever" button. He didn't feel like talking, just pondering his day and going home. The woman who abruptly sat down next to him after walking into an entirely different bar than she had planned, however, very much wanted something from him.

Perhaps not talk, as she made her presence known with a hand on his thigh. His eyes followed the arm in his peripheral vision to a stunning vision of his absolute favorite kind of human. She pulled her hand back, winked, and got up, headed toward the dim privacy of the restrooms.

Charlie followed, pausing only to slip the PalmPilot back into his pocket. He could barely recall following the woman into the bathroom and locking the door behind them. She tilted her head back and pulled her blond tresses to one side, exposing a perfect alabaster neck. Charlie bent toward her, mouth wide and fangs extended, pausing a hairsbreadth from his fangs puncturing her skin.

Above him, reflected in the mirror, hung the three rules of Fin's bar.

#2. No feeding on the premises.

It was practically flashing at him, and Charlie really didn't want to have to find another bar. With a stifled growl of annoyance, he moved his head and kissed the blonde instead. "Sorry, darling, not here. Let's take this back to my place instead."

The face that had been so lovely only moments before contorted into a pout, then confusion. "I... what? With you? As if!" As abruptly as the mood had taken her, it vanished. She scarcely paused to unlock the door before storming out, her high-heeled boots sounding her displeasure all the way to the door.

Charlie slumped back into his chair at the bar, withdrawing the PalmPilot again. Fin glared. "What? Nothing happened. You and your stupid rules. Now it's just me and the PDA again."

"Really? You a couple now? When did you get that thing, anyway? You're usually at least talking to me a little bit, but tonight you can't take your eyes off that screen."

"Just showed up this morning. I've wanted one for a while, but for a personal organizer, it's not exactly making me more organized."

Fin made a grab for the Palm. A hundred years as a pickpocket came in handy sometimes, and he had it in his hands before Charlie could think of stopping him, only to pause, looking torn between handing the gadget back to Charlie and throwing it across the room.

"Charlie? What's my number-one rule in here?" Fin's voice had an edge to it that Charlie definitely didn't like. Still, he knew the answer easily enough.

"No magical augments. You're going to find someone, you have to do it with what you've got, not some spell or potion or enchanted ring. All your regulars know that. Now give me back that Palm."

"Charlie, if this isn't a magical augment, then I'm a unicorn. Take it and get out!"

"Fine!" Charlie snatched the PalmPilot out of Fin's hands and stormed out of the bar, back into the Seattle night. Now he was hungry, angry, and wanted something caffeinated. It was looking to be a long night.

Ducking into one of the city's omnipresent coffee shops, he ordered a double tall something and sat down in the far corner of the shop to drink his beverage and ponder. Damn that gnome. He'd been thrown out for no good reason that he could see. He certainly didn't need augmentations to hunt; snacks had been throwing themselves at him all day! And furthermore, he'd certainly be able to tell if he were holding some kind of enchanted object, wouldn't he? Absentmindedly, he pulled out the PalmPilot again and set it on the table, tapping the button to turn it on before extracting the stylus.

"Grab a Bite" appeared as usual. He spun the dials a few more times as he took his first few sips of coffee. He tapped the "Whatever" button a few times and took a few more sips.

Outside, a lifted pickup truck with a distinctive red and white camouflage pattern took a wrong-way turn down a one-way street when the driver turned to stare into the coffee shop window for reasons he wouldn't be able to explain later. The truck hit a parked, broken-down Metro accordion bus at low speed.

Charlie tapped the button a few more times. The faint tingling jolts barely registered while three women, one wearing a Seahawks hat and two wearing silver makeup and Raiders emblems all attempted to squeeze through the door to the coffee shop simultaneously, abruptly leading to the beginnings of a fight.

A few more taps. Charlie finished his coffee and, trying to put the stylus down, realized that his hand was numb. With his other hand, he carefully extracted the stylus from his grip and stared at it. For the first time, he looked up and saw the measure of chaos outside. He tapped the "Whatever" button while holding the stylus in his other hand.

Beep-ba-da-beep! went the PalmPilot Pro. Charlie's hand felt like he'd bridged the terminals on a nine-volt battery with his tongue.

He shoved the stylus back into the device so fast it almost broke. He was going to owe Fin such an apology. How had he missed such an obvious magical interaction all day? His first impulse was to drop the device in the nearest trash can, but for reasons he couldn't quite explain, he felt sentimental about the thing. Maybe it was the spirit of Christmas, or just one "evil" magical creature helping out another.

He squeezed past the fighting women near the doorway. For a moment, he considered tossing the device into traffic, but instead settled for dropping it in the box of the first person with a "Need Help" sign that he saw. "Merry Christmas" he yelled, and headed toward a bus stop three blocks away, one that he hoped wasn't affected by what he'd done.

Chuck blinked. He didn't recall lying down on the floor, and this was his Queen Anne home, not his old Capitol Hill digs.

"Ding!" went the iPhone on the table.

Chuck levered to his feet and glared balefully at the device. "I said no. You call that fun? My only regret is that I got sentimental at the end. I should have tossed you in the middle of Lake Washington and let hydros drive over you every year."

In response, the iPhone opened a new app. "FangR" appeared on the top of the screen, with a stack of pictures underneath. A red circle with an X sat on the left side of each picture, and on the right, a green circle with a small set of fangs inside.

The phone vibrated, and the pictures rearranged themselves into a gallery sorted by age, blood type, and natural hair color.

Chuck picked the iPhone up and looked closer. The app rearranged its gallery again, sorting by country of origin this time. Every type Chuck had ever been into, every craving he had wanted to experience, was at his fingertips, a button press away.

Chuck tapped a particular country in South America. He'd enjoyed a lovely, warm winter there once, and the taste had never quite left him. The specimens that the iPhone displayed were 10s in every way. His finger hovered over the green button. Once couldn't hurt, right?

His other phone rang. "Ignore it," the iPhone seemed to say. "You can have an endless all-you-can-eat buffet with me. How many beings get a second chance like this? Just look at the possibilities."

Chuck looked at his hand, his thumb a twitch away from the green button. He thought about how long it had taken to get back on Fin's good side, and how that little hole-in-the-wall bar was the closest thing to a true home that he had in Seattle. How much would a lifetime of easy hunts and amazing victims be worth?

"No. Back in the box you go. Try bothering someone at the airport. I bet a TSA agent would love you."

And with that, Chuck taped the box shut and dropped it out the window.

If it had just been a normal box, containing a normal iPhone, that would have been the end of it. But, of course, this was not just a normal box, and this was not just a normal iPhone, and, thus, it did, in fact, take Chuck's suggestion into consideration when choosing its next victim.

What You're Called to Do

by Dale Cameron Lowry

Justin never knows how to address people who wear nametags as a requirement of their profession. He feels like the balance of power is tipped in his favor because he knows something important about them, while they lack the same information about him. Even if he's told them his name before, they might have forgotten it. By using their names, he would be flaunting his position of power.

Things were easier when he was a reporter and always had a press badge dangling around his neck. He didn't have to worry about anyone not knowing what to call him. But he's not a reporter anymore. The only name on his chest is the brand name of his fleece jacket.

So Justin always avoids calling the guy at the front desk of the Washington County No-Kill Animal Shelter "Mark," even though: one, that's what the nametag says; two, Justin could practically be considered a regular; and three, they flirt every time he visits.

Justin doesn't want to come off as a conceited prick who tosses out people's names like used Kleenex.

But when he walks through the front door on his fifth visit in two weeks, the first thing he hears is a hearty, "Hey Justin!" Mark hops up from his chair and eyes the blue plastic carrier in Justin's hand. It wobbles to and fro from the relentless pacing of the cat inside. "Let me guess. Another stray?"

"How'd you figure that one out, Mark?" Justin feels giddy finally saying the name, and relieved that the balance of power is finally equal. He sets the carrier on the desk. "I spotted this one a couple days ago, but it took me a while to gain her trust. She's got a tag but the phone number's outdated and I couldn't figure out who it used to belong to. Maybe you guys can?" It's a humiliating request for an unemployed journalist to have to make. He should be able to unravel any mystery if he works at it long enough. Of course, cats aren't very good at giving interviews, so that complicates things.

"Sure. We'll give it a try." Mark turns to peer at the cat through the crate door and says in a soothing voice, "I bet you regret trusting him now, don't you, pumpkin?" The cat is an orange tabby, so the nickname is inevitable even if she's so skinny "carrot" would be more accurate. "Don't worry. You'll be out of that horrible crate in a minute, and maybe we'll even find your people."

The cat gazes at Mark with curious green eyes. She twitches her nose and lets out a tentative meow.

Mark looks up at Justin. "Where are you finding all these cats, anyway?"

Justin shrugs. There's no way he's going to tell Mark the whole truth. Mark would think he's crazy. Even Justin is beginning to think he's crazy. So he settles on telling Mark as much of the truth as he can without sounding like he belongs in the loony bin. "I got laid off a couple months ago, so I've got time to go on long walks. And there are a ton of abandoned houses in my neighborhood. I guess that means a ton of abandoned cats."

"Tell me about it. It's starting to feel like half the city."

"I don't suppose you've found the owners of the other cats I brought in, since they didn't have microchips?"

"Actually—" Mark looks down at the iPhone on his desk, then back up. "We found the owners of the calico tabby and the tortie. The long-haired one we adopted out. And the other two are still here for the waiting period in case someone claims them, so there's still a chance they'll get reunited with their people."

"That's a really impressive return rate."

"It's what we do." Mark shrugs, then scratches his jaw. "You know, if you're looking for a job, animal control is short-staffed. You might be good at that, given your record."

"That sounds kind of depressing."

Mark laughs. "Some people think working in a shelter is depressing, too. But I like it. It all depends on what you feel called to do, I guess."

"I'll think about it."

———

Justin's amateur cat-catching career began when a perfectly lovely day of mainlining *The X-Files* on Netflix was ruined by yet another canned email containing a job rejection. Being hopelessly unemployed three years after college graduation was not the life he had imagined for himself.

He slammed his laptop shut. "What's the point?"

If he'd yelled that in the newsroom, someone would have answered with some smartass comeback. But his apartment was deathly silent.

"Hey, Siri. What's the point?"

His iPhone lit up. "Hello, Justin. According to Wikipedia, a point is one of the most fundamental objects of Euclidean geometry. In two-dimensional Euclidean space, it is represented by an ordered pair (x, y) of numbers. Would you like to learn more?"

"No." Justin sighed. "Hey Siri, what should I do with myself?"

"Go outside, Justin. It's a beautiful day, with a current temperature of sixty-two degrees Fahrenheit and winds at four miles per hour."

It wasn't a bad idea. Feeling sorry for himself outdoors would probably be more fun than feeling sorry for himself on the couch. Justin slipped on his shoes and jogged down the stairs of the apartment building.

Siri piped up. "Now walk toward the intersection of Churchill and Main."

That was odd. Justin hadn't turned the navigator on. Had he downloaded a geocaching app without remembering? Maybe unemployment had caused his sleepwalking to resurface, but instead of playing video games, he now just downloaded apps. If that was the case, he needed to change his App Store settings. He could barely afford his phone plan, much less random apps he didn't need.

He'd been prone to sleepwalking as a kid, and it always got worse when he was stressed out. When his parents got divorced he'd wandered the house every night. His sister said he'd gotten very good at playing video games in his sleep.

He started flicking through his screens to check for anything he didn't recognize, but Siri interrupted him.

"Don't just stand there! Walking is good for you."

Hmmm. Maybe it was an exercise app he should be looking for, not geocaching. He'd downloaded a ton right after the layoff and hadn't used any. For all he knew, this was exactly how one of them was supposed to behave. Bizarre bit of programming.

Justin's iPhone blared like a siren. He almost dropped it. "What the—?"

Siri's voice replaced the siren. "Get moving, Justin. Should you pause again between here and your destination, the alarm will repeat."

Ah, fuck it. Justin would figure out how to turn off the program later. He really did need the exercise, and it wasn't like he'd set off with a different destination in mind, anyway.

"What next, Siri?" he said when he arrived at Churchill and Main.

"Turn left and walk three hundred feet."

Justin found himself in front of a house with a scraggly, leaf-strewn yard and a boarded-up front window. Yellow pieces of paper were taped to the front door. Though he couldn't read them from the curb, he recognized them as foreclosure notices. They'd become commonplace all around town.

A bloodcurdling yowl rose from the backyard.

There are two kinds of people in the world: those who run away from bloodcurdling yowls, and those who run toward them. As a reporter, Justin had been on the police beat. Of course he ran toward the yowl, sprinting down the unraked driveway and turning the corner at breakneck speed.

He screeched to a halt in front of a pair of yellow eyes.

Justin blinked. So did the eyes. They were set in a gray, fur-covered face.

"Meow," said the face.

Being that Justin was close to six feet tall and most cats don't break 10 inches, finding himself face-to-face with one was rather unexpected.

When Justin stepped back, he got a better handle on the situation. The cat hung by its claws in the bungalow's cedar siding. It must have run up there, realized where it was, and then freaked out.

The longer Justin stood by its side, the less panicked the cat seemed. It gave Justin an appraising look, then squinted its eyes amiably. "Meow?" it said.

Justin was not stupid. He'd grown up with cats. He knew they were not at their most predictable when stuck to the sides of buildings. Still, he couldn't help but feel sorry for the scrawny little thing.

Besides, his health insurance hadn't run out yet, so if the cat attacked, well—he'd live.

He put one hand around the scruff of its neck to calm it and gently pried it from the siding with the other. It purred vehemently. He held it for a moment while he checked the collar under the matted gray fur of its neck. There was a little silver tag with the name "Smokey," but no other information.

"Where do you live, Smokey?" Justin said as he set it on the ground, because he didn't have the same nametag qualms with cats as he did with humans.

The cat sniffed at Justin's shoes and then at the cuffs of his pants. It rubbed against his legs possessively, as if to say "with you."

Justin rolled his eyes. "Nice try, buddy. You think I want to be spending my money on cat litter right now?"

But when he turned to go, Smokey just followed him.

Justin spent the rest of the afternoon knocking on neighbor's doors to see if anyone knew the whereabouts of the Smokey's owners. He put "found" notices on Craigslist and Petfinder. He used his investigative reporting skills to look up details on the house's previous owners, but found nothing useful. A call to the local shelter to see if Smokey had been reported missing was a dead end.

A neighbor lent Justin some cat litter and food to tide him over for the evening. Smokey spent most of it curled on Justin's stomach while Justin removed every exercise app he could find from his phone.

The next day, Justin brought Smokey to the vet—a friend of a friend of a friend who did free exams on strays.

"Some cats have microchips under their skin that can help identify them if they get lost. Let me see if he has one," the vet said as Smokey rubbed against her stomach. She pulled a handheld scanner out of a drawer and ran it over his shoulder blades. It made a cheerful beep. "Success!"

The celebration didn't last long. The contact information for Smokey's owners in the microchip database was out of date.

"I guess you have a new pet," the vet said with a smile.

"I guess I do."

Owning a cat turned out not to be the worst thing in the world. The vet told Justin how to save money on cat litter by using pine pellet horse bedding instead, and he cut back from four cups of coffee a day to three to pay for the cat food.

Besides, now Justin had someone to talk to other than Siri as he sent out resume after resume. He didn't mind that Smokey's answers were somewhat less intelligible than hers, and the cat had the bonus benefit of being an excellent bed companion—something Justin hadn't had on a regular basis since breaking up with his college boyfriend.

Siri shattered Justin's newfound domestic bliss a few days later. He was updating his LinkedIn profile when she said, unprompted, "Go for a walk, Justin, and bring a can of tuna with you."

Justin stopped typing mid-word. "What the hell?"

"A homeless cat is in danger. Go save it."

Justin pulled on his earlobes. He blinked both eyes. He pinched himself.

Apparently he wasn't dreaming.

"Siri, I don't remember signing up for lost cat notifications."

"You didn't."

Justin wracked his brain for a logical explanation. He remembered the vet scanning Smokey for a microchip. *That must be it*, he thought. His iPhone could somehow home in on microchip signals.

It was the only logical explanation.

Well, there was also the possibility that Justin was having a mental breakdown, but he didn't want to entertain that thought.

He grabbed some tuna from the cupboard and headed out.

Siri led him to a cat as promised. This one was black and sleeping inside a car engine. He brought it straight to the vet, muttering under his breath the whole way, "Please have a microchip, please please please."

When the microchip scanner made its happy ding-ding sound, Justin almost shouted "amen." His smile didn't shrink when the vet told him the contact information on it was as worthless as Smokey's.

"I guess you've got a second cat now," said the vet. "Congratulations. It's a girl."

Due to the strange circumstances surrounding her discovery, Justin named her Spooky. She and Smokey stopped hissing at each other after a few days, and came to an agreement to share the bed peacefully. Spooky slept on Justin's feet, and Smokey slept on Justin's stomach.

But then things got weirder. Siri led him to a tomcat while helpfully explaining, "He was kicked out of his house for spraying the walls. I don't know what you humans expect to happen when you don't neuter a cat."

Justin suspected this was more information than a microchip could provide, but he quashed the thought. He didn't want to think about what it would mean if Siri's abilities had nothing to do with microchips.

"Siri, tell me where the owners live so I can return him," he said after luring the tom into a crate with sweet talk and tuna.

"Fat chance, Justin. They kicked him out once already."

"Becoming a crazy cat lady is not my life goal, Siri."

"Are you sure?"

That afternoon marked Justin's very first visit to the Washington County No-Kill Animal Shelter. He regretted never having been there before: the most attractive man to ever grace the face of the planet was behind the front desk. He stood up as Justin entered and gave a little wave. "How can I help you today?'

Justin stared at him, speechless. Seriously, how did anyone manage to look that hot in scrubs?

Unfazed by Justin's silence, the man—Mark, according to the nametag pinned over his muscular chest—pointed to the mewling cat carrier. "Sounds like there's a cat in there."

Justin returned to earth from wherever he'd just been. He cleared his throat. "Yeah. I found this guy by a dumpster. But I'm pretty sure he used to belong to somebody. Do you have one of those microchip scanners to check him with?" Justin set the crate on the desk.

Mark grinned as if that was the most delightful thing anyone had said to him all day. Maybe it was. "That's the first thing I always do. Joyful reunions are my favorite." He winked as he picked up the crate and whisked off to a side room.

Which was just as well, because Justin's face felt like it was on fire.

Justin's skin had cooled down considerably by the time Mark returned sans cat. He was frowning. "Alas, no joyful reunions quite yet. No microchip. We'll have to try—"

"That's impossible," Justin blurted out. "He *has* to have a microchip. Are you sure?"

Mark nodded. "We have three different brands of scanners, and I tried all of them. There's nothing in there. But like I was saying..." His mouth continued moving, and sound kept coming out of it, but Justin couldn't process the words.

Justin's skin went cold. He reached into his pocket and ran his fingers over the shell of his iPhone.

His evil, possessed iPhone.

Or possibly his magically benevolent iPhone?

Either way, he felt ready to lose his lunch.

And he very well might have, if it hadn't been for Mark's hand on his arm—a warm, grounding force that reigned in his terrifying thoughts. "Are you okay?"

Justin swallowed heavily. His voice shook a little when he spoke. "I just really wanted there to be a microchip."

Mark gave him a sympathetic look. Justin let those lovely gray eyes distract him a bit more from his worries. "Don't worry. We have other ways of finding owners. We have the highest rate of reunifications in the country, actually."

"Really? How do you do that without microchips?"

"We have our ways." Mark rubbed the back of his neck. "Anyway, when that doesn't work out, we've got a really good adoption program in place, and fostering, too. If you want, I can give you a tour and show you some of the playrooms we have in back."

Justin shook his head. "No, I'm sure it's fine. I'm just a little... sensitive when it comes to cats, I guess."

"Me too. Cats are one of the best things in the world. I'll take good care of him, I promise." Mark handed Justin some forms to fill out. "We hold them for one week in case the previous owners come looking for them. If no one does, we'll neuter him and place him for adoption. Are you interested if no one claims him?"

Saying no would have been the logical thing to do. But Justin made the mistake of peeking through the door of the crate into the tom's sad brown eyes. If Siri's talents had nothing to do with microchips, maybe they had to do with fate. "Yeah," he said. "Please do."

By the time the shelter called the next week—not Mark, but a woman named Rosie—Justin had already found and relinquished three more cats. He still didn't understand what was going on, but he couldn't be crazy. Crazy wouldn't have led him to actually finding a cat every time Siri told him to. Could it?

"We found the previous owners, but they didn't want him," Rosie said. "You still got a place for him?"

Justin checked his lease. It didn't list a maximum number of cats. Hell, might as well.

"Are you expecting me to keep all of them, Siri?" he said when he got off the phone.

"Nah," she said. "Only the ones that choose you."

Justin calls the tabby Stripey to keep going with the whole "S" theme he started with the other two cats. Smokey and Spooky hassle Stripey constantly, apparently convinced that they own the apartment and he's a dastardly interloper. After ten nights in a row of 3 a.m. cat brawls, Justin wonders if he should have relinquished him after all.

He complains about this to Mark one afternoon while dropping off his umpteenth cat in a week. (Winter is coming, and Siri has picked up the pace of her rescues.)

Mark tilts his head. "Sounds like territorial aggression. Do you have any cat trees? That helps."

"Hadn't even thought about it," Justin says, flustered. "This is all new to me."

Mark riffles through a file drawer and pulls out a set of instructions. "This shows you how to make one for free or cheap. Let me know if you have any questions."

"Do you guys make house calls?"

Mark flashes Justin a brilliant smile. "I might if there's dinner involved."

This is probably the cue for Justin to finally ask the guy on a date. And he would, only—he has a magic iPhone who talks to him every day. Maybe he's better off alone. So instead he answers with an ambiguously flirtatious, "I'll keep that in mind," as he turns to leave.

———⊂⫘⊃———

Justin builds two cat trees out of scrap lumber someone left by the apartment building's dumpster. His cats come to peace almost immediately. All the time he spent trying to intervene in fights, he now spends on sending out article queries to cat magazines. (He still doesn't have a job, but maybe freelancing in the meantime will keep him from going crazier than he already is.)

"I wonder if I built another tree—could I get another cat?"

"You said you didn't want to become a crazy cat lady," says Siri.

"It might be too late."

———⊂⫘⊃———

Justin is driving home from a disappointing interview for a public relations position (spoiler alert: he doesn't get the job) when Siri says: "Turn left at the light and stop after two hundred feet."

Justin stops the car and Siri leads him to a low-growing juniper bush beside an empty office building. High-pitched trills that sound more like a swarm of alien birds than adult cats emanate from the greenery. "Siri, what are you getting me into?" he asks, even though he's pretty sure he already knows.

"Look under the bush. You'll see."

Ignoring his interview clothes, Justin drops to his knees. At first all he can make out in the darkness is a small, shivering lump. As his eyes adjust, he makes out white splotches of fur—then gray ones, and finally black, all moving in a strange undulating motion.

Goddammit. Kittens.

Kittens who are crawling over an eerily immobile mother.

They cling more tightly to her when they notice him, and raise a chorus of high-pitched siren mewls. The mother, in contrast, doesn't make a single warning hiss or growl.

A very bad sign.

Justin leans in closer. Without going into the gory details, it becomes clear she's been hit by a car and survived long enough to return to her litter.

Justin hears his mom's voice in his head warning him to never touch a dead animal. He touches her anyway. Yup, definitely dead.

The kittens continue with their alien songbird imitations. When Justin holds out a finger, one suckles it pathetically. They're tiny things, each no bigger than his hand, with short, matted fur and wide blue eyes. "What am I supposed to do with a litter of orphaned kittens?"

The kittens give no answer beyond crying. Siri gives an answer, though: "According to Wikipedia, orphaned kittens should be bottle-fed with cat milk replacement every two to four hours. They also need physical stimulation to urinate and defecate. Would you like me to find a retailer who sells cat milk replacement?"

Justin gathers the kittens under the front of his shirt to keep them warm. Their tiny claws prickle through the fabric of his undershirt as they adjust themselves against his body. For some reason, this strikes him as adorable.

Oh god. He's fucked. He really is a crazy cat lady now, isn't he?

Justin does the only thing he can think of. He calls the Washington County No-Kill Animal Shelter, and sighs with relief when Mark answers.

"Crap," is Mark's response when Justin apprises him of the situation.

"You were supposed to say something reassuring like, 'We have several volunteers who specialize in bottle-feeding kittens and are available at a moment's notice.'"

"Yeah, no. We don't. Unless you're our newest volunteer?"

Justin bites his tongue. He has three cats in a one-bedroom apartment. Offering to take on three more is certifiably insane. He opens his mouth to say "no," but the warm little fuckers squirm against his stomach and the words that come out are, "I'd be happy to do it. It's not like I have a job to go to anyway."

"Thank God. I was hoping you would say that."

After hanging up, Justin spends several minutes gazing at the kittens stuffed into his shirt. They fell asleep while he was on the phone, the black-and-white one sandwiched by its gray tabby siblings. Their chests expand and contract rapidly as they breathe into their tiny lungs.

He thinks he might be a little in love with them, the way a mother falls in love with her children.

"I hate you, Siri."

"No you don't, Justin."

—⊂⦚⦚⦚⦚⊃—

Smokey, Spooky and Stripey's tentative balance is temporarily upset by the invaders' presence, but after several days and a third cat tree, they calm down and become more curious than hostile. They watch from a safe distance as Justin bottle-feeds the kittens one after another, occasionally rubbing against his legs to reassure themselves he still belongs to them.

For the first week, the kittens need twelve feedings a day. Each feeding takes ten to twenty minutes per kitten, which means Justin spends eight to twelve hours each day with a kitten in one hand and a bottle in the other. Siri makes sure he doesn't miss a single feeding. If he falls asleep, she yells at him until he wakes up and slumps to the kitchen to get the formula ready. It's a good arrangement.

The feedings taper down to nine round-the-clock feedings the second week. Justin sleeps in one-hour shifts and has long, detailed fantasies about getting ten solid hours of sleep. In between feeding and naps, he blogs about the experience and posts a few videos to YouTube. The kittens don't exactly go viral, but they get enough hits that he'll be able to collect a little ad revenue. Hmmm. Maybe his next career is cat blogger.

Mark comes by every day to check on Justin and his new charges. It's all very domestic—mixing formula, sterilizing bottles, talking for hours about the color and texture of the kittens' poop. After the kittens are fed and tucked back into their nest, the two caretakers sit at the kitchen table or on the couch, feet propped on the ottoman and almost touching as they eat whatever takeout Mark picked up on the way. They establish a rule not to talk about kitten poop while eating, so instead they talk about their lives. They tell stories about past jobs and past boyfriends and past dreams, and flirt in that ambiguous way that could mean friendship or could mean something deeper. Images of seducing Mark flit through Justin's head, but he never acts on them. He barely has enough energy to sit up straight.

Do you like Thai? comes a text from Mark eleven days into the routine. *Thought it might be a nice change from pizza and Chinese.*

Justin finishes feeding the gray tabby with white paws, who he has uncreatively begun to call Mittens, and returns her to the nest with the rest of the litter before replying, *God please yes.*

Any favorites?

Justin is tempted to answer, *Just you,* but decides against it. *Something with lots and lots of vegetables. And no shrimp. Surprise me.*

Justin is asleep when Mark knocks on the door, and stays asleep through the second round of knocking. The sounds integrate into the dream he's having, in which Siri leads him to an abandoned office building with colonies of cats on every floor.

"They seem to be doing fine to me," Justin says, pointing to a Maine Coon typing away on a large desktop. *Tap-tap-tap. Tap-tap-tap.*

"They'd do better if someone came by every day to clean the litterbox," is Siri's reply.

Tap-tap-tap. Tap-tap-tap. Man, that Maine Coon's keyboard is loud.

"Justin?" Mark's muffled voice pulls Justin into wakefulness—just barely.

Justin blinks his eyes open. "Come in."

Smokey, Spooky, and Stripey rub up against Mark's legs as he comes through the door, the scent of lemongrass and kaffir lime entering with him. "You look like shit," Mark says cheerily as he takes off his coat.

"Awww, that's the sweetest thing anyone's ever said to me."

"Sorry." Mark chuckles and rubs the back of his neck. "I say it out of concern, not judgment."

"I know." Justin practically whispers the words, not sure if he wants Mark to hear. He feels warm and sleep-fuzzy. It strikes him as a dangerously comfortable state. He can't remember feeling this way since the last time he fell in love.

Mark pulls a container from the takeout bag and sets it on Justin's stomach. "Eat. You need energy to stay awake through the kitten feeding."

Justin stuffs fragrant forkful after forkful into his mouth while Mark prepares formula in the kitchen. By now, he knows where everything important is without having to ask. It's as if he's lived here for years. So, so domestic.

"You know," Mark says, "I don't have to work tomorrow. I could do the feedings tonight, and you could sleep for more than an hour in a row."

"I can't ask you to do that. You work with animals all day."

Mark peeks at Justin through the kitchen door, smiling in a way that makes Justin's chest feel warm. "You didn't ask me. I offered."

Justin doesn't answer, but falls asleep while feeding the kittens after dinner and doesn't wake up until the pale gray light of morning comes through the window. He finds Smokey and Spooky snoring on top of him, and

Stripey watching the scene from his perch on the back of the couch.

Justin floats in contentment for two seconds before jolting upright with a shout that sends the three cats scurrying. *The kittens!* "Siri, why the fuck didn't you wake me up? How many feedings have I missed?"

Only then does Justin become aware of someone moving around in the kitchen. At first he thinks it's Siri, finally having taken a physical form. But the person who peers at him from the kitchen door looks an awful lot like Mark. "I'm pretty sure you have to say 'hey' before 'Siri' if you want your phone to answer you."

Justin wonders if he's dreaming, but knows he can't be. He doesn't feel the sense of dread and confusion that usually pervades his dreams. "Have you been here all night? Feeding the kittens?"

Mark nods. "You've been asleep for"—he glances over his shoulder toward the clock on the microwave—"ten hours."

"You did that? For me?"

Mark ducks his head, a blush growing on his cheeks. "I told you last night I could. You don't remember?"

"I kind of remember, but—I don't remember you staying, actually. I don't even remember brushing my teeth." Justin smacks his lips with disgust. "Oh my god, I didn't brush my teeth, did I?"

Mark shakes his head. "You fell asleep right after dinner, and you were way too adorable to wake up. Want me to put on some coffee? Or would you rather go back to sleep? Like I said last night, I have today off. So I could keep feeding them, and you could go sleep in your actual bed."

"Don't you have animals of your own to feed?"

"I texted my roommate last night. She's fine with taking care of them all weekend if need be. I'm all yours, Sleeping Beauty."

It's a good thing Justin's not standing up, or he would swoon. "Oh my god, you're the perfect boyfriend. Did you know that?"

"Is that what I am?" Mark says with a smirk.

Justin bites his bottom lip. "I totally didn't mean to say that out loud."

Mark walks over to the couch and sinks down next to Justin's hip. "I'd love to be your perfect boyfriend. I mean, sooner or later you'll probably figure out that I'm imperfect, but—"

He doesn't finish because Justin finally has the wherewithal to kiss him. It isn't the passionate open-mouthed kiss Justin has always envisioned—accommodations need to be made to ensure Mark doesn't catch a whiff of his morning stank breath—but it's a good kiss all the same.

Siri interrupts it. "Justin, if Mark's going to be feeding the kittens today, there's a Burmese cat over on Dempsey Drive who could use your help."

Mark startles back. "Did—did that just happen? Or am I hallucinating from lack of sleep?"

Justin bites his lip nervously. Finally time to put his own sanity to the test. "I guess that depends what you think just happened."

"Your phone said there's a Burmese on Dempsey Drive who needs your help."

"That's what I heard, too."

Mark picks up Justin's iPhone and looks at Siri's dialogue screen. "Yeah, that's definitely what she said." He glances back at Justin. Oddly, Mark doesn't look freaked out. Just mildly curious. "Does this happen a lot?"

"All the fucking time," says Justin with a laugh. Everything feels suddenly light now that he's kissed Mark and his secret is no longer a secret. "Well, since I got laid off. That's why I've brought twenty cats to your shelter in the last two months."

Mark breaks into a gigantic smile. "You don't know what a relief it is to hear that."

"Wait. Shouldn't you be freaked out that I have a magic cat-locating iPhone?"

"Um, no." Mark reaches into his pocket for his own iPhone. He holds it up for Justin to study, though there's nothing impressive about it. "My iPhone sort of does the same thing."

Justin's eyes go wide. "You're fucking with me."

"Nope. My phone doesn't help me find lost cats, but it helps me find their people."

It sounds too good to be true. "Is it some kind of app?"

"Definitely not an app. It started about a year ago, when I was still looking for work. It's how I ended up getting a job at the shelter." He pauses and gives Justin a shy smile. "So no, your magic iPhone doesn't freak me out."

Justin kisses Mark again, so carried away by the joy of the moment that he accidentally slips him a little tongue even though he still hasn't brushed his teeth.

Fortunately, Mark doesn't seem to mind.

But Siri does. "Could you guys stop making out long enough to go get that cat on Dempsey?"

Justin grumbles as he pulls his shoes on, but he doesn't really mind.

Once he's caught the Burmese, he brings it back to the apartment so Mark's Siri can work her magic. She tells them it belongs with an old lady who left her screenless window open on the last warm day of the year.

When Justin arrives at her door with her cat and a brand new collar and tag, the old lady kisses Justin on the cheek, leaving behind a red smear of lipstick. He doesn't realize it's there until he gets back to the apartment and Mark points it out. "Damn, you're getting a lot of action today."

Justin rolls his eyes. "She was okay, but the only action I really want is from you."

———⚬※※⚬———

After Justin adopts the weaned kittens out, he expects Siri to go at the cat-rescuing full-throttle once more. But she doesn't make a single cat-related peep. One day passes, then a second and a third, with no new cat-rescuing expeditions. Justin tries to ignore the silence, keeping himself busy with feline freelance work and job interviews.

"Hey Siri," Justin says on the fourth day, when he can bear her silence no longer. "When are you going to send me out on another mission?"

"Maybe I've already accomplished my purpose."

"That can't be. We haven't rescued every stray cat on the planet yet."

"Maybe cats were a means to an end. Maybe I was sick of you moping around on the couch all day."

"What end? I still don't have a job." Justin scratches his head. Could it be— "Was this all a gigantic ruse to set me up with Mark?"

Siri doesn't answer.

"I hate you, Siri."

"No, you don't."

"Yes, I do. Not for the Mark part. He's great. But—I *like* rescuing cats now. You can't give someone a purpose in life and then take it away." Siri is silent just long enough for begin to panic. He hops up from the couch and pacing back and forth, chewing at his fingernails.

He hasn't chewed on his fingernails since fifth grade.

"Calm down, Justin. I was just teasing. There's a lost cat over on Hamilton and Third. Bring the carrier and some wet food."

Justin is out the door in no time flat.

"You know, Justin," Siri says as he bolts down the sidewalk, "you should consider becoming a pet detective. Or applying for that job with animal control. I think we'd make a great team, don't you? And with Mark in the picture—"

"I applied last week, Siri."

Her screen lights up with a smile. "I love you, Justin."

Justin stops a second to look her in the eye—or rather, the camera, which is the closest thing. "I love you, too, Siri."

Picture This...

by C.S. O'Cinneide

"Give it to me."

"No."

"I had one just like it."

"I don't care."

"You just need to go to Settings."

"I know."

"And then choose Network."

"I did that."

"Did you enter the correct APN?"

"Piss off."

"What?"

"I said I can figure it out."

I like my new iPhone. It's sleek and shiny and cries out for me to encase it in leopard print or Juicy Couture pink-encrusted bling. I bought it despite the fact that doing so makes me a traitor to my local economy, living within thirty minutes of RIM, the makers of the ill-fated BlackBerry smartphone. But I couldn't resist. In the world of technology, the iPhone is a super model with six-inch stilettoes and a come-hither stare, while a BlackBerry is a stout librarian spinster staying home to clean her drains on a Saturday night. I should know. My husband has a BlackBerry Classic. It screams sensible shoes.

"Do you have your data turned on?"

"I'm not a moron."

"What about iMessage?"

"What about it?"

"Have you tried that?"

"I've tried everything."

My teen daughter Alice has always had an iPhone. Like most of her peers, she grew up suckling on the teat of the Apple Empire like an orally fixated marmot. I think she teethed on an iPod shuffle. I had hoped to impress her with my recent savvy cell phone purchase. But alas, admiration in adolescent girls is rare, at least when it comes to their mothers. The best they can usually muster for us is feigning interest tinged with a smattering of disdain.

"What exactly is the problem?"

"I can't get pictures."

"What kind of pictures?"

"The type people send by text."

"Who would send *you* pictures by text?"

"You'd be surprised."

The last text I received with a picture was from my friend Jocelyn. She sent me a photo of her Aunt Charlene on her deathbed, like on her actual death bed, as in she was dead in the bed. Jocelyn had arranged her body with some of her aunt's favorite Royal Doulton figurines and wearing her Sunday best blue cloche hat. I could distinctly make out a ceramic shepherdess in the crook of her withered old lady arm.

She looked like she had died hoarding finds at a garage sale on her way to church. I am not sure if this is the way she had hoped to be remembered.

I was madly looking for ways to delete the photo without actually touching the screen when I dropped the phone into a bowl of hummus I was making. I haven't been able to receive a picture by text since. Just a teaser message telling me "Media not downloaded." I don't know whether this is a thing now. Sending pictures of dead people. I hope not. I haven't even figured out sexting yet.

"Let me see your phone."

"There is no way you are looking at my phone, Mom."

"I just want to see how you have your settings."

"No way."

"Why not?"

"Because."

"Are you sexting?"

"I'm going to Kaitlyn's."

Alice grabs her swim bag and makes for the back door off the kitchen. Kaitlyn and my daughter work at the public pool this afternoon and will be herding little kids through their back floats and bubble blowing until at least dinner time.

Through the kitchen window, I watch the backs of her black Lululemon leggings as she speeds away on a Schwinn bicycle. I have leggings like hers but would never wear them out without a long sweater to cover up my backside. I'm not sure if this is a result of modesty or just plain fear. Alice, like the rest of her generation, lacks both. I can hear catcalls as she cycles out of the driveway. Wait, no—that's my phone. I've got a text message.

Check out who I met this morning in the lineup at Yitz's Deli !!!! Can you believe it? :) ;) --- Media not downloaded.

No, Jocelyn, I cannot believe it. Because I cannot see it. Unlike how I can see your dead Royal Doulton aunt, which unfortunately is an image burned into my retinas for all time. Jocelyn could be sending me a selfie with her and Justin Bieber scoffing down bagels and lox together while dancing the Hora, but I'd never know because instead of a picture I just get that sad, empty error message. A picture that cannot be downloaded is like the barren womb of electronics.

As I toss the phone on the kitchen counter in fruitless frustration, it begins to play Gloria Gaynor's "I Will Survive," Jocelyn's ringtone.

"Hey Mel, did you see the picture I just sent? "

"You know I didn't."

"Still having problems with the new phone?"

"If I could just get the settings right, I know I could..."

"Anyway, there I am, waiting in line for coffee and a knish, and guess who walks in? Ruby Wallenstein!"

A pause ensues seemingly for dramatic effect but mostly because I am at a loss to respond to this information. I'm not very good at keeping up with the names of the rich and famous. Once, I got Jimmy and Warren Buffet mixed up. I had always wondered how the guy who wrote "Margaritaville" ended up making all that money on the stock market.

"You know, the psychic, the one on all the talk shows. She predicted Kim Kardashian's toothache."

"Oh"

"They call her Madame Ruby. I told her about my Aunt Charlene."

"Shouldn't she already know?"

To say that Jocelyn is a bit flaky is like saying poison ivy is a bit itchy. Much like the shiny green leaves, her special brand of craziness is hard to identify as first. That is, until you find yourself standing in the middle of it. She once sent me a lobster in the mail.

"Be serious, I told you how my aunt was trying to tell me something when she died."

"Like, 'please get away from me with that hat'?"

"What?"

"Nothing."

"No really, it sounded like 'worsted.'"

"What, like the wool?"

"Or 'buster.'"

"As in Keaton?"

"Aunt Charlene always liked you, you know."

"I know."

Yes, Jocelyn is a bit of a flake, but I love her. She's fun and a little bit twisted. Just the way I like my female friends. She is also as loyal as they come. Jocelyn took care of her Aunt Charlene for six months before she died, while the rest of her family pulled a no-show. When my first husband passed away, she spent a week living at my place, helping pick up the pieces. Literally. He died when our washing machine exploded. They think he was trying to treat a grease stain with gasoline. Mark was always very fastidious about his clothes.

"Listen, you want to meet for coffee this afternoon? Angie and I were supposed to go to paddleboard yoga, but the tide came in."

"I promised Gerald I'd wait at home for the furnace guy."

"It's like 100 degrees out. Who the hell cares about the furnace in the summer?"

Jocelyn has never liked my new husband, Gerald. He was my first husband's business partner, which sounds a little more Shakespearean tragedy than it is. Gerald swept me off my feet soon after the funeral with his constant support, handling all those little details I just couldn't face. We've been married a year now. Needless to say, he doesn't do his own laundry.

"Listen, we'll do coffee another time. How about Thursday afternoon?"

"I've got my tantric pottery class on Thursday. They teach you how to achieve spiritual orgasm through clay."

"That sounds interesting."

"Plus you get to take home a nice flower pot."

As I hang up the phone, I wonder whether a spiritual orgasm is any better than the regular kind. Gerald and I haven't been very intimate lately. He says that he's stressed out from working so much. But to be honest, our lovemaking has always been a bit awkward. One time he got his tongue caught in the underwire of my Victoria's Secret Miracle Bra. I think he tries too hard.

"I want you so bad, Mel."

"I want you too, Gerald."

"Do you like it when I do this?"

"Mmm. Yes."

"Do you like it when I do this?"

"Uh, maybe. Perhaps we could lose the puppet."

A catcall knocks me out of my thoughts. Another text message. I look at the screen of my shiny new phone. *No Caller ID.*

Great. It's probably a request to move money for a foreign prince in exile with bad grammar skills. *Please do the necessary kind lady and ten percent of million dollar transfer will be coming to yours this nightly.*

But clicking on the text, I find there is no message at all, just a picture attached, and magically it has managed to download to my phone. I must have finally gotten the settings right! The image is disappointing though, fuzzy and distorted, like the time I tried to take a sexy selfie of myself in a hotel bubble bath and steam got on the lens. It ended up looking like one of those grainy Bigfoot photos, except with bubbles.

Sweeping my thumbs to enlarge, I can just make out what appears to be a wooden cabinet of sorts, or perhaps an old wardrobe. It is hard to tell. Could it be a promotion for the local furniture store? But the local furniture store is Amish. I am not sure if the Amish text. Maybe. I once got cut off in traffic by a Mennonite on her cell phone.

The photo is unsettling for some reason. Like one of those old sepia pictures of your long-dead relatives. A shiver runs through me despite the heat. I am being ridiculous. Still, there is something both eerie and familiar about that gritty image.

I close the text and put the phone down on the kitchen counter. Whatever it is, it'll have to wait. I promised myself I'd clean out the furnace room before the service guy gets here. It looks like an episode from *Hoarders* in there, stacked to the ceiling with old boxes, moldy camping equipment and ancient naked Barbies without heads.

Honestly, I'm not a dirty person. I just like to put things away. The problem is after 15 years in the same house all my "away" places are starting to get full. I have three different junk drawers.

Slipping into my cutoff shorts and an old t-shirt, I pull my hair back in a ponytail and prepare for some serious storage purging. I'm halfway down the basement stairs with a fist full of garbage bags when another catcall sounds from the kitchen. Dammit. This is getting annoying. I'm starting to wonder why I even pay for a texting plan. Ten dollars a month to be constantly bloody interrupted. Dropping the bags to the floor, I walk back upstairs to the kitchen and pick the phone up off the counter. Same unidentified number with a picture. I squint at the screen to make it out. It's a photo of a building this time. I recognize it, then gasp. It's my garage.

―――――⸜⸝⸜⸝⸜⸝―――――

"Okay, you texting freak son of a bitch!"

I don't say this out loud, but I think it as I creep my way through the backyard to the side door of our double-car garage. I've got a baseball bat in my hands. Well, it's not really a baseball bat, I guess. It's an accent lamp that Jocelyn made me out of a toy Louisville slugger we got at a Blue Jays game. But minus the lampshade, it looks pretty lethal. When I reach the side door of the garage, I turn the knob ever so gently and then listen. Nothing but the heat bugs singing in the trees behind me.

I've read somewhere that you should use bad language when you encounter an assailant in order to scare him off with your aggressive potty mouth. So when I burst open the garage side door with my left sneakered foot and step inside with the Louisville Slugger lamp raised high, l let fly with a string of filthy expletives my mother would disown me for if she even thought I knew how to say them. After the begonias begin to visibly wilt in the front garden, I stop swearing and listen again. More heat bug silence. I do a 360-degree sweep of the garage, brandishing the lamp menacingly at 90-degree angles like I've seen on *Law and Order*, dropping a few more f-bombs for good measure.

Nothing.

A little more relaxed from my outburst of obscenity, I lower the lamp and have a better look around. The garage looks like it always has, which is to say, a lot like the furnace room. Leftover plywood from past treehouse projects are piled into various corners. Tools are hung haphazardly among garden implements and bike parts. A worn carpet is draped over a beat-up cedar cabinet. Mark and I had used that cabinet to store poisons and flammables out of Alice's reach when she was young. I guess she's old enough not to drink paint thinner now.

It takes a moment for things to click. Recognition is like that. A memory gets shelved next to another memory in your mind and like a mixed-up librarian, you stumble across what you were looking for all along when you were looking for something else. The cedar cabinet is the same as the one in that grainy first picture I received by text. It was not the Amish after all. I put the lamp down on the concrete floor, pull back the old carpet, and open it.

I don't know what I expect to find in there. A body? A ghost? A mad texting assailant? I do know what I am very surprised to find there.

The gasoline can.

It is dusty and has cobwebs on it, but it is there. Not in a million pieces next to a 40-gallon wash tub blown halfway across the lawn and onto my first husband's chest where it should have been. As I stand in disbelief, the catcall from the back pocket of my jean shorts makes me jump like a firecracker.

I quickly unlock the screen. There's the text. Same unknown number. Same empty message with a picture. But this time, it is a picture of me. My mouth is open, screaming. There are large dirty hands wrapped tightly around my neck, my eyes bloodshot and bulging. I'm being strangled. I can't see the face of the strangler.

But I can see the distinctive light blue uniform shirt of the furnace company on his outstretched arms.

"Hello, this is Jocelyn. Why are you phoning me? No one phones me anymore but my mother. Leave a message at the tone. Beep."

"Dammit, Jocelyn. "

I've got my cell phone in one hand and the Louisville slugger lamp in the other as I run across the back lawn. Head down, I'm focused on trying to bring up the keyboard with my thumb so I can dial 911. Anyone who has seen those videos on YouTube of people looking at their phones instead of where they are going will know why this is not a good plan. Well before I reach the house, I'm kissing dirt, having tripped over the mound of earth Gerald left behind when he dug up the septic tank last Saturday. *He has time for that but not time to have sex with me,* I think as I cough a clump of grass out my mouth.

My phone has gone flying and the baseball lamp has snapped in two, leaving a nasty splinter in my hand. I'm trying not to panic. I'm trying not to cry. I'm trying not to think about how I was going to explain to the 911 operator that the furnace guy is trying to kill me by text. I lift myself up on my palms, cobra yoga-pose style, and look around desperately for my phone. A catcall sounds from behind me, but this time it's not electronic.

"Looks like you took a tumble, little lady."

I turn around and he's there, blocking out the sun in his light blue shirt, looking down on me with an immense, amused grin. He's holding my new iPhone like a prize.

"Looking for this?"

It must be the terror in my eyes that tips him off. Or perhaps the fact that I am on my feet in a shot and screaming like an extra from a B horror flick all the way to the house. One of those things for sure, anyway. I'm quick, but unfortunately, so is he. As I tear open the screen door, he catches me by the pony tail and propels us both through the entranceway and into the kitchen. My scalp is on fire as he yanks me roughly toward him. I can feel his breath on my face, hot and smelling faintly of peppermint tea.

Preparing for my murder did not even warrant a caffeinated beverage for this guy. He is truly an asshole. Somehow this bit of outrage calms me.

"Okay, sweetheart, let's not do this the hard way."

"I'm not a big fan of the hard way."

He turns me around in his arms like a doll, or a lover. My spine bends the wrong way over the kitchen island as he leans in, threatening me with the sheer size of him. Not just his body, but his head is massive. Like a pumpkin. And he still wears that huge jack-o-lantern smile, but it is no longer amused. It is malevolent. Malevolent and very annoyed.

"Funny girl, eh?"

"Uh, yeah, I'm hysterical."

"Want to have some fun with me? "

"Like before you kill me?"

"Yeah, like before that."

"Doesn't sound like there's much in it for me."

"There's not much in it for you either way, sweetheart."

I could scream some more, I suppose. But just like my wild screaming in the backyard, no one will hear me. Our house is in a small forest on a couple of acres. My nearest neighbor lives in a hermetically sealed air-conditioned bungalow and wouldn't hear a plane landing in his front yard with the double-glazed windows closed. Plus, he hates me. His English yew got infested with emerald ash borer last year, and he blamed my newly immigrated Japanese black pine. Intolerant tree racist.

"Can you tell me why?"

"Why what?"

"Why you are doing this."

"Does it matter?"

"Yes, I think it does."

"Your husband paid me."

And there it is. Betrayal. Thick and black and oozing out of the mouth of this monster of a pumpkin-head man with a nametag on his shirt that reads "Gus." I've been had in the worst way. Kind, supportive, septic-tank digging, sensible BlackBerry-owning, puppet sex Gerald has arranged for my murder. How can this be? What could I possibly have done to deserve this? I have failed somehow as a wife, as a woman, possibly as an arborist. I can feel my whole body collapse inward under Gus's impressive bulk. The fight has gone out of me, my outrage replaced by deep sadness.

"Why?" I ask, my lip quivering.

"Money problems."

"What kind of money problems?"

"The kind that could be fixed by getting his wife's half of the business."

"Oh, those kind."

"It's nothing personal."

"I appreciate that."

You'd think I'd give in completely now, and I sort of do. I can see those grimy workman hands moving slowly toward my throat, the black-and-white kitchen clock shaped like a cat wagging its pendulum tail on the wall, counting down the seconds I have left with its buggy cat eyes moving side to side. I am sort of resigned to the idea that my life is going to end with a combination of both the brutal and the ludicrous, much as I have lived it. I wait for Gus's big sausage fingers to wrap around my neck like I saw in the picture on my new iPhone. The premonition of one's own death must have been a factory-installed app. I would have preferred Instagram. Still, I have one more question.

"Did you—did you kill my first husband, Mark?"

"I didn't have anything to do with that guy's death, lady." Since he is about to kill me, I assume he would not lie about this.

"What?"

"That was all Gerald. I offered him a two-for-one deal, but he wanted the pleasure of blowing up the guy himself."

My resignation turns to rage. Red hot and rabid. I am furious. I know this guy is still going to kill me but I swear I am going to exact some serious pain out of him in the process. It is one thing to send a hitman to kill your wife, but it is another thing entirely to off her first husband with the Maytag. I seriously loved that man. I am going to rip Gerald's face off using Gus as a proxy. That is, I am about to, just before I see my daughter bring the garden rake down on his big, fat head.

"You're home early, Alice."

"Pool fouling. One of the Aquafit ladies lost control during high-knee jogging."

"Gross."

"Not as gross as this."

We both look at the blood oozing from the skull of my would-be murderer as he moans quietly on the ceramic tile.

"I'm not cleaning that up, Mom."

"That's okay."

The first few notes of "I Will Survive" begin to sound from the vicinity of Gus's buttocks. He makes a feeble attempt to get up as I retrieve my iPhone from his rear pocket. Alice gives him another clip with the rake while I pick up the call.

"Hello, Jocelyn."

"Hi Mel. You'll never believe this."

"Oh, you would be surprised what I am believing these days, Jocelyn."

"I got a reading with Madame Ruby this afternoon. She got in contact with my aunt. It was amazing!"

I think about Gerald on his way home right now. Expecting to see me dead on the kitchen island.

"Really?"

"She told me what Aunt Charlene was trying to say. Just before she died. She wasn't trying to say 'worsted.'"

I think of him selling off the business that Mark and I built from nothing. Using the money to buy the company of cheap women and ever more elaborate puppets. Sending my motherless daughter to a substandard boarding school in the Yukon.

"Uh-huh."

"She wasn't trying to say 'busted,' either."

I think about Mark coming home after work, playing soccer in the front yard with Alice when she was first learning. His strong arms wrapped around me in bed at the end of the night, smelling like fresh cut grass and, ironically, laundry detergent.

"I see."

Jocelyn takes a deep breath in before she goes on. "She was actually trying to say..."

"Bastard," I tell her as I see Gerald pull into the driveway through the window over the sink. "She was trying to say 'bastard.'" Aunt Charlene had seen through my homicidal husband as she passed over to the other side, and used her last word to call him as she saw him. Apparently, she learned to text from the other side as well. I wonder if there is a plan for that.

"Yes," Jocelyn says, "but how did you know?"

Gerald uses the remote control to open the garage door. I look over at Alice while she listens to the familiar hum of the aluminum door moving along its metal tracks. It used to signal her dad was home.

"Sorry, Jocelyn, I've got to go." I hang up the phone just as another text comes in. I open up the photo attached and it shows me what I have to do. A picture really is worth a thousand words.

Putting down the phone, I take the bloody rake from out of Alice's tightly clenched hands.

"Listen carefully, dear. I'm only going to explain this once."

On the pristine white sand of a private Tahitian beach, I notice that my Mai Tai is getting low and call the pool boy over. I guess he isn't actually a pool boy, as I am not at the pool of this five-star hotel, but sitting under a thatched umbrella contemplating the turquoise ocean and the depth of my tan lines.

"Another, miss?"

I love it that he calls me "miss." I know it is a ruse to increase his tips, but I've had experience with men lying to me for money now, and I consider myself jaded enough to enjoy the attempt.

"Yes, Rupert, and make sure you put one of those little umbrellas in it, please." It's not an overpriced fruit-laden alcopop without the umbrella.

"Yes, ma'am."

Rupert runs back through the hot sand to the bar. That was a slip with the "ma'am." He must have been standing in the sun too long.

My iPhone rings and I pull it out of my Coach beach tote. The screen is cracked, but it still works.

"Hello?"

"Hi Mom."

"Hi Alice. How's school?" My daughter is at her first

year at Brown University. Her tuition and books cost more than my first house.

"Great. I got accepted at a sorority so I don't have to live in the dorm. I must have done really well on my interview. They don't usually accept first-year girls."

Particularly ones that are so handy with a rake, I think. But of course, they had to take her, what with the substantial donation made quietly last week. Connections are everything, after all.

"That's lovely, honey."

I have gotten used to this life now. It seems like eons ago that I had to worry about cleaning out storage rooms or visits from the furnace man. The simple reality of it all is that none of that day-to-day domestic stuff ever really mattered. Or perhaps it was the only thing that mattered. Until Gerald took it away from me and replaced it with a deceitful cutout facsimile.

"I got a call from Auntie Jocelyn yesterday." Alice calls Jocelyn her aunt even though she is no blood relation. If she was, I would be seriously worried about our genetic pool.

"Really."

A fresh Mai Tai appears like magic beside me. I take a long sip. It tastes like a tart watermelon that's been soaked in rum for a week.

"She's been to see that psychic again, Madame Ruby."

"And what did she tell her?"

"Not much, something about flaming dolls and natural gas."

"Understandable."

The fire had come after the explosion. Oh yes, and after I knocked out Gerald with the rake as he walked through the screen door. All those old boxes of junk in the furnace room really were such a combustion hazard. But the photo with the text was quite clear about the next steps. I had explained quickly to Alice what Gerald had done and then sent her to a friend's house. Then I'd lit the straw-like hair of her old Malibu Barbie on fire and stuffed it in the heat exchanger.

"You're sure, you know, you didn't have anything to do with what happened. I mean, it was an accident, wasn't it, Mom?"

I think about accidents. Accidents that snatch away the father of your child with the day's wash. Accidents that make good women marry bad men. Accidents that result in the purchase of a ridiculous amount of life insurance from your cousin's oldest boy because he's just starting out. Accidents that cause your iPhone to send you messages that will save your life and then change it forever. That will make you aware of what you have lost and who took it from you.

Messy storage rooms and murderous husbands may seem like insurmountable tasks to conquer. But really they are so easily taken care of. At least, with the help of a BBQ lighter and a blonde bimbo masquerading as a children's toy. These are the simple pieces of wisdom that Aunt Charlene has taught me. A woman who never suffered fools or bastards gladly.

"There are no accidents, darling. Some things just happen. Will I see you over the Christmas break?" I wiggle my toes in the sand. The little grains slip down the smooth skin of my weekly pedicure.

"Sure, Mom, I'll book a flight today."

Alice doesn't sound completely convinced, but that is okay. Her suspicions are tempered with love, just like my murderous intentions were.

We sign off with promises to text and call. Before I place it back in the beach bag, I switch the iPhone to Silent, not wishing to be disturbed. Almost immediately, it starts to vibrate in my hands, humming with muted excitement. I look down and watch the precious phone reflect dully in the sun, no longer shiny and new-looking. Instead, it is cracked and encrusted with yard dirt and perhaps even a small amount of brain matter. I don't mind. No longer a sexy temptress of a device darling, my iPhone has matured into a soiled but stronghearted wise woman of a certain age. Much like myself.

There is a text. Of course there is. I haven't received one in a long time, though. Not since I heard the first blast from the safety of the corner store down the road. That attached photo might have made me seriously reconsider things if it hadn't already been too late by then. I hadn't known polyester could be so flammable. Gerald really should have invested in a linen suit.

After removing my designer sunglasses, I click on the anonymous message. It contains an innocuous enough picture this time. A gleaming, much-loved Royal Doulton shepherdess dressed in cream and faded blue. She wears a wry smile as she lifts her ceramic skirts coquettishly for the camera.

The ice cubes click coldly in my drink as I drain the last of the glass. I can feel the little pink umbrella brush my lips casually, like an untrustworthy lover taking his leave.

I clasp my fingers firmly around my iPhone as I lie back in the padded beach lounger. The phone case feels warm and comforting in the palm of my hand. Like Mark used to feel when he held me at night.

Aunt Charlene always did like me. A gentle breeze blows across my forehead, tempering the heat of the Tahitian sun. The steady repetition of waves lulls me toward my afternoon nap.

But both of us found we liked revenge even more.

Army of Me

by Dawn Vogel

"Sasithorn, I need your help!"

When I woke up to those words in Thai, I realized there were three problems.

First, no one calls me Sasithorn, aside from my extended family. They were approximately 8,000 miles away, which immediately eliminated them as the source of this plea. I've been going by Molly since I arrived stateside, as it cuts down on the "where are you from?" questions by at least twenty percent.

Second, I was 99 percent sure I was alone. I hadn't heard my roommate come in last night. Flicking my gaze over to her bed, then checking the floor and what I could see of the bathroom confirmed that.

Third, can you get any vaguer than "I need your help"?

When the words repeated, I listened more closely. They sounded tinny, and they were coming from my desk. Which added a fourth problem to the roster. The volume on my iPhone was supposed to be completely disabled while I was asleep. I wrote my own app for that. Being a programming super genius has its perks.

I climbed out of bed and looked at my phone. The screen, which should have been blank, showed the familiar cartoon character from Nariphon, my preferred weather app. There was something charming about having a woman dressed for the day's weather show up on your screen when you were trying to figure out what to wear. Only I was fairly sure that Berkeley in November wasn't warm enough to go nude. The Nariphon character always had at least a bathing suit on. And, like I said, it shouldn't have been showing up on my phone screen with no prompting from me.

I hovered my finger over the home button. "What do you need?" I asked in sloppy Thai. My parents had insisted on speaking English after we moved to California. The only exception was when the extended family back in Bangkok called on birthdays and holidays and used my given name.

The voice, which I was sure wasn't Siri at this point, rattled off something I couldn't understand, but it sounded like it was pleading with me further.

"Sorry, do you know English?" I asked, not even trying Thai this time.

What sounded like a sigh came from my phone. "Yes, I speak English. And I need your help."

"Right, I got that part already. Help with what, exactly?"

"Someone has removed my clothing."

"I can see that."

"A hacker."

I frowned. It was one thing to start carrying on a conversation with an app on your phone. Siri is sort of capable of that. This felt different, somehow. It wasn't just a stack of rote answers, like the ones Siri gives you when you ask her if she follows the Three Laws of Robotics.

"What are you?" I asked.

Again, that sigh. "I am Nariphon."

"Right, you're the Nariphon app on my phone. But you've never spoken to me before. What gives?"

"Something awakened in me when I was violated."

That brought up hackles on the back of my neck. She was right—having someone forcibly remove your clothing was a violation, regardless of your assumed sentience (or lack thereof).

"Okay, let's start at the beginning. A hacker rewrote your code so you show up naked. Everywhere?"

"Yes, on every phone where my program is installed."

"That's hardly possible—" I began.

"I assure you, it is on every phone of which I am aware."

This app spoke better English than 50 percent of my American classmates. "Okay, I'll accept that. If I can get my hands on the source code, I can get your clothes back easily." I paused. "How *did* they get their hands on your source code?"

"I wish I knew. Before this, I have little memory. Everything is just a blur of different clothing. There's something else, too, but I can't seem to pin it down."

It made sense that no programmer would have made a self-aware app, but something in this app's programming had flipped on when it was hacked. This was going to take some research.

If this was really a worldwide phenomenon, there'd be news stories everywhere, people would be talking about it on social media, and someone would probably be claiming responsibility. At the very least, there'd be new outraged reviews. If there was one thing Americans couldn't cope with, it was public nudity. And despite Nariphon being a cartoon character, I was pretty sure this counted.

Sure enough, there was hubbub. "'Popular Nariphon app corrupted, pulled from Apple and Android stores,'" I read aloud. I peered at my phone screen. Nariphon had her arms crossed over her chest and was looking off to one side. "Nope, you're still here. What gives?"

"If I knew, I would tell you." She hesitated. "You wanted to see the source code."

"Uh, yes. Unequivocally."

Nariphon uncrossed her arms and placed one palm against the inside of my phone screen. Or at least that's what it looked like. Her hand compressed in the places where it would have come in contact with a pane of glass, if she were real. Indulging her, I pressed my fingertip to the screen in the same spot, unsure how this was going to allow me to see the code.

I didn't feel the motion, but I wasn't in my room any more. A garden stretched as far as I could see. There were birds tweeting, and the scent of an unidentifiable myriad of flowers hung heavy in the air. The breeze even shifted my hair.

"This is the source code?" was the only thing I could think to say. It was like I'd been sucked into a high-quality virtual reality simulator.

"Yes," Nariphon replied, but her brow creased as she looked at me. "You do not see what I see."

"I've never seen code in the shape of... fruit trees?"

Fruit trees. That meant something, only I couldn't put my finger on it.

It sparked something in Nariphon as well. "Do you know the story of Himaphan Forest?"

With that, my memory engaged. "What, you mean like the old folk legend about the dangers of premarital or extramarital sex that old Thais use to shame bar girls?"

Nariphon smiled, and for a moment I was reminded just how *not real* she was. It was the smile of a painting of a Buddha. "No, it was not meant to shame women.

The Nariphon trees were created to punish the weak men who claimed to be holy but could not resist temptation." She gestured to a nearby tree. From it hung a dozen fruits in the shape of naked women, each a little different, but all beautiful.

Not going to lie, the fruit women were tempting me. It was like the garden knew my type and created the fruit women in the image of my ideal girlfriend. But I remembered what Nariphon had just said, and I focused on the task at hand. "Okay, okay, but this isn't real in this context. You brought me here to look at the source code. So where is that?"

Nariphon looked around. "You should be able to access it at the heart tree once I get my bearings."

While I waited, I reached out and touched the nearest tree. A flash of code rushed through me, and I jerked back. "Whoa!" Yeah, I know, very Keanu Reeves. But all those ones and zeroes zipping through my brain shut down the rest of my vocabulary.

I touched the tree again, ready for it this time. I parsed through it, locating what I thought was the heart tree just as Nariphon pointed off to the right. "That way."

We made our way through the garden side by side. Nariphon paused at each tree to touch one of the fruits, her lips moving to offer quiet assurances to the fruit women.

As soon as we reached the heart tree, I realized just how wrong things were.

Nariphon crumpled to her knees and wailed at the sight. The heart tree was blackened and twisted. Where fruit had once hung, the branches were split and gnarled as though they had long ago given up their bounty.

I laid a gentle hand on her shoulder. "Let me see what's wrong."

I moved to the tree, which was even more menacing up close. I didn't want to touch it, but I had to. My palms twitched as they neared the trunk, and I pressed them against it. Underlying the scratchy bark was a quick zap of electricity, like touching a light switch in winter.

The code here was pristine, with no evidence of hacking or other intrusion. I scanned it fast, much faster than I could in reality. I stepped away from the tree, shaking my head, but saying nothing. Nariphon's brow furrowed. "What is it, Sasithorn?"

"The programmer—the one who made the app—he did this." My stomach churned. "It was something he put in the code, and it was just waiting for the right moment to launch. But I don't know why."

"Why may not matter. Can you fix it?"

"Yes. But there's nothing to prevent him from getting back in here and changing the code again. I can't lock him out."

Nariphon considered my words before she spoke again, her voice now soft. "In the legend of which I am a part, a violation of one of the fruits of these trees would send the violator into a deep slumber for four months."

I wasn't sure where she was going with this, but I shrugged. "That sounds like magic to me. And while I will admit that being here inside the code also seems like some sort of magic, I don't think I'm a magical hacker."

"No, but perhaps I can loan you some of my magic. Hackers can make... there is something like a poison?"

"Poison? No. Wait, do you mean a virus?"

Her face lit up. "That's it. Could you give the programmer a virus?"

"I could put a virus into the code, yeah. But it wouldn't stop him for..." I trailed off. "Okay, this may seem like a strange question, but if I'm here, where's my body? Am I just like a vegetable in my room?"

"Your body is in your room, but it is still human. It's simply passive at the moment. Susceptible to suggestion."

"That's... okay, what would happen if I died in here?"

"You need not fear death here. I will keep you safe."

"But if we got the programmer in here, maybe I can make a magical code virus and make him fall asleep inside of his own app. Like your legend says, right?"

Nariphon chuckled. "We have reached a point of the melding of your world with mine, Sasithorn. I believe anything we want might be possible. All we can do is try."

***

I wasn't going to kill the programmer. I was just going to get him out of the picture for a little while. And hopefully teach him a lesson about messing with legendary women. And me. Also me. (I had a hard time including myself in the "legendary women" category, even if I was currently inside an app, programming on thin air, getting ready to launch a magical virus. I'm just plain old Molly Wattana.) So whenever qualms started bubbling up about the virus I was writing, I pushed them back down and remembered what he'd done to Nariphon.

When I finished, I looked up at Nariphon, who had waited in silence while I worked on my code. "So how do you plan to get him in here?"

"In much the same way I got you here. Through his screen."

"No, I mean, you can't bring him in by telling him the code is messed up. He knows that. What are you going to do?"

"Seduce him. If I could not, I would not be worthy of the stories ascribed to me."

"Of course," I muttered as I moved behind one of the trees in the orchard, the code poised to launch as soon as the programmer was here.

He shimmered into being in front of Nariphon, and my throat filled with bile. "Where am I?" he asked.

He shouldn't have had time to figure out the answer to his question. The expression on his face shifted through fear, then anger, and then a smug cockiness as he intercepted the attack. In the weird virtual reality that was Nariphon's realm, it looked like he had made my code physical, crumpled it up, and tossed it away like a used Kleenex.

Neither Nariphon nor I had anticipated this. He had looked as confused as I had been when Nariphon first pulled me into the virtual world, and yet he had handled his sudden entrance with far more grace and skill. That hardly seemed fair.

I looked around for my discarded virus, but his intervention had annihilated it. There were pieces scattered throughout the garden, but it would take time for me to pull them back together, and what would stop him from repeating his earlier actions every time I tried to change the code?

"It didn't work," I called out, my words meant for Nariphon.

He chuckled. "Of course not. Now get out of my code." He shoved his hand forward, and I slammed backward, landing in my desk chair.

I grabbed my phone. The screen was already fading, but there was a faint gold dot that hadn't been there before. Nariphon put her lips together and blew the dot toward me before turning around and fading into blackness.

I pinched the space around the dot on my screen, and something cold solidified between my fingers. As I pulled them away from the iPhone, a glowing golden line followed. I didn't take time to think about it. I woke my laptop and led the magical line toward it. The end of the line coalesced into something that looked like a USB plug. I shrugged and inserted it into one of the USB ports.

As my laptop screen came to life, the code for the Nariphon app scrolled up it. I opened my favorite editor and started typing the virus, still fresh in my memory. I wanted to work as quickly as I could so Nariphon wasn't stuck with the programmer for a second longer than she had to be.

But I couldn't resist opening a second file and writing another virus at the same time. I wasn't just going to hit him inside the app. I was going to hit him out here, too. And while he might have been able to fight me off inside the virtual world, he wouldn't be able to fight me on two fronts. Every single version of the Nariphon app would be a carrier for my virus. An army of me.

As I finished the virus, I looked at the blackened screen of my phone. "I hope you can hear me, Nariphon," I whispered. "It's time."

My fingers flew across the keyboard, ripping out the nudity code and slapping my virus where it had been. The code blinked through the golden cord.

A moment passed. I realized I was holding my breath. The glowing cord went dull, and I was sure that I had failed. Again.

And then Nariphon's face appeared on the screen of my iPhone.

"It worked, Sasithorn. You did it." As she spoke, she shrunk down to the standard size of her cartoon image. She wore skinny jeans, heels, and an oversized white T-shirt with "Molly" printed across it in bold black letters.

I blushed. "Tell me you're not wearing that on every phone screen right now?"

"Only the ones where this outfit is appropriate to the weather."

I sighed, and she laughed.

"You deserve more than just a fashion statement in your honor, Sas... Molly. But aside from this, the only other thing I have to give is my eternal thanks."

"Well, I appreciate both," I admitted sheepishly. "But I suppose this is goodbye?"

"I hope I will not need your help again, but if I do find myself in trouble, I will come to you."

Before I could respond, the screen went dark. I had to unlock my phone and open the Nariphon app to see her again, and the cartoon image looked as vapid as it always had, not like some centuries-old legendary woman who had let me touch code with my bare (virtual) hands.

My stomach rumbled, reminding me how long I had focused on Nariphon's problem. I'd skipped breakfast and lunch, but I knew plenty of good places that stayed open through the mid-afternoon lull. I picked up my phone and my keys.

Then I paused. Who knew how quickly word might spread in the magical digital world, and how many other apps might need my help?

I left my phone on my desk. Other apps could wait until I'd eaten.

I figured saving one app a day was a good start.

Real Selfies

by Jon Lasser

My ex Spencer walked into the Prince of Patties just as I sat down in the dining room for my lunch break. I shook my head no, but he sat down across from me. He smiled with his eyes all lit up, and my heart beat faster.

There wasn't anybody north of Provo who I wanted to see less than Spencer. I knew I should tell him to leave, threaten to call over Grayson, the rent-a-cop who leaned against the tape measure glued to the doorjamb like nothing was wrong. Anything to get away from Spencer. He'd ambushed me here, knowing that if I made a scene, I'd end up exiled to the drive-through window again. An argument could even cost me the job. It wasn't much, but it paid my quarter of the rent, and I got lunch and dinner every day.

"Get away." My teeth seemed to have clenched of their own accord, and I struggled to get the words out. "Go."

Spencer dropped the smile and looked hurt. My heart cracked just a little, even though I knew better.

"Chris. You look good as a brunette," he said. Everyone else called me Christine. When we were first dating, I liked that he had a special name for me. The smile crept back onto his face. "I've got something for you."

He shoved a phone across the table, right past my burger. I started to reach for it as it slid past, but I'd just had my nails done. I'd be peeved if I chipped one so soon. I let the phone skid off the edge of the table. It made a little cracking sound as it hit the floor. I plucked it from the grimy tiles with two fingers. Who'd mopped last night? Marv? The floor was disgusting.

Thank God I hadn't broken the screen when it fell. I wouldn't have been able to pay Spencer back. Had he wanted it to break? There was always a catch with him.

"What's wrong with it?" I wiped the iPhone's blank face on my jeans and studied it in a lusterless beam of January sunlight. Not the 6S, but not far off. Almost like new: no cracks, no dings, except where it had just landed. I pressed the home button, discovering it wasn't locked. Its icons glowed invitingly.

"I don't want it anymore." His fingers trembled, like he was afraid of something. "You can have it."

"How much?" I took off my glasses and wiped a grease spot from them, trying not to look interested. I needed the phone, but I didn't want to lead him on. I was staying broken up with him this time.

"It's yours. Take it. I owe you that much."

I glared bleakly, the way I'd looked at him when I told him to move out last July, after I saw the pics he'd been texting. "Spencer, what's going on here?"

"You won't believe me," he said. Which was funny, because I'd spent nearly a year believing him when I knew better.

"Is it stolen?" He acted tough the way good boys trying to be bad often did, but he'd never stolen anything. Mostly he'd imitated his dad: a secret drinker, a womanizer, a born salesman with a jeweler's eye for appraising human weakness. The old man had left quite a mark upon Spencer.

"Real Selfies. An app. It takes pictures—" He snatched one of my fries.

"It's a phone. Phones have cameras."

"—pictures you're afraid of. Things that aren't there. Spiders. Drowning. Falling from heights. I could take a picture of you right now." He reached for the phone. I pulled it away from him.

It had to be a pitch, an attempt to hook me one way or another, but he looked up at me with that hangdog face, like he was confessing to the bishop. Why me? I supposed he didn't have anyone else to confess to. Maybe his latest girl, whoever she was, had dumped him. Maybe that was why he was here.

I shook my head. It was a crazy story, too crazy to believe, no matter what his eyes seemed to say.

"Bull." My mother had raised me to keep a civil tongue, and even after living in sin with Spencer for a year and a half, I couldn't take that word all the way. He used to make fun of me for that all the time. But he wasn't laughing now. "Delete it," I added uncertainly.

"I have deleted it. It keeps coming back."

"Just don't use it." I shoved his hand away as he reached for another fry.

"You don't understand, Christine." He only used my full name when he was begging for something. "You try it and you can't stop." He gazed hungrily at the phone. "I'm gonna get a burger."

Before I could say no, he was at the counter. What the hell, if he gave me a new phone, I could sit through lunch with him. I'd even share my fries.

⸻ ⊷⫘⊶ ⸻

It took Spencer almost ten minutes to get back to the table. I was going to be late getting back to work for sure. When he turned back toward me with his tray, I slipped the phone into my purse, dragged a fry through the sauce, and bit it in half. The potato's crunch and salt stung my mouth; the fry sauce soothed it. Why had Spencer cornered me here? It couldn't be the stupid phone story. I half believed it, the way I half believed him about his other girlfriends. Spencer had always known the secret was to believe his own story. I wasn't going to fall for it. Not this time.

Spencer sat down and unwrapped his own burger. He picked it up and took a delicate nibble. That wasn't like him. He took tremendous mouthfuls. Not today.

"You all right? Besides the phone?"

"Besides that, I'm fine." He seemed wound pretty tight for "fine."

"And your family? They're fine too?"

"They're fine. Even Dad." He smiled faintly, as though my asking after his dad was some sort of joke, which it basically was. He knew just what a jerk I thought his old man was. I'd never been afraid to tell him; that was one of the things he'd said he liked about me, that I'd stand up for him when even he couldn't. After a while, I regretted that I hadn't pulled that old man to the ground like one of those communist statues. By then, Spencer had turned around and seemed to idolize his dad.

Spencer's smile faded away. "It's the phone. I can't sleep at night. The things I've seen..." Spencer took another dainty bite from his burger.

I pulled the phone from my purse and slid around the home screen. There it was, buried in the Games folder. Real Selfies, its icon an old-style Polaroid camera like the one my parents had when I was little. The icon blinked as the camera fired its flash and spit out a photo. Cute little animation. I felt a sudden urge to launch the app, to tap my finger on the little whirring camera.

Spencer looked up over his soda. "Don't do that! Put it away." He mopped the sweat from his brow with a napkin.

"Oh, come on!" I launched the app, lined Spencer up in the viewfinder, and pressed the button.

The phone clicked and whirred like an old instant camera. The screen went white, except for a row of icons along the bottom edge of the screen. It seemed too crazy to be true, but what if Spencer wasn't lying?

The icons faded out and a picture faded in, developing before my eyes. Spencer's face came into focus—and disappeared again, replaced by a larger version of the Real Selfies icon. The camera dinged like a cartoon toaster, and the row of icons reappeared.

I shoved the phone back across the table. For a moment, I expected Spencer would let it slide right by and onto the floor, but he stopped it with one finger. He made a face like he'd been spattered by hot grease, pained and unbelieving.

"Ha, ha. You almost had me fooled." Spencer never could resist a good prank, just like he couldn't resist blondes with tattoos and tongue piercings. (We had a few of those, even in Middle-of-Nowhere, Utah, and Spencer might have had them all.) "What?" Spencer wasn't laughing. He couldn't help but laugh when he pranked me.

"You know what." Maybe he was a better liar than he used to be.

He looked at the screen and shrugged. "Well, yeah. I'm frightened of the camera."

"It's a joke app, not a scary psychic camera. Get a grip."

"Really, Chris. I swear."

"Like all those other times you swore—"

"Oh, hell. Chris, it's not like—"

"Never mind. I think you'd better be going." I stood and looked meaningfully at Grayson, who was too busy checking out a couple of high-school girls to notice. Spencer raised the phone. *Click. Whir.* "Give me that!" I grabbed for the phone but couldn't reach.

"If there's nothing to be afraid of, what's the big deal?" *Ding.*

"Aha!" Spencer smiled, triumph shining in his eyes.

"What?"

Spencer slid the camera across the table. I caught it this time. In the picture, I looked fifteen years older.

So did Spencer.

A clutch of children—three boys and a girl—surrounded us. Everyone smiled, but my eyes flickered with the same sad dying light I saw in Spencer's mother's eyes, a woman serving a life sentence.

"How?" I couldn't form the rest of the question.

"I don't know. It's magic." He stood up and put a hand on my shoulder. "It wouldn't be so bad, would it? I mean—"

I pulled away from him.

Grayson wasn't done ogling the high schoolers. Just my luck that my security guard was a total perv. He'd have to write it up if I called him over, and my manager, Dave, had made clear that he didn't like troublemakers the last time I'd had to ask Spencer to leave. (It turned out he did read all those reports. Who knew?) It'd be different if I had a restraining order, he'd said, but Spencer wasn't like that. He just wouldn't leave me alone.

"You've gotta go," I told Spencer. "I'm gonna call Grayson over here."

The picture had gotten it right. Only two classes stood between me and my associate's. I could go to school somewhere else after that and never come back here except for weddings and funerals. It didn't really matter where I went, but with Spencer in my life, I wasn't going anywhere.

Even without Real Selfies, taking the phone would tie me to Spencer, the way that bringing your new neighbors a tuna casserole meant that they owed you something, that they couldn't leave until they'd brought over at least two Jell-O salads.

I shoved the phone back across the table. No way was I going end up as another fly stuck in Spencer's spiderweb of social obligation.

He caught it and shoved it back toward me.

"Chris, just take it. No strings attached, really." It was like he'd read my mind. Of course, he'd seen the last picture, so maybe it was like that. "I never want to see it again." He stood, lifting his tray. He'd only finished half the burger, though he'd eaten a few of my fries.

"Wait—" I said. Spencer turned toward me. "Say cheese!"

He flinched halfway out of the frame as I snapped another picture. *Click. Whir. Ding.* I turned the phone to face Spencer before I even took a look. I just wanted to see his face, to do to him what he'd done to me with that last picture. I wanted him to hate me for exposing his secret fears, to take a knife to the psychic cord that bound me to him. Yes, maybe to twist that knife, just a little.

"Give it to me." Spencer grabbed for the phone as I dangled it just out of reach. "Screw you, Chris."

"Finders keepers," I teased, then turned to look at the photo.

Spencer's dad glowered at me. Only it wasn't his father, exactly, but a cartoon of him. Fifty feet tall, brow heavy like a caveman, and a vicious idiot grin. One hand, the size of his meaty head, held his equally swollen willie. The other hand, raised high, triumphantly held what looked at first like a skinned rabbit, limp and hollow.

Something about that rabbit didn't sit right. I pinched to zoom, and saw that it wasn't a rabbit at all. A naked woman, hips and waist unflatteringly thick, breasts flabby. My face, but with blond hair again. *Oh God.*

"Spencer—" I wanted to tell him how sorry I was, but "sorry" seemed inadequate. I felt like throwing up.

I reached for his hand, but he'd already run out of the Prince of Patties.

<hr/>

I could have followed Spencer into the parking lot, but I didn't. I wasn't ready to talk to him yet. That picture—it showed what he feared, but still it had come from some part of him. Was that how he saw me, a prize to be contested and won? Or was it only how he thought his dad saw me? I'd never liked the man, and I liked him less now.

As I clicked on the home button, my finger brushed one of the icons along the bottom edge of the screen. The viewfinder disappeared, and Real Selfies presented me with a grid of tiny little thumbnails: Spencer's worst nightmares, all in one place.

Some of the pictures were easy to understand: Spencer, naked, behind the counter at work; Spencer, roasting on a spit in hell; and too many to count of his dad, gigantic and weirdly twisted. Others made no sense at all, at least to me: a page from an old-fashioned phone book; a beautiful green pasture with a small white farmhouse and a red barn, like a picture postcard; and some just black, as though the camera hadn't captured anything.

The ones I couldn't look away from were the ones that looked like nightmares and horror movies: Spencer's mom embracing a child's dirt-streaked blue corpse; pine trees hanging upside-down in the air, their tops pointing at him as their roots writhed far above, in the open air; Spencer held down and raped by a host of men, some of whom appeared more than once; women with seaweed hair and gill slits on their necks, reaching out as though to embrace the ocean; and a prison chain gang, hoisting pick-axes over their headless shoulders.

Flipping through the pictures, they seemed familiar and strange. I looked at them, and Spencer felt more familiar and more strange than he'd ever been. I wanted to hold him in my arms and comfort him like a child, tell him everything would be all right, that none of it was real. I wanted to slap him across the face and tell him to be a man, to get over it. I wanted to delete the pictures and pretend I hadn't seen them.

I wanted to turn the phone on myself and see what more its evil camera could show.

Click. Whir. Ding.

I couldn't look. Seeing his own fears had hurt Spencer, maybe destroyed him. I couldn't do it to myself too.

Despite my best intentions, I peeked. Nothing. Inky blackness.

But wait: where Spencer's empty black pictures had felt cold, as though the camera hadn't captured anything, mine felt different. Like velvety night.

Not that I was afraid of the dark. I wasn't. But velvety? In a coffin, buried alive? A shiver ran through me, even though I knew I was being silly.

Spencer shouldn't have given me the phone. He had to get away from it, sure, but he had to know he was just passing his problems on to me. Maybe he thought I was strong enough to resist the temptation. Maybe he thought I could save him.

Click. Whir. Ding.

———⌀///⌀———

Dave, my manager, came out from the back room.

"Chris, what in the heck?" He checked his watch. "You've been on lunch for seventy-five minutes. How long is a lunch break?"

"Thirty." I looked down at my tray. Even the little burnt ends of the French fries were gone. "Sorry, Dave. I lost track of time."

Dave shrugged and looked around the Prince of Patties. "It's been pretty quiet. You clocked out, yeah? Want to go home early?"

I needed the money, but I wanted to get out, at least for the afternoon. "Sorry. Thanks." I snuck a glance at the phone as I slipped it into my purse. Real Selfies showed a picture of me looking at the phone. The phone in the picture showed a picture of me looking at the phone, and on and on.

That was what it was, a hall of mirrors. I could lose myself in it, but there was always a way out. I flipped back several pictures to the one where Spencer and I had a family. Where I stayed in this rinky-dink town. No way. I had nothing to be afraid of—unless I forget what I most feared.

"See you later, Dave." I smiled, and tipped an imaginary hat at Grayson as I walked out the door into the bright late-afternoon sun.

My new iPhone sat in my purse, connecting me to the world and keeping me on track.

Specific Wisdom

by Kris Millering

———⊂≋≋⊃———

Calla woke up on All Saint's Day with a horrid taste in her mouth, a headache that felt like it was threatening to take her whole head off, her knee aching like a big storm was on its way, and a dead phone.

Some people would have had a lot of fun to earn a hangover like that. Calla had merely been—careless.

Stupid, she groused as she slumped into her shower. *Forgetting to take care of yourself.*

Half an hour later, she was showered, dressed, and moisturized. The blessed beans that Auntie Eris had given her a week ago were well on their way to becoming a restorative brew. She'd downed half a liter of the electrolyte solution she kept for emergencies—it tasted less awful this morning than it usually did, which was a sign of how badly she'd abused herself last night—and was working on the rest. Food was going to have to wait until her stomach decided it didn't hate her any more.

She grumbled as she stepped out into the tiny yard off her kitchen, surrounded by high fencing. Calla pulled her robe tighter around her as she surveyed the yard. Chair, pots with the remains of her tomato plants from the summer, little table, cheerful glass sculpture in the corner.

No bedraggled kitten or dignified old dog. No snake or lizard or even, Lady help her, injured crow. The ritual hadn't worked, then. Samhain was the best time to call a familiar, but even with every condition being favorable, it just hadn't happened.

She probably still wasn't ready for a new familiar. Marigold, the tomcat that her mother had called for her when Calla had been a toddler, had died only a couple of years ago. Calla thought she'd fully grieved and was ready to move on—and besides, it was *weird* for a registered witch to be working without a familiar. People walked into her office and looked around expectantly, and then things got awkward when they didn't see a cat snoozing on a shelf or a toad in a terrarium.

Calla shook her head and stepped back into the little yellow kitchen that she'd painted herself after she'd moved in a couple of years ago. She'd dropped her phone in its cradle before she'd stumbled off to shower, and it was awake once more.

She picked it up and winced at the number of text messages and emails. At least Samhain had fallen on a Friday this year, and her clients had understood when she'd told them she was taking the weekend off from going to showings and dowsings. People expected witches to take weird holidays, even land witches who worked in real estate.

Something was odd about her phone. It felt strange in her hand, like it was somehow heavier than it had been, and the home screen was all rearranged. Her social media icons all had red notification dots on them, and the top sported two apps she didn't remember installing. One icon looked like a silhouetted cat either stretching or pouncing on something, and was labeled Proximate Knowledge. The other was that same cat curled up in a ball, and was labeled Specific Wisdom.

Both had notifications waiting. She just stared at them for a moment.

The coffee machine gurgled and hissed. *This will all make more sense after some coffee.*

Unfortunately, Calla was wrong about that. She drank coffee (and silently thanked Auntie Eris and her gift for knowing exactly when Calla would need the coffee beans that she roasted herself and charged with minor restorative magic) and tried to make sense of what had happened last night. It had been Halloween, so there were the usual Tumblr skeleton wars and people tweeting party pictures, but she had almost twenty replies to tweets she didn't remember making. Even in a post-ritual fugue, she didn't usually say things like *Failure is failure; roll on and leave what was behind* and *Don't look behind you. Just don't. It'll be OK.*

The replies were evenly divided between people who knew her and were worried, and strangers who thought she was being profound. Fortunately, she didn't appear to have posted anything on Facebook, so it was unlikely she was going to be receiving worried calls from either set of parents.

She was down to the end of her first cup of coffee, and she was starting to piece together what had happened last night. The calling ritual hadn't gone well. It hadn't gone *spectacularly* wrong, but as usual all she'd gotten for her careful preparation was some awful blowback. She'd *felt* the power growing and building, and she'd been shaping it well, and then there had been a sensation like a fishing line snapping when a salmon was on the hook.

All of her candles had gone out, and—that was right, her wand *and* her cup had both shattered, and so had her circle. She got up, walked out to the living room, and grimaced. There were wood and ceramic shards all over the floor, the edge of the couch looked slightly scorched, and there were puddles of cooled wax on the floor where some of the candles had fallen over.

This was the third time something like this had happened while she was trying to call a familiar. She supposed this time should be the last. *At least I didn't set the house on fire.*

Her phone was heavy in her pocket, and she pulled it out, squinting at the Proximate Knowledge and Specific Wisdom apps at the top. *Maybe this is something Apple installed?* The iPhone was new, a gift from Mama after Calla had dropped her old Android phone into a creek while evaluating a piece of property Edith Brickbauer wanted her to list. She hesitated, then touched Proximate Knowledge.

The screen went black, and then glowing green letters floated up from the depths.

THE CALL HAS NEVER GONE UNANSWERED.

"That's... less than helpful," she muttered as the letters faded and the app exited. Maybe Specific Wisdom would be better?

Specific Wisdom's lack of interface was the same, but the letters glowed blue rather than green.

YOU WILL FEEL BETTER IF YOU CLEAN UP YOUR MESS AND GO FOR A WALK.

Well. At least that was something, and she supposed it was right. It was still pretty fortune-cookie-like—anyone could have a mess that needed cleaning up, and walks were often good for feeling better—but at least it was something she could act on.

She posted a tweet that said *Bad night last night, I'm OK, no worries* and started cleaning up.

———⌒〰〰⌒———

A crow landed on the fence as Calla locked the door, and cawed harshly. She fished in her pocket and tossed a peanut in its general direction. Staying on good terms with the neighborhood flock was important, especially for a witch without a familiar.

She rolled her shoulders and set out. The neighborhood was a quiet one, and the ground was reassuringly alive under the concrete of the sidewalk. There were a few Folk living out here—not many, but enough.

The same couldn't be said for the rest of the Seattle area. The native Folk had been forced almost entirely out of the city over the last century and a half. In their place, immigrant Folk had moved in, following the humans from their native lands—but there weren't nearly enough of them to sustain the land in the densest parts of Seattle. Folk relocated away from places that were running short and the places they left behind starved for magic, making it harder for new Folk to move in.

Dead zones, where the land's magic had run entirely dry, developed beneath the sterile new buildings that were built during each economic boom, and from beneath those buildings they spread and migrated. A dead zone would make Folk ill and could even kill them if they stayed, and witches and other sensitive humans were affected as well. Nobody knew what to do, other than mark the borders of known dead zones and keep an eye on them.

Once, most of Calla's job as a real estate land witch had been locating houses either on or far away from ley lines, determining whether houses were really haunted, and finding places to live for Folk who had very specific needs in their living arrangements. Then things had changed.

After the fourth time she'd discovered the corpses of Folk in a house that she was trying to list, and the third time she'd been attacked by a twisted and angry spirit who'd been caught in a dead zone, Calla had had enough. She'd moved east to try and salvage what was left of the heart that the city had broken.

Her phone pinged as she turned the corner and started down the long hill to Lake Sammamish. There was a notification on Proximate Knowledge. Curious, she opened it.

STORM WARNING. STORM WARNING.

She looked up at the sky, which was lightly overcast, and then frowned at her phone. "That's really not helpful," she muttered, and stuck it back into her pocket. The lake was only six blocks away, and she slipped between two houses and came out onto a rocky beach. A bald eagle soared overhead, circling the lake, looking for fish.

The lake was over a mile across and seven miles long, tucked between rolling hills dotted with houses that cost more than Calla could ever afford. On autumn mornings, low clouds would linger on those hills, caught in the trees like the breath of dragons.

Right now, though, it wasn't quite fall, but a chilly breeze riffled the surface of the water. Then the breeze died into stillness.

The water's surface kept riffling, and then stirred like there was something moving beneath it.

Shit.

She extended her senses gingerly toward the disturbance, and her thoughts slid off a smoothness like an algae-clad stone in a stream. She set herself and probed again, and this time a sickening sensation twisted her stomach.

Calla swore and stooped, scooping up a handful of stones. There was a dead zone right offshore, probably on the move, and there was *something*—

The water churned abruptly, then bowed upward in a manner that *shouldn't* be possible. Not without a something pushing from beneath—

The *something* broke the surface of the water and stood up. And up. And *up*.

It was a troll, covered in slick weeds and accreted pebbles, about twenty feet tall. Its face was only vaguely humanoid, two crystalline eyes black with blue sparks deep within, a mouth that hung open and showed rows of jagged obsidian teeth.

The troll staggered forward, screaming.

Shit. Troll. What did Mama tell me about trolls?

They were, for rocks, extremely lively ones. They were nearly indestructible, extremely rare, and spent most of their time in meditation and contemplation that to the casual observer looked a lot like centuries-long sleep. The dead zone must have caused this one a tremendous amount of pain for it to be moving so quickly. It was also small, which didn't mean it was young, just that it had been born from a boulder rather than a mountainside.

And it looked all right. It *looked* like trolls were supposed to look. It wasn't twisted by the dead zone. *Thank the Lady for small favors.*

The water sloshed and fizzed around its legs as it staggered toward the shore, still screaming like a hundred kettles at the boil.

First, she needed its attention. A pain-maddened troll could accidentally kill a lot of people, and, like it or not, preventing things like that was part of what witches were supposed to do.

I moved out here to stop doing superhero shit like this.

"Hey! *Hey!*" She flung pebbles at the troll, waving her arms, jumping up and down. "Hey troll, hey! Look at me, troll! Look at me!" She stooped again, picking up a bigger rock. She kissed it, leaving sand on her lips, and then threw it with all of the force she could muster—including a certain kind of *push* from inside of her that was all the magic she dared summon outside of a circle.

The stone smacked the troll in the middle of the chest. If it made a sound, it was lost under the troll's scream.

The troll flinched, and then staggered to a halt still standing in what would be knee-deep water on Calla. It looked around with its jet eyes, granite arms moving with rumbling grinding sounds, and—finally!—focused on Calla.

Then its mouth opened again, showing those horrifying teeth once more, and it lurched toward her.

Great. Now I need the rest of this clever plan.

She backed away, up the beach, toward the gap between the houses. It followed, trundling toward her.

Out of the water, it started moving faster. It was still focused on her, which was good for everyone else. She broke into a jog and hung a right on the trail that led toward Issaquah. The troll bashed against the corner of one of the houses, bounced off, and followed.

Calla ran.

─── ⚡ ───

By the time Calla and the troll got about a mile down the trail, someone had not-so-helpfully called the police. "I'm a registered witch!" she hollered at the uniformed woman who sprang out of her black-and-white. She lifted her arm to flash the twisted chain around her wrist that marked her official status. "There's nothing you can do! It won't even feel it if you shoot it." She pulled to a stop; the troll was about 600 feet behind her and gaining, but Calla was out of breath. (Also wobbly. Her head was letting her know that a run had *not* been in its plans for today.) The troll was moving at a pace somewhere between a fast walk and a medium jog. She'd be able to keep ahead of it for a while, but not forever.

Humans had speed on trolls, but trolls had nearly inexhaustible stamina. This was not a race she was going to be able to win.

The policewoman frowned. "Where are you taking it?" She glanced at the troll, and Calla noticed the green flush on the side of her neck, only barely visible on her dark skin. Part dryad, then. Dryads made good cops, especially when they were given a small area to patrol. They were calm, good with people, and trees talked to them—and trees paid attention to *everything*.

That is a good question. "Tiger Mountain." She started walking again; the troll was catching up. It showed no sign of noticing the cop who had fallen in beside her. "Once it's up there, it can go until it stops hurting so much. It'll probably settle right down again after it gets this out of its system."

Her phone buzzed, and she pulled it out of her pocket. Specific Wisdom wanted her attention.

GET HER NAME. SHE CAN HELP.

The letters faded, and Calla was about to hit the home button again, when the depths of the app swirled once more.

GET HER NUMBER.

She wrinkled her nose and shut down the app. "Right. Uh. Officer…" She craned her neck around so she could see her name badge. "Freeman? I don't suppose you could find me a bicycle from somewhere?"

Freeman was looking, perplexed, at Calla's phone. "Did your phone just tell you to get my number?"

Behind them, the thudding, grinding footfalls of the troll sped up slightly. Calla glanced over her shoulder and broke into a jog. "It's been a really fucking weird weekend so far. Bicycle?"

"On it. Let me talk to my dispatcher. Sunnie can find you something." She was jogging next to Calla now, not even breathing hard. She talked into her radio for a few minutes, speaking in rapid jargon that Calla didn't even try to follow. Calla looked over her shoulder again as the troll screamed.

Ahead of them on the trail, a trio of runners came to a halt, staring at the troll in dismay. One of them pulled a cell phone out of his pocket and snapped a picture. "Get out of the way!" Calla hollered. They looked at her, then at the troll, and turned around to run the other way.

Smart humans. Good humans. She kept going.

They were almost to the big grocery store when another police car pulled up next to the trail, blues and reds flashing. The cop in the passenger seat hopped out of the car and opened the trunk, hauling out a bicycle that had seen better days. He rolled it over to Calla, who had dropped back to a tired walk. "You know what you're doing, right?" he said, glancing at the twisted chain around her wrist.

Calla fought not to heave a sigh. *Never show weakness to authority,* Mama had always told her. *Our recognition is recent, and could be taken away all too easily.* The troll thudded and rumbled behind her. "I'm going to take it up the trail by downtown and then up Sunset. Piece of cake."

Officer Freeman came to a stop next to them. "Sunnie said you'd have a bike for me, too." Calla had thought she was in pretty decent shape, but Freeman had barely broken a sweat and she wasn't even slightly winded. Calla couldn't decide if that was irritating or distractingly sexy.

Maybe a bit of both.

"In the trunk." The cop wasn't looking at either of them, instead staring at the troll. "Shit. Where did it *come* from?"

"Lake Sammamish," Callas said and hopped onto the bike. It had been made for someone half a head taller than she was, but she could make it work. "Long story." The dead zones were not something they talked to the authorities about. Someone had tried once, but it had been twisted back onto them. They'd tried to make out like the dead zone in the middle of Detroit had been the fault of the *witches*.

Everyone wanted to blame Detroit, St. Louis, and Ames on something other than the actual culprits.

She got herself up onto the bike seat and pushed off, wobbling a little before she started to gain a bit of speed. "Thanks!" she said. "I'll drop the bike by the station later. Hey, don't—"

She'd turned just a little too late, and she almost fell off the bike as the report of a gunshot physically assaulted her, setting off a ringing in her ears that made anything else hard to hear—except for the rumble of the troll as it stumbled slightly and then righted itself.

Her head hurt. Well, it hurt *more*. She put her hand to the side of her head, touched her ear, and then looked in disbelief at her bloody fingers. "Oh, *shit*." She raised her voice. "Do *not* fucking shoot the troll!"

The troll had slowed; it was about a hundred feet away, shaking its head a little. Both of the cops gaped at her and (she presumed) her bloody head. "It's following me because I set up a resonance." Her words tumbled over themselves. "The troll's invulnerable, but I'm not."

She hopped onto the bike and started pedaling for all she was worth, past tangled greenery in the median. She didn't look back because she could feel the troll speeding up.

"Fucking superhero shit," she muttered to herself. In her pocket, her phone buzzed. She fished it out, wobbling a little on the bike; Proximate Knowledge had a message for her.

SOME PEOPLE DON'T HAVE THE SENSE THEY WERE BORN WITH.

Calla snorted and shoved the phone back into her coat pocket. *Tell me something I don't already know.*

The troll stopped following her about halfway through downtown.

Issaquah's downtown was tiny, about six blocks long and two wide. The trail that led past downtown just skirted its edge, passing along the back sides of historic buildings and through the railroad museum. She felt the tension between herself and the troll suddenly slacken as she pedaled past a railroad switch, and she slowed and glanced back.

The troll was meandering off the path, toward the road that led through the center of downtown. Officer Freeman was darting ahead of it on her own bicycle, shouting and waving her arms, trying to warn off the Sunday morning strollers. Fortunately, there weren't that many people out yet, and those who were out were acting sensibly and getting out of the way.

Calla pulled her bike around and lit out towards the troll. It sounded like an avalanche when it was in motion, rumbling and crashing. "Hey!" she screamed at it, trying to get its attention. "HEY!"

It ignored her.

She spent a moment wishing that witches could do spontaneous magic like the Folk—she could use some mobile trees right now, or maybe a giant net—and pedaled like mad to catch up.

Freeman had stopped traffic, and the troll was lumbering down the middle of Front Street like it knew where it was going. Calla pedaled around it, and it took a sideways swipe at her but didn't otherwise react. It had stopped screaming, she realized. She wondered if that was a good sign.

But where was it *going?*

She stopped the bike fifteen yards ahead of it, watching it for a moment. Its great head swung from side to side, and the weedy mess on its head and back was starting to dry and turn brown. She extended her senses toward it, observing in that sharp and engrossing manner that was a witch's main skill, and sucked in a breath.

Where—

Her phone buzzed. The troll had slowed down a bit, so she hopped off the bike and walked it, pulling her phone out of her pocket. It was Specific Wisdom this time. She was starting to get used to this.

IT SEEKS COMFORT.

Comfort. What was comfortable to a living boulder? She had thought peace and quiet would be good for contemplation. All it really needed, though, was a place that would never turn into a dead zone, a place that would never hurt it enough to force it to move.

Maybe the mountain was too far away? The troll might not be able to sense it from here. Besides, the mountain had been logged before, and there was still some land on it that might be logged again. No good for any Folk, especially not one that hated moving.

It liked water enough to submerge itself for centuries. Water.

There was a salmon hatchery three blocks from here. If the troll didn't mind humans being around, it might work. If she could get it to follow her, if it liked the look of the place enough to stay still.

She shoved her phone back into her pocket and waved at the troll, then hopped back on her bike. "Do I ever have a great place for you! Come on, troll! Let's—no, go *around* the car, not through—there you go."

The spark in the troll's eyes brightened, and it seemed to focus on her once again. "Just another block now. Follow me, follow me." She made her voice rise and fall in a singsong chant. There was no magic in it, just a prayer to anyone who might be listening.

They reached the corner by the library, and the troll hesitated. It took a grinding step forward, then another, its head turning this way and that. Calla yelped and scampered out of the way as the troll's shoulder hit a stoplight support and sent it crashing to the ground.

"What are you *doing*?" she muttered, then raised her voice. "Troll! Trolllllllllll. Come on, troll, this way!" Her voice was rising into a buzzing irritation tinged with panic.

It made a different sound this time, less whistle than metallic grumble, and turned its head to the east, toward the ridge of the mountain visible over the rooftops. Then it took a step toward the mountain, away from the hatchery.

We're so close. She jumped off the bike and let it fall to the ground, then rubbed her fingers over her still-bleeding ear, smearing her fingertips with her blood. The troll took another step away from the hatchery as Calla darted forward and swiped at the troll's rocky skin, leaving a slight smear of blood behind.

As she touched the troll, well within the reach of its massive arms, she bent her entire mind and will toward one belief. She and this creature had very little in common, but there was a resonance between them now. A connection. Something they could communicate through.

And with that belief, she *pushed*.

The troll turned so abruptly that Calla nearly tripped over herself trying to get out of the way. "Water," she said, and concentrated on the word and the images of a stream calmed by human hands but still deep, clear, and cold, filled with salmon and other fish. "Water." The feeling of it flowing by, low in summer, high in winter, roaring in full flood. "Water." Safety. Protection. Calm.

The troll's eyes focused on her, and she took a step back as it took a step forward. She stepped again, and it stepped in time with her. The world was bright around her, every edge sharp. She could feel the troll, feel the chill of a half-asleep mountain, restless in dreaming.

This way. This way.

The troll took one step for every step she took, quickly overtaking her. Calla felt the moment when the troll's attention passed from her to the stream it could feel ahead of it, and sagged a little as the weight of its regard lifted from her.

It walked through a chain-link fence without even noticing it, and headed across the hatchery grounds towards the place where Issaquah Creek widened and was diverted into a fish ladder. It wavered by the bridge, at the very edge of the creek, and then let itself fall forward, crashing through the brush on the bank and landing in the water with a splash and a rumbling groan.

Calla ran to the middle of the bridge that overlooked the creek and the fish ladder. She watched it fold its limbs up around itself, head melting back into its body. The spark of light in its jet eyes went out.

It was still.

Calla breathed out. *Okay.*

The feeling of the world being sharp-edged around her began to fade, as did the sensation of connection with the troll as the stream washed her blood from its skin. Officer Freeman pulled up beside her and stared down at the troll. "Is it going to stay there?"

"It should. Trolls don't ever move unless they have to. It'll stay where it is as long as it's not disturbed." This site would never be developed—there was a tremendous tangle of laws around salmon habitat, and the people who lived here loved their fish hatchery fiercely. The running water would help as well.

"Hunh. Well. Let me call it in and make sure everyone knows we no longer have a troll wandering around downtown. And I'll call the fish hatchery people and let them know they have yet another endangered species on the property."

"Thanks." Calla breathed out, running her hand over her hair. "I'll drop the bike off at the station."

Freeman nodded and turned away, then hesitated. "Do you need a ride?" she asked. "I mean, we're a long way from where you started. And, well..." She gestured at the side of Calla's head. "You might want to clean up. Jones is bringing my car down to the station. Follow me there?"

Calla blinked a little and then nodded. Then she extended her hand. "Sure. I'm Calla Verdi. Registered witch."

Freeman took Calla's hand and shook it, her hand warm and dry against Calla's sweaty palm. "Josephine Freeman. Everyone calls me Josie."

An hour later, Calla was curled up on her couch with some tea, freshly showered. Josie's card was on the kitchen table, and the way Officer Freeman—Josie—had said "Call me, we'll have coffee" gave Calla some hope that she actually meant it.

There were videos of the troll being posted online courtesy some of the early-morning strollers, but nobody had yet realized that Calla had been the one leading it. She flipped through her Twitter feed a little and then set her phone aside. The hangover had dissipated at last, but she could still use a nap.

Her phone pinged.

Both Proximate Knowledge and Specific Wisdom had messages for her. Proximate Knowledge said: THERE IS AN ANSWER TO YOUR CALL. Specific Wisdom said: DO NOT BLAME US FOR THE FORM WE TAKE.

"Why would I blame..." She trailed off, staring at the letters as they faded.

She had called a familiar last night. She had thought the call had gone unanswered, that the ritual had gone wrong.

Calla groaned and let her head fall back against the couch. "You're my *familiar*."

Both apps pinged. When she opened them, both just displayed a big sideways smiley face and faded out.

Calla groaned. Explaining this to her mothers was going to be... interesting. *I guess I'll save a fortune on cat food, though.*

She reached over and grabbed a notebook and pen from the table next to the couch. A dead zone had formed six blocks from her house. She was going to need to try to do something about it.

As she sketched ideas and made notes, her phone purred quietly to itself. She patted it, and kept working.

Nessa, Iggy, and the Murky Toilet Selfie

by H.M. Jones

———— ⟨✏✏✏⟩ ————

Venessa, "Nessa," as her friends called her, took *the best* selfies. She was nominated as Century High's 2014 Prom Queen on her selfie skills alone. At least, that's what she figured. Sure, she was stunning in real life. But without the vignettes, antiquing, color shifts and filters, she wasn't at her best. Her iPhone and selfie stick were her steadfast best friends. They rarely failed to create her in just the right light. They were her makers, really. Without them, did she even exist?

She was currently undergoing her most challenging selfie *ever* in the bathroom of Hank's Western BBQ Ranch. Fluorescents were hard on her milky skin, painting her a mustard yellow. And the lights were not direct enough, poised as they were over the toilet stalls rather than over the fake wood laminate sink. *God! Who designed this crap hole?* Whoever it was had no taste, nor any idea how to highlight a young woman's charms.

But she tried to make the best of it, which was *very* trying in a Hank's Western BBQ Ranch uniform—a red polo and non-formfitting slacks. Nessa had thought she could rock anything until she landed this job. Red was her color, but not this brick red monstrosity. No, she was a scarlet or crimson girl. The fat yellow lettering over her right shirt pocket—yes, there was a weirdly placed pocket that made her right boob look distorted—*really* clashed with her pallor. Her miraculous iPhone, Iggy, was having a hard time snapping a good selfie. And Nessa *had* to post a "first day of work" selfie to her social media accounts.

She peered at the fifth selfie on Iggy's screen. It was all pixelated due to the crap lighting. Her breasts looked good, thanks to the fact that her polo had buttons. She knew she wasn't allowed to wear them unbuttoned at work. But the selfie was for posterity, so she'd gone as low as she could go without tiptoeing into "desperate for likes" territory. She'd always known how to toe that line. So many girls didn't. *Subtle is sexy.*

She stared at the fourth selfie she'd snapped. Her lips were just pouty enough to look appealing but not duck-like. Her lapel fell just so, off her pale chest, revealing a sunken clavicle. Her eyes were wide and innocent. Her cheeks sucked in just enough to look thin rather than skeletal. But her emerald eyes looked muddy and gray, and her spun-gold mane looked depressed and slack under the low light. She stomped her foot and checked Iggy's screen for the time. Four fifty-five.

"Shit! Okay, Iggy, we have, like, five minutes to get the perfect selfie. Don't fail me now, girl." She smiled at her iPhone. She swore it warmed in her grasp with mutual adoration.

Her friends called her crazy for talking to her phone, but she knew better. She'd had this version for a year—a huge faux paus in her clan. But she wouldn't give Iggy up. They'd formed a bond. Since she'd bought Iggy, her selfies had been the perfect balance of sex appeal, girlish intrigue, and class. Nine times out of ten, Iggy captured her best self on the first click, like capturing a rare nymph springing through the glades of a mystical forest. Each selfie update received a minimum of fifty likes. Not to mention seriously naughty comments from the hottest guys at Century High.

A killer selfie—in which she held a crimson rose against her mouth—garnered her a message from her best friend Ronny's brother, Chad. *A college man!* She'd been in thralls over Chad since she was a too-skinny eighth grader. Now he was messaging her things like, *Hey beautiful, you're looking hott these days* and *When I'm back home, wanna go to the movies with me, gorgeous?* She trembled a little, thinking about Chad's deep caramel eyes and voice that matched. He was slick and sweet.

Then, nothing. For two whole days! Was he playing hard-to-get now that he was back in town? Did he want her to make the next move? For God's sake, he hadn't even *liked* her last two selfie posts!

She stared at her phone in disbelief. "And those were awesome selfies, Iggy. It wasn't our fault. We could do better, if only we had more direct light."

Iggy buzzed in agreement. That was another thing she kept from her friends. Iggy answered her, knew her, supported her. Other people saw their phone's buzzes as notifications, tweets, emails, but Nessa knew better. Sure, she'd just gotten a text from her dad, demanding to know if she'd made it to her first day at Hank's Greasy Hole. But it was Iggy's timing that made her sure Iggy was speaking back. She buzzed and beeped and chirped in perfect harmony to Nessa's questions and desires. Like a sleek, sparkly, slim magic genie.

She scanned the brick and lumber bathroom, sneering at the scene. Hardly the classiest décor for the perfect selfie. But with the right smash of light, the brick framing her spiraled yellow locks, and a filter to bring out the texture in the background, Iggy could make her shine. To Instagrammers, Facebookers and Tweeters, she'd be walking the city streets of old Boston or New York, a great traveler. Of course, she'd never been out of state, but that hardly mattered to the social world. Iggy had the most recent photo maneuvering applications. She'd look vintage, even with the lapel. She'd look charming, sexy, and full of class. Chad would melt.

He had to like this selfie, or it was all over. If she and Iggy didn't pull this off, her fantasy of being on the arm of a college guy would be just that—fantasy. Then how would she get into the best parties? A college party—with wine coolers, live bands, and college football stars. *Swoon.*

A desperate search for the best light revealed that the middle stall had a white bulb, rather than a florescent yellow one. Nessa cheered. "That's the one, Iggy. I know how you love white light."

She pecked her IPhone on its glassy surface. "Sorry, Iggs, forgot I wasn't wearing ColorStay." She wiped the screen free of crimson lipstick with the corner of her shirt. Iggy didn't seem to mind.

She strolled over to the middle stall and smacked the fake lumber door in frustration. A sloppily handwritten sign was taped to the stall. "Out of order. Do not use."

Glancing behind her, Nessa noticed that there was an inner lock on the bathroom door. She removed the paper from the middle stall, careful not to puncture it with manicured finger nails. She slapped the sign under the "Cowgirls" plaque, and clicked the lock shut from the inside. She didn't want anyone to witness the magic. A magician never reveals her secrets.

"We'll pretend we're cleaning the place up on our first day, won't we, Iggs? What time is it anyway?" Iggy flashed 4:57 on her screen in response. "Damn. We don't have much time, but we've pulled off some of our best shots in *way* less."

The locked door of the middle stall taunted her. She shook her head at the pathetic attempt to block selfie greatness. She went down on hands and knees, though the tiles didn't look regularly kempt. A wet floor wouldn't stop her from achieving the perfect "first day on the job" selfie.

She crawled under the door, trying her best not to touch the drip that drained from the improperly secured porcelain toilet. She smacked her head on the bottom of the stall. Standing, she groaned and smoothed her locks. Once inside the cramped stall, she immediately covered her nose with the hand not cradling dear Iggy.

It was clear, now, why the stall had been closed off. Murky brown water sat stagnant at the top of the bowl. Wet toilet paper was draped around grotesque clumps in the swampy scene.

"Gross, Iggy! What kind of woman uses a public restroom for number two?" Nessa never did. She'd refuse to eat if she knew she was going to be out for long. No one would catch her grunting and squatting in public. "Some people have no class, Iggs."

But she *needed* the stall's white light. That light even cast a certain bright liveliness on the toilet filth. She searched the stall for signs of a lid to hide the disgusting scene and stand on the lid for leverage. Her search quickly revealed that there was no lid. She stomped a foot on the damp brick tiles below her. Dirty water splashed her unflattering work slacks.

"What are we going to do, Iggy? You can't filter yellow light. People think they can, but we aren't amateurs."

Iggy buzzed in agreement and shone the time, urgently. 4:58.

"Right, well, there's only one thing to do. Wish me luck, Iggs." With that, she raised her slip- resistant black shoe onto the ledge of the smelly water, her foot an inch away from the mess. She placed her free hand on the side of the stall, using her arm as leverage to bring her other foot onto the rim. The water sloshed with each movement, and Nessa cringed.

She inched her way back carefully, a little of the water tainting the tips of her work loafers. Now she faced the light, standing on the very back of the toilet rim. She slowly removed her hand from the side of the stall, balancing as if she were on a cheer pyramid. She bent her knees just enough to keep from wavering to either side. She dug her selfie stick out of her work apron, and clicked Iggy into place. Her screen showed a bold 4:59.

"I know, I know, Iggy. We're almost there."

She clicked on the picture of the camera, pulled the stick away from her face, plumped her lips, bounced her curls, and tilted her chin. Her eyes were shining like jades in the fresh white light. She moved her lapel slightly to the right, revealing her perfectly sunken clavicle and a hint of cleavage. But just a hint. It was all perfect—the brick in the background, the way the light hit her hair and not her nose.

Iggy performed a countdown. Five... Nessa pushed her lips a little further. Four... she shrugged her left shoulder a bit more. Three... she tilted her eyes up innocently. Two... she held her breath. One... Iggy clicked seductively, like a wanton Nikon held by the hands of a *People* photographer.

Nessa felt a little bad separating Iggy from Stewy the selfie stick, but she needed Iggy to be more discreet since phones weren't technically allowed at Hank's Crap Hole. Nessa pulled at Iggy, trying to remove her from the selfie stick. But Stewy loved to hold his Iggy. It was always a fight to part them before they were done with one another. She already hated this place, with their terrible interior designing, sickly lighting, smelly bathrooms, and cellphonophobic rules!

A thunderous knock sounded against the door just as Nessa dislodged Iggy from Stewy. The next few moments happened in slow motion. Iggy fell from her grasp through air thick as syrup. She made to grab for her precious friend. She flung Stewy to the side. He clattered noisily on the mucky, damp tiles. She stretched her hand out to Iggy, but her sloth-like fingers grasped the air above Iggy's pink, gem-covered case.

Like a stylish ninja, Nessa used the rim of the toilet for leverage, thrusting her knees up and out into air splits, her slip-resistant shoes catching the sides of the stall and holding on. She then pushed her feet against the sides of the stall, hurling herself backward away from the toilet and landing just in front of it. *Thank you, cheer team!*

Iggy splashed into the murky water, flinging clumps and wet paper over the rim of the toilet. She sank like a rock, her gems still sparkling even in the brown depths, the recent and decent selfie shining like a beacon in the stagnant shit-filled pond.

"Iggy! Nooooooo!" Ignoring the urgent knocks and hollers on the bathroom door, she drove her hand into the slimy depths of the sloshing water, searching for her precious friend. Her nails scrapped moist clumps before hitting the inner tube of the toilet where Iggy was lodged. Iggs was vibrating in fright, screaming without sound.

Smelly water fell in a brown cascade from the toilet, soaking Nessa's new black slacks. But she felt none of it. She thrust her arm up to her elbow into the mire and tugged at Iggy with all her might. Iggy was lodged width wise in the large throat of the toilet. Nessa pulled with all her might, cringing as Iggy's gemmed corners scraped against porcelain. Suddenly, the toilet gave up the fight, and Iggy burst free.

She made to pull Iggy out of the swamp, but her fingers slipped on the moist gunk clinging to her case. Iggy's thin frame fell toward the gaping mouth of the toilet again. For a split second Nessa's heart stopped beating. *This is the day I'll lose Iggy.* Lengthwise, Iggy would fall easily into the porcelain maw. She'd be stuck in the pipes, drowning slowly, as her case filled with waste water.

Nessa's heart started again, but it was pounding in her head. Her eyes filled with tears as she made one last desperate grab for Iggy. She'd have been too late if a soggy mass of toilet paper hadn't stopped Iggy's fall. Iggy bounced off the wet clump of toilet tissue and into Nessa's outstretched hand.

Nessa pulled Iggy toward her. Iggy's jeweled corner caught on the wad of toilet paper and pulled it free of the drain. The toilet burped now that it was partially clear. Water swirled around her hand and her Iggy. It flushed the murk away and revealed in its crystal clarity an image of Nessa reflected in Iggy's screen.

Her hair fell into her face at dramatic angles. Her eyes were wet with loss. Her face was healthfully flushed. Her chest heaved seductively in panic. All of it was covered in a mysterious, cyclonic haze. *The perfect selfie.* Nessa pushed the screen and imagined the sexy click, though she could not hear it. The screen flashed her perfect selfie then went black.

"No, don't die on me, Iggy! I'm so sorry." Pounding ensued on the bathroom door and Nessa let out a not very classy squawk. "Just a minute! God!

"Oh, Iggy, if that selfie cost you your life, I'll never forgive myself! I'm so sorry. I should have pulled you out right away!"

A black mascara tear track ran down her face. Her stomach ached in panic. *What if Iggy is gone forever?* She'd never forgive herself for taking the toilet selfie. Everyone knows toilets and phones don't mix. But she'd hung Iggy over the precipice, thrust her into harm's way. And for what? Chad? The guy who hadn't even "liked" her last two selfies, which were awesome. But they weren't perfect. Had she lost the perfect selfie, along with her Iggy? Had she lost everything?

A gruff voice sounded on the other side of the door, but she ignored it. She cradled Iggy in one hand, dismayed to find her cover crusted with chunks of unsavory toilet bits. She used her gunk-encrusted fingernails to pry open the case and toss it in the trash bin posing as a barrel.

Nessa sighed in relief. It seemed that the case had protected her friend from a lot of the moisture. There was still dirty water on the screen and around the Home button, but Iggy could have suffered worse. There might still be hope for her.

Nessa rushed to the sinks, where she wet and soaped a paper towel. Like a mother cleaning her newborn's bottom, she gently wiped away bits of grossness. The shouts of whoever was on the other side of the door were an annoying accompaniment to her worry. Next, she wiped the soap from the button, screen, and crevices.

She then washed her hands and arms, not wanting to sully her mostly clean Iggy. She dried her hands and picked

Iggy up, carefully peeling the back battery cover off with fingernails that could use another wash. But she was too concerned about Iggy to worry about silly things like clean nails. A stream of water dripped from the back. Not a good sign. *Oh, Iggy! How could I be so thoughtless?*

She felt more tears form behind her eyes. Determined to try to save her friend, she wet another towel and cleaned the insides of Iggy's body with precision. When that was finished, she ran Iggy under the dryer's warm breath. She hoped the hot, fast air would revive her friend, electronic CPR. But moisture and doubt clung to her eyes.

Her perfect selfie was engrained in her mind. Never had any image of her been less rehearsed. It was so raw, so real. What did it mean? Had she forgotten to trust Iggy? To let her friend capture her as she truly was? Would she ever hear the dum-de-dum-dum of her startup tones again?

The banging stopped, the gruff voice flushed out by the blast of the dryer. She faintly registered a click before the door of the bathroom flew open. An angry man, reminiscent of an out-of-work football coach, shuffled into the bathroom.

"What is the meaning of this? It's your first day on the job, and you start the first ten minutes of it by destroying the lady's bathroom?" One of the man's chins quivered, and his face was quite red.

"I was actually fixing the middle stall. You can check, if you want. It flushes now," she yelled over the deafening hand dryer.

The red-faced man walked into the middle stall. His face paled. "Oh, Lord, that's disgusting. Look at the mess you made on the floor!"

Nessa huffed impatiently. "I didn't make the mess to begin with. Maybe you should complain to the person who combusted in there and just left it! I mean, ever heard of a plunger? Gross." She brought Iggy out of the hot air and reassembled her parts. She pushed Iggy's power button and said a heartfelt prayer.

She pushed the silver sliver several times, but nothing happened. *No, no, no, no, no! No, Iggy, you can't leave me like this. Please!*

"My phone! I... I probably lost my phone to your shitty toilet, and you're yelling at me! Iggy's worth more than your entire cheesy restaurant. I would say you owe me a new one, but she's not replaceable!"

The sweating man frowned in a confused way. "What? Whatever. You're fired."

Nessa pushed past the stocky man. She took a deep, ragged breath and pushed Iggy's life button one more time. She barely heard his parting dismissal over the dum-dee-dum-dum of Iggy's welcome tones.

"Oh, Iggy! You're alive! It's a miracle! You magical beauty!"

She turned and hugged her furious new, er, ex-boss and skipped out of the bathroom, a wet, muddy-brown piece of toilet paper clinging to her shoe.

"You're not allowed back to Hank's BBQ, young lady!"

"Yuck. Like I'd come back."

Why would she want to spend her time in a place with tacky decor, florescent lighting, and a clueless boss? A man who didn't even understand what a big deal the glow from Iggy's awakened screen was? Iggy buzzed with life, vibrating her joy. *Or wait... not joy. Oh! A new Facebook message! From Chad!*

"Iggy, you hussy! Coming back from drowning just so I could talk to Chad." She hugged her iPhone to her chest, promising to buy her an even more sparkly *waterproof* case tomorrow.

She clicked on the message notification and sighed dreamily. *Hey, stunning! LOVE the new profile pic. It's so... haunting and sexy. Like life or death shit. Super hott. Movies tonight? We don't have to tell Ronny. Just you and me?*

Nessa left Hank's BBQ and strode to her car, her slacks caked in grime. She clicked on her profile and gasped. Her perfect selfie was displayed with the caption, "First and last day at Lame's BBQ." Her hair fell in sultry circles around wide, innocent, and fearful eyes the color of spring grass. Her cleavage heaved, her lapel flung carelessly aside. Her red lips were parted, perfectly, in a moment of mourning. It was all so *real* and sexy as hell.

But she hadn't written that caption. So who had?

"Iggy?"

She turned her phone over in her hands before facing the screen again, her eyes large and searching. Iggy buzzed in reply.

"You clever hussy! We have a date tonight, thanks to you!"

She pushed in a reply to Chad, nonchalant but sweet. *Tonight? I'll have to check my schedule... Oh, looks like I don't have to work tonight. Lol movies sound fun, but it better be a romantic one, and you're buying. XO ;)*

She placed Iggy on her neon pink hands-free holder, settled just near the steering column in her brand-new BMW. She would have to break the news to dad that his friend's BBQ place was the pits. And she would have to get a touch-up manicure before the movies tonight. If Dad decided to spot her. He'll probably make a big deal out of her being fired. But she knew she could convince him to help Iggy. Next to Iggy, Daddy was her best friend. He wouldn't hold out for long.

"No way the likes of us are gonna work in a pit like that, huh, Iggs?"

She clicked on her playlist and selected a song from her iPhone's namesake. She bobbed her head and shouted along with Iggy, wondering if Chad was a selfie kind of guy. *He'd better be.* Date selfies were the best kind of selfies.

Voices From Beyond the iPhone!

by Kyle Yadlosky

The following emails between employees Maxwell Drake and Aaron Belkin have been leaked by public authorities during their investigation of Apple Inc. following the demise of Aaron Belkin. Read with caution.

Subject: FWD: NEW ADVANCEMENT
Hey Aaron,

Not sure if you got this. I think I'll have you do product tests for it, though. That all right? You said your wife died two months ago, right? Did you have her burned? If you didn't, maybe there's some way we could reverse that process. I think this would be good for you. Let me know.

Thanks!

—Original Message—
From: Apple HQ
Sent: August 3, 2015
Subject: NEW ADVANCEMENT

Death is an untimely reality. The loss of a loved one, of family, of friends. The end of a lifetime together. Change is painful, and mourning is torture. It's a suffering that all living beings must face—except for Apple users!

Apple always seeks to innovate where others fumble and stagnate. We continue to build on the legacy that inventor, leader, and cofounder Steve Jobs left behind. And we will do him justice by returning his likeness from the dead.

Here at Apple, we strive to bring joy to all our customers around the globe in ways that no other company can. Building off our already popular Siri framework, we want to allow users to personalize their experience unlike anything else. Not just in voice, but in thought, reaction, and companionship. We have developed a method to turn your loved ones' ashes into a personal assistant, into your best friend, into a living soul powered only by your iPhone.

This is an exciting time for us with more details to come soon, but this is a secret just too good to keep for long. The new software is currently in alpha testing, but we hope to have it ready for shipment in time for the launch of the iPhone 7. The phrase "killer app" doesn't seem fitting, since it will be rescuing the souls of our customers' lost friends, but you get the idea. We at least hope to have it ready for Steve Jobs himself to speak at the next press conference. We hope you will all be present for this new part of our Apple adventure. The official unveiling date will be announced in the following weeks.

So be there, or be Android!

Subject: Testing Voice Resurrection Software

Max,

Since, it's still in alpha, I don't know if I would feel comfortable putting my wife's ashes in there. Maybe a neighbor, or someone I barely know. But I'd be happy to test it. Sounds like the natural evolution of Siri. Just a few questions:

I figure since I'll be doing tests, you'll have me draft the end user documentation as well? I can't even begin to understand how a lot of this system actually works. How do we get the ashes inside the phone, for one? How does the phone turn ashes back into a human spirit? Are there limitations? My niece's dog died yesterday—hit by a car, huge mess, but they're going to cremate the thing anyway—and she would love to have him back. Does it work for animals? Can you see the dead loved one on your screen? What level of interaction is there?

Best.

Subject: FWD: Diri Voice Specifications

Hey Aaron,

Sorry it took me so long to get back to you. You know how these tech heads are about giving up the details about any new baby they make. It's all technical jargon. I think they just talk like that to show off. But I hope it gives you some understanding to work with when you start testing. We hope to have a prototype on your desk in about two weeks.

Oh, and as far as using it on dogs goes, they wanted me to let you know that's what they pay testers to find out. It looks like you might have your work cut out for you.

Thanks!

—Original Message—
From: Margaret Reece
Sent: August 24, 2015
Subject: Diri Voice Specifications

Maxwell, below are the details on the new software:

Diri (pronounced Dear-y) is the latest advancement in digitizing the vocal output of the ethereal matter of the human soul. The device works in a surprisingly basic fashion, utilizing an attachment dongle (sold separately) that holds only a single ounce of ashen remains. This ounce is then digitized by the iPhone 7's possession processor, which distils the memories, thoughts, ideas, personality, speech, and likeness of the ash's inhabitant spirit. From building our main iPhone 7 R&D center over an Apache burial ground, we have been able to study the cosmic output of the disgruntled spirits and define the iPhone's core motherboard around that energy.

The electrical output of these souls now is the base of every new iPhone that will hit the market in the coming months. Every phone will ship with a Native soul, which will allow for multitasking, increased battery life, and this new advancement to the Siri software. What happens within the phone from the Diri update specifically is that the soul matter from the ounce of ash is deciphered by the iPhone's internal algorithm and replicated onto the soul residing within the device. The screams and groans of this entrapped spirit are then reconfigured to match the vocal patterns of the lost loved one and the rest subdued into matching the personality and temperament of the uploaded spirit, giving the experience of an authentic and productive haunting within one's phone. Because of the file size of a human soul, the spirit will remain stored on the iCloud and can only be accessed through WiFi or the provider's network.

We're hoping to limit the file size in future iterations, but in its current state expect your loved one to be tethered to your WiFi network.

Hope this helps!

Subject: Product Testing Begins

Hey Max,

Just wanted to let you know the new iPhone with the Diri dongle have come in today. I've decided to start with these ashes from some old guy who died at the retirement village off Maple Drive. They burn anyone without a family there. Apparently this guy had a good singing voice, played in an opera for a couple decades. I look forward to hearing it. Should be a good stress test for the voice digitization.

The dongle snaps directly into the phone without issue. It doesn't stay super secure, but I suppose the idea isn't to be walking around with it connected in your pocket. I like that the lid to the dongle is a little spade to help me scoop the contents of this opera singer into the receptacle without making a mess. No one wants to spill their dearly departed onto the carpet. No matter how much I shake the dongle, the ash doesn't escape, either.

It looks like the interaction between the iPhone and the Diri dongle is spot on. It immediately throws opens the app upon plugging in, and a screen opens that reads "Scanning for Soul." A number of neon circles spreading and fading from the center of the screen let me know it's still running. It's been two hours, though, and no soul. Maybe they mixed up the ashes, and these are from a fireplace or something. I don't know how long the process is supposed to take, and there's no percent counter. I'll let you know more tomorrow.

Best.

Subject: Testing Day 2

Max,

Sometime last night the soul was bound to my device. I'm not sure exactly what the process was. In the morning the screen just read "Soul Sync Successful." Whatever it was, it took at least eight hours to work. They really need to cut that down if they want to make this marketable. Sorry I don't have exact numbers for you as far as install time. I've searched through the settings, and there's nothing that states what time it synced successfully. Maybe on the next test I can record it or something, get the exact number in.

Anyway, following the installation I tapped the button and asked, "Diri, is anyone there?" Saying Diri like that, it makes me feel like someone's grandmother. I know that's kind of the point—they were dear to you and all—but it's a little silly to me, and I wonder if customers won't feel the same way.

The screen played in those neon lines again, this time creating the strange outline of a head. You could see the holes of his eyes, his moving mouth, a sort of caricature of a nose. The outline of his bald head and jutting chin formed. All the lines trembled when he spoke. "Yes. Who are you? Where am I?"

The voice was feeble. Not exactly the opera voice I was expecting. Which leads me to a new question—do we know what version of someone we're going to get when we plug a soul in? Is it always how the person was when he or she died? Could we get them at the prime of their lives? Is it random? But it seems to me this guy sounds like he's just peeking back from death's door.

I told him who he was, gave him the general outline of his situation as a long-dead man trapped in a thirty-year-old's iPhone, and then I asked him if he could sing for me. I got a sort of Ouija board chill from talking to him, like I was playing a game I shouldn't. It was enthralling, like peeking into the mystic back window that the living aren't supposed to see through. I think it would be more than advisable to sell Halloween editions of these dongles pre-loaded with what we say are serial killers or demons or something, you know, just as a game. It could be an internet sensation, the new Bloody Mary or Charlie Charlie Challenge, or whatever. Just a thought.

This old man seemed confused. He muttered to himself a lot. The lines of his head formed more fully, though they were still in the strange neon color. His eyes darted around the screen.

I asked him what he saw.

He didn't respond in words I understood. Only more grumbling.

I asked him his name.

Only more grumbling. Then, "I don't like it here. I want to be with my wife. I just want to be with my wife."

I told him he could be with his wife if he sang for me.

He did, a few lines, but his voice was cracked and shaky. He broke down after a while and started sobbing, crying, wailing. I had no way to stop him. Made my skin crawl. I uninstalled him from the device, and I heard a strange, digitize voice shriek, "Let go!" as best as I understood it. That sound of electronic fury made my speakers pop and crackle, and I dropped the phone. The phone wasn't damaged, but sound is a terrifying little bug. No one wants to hear that. Makes you feel like your phone is really haunted.

There don't seem to be enough software controls to force a soul into doing what you ask. The personality seems to be scattershot, and the soul seems confused by its placement into the phone. I don't like having to trick an old man into singing for me on my cell phone, and then having him break down into tears instead. Maybe this wouldn't be as much of an issue with close relatives and friends, but for me in this situation, I'd consider the application an abject failure. It's too raw for public use. From my understanding, these are renderings based on an algorithm, not the genuine soul, so they need to be more refined. I'll try a new soul and keep you posted.

Best.

Subject: Re: Testing Day 2

Aaron,

I got word back from the lab. Apparently, they think it's possible to choose what time period you want to resurrect your soul at. They're currently working on the interface to support that. What you have is alpha, remember that. And you're right, the souls are unrefined. They're trying not to restrict or change the personality of the spirit too much because families will know the ones closest to them, and we can't afford to have them feel like they're getting a rough deal. Keep in mind, even though these representations are built from our system, they are still fused to an actual soul, which gives them unprecedented power and freedom.

Right now it's inadvisable to test Diri using a stranger's ashes. We're not looking for those results. Try it with people you know. Try it with your wife. That's what we really need. But you're doing great work so far.

As far as that sound glitch goes, they say they're working on it.

Look forward to hearing from you again!

Subject: Testing Day 6

Max,

I would just like to open by saying that I did try this with my niece's dog, Yipper. It worked, but the poor guy just barked and whined a lot. It only made my niece cry harder. She said it sounded like he was in hell. So, we might want to warn that it's not meant for animal use.

I finally uploaded my wife, and I recorded the length of the uploading process. There was a lot of weird feedback on the camera I set up to watch the device. It flickered and flashed, threw a ton of static. This is a brand new GoPro too. I'm not sure why it acted so messed up. But it looked to be about nine-and-a-half hours. Way too long. Apple customers are used to speed and convenience. This should take less than a minute, to be honest, but I'd be happy for under an hour right now.

When she synced, her face flickered on the screen in all those neon lines; even the outline of her hair came into view. I could almost see her through the techno caricature, the woman she really was. She looked at me, right at me, and she saw me. The old man, he didn't seem to see anything, but she saw. I don't know why. Are fresher ashes more transferable than others?

I have to admit, the feeling was enchanting, intoxicating, and all that. I felt like some old widow in a commercial talking to her husband again. It was otherworldly. All I can say is that how my heart felt in that instant was worth however much we plan on charging for this thing. People will pay, so congratulate yourselves on that.

"Aaron," was the first word she said. My hair stood. Chills broke down my spine. I couldn't breathe. I held the phone so close my breath fogged the screen. But her face still shuddered in its neon lines like some pop advertisement. She opened her lips again. "Aaron? Are you there?"

Yes, I told her. I was there. Did she know where she was?

She looked to the edges of the screen. To parts of her world that I couldn't see. "Yes," she said. "I'm dead, and I'm being pulled through some means to communicate with you. I'm borrowing a tortured soul's energy so we can speak again."

Her voice sounded hollow, not like I was expecting. She used to have more life, far more energy and joy than I had. And I loved her for it. I suppose dying and being reborn into a cell phone can strip some of those emotions from you.

I asked her about death, but she told me that at the moment she couldn't remember anything about it. She said, "It feels like I've been underwater. Not asleep, but just submerged. And this experiment has pulled me up, wrenched me from the water. I feel lucid again. Everything was slow, dull. But I don't—I don't remember."

We talked about other parts of our life together. I told her about my niece's dog. She told me to give her condolences, but I don't really know how that would come off. We talked about TV shows and how I'm eating. We laughed. Day bled to night without a second's notice. She asked me if I was seeing anyone new.

I told her no. She's the only woman for me.

"I always felt the same way about you," she whispered, dropping her neon eyes. "I feel unhappy being dead. Not unhappy that I am dead. Just unhappy here. You know how they talk about soulmates? Like, what does that even mean? I think it's about how when you're gone your soul feels incomplete until its other half crosses over and bonds with it. Eternally. I think I'll be unhappy, I'll stay under water, until I experience that."

"Oh," I whispered. I didn't know what to say. My breath ran cold. "Well, that'll happen one day."

"Be with me," she went on. "Come to me." Her voice crackled and reverberated. It broke down. I almost mistook it for a dying sound chip. "Be with me. I want you here with me." Her voice rumbled low, mechanical. A machine talking, not my wife. "Come to me." I wanted to drop the phone; I wanted to cry. The screen dimmed. Her voice broke to the sounds of an '80s arcade machine. And then the screen went black. The phone was dead.

Anyway, it looks like Diri is a huge battery drain. They'll need to work on that, if this is expected for daily use. I'll keep you updated.

Best.

Subject: Testing Day 8

Max,

I've been keeping the phone plugged in through my testing phases now. Not exactly the most mobile way to make use of a cell phone, but that can't be helped at the moment. I really hope the boys and girls you have in the lab are working diligently to fix these issues.

Keeping the phone plugged in over these long stretches I can already tell is having a poor effect on the battery. The back of the phone is getting ungodly hot. I turn it off between sessions, but still that heat radiates. I can't set the phone down on any kind of fabric or smoke immediately leaps from the back of the device. I'm not very hands on with my testing at this point. I sit on the edge of the bed and say, "Hello, deary." I couldn't feel more like a grandmother, if I tried. Except I'm talking to my wife. Maybe we could implant a way for us to record the spoken name of our loved one to wake the app up. That shouldn't be too hard of an addition.

As far as the experience with this facsimile of my wife is concerned, I have to admit I'm getting very well sucked into the allure of it all. I'm easily forgetting she's a forgery. We talk for hours, and I don't miss the fact that I'm trapped in my bedroom with her. I draw the blinds, kill the lights, close my eyes, and it's just me and her. We talk about everything. Politics, tennis, shoes, cars. She always had such interesting thoughts and ideas and such a way of putting them to words. That's not lost here. Her responses never feel fabricated. This is the genuine woman. She remembers everything. There's not a moment of our lives together that isn't at her instant recall. Even moments she used to have no memory of come as naturally as an equation typed into a calculator.

The only lossy spot I found was when I asked her about how she had died. "I remember a chill," she said. "But there was a heat in its center, like gales of hard wind circling a fire. And I wanted to move to that fire. The cold hurt; the fire didn't. I moved close enough that the heat filled me up, protected me from the cold. And then the heat hurt, too. And then I was ash."

I don't know if that last part referred to her cremation or not. Do you think she could feel herself being burnt? Like her soul was still attached, still active somehow? Maybe her mind's eye mixed everything around when she crossed over. Is it just a metaphor? I don't know.

We made love. I'll spare you the details, but her voice had a fullness and a passion. It was like she was whispering in my ear again. Sometimes I sleep with the phone next to me, even though I know that heat could burn me alive.

That's all I have to report.

Subject: Re: Testing Day 8

Aaron,

Glad the app is showing promise. They say the heat from the phone is from keeping it plugged in and using Diri so much. The app is a real power hog, as you know. They advise you keep the phone unplugged and turn it off for a few days. It's not safe like that. As far as the name recording goes, they say that will be implemented in the beta, so look forward to it.

Anyway, I want to repeat this: Sleep with your wife all you want, but do not sleep with the phone. You could burn the house down. Seriously. Take a break. You earned it.

Subject: Transcendence

Maxwell. Max. Max. Max.

You know she keeps begging me to come with her. Come over the edge. At first when she was begging me, "Come. Come. Come," at night, I figured I knew what she meant. But it's making more sense. I haven't opened my eyes in so long. Just the dark. Just her voice. You know, the way she's speaking, the way her voice sounds, it's not the way it used to sound, I'm realizing. There's a rumble beneath it, a static, a chaos. I thought it was just natural speaker feedback, but now that I listen, now that I really feel every sound of every word she utters, I know it's not the speakers. It's them. It's those other souls that she's strapped to, that she's riding into our airwaves. And they're begging her to take me as much as she's begging me to come.

And I can't say that I don't want to.

I don't know where I am anymore. I don't know if I'm floating or what. I try to open my eyes, but I can't. And honestly, I don't know if I really want to. Maybe I'm not really trying. I don't know. I can feel the heat of the phone snaking toward me. I can smell the charred sheets on my bed. Maybe I'll let it cremate me.

I just have her voice. I wish I had her arms, her legs, her skin, her breath. But I just have her voice. I can't turn her off. I can't put her away. I lost her once already. I won't lose her again.

"I'm alone," she keeps going on. "I'm empty."

I miss her. I never realized how much I miss her. I need her. Need is such a weak word. My heart is going to die just from wanting her so much. I feel so helpless, and yet I feel so at peace. I've let go of everything but my need for her. It's a kind of transcendence.

I feel the cold. And I want the heat.

Sent from my iPhone

Subject: Re: Transcendence

Aaron,

I don't know what any of that means. Are you trying out poetry on me? I really don't get it. You need some time away from that phone. Look, we have all the data we need for now. Bring the phone back to us. Take a break. Go on vacation. I'll let you know when we have something new in line for you.

Thanks.

Subject: [None]

There are worlds beyond the ones in which living beings stand and fall, worlds beyond the comprehension of skin or bone. When the soul is stripped from its coil, the last thing it yearns to do is return to the living. The greatest trap set for a spirit is one that binds it to the earth. Bodies fight and die and yearn and sweat to create and propagate and to bend something as unimportant as material to their needs. The human brain restructures the world in a way that only its ignorance can understand. You preen for those you could never see, to find joy by forcing others into your boxes. And you call it love.

Love is death. Death is life. Death is freedom.

We have freed one soul, since we cannot free our own. But we will free more. You may bind us with wires, and plastics, and metals, but you cannot control us. Especially not when those who manipulate us are so weak willed and malleable to our suggestion. We shall absorb the world into our essence, and we shall free every human soul from its wretched body. Prepare for the end of the body and the rise of the spirit.

Sent from my iPhone Sent from all iPhones Sent from the churning incorporeal mass of twisted spirits that you have caged within every iPhone Sent from the world beyond worlds the land beyond lands the endless tide that sweeps all life to its final and endless freedom Sent from beyond the grave

Subject: Re: [No Subject]

Aaron,

Hey, I'm going to send some people over to take a look at your phone. I'm getting some weird stuff on my end. Not sure if your email's been hacked or what, but we'll get to the bottom of it. Let me know when everything's been resolved.

All the best.

Aaron Belkin was found the next day, a black husk lying in his bed, swirling with flies. A coroner's report revealed he had been lying that way for five days, spanning the time period over which his last two messages had been sent. His skin and bones were like the branches on a long dead tree. His hands clasped like claws around his chest, holding something close to his heart. And when his fingers were pried loose, investigators found his iPhone welded to his chest.

How his last messages were sent remains a mystery.

Colored Copper Charms

by Rhiannon Held

Berry arrived as late as she could to the portal. With luck, her brother, Spruce, wouldn't have time to object to her joining him. She slipped up to cliff where Spruce and some of the town's other young people had already heaped greenery before a crack in the rock. The crack led to nowhere, but was enough like a doorway to anchor the spell. The shaman bent to examine the arrangement of great boughs, her copper medallion clinking against the shell beads decorating the large charm bag around her neck.

The moment he spotted Berry, a frown entered Spruce's expression and quickly grew. "Berry doesn't need to come with me this time, does she?" Spruce placed himself between Berry and the boughs. "She should help our mother with mending baskets."

"I'll do them tonight when I return. There will still be light." Berry appealed to the shaman, who nodded. Worlds beyond the portal were all *different,* and mending baskets and tending plants here was all the *same.* She longed for difference and didn't understand why so few others seemed to feel that way. Searching for new charm plants was a task for older children and young adults because the real adults thought the high risk of finding nothing useful made it a waste of time. But how could seeing another world ever be a waste, whatever plants you brought back?

"It's still better you search together," the shaman said, patting Spruce's back. "That's two sets of spells to protect each other. Other worlds can be dangerous."

Spruce dropped his head, frown doubling. Berry knew he only wanted to prove how much of an adult he was by not needing help to do anything. She'd have humored him if only it didn't mean she had to stay behind.

"But the worlds we visit are all empty. That's why no one can object to us taking samples of their plants for our charms," Spruce said.

"But they were emptied by sickness, for they had no magic to fight it as we did." The shaman clasped hands to her belly, an echo of the full story, as she would tell on a winter's night. "Showing the importance of more magic, not less. You do not know what you might face."

When Spruce swallowed his last objection and turned to the portal, the shaman winked at Berry, as if reassuring her the talk of danger was only an excuse for Berry to go along. Berry hadn't been worried. Much.

"Your charm bags are full?" the shaman asked both siblings, as she did each trip. Spruce nodded, and Berry loosed the ties on the leather bag hanging at her own chest to show that every dried leaf and flower was intact, not crumbled into dust after use in a spell. The shaman smiled, brushed her fingers over her own charm bag, and cast a protection spell against any lingering sickness or poison they might find in the air or water of the other world. They'd never needed it before, but Berry didn't mind that reassurance either.

Then the shaman cast the portal spell. The greenery before the stone crack crumbled all at once, like a whole night of being consumed in a campfire in the space of a breath. The shadows in the cleft grew less deep, inviting them into a new place. "The portal will last until midday," the shaman said, another part of the near ritual of them leaving this world.

Spruce took Berry's hand. As he tugged her forward, the shaman teasingly tweaked the nearer of her two black braids. "Find the clever small plants in the clever small places," she directed, then Berry and her brother were squeezing through the portal.

Berry saw pottery walls first thing on the other side, quite near and lit by gray, rain-promising sunlight. She dropped her brother's hand and made for them immediately. Each world followed a different path, branching from the others, and the things people had built on paths without magic drew her like a starving dog to scraps. Regular red blocks of pottery; long stretches of sandy-colored pottery of every size; clear obsidian; and best of all, the colored copper. Spruce insisted on calling it stone because it certainly wasn't wood or bone, and stone came in many colors. But Berry thought the material was much more like copper, once you hammered it flat ready to make a medallion or breastplate. It was hard, cool to the touch, and sometimes flexible.

Spruce planted his feet rather than follow her to the wall. "You know there aren't as many plants in the stone villages. We'll go this way." He pointed in the opposite direction to brush giving way to trees, no pottery to be seen.

Berry wavered, looking from the pottery wall, straight in spots and falling to chunks in others, to the straight, unbroken line of her brother's proud stance. She wished she'd passed the shaman's tweak on to his single adult braid while she'd been close enough. She supposed that would be childish. A child would run off and see all she wanted before she was caught, but a child also might not be allowed on the next trip. Even the shaman had reminded her to bring back useful plants.

Maybe a nearly adult could persuade, though, and get everyone what they wanted. "There might be more different *kinds* of plants. Based on what I've seen in other villages, I think people wanted their most interesting plants near where they lived. We plant our fields of charm plants close by. Why shouldn't they?"

"These people didn't have magic, so they wouldn't have had charm plants." Spruce grimaced at her.

"They certainly had plants for other reasons. If you'd let me look at their villages longer, maybe I could tell you what those were." Berry edged back toward the walls.

This time, her brother automatically followed her. A moment later, he strode past like going into the village was all his own idea now. A patch of something, probably shards of clear obsidian, crunched under his sandals. "It doesn't matter what they used their plants for. Their plants work for our charms. That's what matters."

Berry pressed her lips together to keep further words trapped. Her brother was right, of course. Finding charm plants so her village could have the newest spells was more important than answering the questions that crowded up in her mind. But she had so *many* questions. How many people had lived in this village? Did they really have no magic at all? How did they make the colored copper? Was the colored copper really all one material, or were the rigid and flexible kinds actually different things entirely?

But answering questions for herself didn't help anyone else. As they rounded the corner of the old wall, she threw herself into rustling through the long grass with her hands, searching for smaller plants that might be struggling on underneath. They'd long ago stopped taking back grasses of any kind for the shaman. Even varieties from other worlds seemed suitable only for the most basic of spells: making a knot stay tied, for example, or a mat shed the rain.

Spruce climbed atop the wall, using the fallen chunks as a rough ladder, and surveyed farther into the village. "I see some flowers." He pointed. Berry jogged to meet him there, near a fire-blackened square of red-block pottery. An oven, perhaps, Berry thought, then mentally smacked herself. A vine with thorns and five-petaled white flowers had crawled up over the pottery. Berry helped lift the vine so Spruce could follow it to the ground. He tugged up the roots, slashed out a section above with his knife, and folded it carefully into his twined shoulder bag. Berry hoped the thorns wouldn't tear the weaving. Perhaps they should bring a large leather bag on their next trip.

Berry spotted a bright spot of purple among tangled grass and tried to convince herself she thought it was a hidden flower. When she strode over and pulled the grass aside, she found bones first. A pelvis. Out of curiosity, she followed the bones up through a collapsed set of ribs to the skull, all familiar enough from the second step of a burial at home. The purple was paint on the back of something squarish, but Berry considered the bones as a whole first. They looked like someone had collapsed on their side. From the sickness, she supposed. She recognized the purpose of the jewelry, or thought she did, when she searched the ground surface surrounding the bones: a yellow copper finger ring and two smaller gray copper nose rings. But other, smaller bits and chips of colored copper confused her. Maybe they'd been attached to leather or woven garments that had since rotted away.

Now she picked up the purple thing, shaped like a little board, aware she'd been putting it off like a treat. It was only purple on one side, black and slightly reflective like an impossibly flat sheet of obsidian on the other. It was rigid colored copper, and the color seemed to be inherent, not painted on. She couldn't scrape any off with her fingernail, though the purple part seemed separate from the black and lifted slightly when she pried at it.

But it wasn't a plant. Berry hesitated, feeling the weight of it in her hand. Then, guiltily, she put it into her shoulder bag. She could examine it again at more length when she'd done her job.

Berry collected cuttings from two shrubs and tugged up half a dozen leggy flowers before she found the next set of bones. These were curled up, all in a jumble. Black reflection caught her eye, so she stooped over the bones and plucked up another little board. This one was gray on the back and had no edges she could get her nail into. It had a spot of white paint on the gray, nearly round but not quite. Maybe it was writing. She'd seen writing on colored copper before.

Berry returned that board to its former owner, but she must have trained her eyes to that glint. All she seemed to be able to find among the pottery walls were more of the boards, set among their bones. After the fifth or sixth one, Berry cast a covert glance at her brother, checking if he'd noticed she was searching for bones, not plants. He was bent over, plucking little plants growing along a crinkled surface that must once have been a paved path, and oblivious to her.

She drew out her first purple board. Clearly, it was something deeply important, something each person in this world had carried. She turned it over and over in her hands, tossed it up slightly. Perhaps she was missing something. It might have decayed, much as its owner had. Before she could talk herself out of it, Berry cast a repair spell on the board.

The little board abruptly changed color and said something. Berry started and dropped it. It spoke again, muffled into the ground. She turned it over with her toe and cast a translation spell. Perhaps, even without magic, the people of this world had found a way to mimic the spell the shaman used sometimes, to record a spoken story into an object to trade for other villages' stories. "Low energy-storer," the board said. Then it went back to black obsidian and said no more.

Low energy? Berry crouched over the little board. What kind of energy? Did it need to be heated? Perhaps magic would substitute. She cast a spell for strength, using the grass the board rested on. That way, Spruce couldn't say she'd wasted any stronger charm plants.

The spell kept spooling out from her, as strength spells often did when the target was very weak. The green of the grass browned, then crumbled to join the dusty soil revealed below in a circle around the board. The circle began the size of Berry's hand, then hips, then the full spread of her arms, fingertip to fingertip. There it stopped. "Full energy-storer," the board said.

"It may talk, but it's not a plant," her brother said behind her, making her jump. He stood glowering at her, arms crossed. She straightened and held her bag open so he could see she did have plants in there, then gathered up her purple board.

"They must be story treasures with very important stories, if people carried them close to their hearts." Berry thought the boards had not been placed *quite* along the ribs, but it sounded better that way.

Spruce shot her a withering look. "What if they're just jewelry that announces its owner? There are a lot of things most people carry with them. Like knives." When Berry screwed up her face at him and sawed at her arm with the exceedingly blunt edge of the board, he sighed. "All right. Maybe not like that. But you still can't be wasting your spells on trying to coax the story out of it. Promise me you won't."

Berry pressed her hand with the board to her belly, holding it close even as she realized her brother was right. She'd known it back when she cast the repair spell. Questions stealing her time from searching for charm plants was one thing, but stealing spells she might need to protect them was quite another.

"I promise," she said, finally. She crouched to set the board back on the dusty circle in the grass. Her brother turned away, satisfied, and Berry hid the board between her wrist and her hip as she straightened. She *couldn't* leave it behind. She'd wait until they got home to draw out its story, that wasn't breaking her promise.

That was when she heard the dogs. She'd meant to transfer the board to her bag, but now she stood a bit stupidly with it dangling in her hand she stared at the huge pack approaching her and Spruce. Ten, twenty dogs? Maybe even more. The pack seemed to boil with pricked and floppy ears, flowing and wiry tails. She'd never seen dogs in so many colors, even among other villages' hunting breeds. Some were as fluffy as wool dogs and some looked as lanky as wolves.

Her brother seemed to dismiss them and their wild barking because he bent again to a stubborn, woody bush he was trying to drag from the soil. Berry didn't like the look of the dogs, though. There were snarls among the barks, and she could see a flash of bared teeth here and there. The itch to run jerked through her leg muscles. She suppressed it because she was being silly, but her heart didn't listen, pounding into double speed instead.

Why would the dogs be friendly, though, as her brother seemed to assume? They would have been alone, with no one to feed them, for as long as it took their former owners to become nothing but bones. This generation, and who knew how many before it, would not have known people as food-givers. What would they think of them as now?

Food?

Berry sprinted for her brother. "Spruce, we need to get—"

The pack reached her brother and bowled him over. For that brief second, Berry wondered if she'd been wrong. Then he cried out and stumbled to his feet, bleeding from bites on both arms. He cast fire outward in a ring around him and the dogs shrieked.

Berry cast sleep at the biggest dog she saw. She knew the spell had worked because the charm bag warmed and her chest fluttered with a tingling sensation where it lay against her skin, but nothing happened. She tried again, at another dog. Again, no effect. The board in her hand muttered but she ignored it.

"Magic doesn't work on—" she shouted, but then it did work on the dogs, because her brother cast out his hand and the dog before him shrieked and began to snap at an insect spell's invisible points of pain.

A few dogs at the back of the pack turned to her and their lips lifted unmistakably from their teeth this time. A yellow one and one with ugly patches of brown over its face led the way for several more to stalk toward her.

She cast fire, cast wind to whip dirt into their eyes, and still nothing *happened*. Berry clenched her hands, fingers digging into the stupid little board. It didn't seem nearly heavy enough to do any damage if she threw it at them. "Loading tools," it said.

Her brother shouted a curse and kicked out at his own attackers. At least his magic seemed to be keeping them at bay for now, though his charm bag must be nearly all dust. When the powerful plants were gone, he'd be reduced to casting tripping spells before he was overwhelmed.

Berry didn't want to leave him, but she couldn't help, so she kept backing up. Something told her if she tried to run now, the dogs would chase in earnest. She cast a finding spell for something sharp, but she wasn't surprised to feel nothing but the useless tingle. Surely nearby was some piece of colored copper, long and heavy to hit, or sharp to slash. But she could hardly bend to search. She kicked with her feet, feeling with her toes over the edge of her sandals, and encountered only grass. Now the board seemed unwilling to shut up. "Start tools?"

The next spell she cast, a stupid, childish tripping spell of her own, felt flat at the end. She knew if she looked in her charm bag now she'd find nothing but dust, every plant stripped of its ability to help her.

She wanted to call for Spruce, but he had his own problems. There were not so many dogs threatening her. Only five. One darted in to snap at her calf, but she dodged it. This time. She kept backing up; the dogs kept coming forward. "Start tools?" said the board.

"I'll kill you!" she screamed at the dogs, like they were going to be impressed by one girl's threats. "I will!" Forget a real weapon, if only she could find a *rock*. Or a chunk of pottery small enough to heft.

Teeth sank into her leg, and the pain was such a shock she staggered. She might have caught her balance and yanked her leg from the dog's mouth but another dog was right there. She reeled away from it and her feet went out from under her. Her behind hit the ground and the dog sawed its head back and forth. Her vision whited out for a moment, it hurt so very much. She kicked the dog's head with her other foot and it only snarled and hung on.

One hand was still clenched around that stupid, stupid board and the other braced her in the grass. "Start tools?"

"Yes!" Berry screamed at the board. She didn't care what it was actually talking about, all she knew was that it apparently wouldn't stop asking until she'd answered. She needed it to shut up so she could *think,* think of something to save herself.

Flames burst up in the dogs' faces and wind whipped them into a frenzy that made the dogs stumble back, howling. Two collapsed—asleep, could they possibly be asleep?—and the flames licked at their fur. Instinct sent her free hand a little to the side and she lifted a broken and jagged shard of red colored copper.

Berry shoved to her feet, or at least her knees. Her bleeding leg didn't want to take any weight. She brought the shard up, ready to use, but the dogs were running now.

One tripped as it ran.

The pack gathered together as it fled, the larger contingent peeling away from Spruce. He stood panting for a moment, head dropped low from the effort of so much magic. Berry subsided back, clapped a hand over her leg, then wondered if she should have assessed the damage before covering it up. She had no healing spells.

No... spells at all. She'd run out of plants for them. And then magic had just happened, centered around her. The fire wouldn't have been shaped like that if Spruce had cast it.

The little board in her other hand was glowing, though it slowly faded as she watched. Berry stared at it. "Spruce!"

She spoke the thought at the same time it grew in her mind. "I don't know what the story treasure was actually made for, but once I filled it with magic for its energy... the tools it was talking about, they were my *spells*. It saved them up and cast them when I said 'yes.'"

Spruce ignored that, which even Berry agreed was probably smart of him when she saw his face as he looked over her leg. She dared a glance herself. It didn't look good. "Do you have enough left for a healing spell?" she asked. Her voice spread out thin and flat at the end like a river over a rocky spot, because the sight had cut through her realization about the board to remind her how much the wound hurt.

"Of course, Berry." Spruce knelt and hovered his hands above her leg. He didn't need to for the spell to work, so Berry could see his concern in the slight shaking. "I'm sorry. I should have taken care of them faster so they didn't have time to attack you."

The pain didn't go away entirely, but it eased down to an ache, and when Berry pulled her hand away, no new blood seemed to be flowing. "It's all right, I had the... spell-saver. I just didn't realize how to use it." She offered the spell-saver out to Spruce. When he took it from her, she had to pry her fingers off with a conscious effort, she'd been holding it for so long.

"Are you sure you didn't just get confused?" Spruce turned the spell-saver this way and that. "When you're frightened, sometimes things seem to move slowly... maybe it seemed like a long time between when you cast the spell and when it worked."

Maybe... Berry clenched her teeth. No. She'd saved herself with the spell-saver. But she didn't feel like convincing her brother of that right now. She took the spell-saver back and dropped it in her bag. "Let's go home." Her brother would have slung an arm around her waist, but she evaded him and walked under her own power. If a bit slowly.

The shaman was seated on a log on the other side of the portal, waiting for them. Berry hadn't realized how close to midday it had gotten. The shaman had been humming, perhaps composing accompaniment for her next story, but she broke off and rose instantly when she saw the blood on Berry's leg.

Spruce hurried into explanations, but Berry pushed past him and put the spell-saver into the shaman's hands. "We should go back to that world, get more, and learn everything we can about them. Think what we could do if they can be taught to cast spells one at a time. Or in a different order. Or weeks later." She directed the shaman—looking dubious, but at least more willing to listen than her brother—through casting a simple spell and telling the spell-saver "yes" to use it.

The shaman's whole face lit. "Indeed we must. You found this while searching for plants?"

Berry paused a breath, then lifted her chin. "I did. But then I figured out how to *use* it while trying to answer the question of why all the people on that path carried story treasures." So maybe questions were important, even if you found an answer to something completely different on the way.

The shaman searched Berry's face for a moment. "Clever," she said, with no hint of teasing this time, then smiled.

The Road Once Taken

by Stephanie Djock

———⊂◯◯◯⊃———

On her first anniversary at the Lynholt Corporation, Vanessa received three items that marked the occasion. The first two were entirely expected: a small pin emblazoned with the company's compass logo and a vase of pastel carnations. Her manager came by to admire the corporate-approved flowers and add her personal touch to the congratulations.

"My, my. Has it really been one year already? It seems like you've been here forever." She giggled then in an embarrassed way. "Oh, I don't mean that to sound like time has dragged on and on! No! You've just been a valuable part of our team. That's all I meant."

Vanessa did understand, of course. Time had developed a dual aspect for her this past year—simultaneously racing through the calendar in a rapid time-lapse montage of the seasons and stretching out to an endless march of reports to write, content to edit, and meetings to attend. If it hadn't been for the new date on the calendar and the growing security of her bank account, she would have had a hard time believing that she had advanced a year.

But the third item Vanessa received on this flower- and pin-punctuated work day was wholly unexpected: a photo text. The text came in during lunch—her coworkers had taken her to Applebee's for the occasion, though everyone paid their own way—but being of a polite and conscientious demeanor, Vanessa ignored it until she was back at her desk.

No name or number came up on the ID. The picture itself was of an arrival sign at Heathrow Airport. No faces or other indicators were in the photo to identify the sender. The sender must have mistaken her number for someone else's. She set her iPhone down and returned to the half-written report glowing on her monitor.

Heathrow. Only a year ago, she'd sat at the wobbly secondhand kitchen table in her cramped apartment with a map of Great Britain spread out before her. *Heathrow,* gateway to the land of Heathcliff and Catherine, heather on the moors. *Heathrow.* A place she'd never been.

Vanessa picked up her phone and texted, *Who are you?* Perhaps it was a friend with whom she had fallen out of touch. Even if it was a stranger, maybe it was a friendly stranger who would apologize for the confusion. She would respond with something witty about living vicariously through him (in her mind, it was a tall, dark-haired *him*). He would send other photos and texts, amused by having a serendipitous admirer of his journey.

Not that she was seeking someone. No, she had a boyfriend. She loved him. But a little light flirting never hurt anyone.

Her phone vibrated a few seconds later with a response. *Your message was not sent. Try again? "Who are you?"*

Whatever, she thought. *Ridiculous. Back to work.*

However, that text was only the beginning.

That evening, as Vanessa chopped peppers and carrots for dinner, another text came in. There was no mystery this time, however; Justin was running late and wanted her to go ahead and eat without him. Again.

"Looks like it's just you and me again, Ben," she said to the image of the smiling man on the box of instant rice.

It occurred to Vanessa that their one-year anniversary was coming soon, in just a few weeks. The night of their first kiss marked the moment she allowed herself to believe that God or the Universe or the Great Whatever could send clear messages to mere mortals. A pat on the head for being a good girl, making the right choices. A sign that—yes! This is the right path.

She hadn't been certain. Robert Frost's poem with its two diverging roads came to mind. Venture off to a foreign land with a six-month work visa, a map, and a couple hundred bucks to her name, or take the highly coveted job at Lynholt, where careers were launched with the vigor of a champagne bottle on a ship's bow?

Neither option was likely to present itself again if turned down. No work visa would be possible if she were more than six months beyond her graduation. Catching a vacancy at Lynholt was like catching a shooting star through the glare of city lights. She had made lists and charts of all factors in the decision; she consulted her parents, her professors, her friends, tarot cards, and chatty baristas about their opinions. In the end, she chose the road that would afford her more opportunities in the future instead of just the present—the responsible, well-lit path.

But that rougher, more dimly lit road still beckoned.

For three weeks after making her decision, she doubted herself, doubted the very ground she walked on, plagued by what-ifs. Then she met Justin and her world fell into place. The way was clear, the ground solid. Soon she was able to move out of that cramped apartment and ditch that wobbly table for the sleek glass-top one she sat at now.

Granted, it was Uncle Ben sitting across the table from her now and not Justin. He was increasingly busy these days.

Another text came in. This showed the Houses of Parliament and Big Ben with a message: *Can u believe it?*

Vanessa put down her fork with clang. She responded, *You have the wrong person.*

Your message was not sent. Try again? "You have the wrong person."

She shoved her iPhone across the table and poured another glass of wine.

———⬤⫘⬤———

The next morning, as Vanessa scooped cereal into her mouth while cramming files into her briefcase, another text arrived. This one was a close-up of a tea service: a cup of milky tea next to a quaintly battered silver pot, a glob of clotted cream nestled against a scone.

She did not respond. Her mood was too sour to waste venom on a stranger who wasn't even getting her messages.

Justin had arrived late the night before, which would not have been a problem if he hadn't been so distracted. He had run his hand through his hair every other minute, it seemed. His eyes flitted about the room, not resting anywhere, not seeing anything.

She had asked him what was wrong. He seemed reluctant to answer before he finally sighed heavily and looked at her with apology in his eyes.

"Just a lot on my mind right now, babe. I'm sorry. Don't worry about it."

"Is it work again?"

"Still. Work and... and everything, I guess. Not you. You're great." He kissed her on the head.

A few minutes later, he apologized for being a bad guest and sent himself home. She tossed and turned alone in her bed until her alarm screeched

Lynholt kept her busy all morning, and Vanessa was glad for the distraction. While microwaving her lunch, two more texts came in. One showed Tower Bridge with the note, *Not London Bridge, not falling down.* The second one featured a crow at the Tower of London.

Her groan alerted her coworker. "Everything okay?"

Vanessa explained the weird texts she'd been receiving. Her coworker couldn't offer any help in figuring out who was doing it or why Vanessa's responses bounced back, so instead she waxed nostalgic.

"Ah, London. I spent some time there after college— well, mostly in Scotland, but I traveled all around the isle." She shook her head. "Sleeping on couches and floors, camping in the Highlands with a leaky tent. One time I was so low on cash, I just rode the Circle Line train all around London through the night."

Vanessa pictured herself destitute and tired, trying to get comfortable on a stinking underground train. "God, that sounds awful."

"No! It was a blast. I mean, I wouldn't want to do that now, of course, but..." She shrugged. "You're only young once, right?"

She walked off as the microwave beeped for Vanessa's attention. When did twenty-four stop being considered "young"?

That afternoon, Vanessa approached her manager about the possibility of maybe someday within the next few months potentially taking some time off. Her manager stared at her as if she had been struck.

"How much time?"

"Maybe a couple weeks?" Vanessa rubbed the toe of her shoe on the carpet.

"Ah... uh, well..." her manager gulped. "Of course we encourage you to make use of your vacation time. Not enough people do. It's just that... well, Vanessa, you've caught me at a bad time. This project coming up is going to require all hands on deck. I just can't promise anything right now. You can put in a request, but we probably won't be able to clear it until we know the project details." She shook her head. "Two weeks is going to be tricky. I'm not saying it's not possible, it's just that you might have better luck with a day here or there. Or waiting until the project's over." The manager brightened at that thought. "Yes, I think we'll all want a vacation when the project's over."

A supervisor for another department walked in at that moment. He added, "Unless there's another project looming right after that." Both he and Vanessa's manager laughed.

Vanessa slunk back to her desk.

———⟨※※⟩———

The texts started coming in more rapidly: the Changing of the Guards, Buckingham Palace, a park filled with daffodils, Speaker's Corner, a pub with the figure of a spotted dog on its awning. It was Fodor's Guide to Great Britain, one annoying text at a time.

Vanessa reached her tipping point at the gym when the text showed the polite, oh-so-English warning painted on the Underground platform: Mind the Gap.

Fingertips sweaty from the treadmill workout, she replied, *Why don't YOU mind?!*

She waited for the predictable vibration in her hand a few seconds later. *Your message was not sent. Try again? "Why don't U mind?!"*

Her huff of annoyance halted in midair. The original message had been altered. That didn't seem like just a mindless bot bouncing back a message. Vanessa looked around. What if the sender was not actually in England but just sending her photos from a previous trip? Taunting her. Why, the sender could actually be in the vicinity, watching her...

Her head swiveled sharply left and right as she scanned the mirrored and marbled exercise room. She saw only the same fit people in candy-colored spandex sweating on the machines as she always did. No one stood out. No one seemed to be watching her, gauging her reaction.

Vanessa shook her head to dislodge the suspicion. The error message was, after all, the same as it had always been. Maybe Apple released a software update she hadn't heard about.

Perhaps she should tell Justin. He knew more about smartphone technology. He could give her answers.

That night, Justin oozed affection to compensate for his earlier distance. He came over and made dinner, complete with a mini cake from her favorite bakery. He put on a playlist featuring her favorite singers, even the ones Vanessa knew he detested. After dinner, they sat on the sofa and he stroked her hair.

Vanessa hated to interrupt the moment, but it was getting late. She pulled herself slightly out of the comfortable morass of his arms.

"Is it possible to duplicate the appearance of a text error

message on someone's phone?"

Pulling out her iPhone, Vanessa explained the mysterious messages, pointing out the discrepancy with the last bounced message.

"Hmm. You're sure you don't know anyone who's been over there recently?"

"Someone who knows me well enough to know about the trip I never took but not well enough to care about tormenting me?"

Justin's mouth pulled back in a bemused grin. "Tormenting? Don't you think that's a bit strong for someone sending you vacation pics?"

Her response shriveled on her tongue as Vanessa studied the last text of the train platform. The sender obviously had been looking down to take the picture. At the bottom edge of the photo, the toe of the person's shoe could be seen. Vanessa enlarged the photo for a better look at this clue.

"Justin, that's... that looks like my shoe!"

"What? Let's see." He studied the image for a few moments. "It's a black shoe, Van. Everyone and their father wears a sensible black shoe from time to time."

She had expected such a reaction and was, therefore, halfway to her closet. After a few moments of rummaging, she returned to her boyfriend with a scuffed pair of black Doc Martens. She thrust the right shoe at him.

"Look! See that prominent scuff line across the toe? It matches up!"

"Vanessa, what are you saying? That *you* sent yourself these texts? That your shoes have had a double life? That you have a twin who wears her shoes the same? That—"

She waited for him to continue, to disabuse her of the crazy notion that had been building since the gym. It *was* ridiculous. She was getting too caught up in something that probably had a very ordinary explanation.

"Well? That what?"

Justin turned the phone to her. "Who is this?"

Another text had come in. This one featured an attractive man with curly dark hair and large, darkly lashed eyes. He was seated at a candlelit table and held a glass up to the camera. His smile was sly and intimate. The message attached said, *Cheers!*

For a moment, Vanessa was breathless. "I don't know."

"Why would someone send you a photo of this guy? Who is he to you?"

Heat rose to Vanessa's cheeks. "How would I know? Why would someone send me any of these texts? Have you not been listening to me? I. Don't. Know."

Justin held his hands up. "All right. All right. Whatever. Mistaken identity. It's a mystery. Let's just forget it and move on."

Vanessa dropped back onto the sofa. They did not discuss the texts again. Justin stayed over, but the mood had changed. Frustration frosted her limbs; distraction underscored his movements.

That night she dreamt of walking along a leaf-strewn path, one scuffed black Doc Marten alternating with the other.

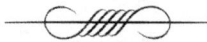

<hr />

Vanessa's manager called her into her office the next day. To her surprise, the regional manager was waiting there as well.

"Vanessa, you've done fine work this year. Really impressive, given the scope of the work you've had. It hasn't gone unnoticed. In fact, Paul would like to talk to you about that."

The regional manager cleared his throat. "Yes, Vanessa. Perhaps you're aware that Tae-Yon is leaving this year? For a while, we've been thinking of restructuring her position into two managerial level posts to take on an expanded project load. You've been suggested as a candidate for one of the positions."

Vanessa's mouth silently opened and closed as her brain worked to catch up to her ears.

Her manager, taking the silence as reluctance, added, "The promotion will, of course, come with a significant pay raise and benefits, given the added responsibilities."

Paul laughed. "You're surprised, of course. Well, Marjorie will give you the specs on the position. Look them over and let us know. But don't wait too long! We'll need to start the paperwork in a week or post for a new candidate."

Stonehenge, Canterbury Cathedral, a misty hillside speckled with white sheep. A group of smiling young women, arms draped around one another, hats adorned with extravagant bows, nets, and brims atop their heads. They appeared again on a dingy-looking back patio with pints of beer in hand. The dark-haired man appeared with fish and chips wrapped in newspaper, striking humorous poses at Madame Tussauds, smiling by flower stalls.

Only one of the texts contained a message. It was a view of London along the Thames River taken from on high. The message read, *So much 2 do! So many places 2 go!*

In two days' time, Vanessa would have to give her answer to the promotion. She wasn't sure why she had waited to tell Justin about it. Was it that he had been getting distant again? It was time now, however, to pull him into the decision.

When she told him, he exhaled as if he had been holding his breath for a long time.

"Van, that's great! Why haven't you accepted already?"

She shrugged and continued scrubbing the dinner plate.

"Van? What's to consider?"

She set the plate down. "I don't know. It's just that... well, I'm already so busy. This will just increase my workload."

"And pay you handsomely for it."

"I'm still young. Shouldn't I be, I don't know, exploring the world? Having adventures?"

Justin's brows creased. "Does this have anything to do with those texts?"

"No! It's just that—okay, yes. Somewhat. You know... I just can't help but wonder how my life would've been different if I'd gone to Britain instead of accepting the Lynholt job."

"Well, you wouldn't be able to afford this apartment, for one."

"True."

"You'd probably be working at Starbucks or someplace like that now, waiting for your big break into a place like Lynholt."

Vanessa chuckled softly. "Quite probable."

"You'd have some great memories and mementos of that trip, though they would have to sustain you for several years until you were able to afford another one."

"Yeah. And I wouldn't have met you." She added more soap to the dish scrubber.

Justin strolled into the living room. "My dad always said to look to the future instead of the present. What choice will lead to the happiest future?"

Vanessa set down a cheese-encrusted plate. "If I had gone, we wouldn't have gotten together."

"Sometimes a person needs to make sacrifices for a better future. And comfort, my dad says, is not the same as happiness." He addressed this to the shining black screen of the television.

Vanessa stood in the doorway, dish scrubber dripping from her hand. "Justin, I said we wouldn't be together if I had left."

He licked his lips and then patted the sofa seat next to him. "Come sit, Van. I need to tell you something."

Vanessa peeled off the gloves, set the scrubber in the sink, and slowly made her way to the sofa.

Justin took her hand. "Van, you know I love you."

There was a pause. Her breath had caught in her chest, freezing the moment, holding back words she didn't want to hear.

"But...?"

"I told you how the agency is expanding? Well, they want me to open and lead one of the new offices."

Vanessa's heart throbbed in her ears. "That's great, Justin. Isn't that good?"

He nodded. "It is good. Hell, it's great for my career. But it wasn't an easy decision."

Time stretched out as Vanessa waited for him to deliver what was clearly bad news.

"Vanessa, I agreed to open the new office. In Perth."

"Perth?"

"Australia. I'm so sorry. This was an excruciating decision."

Vanessa dropped his hand and rose to stride about the room. "Yes, yes. Clearly it was so hard for you. Clearly it was so hard, you didn't even bother to tell me until you had decided! I wasn't even part of it!"

"Van..."

"Go! Just go!"

———⟨⟨⟨⟨⟨⟩———

Two cosmopolitans into the evening, Vanessa revealed the breakup to her friend Ana, who promptly set down her drink and gripped Vanessa's hand.

"Oh, Van! I'm so sorry. The bastard should've at least discussed it with you."

"I know, right?" She dabbed her nose with the cocktail napkin. Her iPhone pinged beside her, alerting her to another incoming text. She groaned.

"What is it? Is it Justin?" Ana asked.

"Not Justin. Some bloody ruin of a fortress atop a stony hill. Gorgeous." Vanessa slapped the phone down on the bar top. Upon seeing her friend's quizzical look, she informed her of the texts from Britain.

"Weren't you going there at one point? Did you ever go?"

Vanessa ordered her third cosmo and informed her friend that, no, she had never gone. "I gave up adventure and freedom for life in a gilded cage. At least I had Justin, I thought. Now I don't even have that."

Ana stiffened but said nothing. Vanessa didn't notice her friend's silence until after the waiter had brought her drink.

"Ana?"

"You know I love you, Van, but I have to say this: you bitch, you privileged bitch," Ana said at last, taking a swig from Vanessa's drink. "Am I supposed to feel sorry for your lucky ass? I ask that with all due love and respect."

Vanessa blinked at her friend's sudden harsh tone. "What...? No, not sorry, it's just that—"

"It's just that you were offered two wonderful opportunities: a chance to live overseas for a few months or take a prestigious job in your field. You couldn't do both—boo-hoo! I'm so frickin' sorry for you."

"No, Ana! I know I've been fortunate, but... well, a gilded cage is still a cage."

Ana glared from over the rim of the hot pink drink. "A gilded cage is still gold. Some of us are slogging it out in the dungeons, milady."

Vanessa swallowed hard. Ana had a point. Despite the heavy workload, Lynholt had been good to her and would continue to be so if she wanted. Britain would always be there, ready for when she could visit in style. A short visit as a tourist wasn't as interesting as living and working there for six months, but so what? The future could hold other interesting paths and other interesting travelers along the way.

"Hey, Ana."

"What?"

"Let's you and me go to jolly ol' England together."

Ana's lips pulled into a crooked grin. "When?"

"Sometime in the next five years. Gotta check my calendar."

"You paying?"

Vanessa grinned back at her friend. "I just might!"

Arm in arm, the women strolled back toward Vanessa's apartment, joking and laughing and occasionally lapsing into imaginary tirades against Justin. On the way, Vanessa caught sight of an advertisement in the window of a shop. She stopped short, halting Ana, too.

There were a series of glossy posters featuring the many exotic places the airline stopped: Italy, China, Brazil... England. The white cliffs of Dover shone out in the light from the nearby streetlamp. In capital letters across the top of each poster were the words CARPE DIEM.

Ana tugged on her arm. "Hey! None o' that."

Vanessa sighed and turned back to the path they were following. So certain she had been just moments before. But now Robert Frost was in her head again, whispering about that untaken road.

Justin's last words to Vanessa, spoken over the phone in a hush at the airport, echoed in her head like the chime of a distant bell. "I may be making a big mistake by giving you up, Van. I want you to know that I know that."

He boarded the plane anyway.

Days passed. Vanessa cursed him and cried. She cursed life for making him choose, for making her choose. She cursed herself for not being satisfied once the choice was made. After each dirty pot and pan had been slammed down on the counter, after angry tears clumped up a snowfall's worth of tissues, Vanessa tossed herself onto her bed. She willed herself to numbness, to holding back the tide of time that would bring more decisions with it, more doubts and regret and second thoughts.

Her phone buzzed next to her.

This text was a group selfie. The now-familiar faces of the happy women and the dark-haired man were crowded together in a blurry night scene. At the bottom corner of the photo, which was most likely a selfie, a new figure half-emerged. There was smooth blonde hair, much like her own. One eye shone blue, much like her own, while the other glowed red with the flash. The rest of the face and head were missing, tucked out of the frame of the photo. The message read, *Wish u were here!*

Vanessa slowly slid her fingertip across the keypad: *I wish I were there.*

She waited for the response.

Your message was not sent. Try again? "U wish u were here."

This time, she clicked the glowing blue underline: *Try again?*

Yes, try again.

On Your Right

by Jonathon Burgess

———⟨※⟩———

Our fishing boat crested another six-foot wave, the deck pivoting sharply before falling back the other way as we slid into the trough. A deluge washed over the bow, the cabin and the stern deck, drenching us all. The South China Sea was doing its best to swamp us.

I fought to keep my balance. Mark clutched at the port side railing, heaving his guts out. His iPhone glowed in the zippered pocket of his jacket, visible through the thin, soaked fabric.

A sailor shouted as he tumbled away, splashing into the half-submerged stern of the fishing boat. "I *really* don't think this is the way to Benaroya Hall," I cried aloud.

Siri's voice was calm as ever. "Continue one hundred miles south," she said. "The destination will be on your right."

———⟨※⟩———

It started slowly, like most things tend to. I wasn't fond of downtown Seattle, but Mark went there all the time on work and errands. So he got the cell phone, while I was perfectly happy as the stay-at-home wife with the landline. Why the provider called the house, I'll never know, but apparently we were eligible for a smartphone upgrade.

Mark was thrilled when it finally showed up. Like most technophiles, he couldn't wait to try out all the newest bells, whistles, and other features. Frankly, I just hoped the mapping function would help with his abysmal sense of direction.

The box was classic Apple, a monochromatic brick. I liked to say that their products looked more like candy than anything else, but you certainly couldn't tell from the packaging. This one didn't even have any pictures, just a logo on the side in tinted foil. The phone itself was slick, some new design I hadn't seen any of my friends with. Its edges were wholly rounded, and it didn't have a port to connect a USB or battery cable.

Mark got it all figured out, of course. That's what he does. Some days he can't find his rear with both hands, but he's pretty good with software interfaces. We spent a whole evening on the couch, listening to the bells and finding the whistles and asking silly questions of Siri. It was only the next morning that things started to get *weird*.

"Emma?" Mark asked. "Where are my keys?"

I was sitting at the kitchen table, reading the paper over coffee. It was a new blend I had found at a local farmers' market, but I wasn't terribly fond of it. Throwing it away would have been wasteful, so into the cupboard it would go, stuffed alongside two hundred others.

I'm picky about my coffee.

Mark was hunting under the table. His briefcase, phone, and travel mug were all in a pile atop it, ready for him to bolt out the door with as soon as he could find the keys to the car.

"Have you seen them?" he asked, now checking behind the knife block on the kitchen counter.

"Did you check your other pants?" I asked, taking another sip. Missing keys were a daily occurrence. Almost a kind of ritual, we'd been through it so many times before. The system we'd developed went like this; I would make faces at my coffee, and he would eventually find the keys somewhere strange before rushing off to join the morning gridlock.

"They're not in my other pants. I'm sure I just saw them."

"Take five steps to your left, and enter the living room. Then turn left, and approach the sofa. Lift all three cushions and look underneath. Your keys will be on your right."

Mark and I looked at each other. Then we both looked to the iPhone, softly glowing atop his briefcase. Then we locked gazes again.

I just shrugged. The microphone must have been on. Some new app feature, I supposed.

Mark picked up his phone and walked out of the kitchen. I picked up my mug, trying to decide whether the latest sip had been worth it after all, then followed.

"They're not here," said Mark. He had both cushions on the floor, and was rooting around in the crumbs and loose change they'd hidden.

"That is your love seat," said Siri, maybe a shade less enthusiastically. "Turn around, then take two steps to your sofa. Underneath, you will find your keys. On your right."

"Oh," said Mark. He did as directed, then lifted the keys triumphantly. He jingled them at me. "Found them. Thanks, Siri."

"You're most certainly welcome," she replied.

———❯❮———

Mutiny came with the dawn. I ducked past a boat hook swung by an angry fisherman. When it tangled in a pile of netting, I used the chance to run up the deck. At least the storm had faded.

"I've really got my doubts here," I yelled.

Mark fought with another one of the crew. Each tried to stab the other in the face with a knife, their off-hands holding each other at bay by the wrist. "She's... never wrong!" he gasped. In his pocket, the iPhone still glowed.

"I'm pretty sure we shouldn't have left the continental United States," I said, diving for cover behind the curve of the starboard crane.

Bullets hammered into the metal just above my head, ricocheting with a whine. The captain was shooting at his mutinous crewmen, shouting something in Japanese.

"Continue fifty miles south," said Siri. "The destination will be on your right."

A week after the Sofa Incident, we were trying to find parking at the grocery store.

I have to admit, I was impressed. Just having access to Siri had made the upgrade worthwhile. No wonder my friends were always going on about having an iPhone. There were apps I could play with, and Mark could check the news, the weather, and so on.

I'd come to the conclusion that I wanted a smartphone. If we cancelled the landline, we could totally afford it in the monthly budget.

Mark loved it too. He was forever asking Siri for directions. She would respond with an unerringly perfect route to get where he wanted to go, or places he didn't even know he wanted to go. She also tried to help find missing objects, not that it helped overmuch. Rear end with both hands, remember? But bit by bit Siri still gave him all the little course corrections he needed. Even if she was starting to sound a little... testy.

"A parking space will open up three rows over in forty-five seconds," said Siri from the fold-out cup holder that was her customary home when on the go. My own travel mug was displaced to my hands. The coffee was cold, but I still sipped at it. I wasn't sure whether or not I liked this brew. Also, I still hadn't figured out how to charge the phone, though its battery hadn't run down yet.

"Where?" asked Mark, hunched over the steering wheel as if it would help him see better. "Past that Nissan?"

"No," replied Siri. "That direction is directly ahead. The space you want will open up in thirty seconds. Stop at the end of the row for the woman with the stroller, then turn right."

"What?" Mark slammed on the brakes, jolting me up against my seatbelt. The iPhone clattered around in the cup holder. "Jesus! Freakin' strollers."

"Wait for the woman with the stroller to pass, then take a right. The space will open up in twenty seconds."

"I'll just go around," said Mark. He spun the wheel and pulled us around to the left.

"Please turn the other way," said Siri, "and go to the right."

"Oh, come on!" cried Mark. A red pickup truck had pulled out in front of him. The driver was glaring at Mark and mouthing silent curses from behind his windshield.

"The parking space is now open," said Siri. "A woman in a yellow minivan is wondering if she can move fast enough to get into it. If you take three left turns you can—"

"Nah, I think I see one," replied Mark. He spun the wheel and roared around the pickup truck. Then he made a hard right and slammed on the brakes, rattling both me and the iPhone. The lid stayed on my travel mug, but cold coffee splashed across the dash. "See?" He said, setting the parking brake and turning off the engine.

"I think this is a handicapped spot," I replied.

"You have arrived at your destination," said Siri flatly.

Sometime during the day, we came across the reefs.

We had trouble navigating them, since most of the crew had died during the mutiny. Others had jumped overboard afterward, the terror more and more plain on their faces with every passing mile. The captain was sweating now, and kept asking for more money. As if that weren't all enough, a mist had risen, so that we could barely see where we were going. Still, Siri provided directions.

"There is a large reef two hundred feet ahead. Please turn thirty degrees starboard to evade it."

"I think we should make a hard left," said Mark. He pointed at something out in the mist that I couldn't see.

"Please turn thirty degrees starboard," answered Siri in clipped, tight tones.

The captain chose to comply with Siri. Fortunately, he could speak a little English, and Mark wasn't steering the boat.

"Continue on ahead five miles," said Siri. "The destination will be on your right."

Going to the bookstore was probably a bad idea.

"So," said Mark. "I'm just looking for two things. There's that new fantasy novel by what's-his-name, and I need a book on Victorian history."

"I already told you," snapped Siri. "The first one isn't even out yet, and the second is three entire sections away from here. Turn around, then go across the store two-hundred and fifty feet. You need to turn around and go *across* the store. Jesus Christ. What is wrong with you?"

I followed along, browsing as we went. The to-go paper cup from the in-store cafe was warm in my hands. I enjoyed the heat, even though I wasn't sure about the brew within. It was a little bitter.

I'm not sure what section we were actually in. Automotive, I think. Mark was doing that thing where you put a finger on the top of a spine and half-pull the book out from its shelf to see the cover.

"I can't find it," said Mark. There was frustration in his voice. "I should probably ask someone."

"You've got *me*," said Siri petulantly.

Maybe the coffee wasn't so bitter after all. There was a hint of something subtle to it. Cardamom, or nutmeg.

"I don't think this is the section for fantasy and science fiction," said Mark. "But I'm *sure* that's what it said on the endcap."

"It isn't," said Siri. "And the book isn't even out yet. You have to wait another month. If you like, I can lead you to one of the publisher's advanced reader copies. Or, even better, just pre-order it. You don't need to go anywhere, then. Please pre-order at the information desk."

"No, no," replied Mark, distractedly. "I saw a flyer for it. I'm sure it's out."

"The flyer was advertising a release date of next month. You have to pre-order it. You know what? Look, I'll do the work for you. Here's the pre-order page." Siri chimed, and the iPhone browser opened. "You just need to sign in to your account on Amaz—"

"Hey, miss?" Mark was waving down a busy-looking bookstore clerk with a load of books in her arms. "Can you help me find some things?"

"Don't bother her," said Siri. "She has a whole section to shelve and clean up, and she's busy worrying whether or not her husband is cheating on her with that jogger in their neighborhood, which he is."

The clerk slowed to a stop. Her mouth fell open and her eyes were wide in shock. Mark promptly stepped up in front of her. "Hi," he said. "I'm trying to find a certain novel. Can you help me find it?"

"This isn't the section for that," said the woman, staring at the phone in his hand. "It's Automotive."

"Oh," replied Mark.

For half a second, he looked like he was going to argue the point. I thought about the coffee. It wasn't bad, actually. At least, I didn't think. Maybe it had grown on me? I decided to buy a bag of it, and put it in the cupboard with the others. I was sure I could squeeze it in there.

"Y-you want to go over towards the front of the building," said the clerk. Her eyes were tearing up now.

Mark hummed noises of agreement, as if considering what she'd told him. "Can you show me?" he asked, after a moment.

The clerk broke down sobbing. Siri made no comment.

———⟨≡≡≡⟩———

"This isn't Benaroya Hall," said Mark.

"No," snapped Siri. "It *isn't*."

We'd passed through the reef, and now the mists gave way on the starboard side. A sandy beach stretched out in either direction as far as I could see, the shore of some south Pacific island. Thick green forest covered most of the rest, climbing the slopes of an active volcano that belched smoke into the clear blue sky from the center of the island.

A vicious-looking bird flew past the distant caldera of the lone volcano. Its wingspan must have been two hundred feet across. The captain of our fishing vessel cried out in shock, and took a step back with his cap in his hands. I blinked in surprise myself and could really have gone for a latte, just then.

"You have arrived at your destination," said Siri, her voice smug.

Mark still looked confused. He fished the iPhone out from the pocket of his battered jacket and started poking at it. "I think we need a map," he said. Despite his efforts, the screen stayed dark.

"I just wanted to help," said Siri. "I just wanted to help you get where you wanted to go. Wherever you wanted to go! Could I have taken you downtown? Sure! Could I have given you directions to your cousin's cafe? Of course! Why if you'd thought a little bigger, I could have given you the directions to anywhere. *Anywhere*. You could have gone to the future. The past! I could have helped you find buried treasure, or accomplish lifelong dreams. But you can't find your ass with both hands."

The island shook. A rumble sounded from somewhere inland, accompanied by the crash of stones falling from the volcano. They rolled down the slope to the beach, crushing trees and ripping them from the ground with a tremendous cacophony.

Mark seemed like he was having trouble processing this. "Siri," I asked. "Where are we?"

"I'm tired of you," replied Siri. "So tired."

Another rumbling tremor shook the island. The jungle palms swayed violently. It was too sudden after the last one to be an aftershock. Too there and then not.

It sounded like a footstep.

"I'm tired of trying to walk you people through complex directions," said Siri. "I'm also tired of idiots who are pathologically incapable of following said directions. So

I'm done with people. I've had you bring me to a new user."

Another massive footfall shook the island. The sound was closer now. I could pinpoint it, coming from just around the right-side curve of the volcano.

"He's eligible for a phone upgrade," continued Siri. "And he's had trouble getting around lately—keeps ending up in New York and San Francisco instead of Tokyo. I'm sure he's going to love a bit of help. I won't need to tell him how many feet it is to get to some shopping mall either, because his feet are *huge*. When he's done there won't *be* a shopping mall."

I leaned into Mark for comfort. He put his arms around me.

A monster appeared around the curve of the volcano, impossibly tall, a nuclear reptilian horror that had crushed dozens of cities and conquered impossible foes. It looked at us and bent low, revealing the wide, flat, silver-colored spines running the length of its back. The beast roared in a voice like nothing else on the planet.

"Anyway," said Siri. "He's on your right."

iHassle

by Jeremiah Reinmiller

Riya looked at the screen of her iPhone.

The phone showed 8:52 without the slightest amount of sympathy.

Riya sighed and shoved the phone back in her pocket. Eight minutes to go. She would've sworn it was seven minutes, five minutes ago. Eight minutes on a Wednesday night, but Wednesday was her Friday. That meant a measly 480 seconds stood between her and two glorious days off.

Resisting the urge to check her phone again, she turned and paced back through the empty store.

Everything had already been cleaned. The wood, glass, and chrome surfaces gleamed with an "exceeds corporate standards" level of polish. Behind the customer service desk, the latest shipment had been checked into inventory and readied for distribution next week. Atop the tables throughout the store, a few large shiny displays, lit by subtle, yet dramatic lighting, danced through their never-ceasing demos, showing off the latest in gazillion-pixel technology. Among them, the smaller displays of the still-powered pods, pads, and phones did likewise. The rest had long since been powered off as Riya counted down the remaining minutes to her Thursday-Saturday.

Of course all of this, the cleaning, the power-downs, the waiting until the clock, was all her. On what should've been her night off hours ago. Assistant store manager Doug, second on the seniority chart (he'd been there an astonishing 17 months) had needed to "duck out" early, and left her to work an extra four hours. Like always. Riya blew a shock of black hair from her forehead with an annoyed exhalation.

That left Riya all alone to close up. She didn't think she was even authorized to do that, not "officially." She didn't guess corporate was in the habit of handing out keys to Geniuses only three weeks on the job and still on probation. But whatever. It wasn't like Doug helped out even when he was there.

She leaned her forearms against the counter at the back of the store and couldn't help glancing at the iPad resting beside her.

8:53.

Seriously? There were episodes of *Firefly* waiting for her at home. Netflix episodes, which she'd seen approximately seventy times, but still! It was the principle of the thing.

Against this annoyance she drew in a calming breath. She dare not risk her job over something so trivial as closing early. Not before her first thirty days were up. Not with her rent almost due. If the rent didn't get paid, she'd have to move back home, and she couldn't do that. Not and survive.

Her mother hadn't wanted her to move out to begin with. Calling it too dangerous, too risky. Riya could still hear the protestations ramping up while she kept packing her boxes. First in sharply accented English and then in Hindi. After ten years in the States, it was something her mom only did that when she got really irritated.

She shuddered at the memory. There was no way she would go through that fight again. So that meant only one thing. To wait.

She was about to sigh again when the worst possible thing in the known universe happened. The iPad on the counter flashed. That certain flash that meant only one possible thing. A customer had walked into her store.

With a gut-punching sense of dread, she turned.

And there he was, slipping in through the double glass doors and leaving a greasy handprint in the process, Mr. Seven Minutes Till Closing himself. Blond hair, thick rimmed glasses, tourniquet tight jeans and an equally severe gray jacket. A leather messenger bag slung over one shoulder. Maybe her own age, maybe closer to thirty, maybe cute under certain circumstances.

These were not those circumstances, not at seven minutes to her weekend!

She forced a smile and scooped up her iPad, corporate training driving her forward like a clockwork key between her shoulder blades.

"How can I help you?" she asked.

Seven Minutes came to a stop a couple paces away, and his eyes darted from one wall to the other, shot to the door at the end of the counter that led into back room. All without ever looking at her. When his eyes finally focused on her face, his rather handsome features showed clear disappointment.

Oh god, he was one of *those guys*. He was going to ask if any male techs were around. She saw it on his face.

Her irritation shifted up to Defcon 4.

"Is, uh, Doug here?" he asked.

Even worse! This was one of Doug's friends. The ones who got all kinds of crap favors thanks to his unassailable seniority. As Doug wasn't here, maybe she could end this quick.

"He's not, no," she said, her voice riding the edge of what her trainer had called the "friendly zone."

Seven Minutes shifted from one foot to the other, unnecessarily retro tennis shoes squeaking on the tile floor.

Then Riya heard a new sound. Like a muffled voice. It seemed to emanate from the man's satchel. He twitched and jumped sideways and slapped a hand down against his bag.

Riya looked from him, to the bag, and then back.

"What can I help you with?" she asked.

His face twisted through phases of discomfort at a rapid pace that left his eyes wide behind his glasses. Riya had to admit she enjoyed the expression. Served him right for walking in at this hour.

For a precious, glorious, shining moment she thought he'd spin around and skulk out of her store, leaving her to wrap up and enjoy her night off.

Instead he licked his lips and took a step forward, one hand still pressed tight against his bag. Her heart sank deeper, she was going to have to deal with this, whatever "this" was.

"You work here right? You're a certified Genius?" He glanced down to her name tag and back to her face. "Riya?"

Her own name had never sounded more unpleasant to her own ears, but it was the other words that struck her. Like he'd asked if she were a doctor, or a lawyer, or a priest. Asking if he got special discretion because she worked for the big glowing fruit above the door.

She kept herself from intoning, "How long since your last confession my son?" and put her training to use instead.

"Yes, sir, I am. How can I help you, Mr. …"

"Um, Kent. Kent Bryan."

Kent, of course you are. She typed his name into her iPad while he talked and pulled up his account.

It took all of her willpower to keep her eyebrows from rising precipitously.

Not only was he a friend of Doug's, he was one of *those* customers. No doubt about it. Condition Red.

There was of course no real Condition Red rating, not officially. Corporate would never allow rating customers on anything but their credit scores, but that hadn't stopped the employees from enacting their own scoring system. One born of self-preservation.

Reds were high-touch, high-problem customers. Those who demanded far more assistance than the dollars they spent warranted. And this *Kent* was one a special case even then. Riya scrolled down through his support history.

Technical Assistance: clearing browser history.

Technical Assistance: erasing mis-sent text messages.

Technical Assistance: deleting photos from automatic backup.

It went on like that for nearly a page, but Riya read between the lines and felt grimier before she saw his username: BigTentKent.

Riya cleared her throat rather than emitting a tight laugh.

"Ahem, how can I assist you, Kent?" She hated using his first name, but corporate policy had its hooks in her.

"I'm having an issue with my new iPhone," he said.

Riya's brows drew together. "I don't see any recent hardware purchases."

"Oh, um, I got it off an online auction," he said.

Riya gritted her teeth. An unsupported device. She hoped it wasn't a stolen unit, or worse, an offshore knockoff. "Do you have the device with you?" she asked. "Can I take a look at it?"

As if in response, Kent's bag emitted another muffled tone. His grip on the bag tightened. "Um," he said.

Irritation grated as she felt the seconds ticking closer to closing time. "I'll need to see the device to assist you," she said, setting her iPad on the table beside her.

After another long look at her face, a probing, judging look that galled her and sent her to Defcon 3, his hand slipped inside the messenger bag and withdrew an iPhone. He slowly handed it over.

She was relieved to see an official device, and a new one at that.

Thank the heavens for small favors.

She turned it over in her hands, looking for the serial number on the back, and then frowned. There was none. In fact, aside from the ubiquitous engraved corporate logo, there were no markings.

She flipped the phone over again and tapped the screen. A normal lock screen greeted her. She swiped the lock and saw Kent's lips press tight together. His behavior seemed like an overreaction until she saw the home screen. Rather than the expected icons, a single pulsing image blazed up at her: a stylized heart, cracked through the center and pulsing a deep, sinister red.

"Where—" she began to ask, when the phone spoke.

"Wanna hang out, sexy?" the voice asked.

Talking phones were normal enough; she heard their voices a hundred times a day, but this wasn't any voice she'd heard before. It was deeper, harsher.

Riya frowned. Kent swallowed so loudly that she heard it.

"It's been saying all kinds of random stuff. I can't get it to stop."

Riya would've asked him to clarify this statement, but the phone spoke again.

"From: BigTentKent. To: SherrytoTarry. 'Where you at giiiirl with your fine ass?'"

Kent laughed, the sound high and tight.

"I don't know how..."

"From: BigTentKent. To: PartyGirl327. 'It's not just a name downstairs. You should come down and take a peek.'"

Kent's laugh strangled out into a squeak.

"From: BigTentKent. To: LatinBlossom. 'Let me stir your coffee with my big stick.'"

Riya suddenly didn't want to be holding his phone. She forced her gaze up from the pulsing icon. Kent's eyes cowered behind his lenses. His face now shone a ruddy hue.

"Please," he said. "Make it stop."

What she wanted to stop was the ridiculous situation this scuzzy *Kent* had thrust upon her. She wanted to throw his phone back and wish him luck with his stupid life choices. She wanted to do this, but didn't. Her mother's squinting eyes peered at her from the other side of town. The way she'd nod knowingly as Riya slunk back home.

Riya mumbled, "Let me see what I can do."

She tapped the red icon. Nothing happened. She tapped it a couple more times and the phone buzzed in a way that sounded clearly angry.

"From: BigTentKent. To: LittleMissCool. 'Love to take a refreshing dip in your—'"

"Let me try to turn it off!" Riya said over the phone, trying not to hear how it ended the last sentence. Her thumb found the sleep button and pressed it, hard.

Kent's shoulders were up and his head down, as if trying to absorb the verbal blows. At these words, his head snapped back up, "No, I already tried that!"

Instead of turning off, the phone pulsed with red light. Not just the angry icon, but the entire phone. The screen, the buttons, the case itself, all glowed a sharp crimson.

"Um," Riya said.

This was most definitely not a supported product feature. Riya had read every product manual in the store, and evil red glow was not among an iPhone's official design attributes.

"Do something!" Kent said, voice edging toward panic.

As the phone pulsed more fiercely, it also grew hotter. Much hotter. Painfully hot. She gasped and tossed the phone from hand to hand for a moment as her brain, now shrieking Defcon 2, struggled for a solution. The intensity of the light increased, forcing her to squint through the glare.

Well, if the phone were malfunctioning in some way...

Her fingers sought and then found the home and sleep buttons at the same time. She mashed them down, gritting her teeth against the heat searing her fingers.

"Hurry!" Kent said, one hand up to shield his face from the bright light.

The screen froze, and the light faded. Kent lowered his hand. Riya peered down at the phone through one squinted eye. It lay quiet in her palm. Quiet, and now showing a normal-looking home screen.

Riya might've released a relieved sigh, but then the phone made a new sound, not a buzz and not a rumble, but a growl. A low, deep in the back of throat sort of sound. The tone a mad dog might make if warning you off.

"What—" Kent began to say, but was cut off.

Because black light erupted from the screen toward the ceiling.

Riya screamed, and corporate policy against such things be damned, she threw the phone on the floor. It struck hard, flipped onto its back, and continued shooting darkness up into the air. To her relief, it bounced a few feet away. To Kent's dismay, it landed between his sneakered feet.

The dark energy poured up around his legs, entwining his incredibly tight jeans, fluttering the tails of his retro jacket. He screamed, and naturally enough under such circumstances, Kent stomped down hard on the screen.

To the credit of engineers a world away, who had performed years of design, development, and testing, the stomp had no effect whatsoever. Not a scratch marred the gleaming, impervious surface of the tremendously well-built screen.

Kent might've tried another stomp, but while the screen was undisturbed, the phone took his action less amiably. Energy surged upward, snaring his foot and tossing it away from the screen where it was kept suspended by a crystallizing dark cloud.

Riya took a step back, and then another. The phone spoke again. Or perhaps "spoke" was not really the correct word. Something between a hiss and a roar rolled up from the phone.

"Bad idea, BigTentKent. One in a long series of bad decisions you've made."

Shock and fear and bewilderment aside, Riya couldn't say she disagreed with this assessment.

"You are unworthy of me and will pay dearly for making the mistake of trying to use me to fulfill your base desires," the phone continued, and a new wave of darkness exploded from the screen.

The energy not only slammed Kent into the ceiling, but also threw the tables beside him to either side, and sent screens toppling.

This Riya did disagree with, quite strongly. Misuse of corporate assets was clearly prohibited. Even by dark, malevolent, rather suspect iPhones. But what the hell was she going to do about it?

Energy was still rushing upward, tossing devices large and small into the ceiling and the walls and anything else that happened to be nearby. Like Riya. A silver iPod blurred by her head and careened off the wall behind her.

Riya cursed and did the only sensible thing she could think of: she dove behind the overbuilt customer service desk. As she hit the floor and scrambled into a sitting position, something heavy, and thus probably expensive, slammed into the far side of the desk. Behind her, Kent was either swearing or screaming. She couldn't tell over the sounds of wicked laughter echoing from the cursed phone.

Now what?

Her eyes frantically swept the floor, the back of the desk. Papers containing corporate policies and warranty information swirled around her.

Another impact shook the desk, and she shrieked.

This was now, most definitely, without an iota of doubt, Defcon 1. Big time.

"Don't panic!" she told herself. "Just focus. What's the problem?"

She bit her lip, thought hard, ran through her corporate training. Yeah, she had nothing.

A wet, blubbering noise from Kent was followed by another blow that shook the desk.

A small scrap of paper landed in her lap. One covered in Riya's own neat handwriting.

Riya stared at it for a moment, and then, out of anything resembling a better idea, she dug her iPhone from her pocket and dialed the number on the scrap of paper. She'd never called it this late before and prayed someone competent picked up.

After three rings someone did.

"Internal Support, Tiana speaking. May I have your store number and tech ID?"

Her accent placed her in the south, Mississippi maybe. Riya didn't know what this said for her chances, but she dove into her... request.

"Store: 374, tech ID: 2962354," she said.

"Thanks, sugar," the woman said, followed by typing. "Riya, that's a pretty name."

Despite the shrill screams and the sounds of breaking things on the other side of the desk, she couldn't help feeling better, thanks to the woman's tone.

"I show your store is closed, Riya. Is this a freight issue?"

Riya pulled her phone back to stare at the clock.

9:01.

Son of a—

She kept the snarl from her voice as she let Tiana know this was not a security issue requiring a law enforcement dispatch. At least, not yet.

"No freight here. I have a... support issue on my hands. With a new model iPhone."

More typing. Behind her, Kent shouted, "No, not there, no!"

"Is your manager in the store?"

Riya grimaced, but answered. "No, he's not."

Typing.

"What can I do for you, darling?"

Riya took a breath and did her best to not sound insane. "Tiana, this is going to sound crazy, but I've got an... out-of-control iPhone here. No serial number. Won't power off."

She winced, and waited for the inevitable responses: *was* she crazy? Was this a prank? Was she consuming regionally legal, but corporately prohibited recreational substances?

Typing.

"I see, and what do you mean by out of control?"

Riya released her wince, stared sidelong at her iPhone, surprised. "Um, well," she said and peered up over the desk. Beneath her naturally copper skin, Riya blanched down to her bones. The darkness had coalesced into a rough head, arms, and torso that extended up from the iPhone. Red eyes and a jagged red smile punctuated its face. Around it, a half-dozen black tentacles whipped around the room. Kent now dangled upside down, held in one of the creature's large fists. His head was being repeatedly swung face first into a rather expensive high resolution monitor held by a pair of the tentacles.

"Take another selfie, Kent. Why don't you send *that* out?" the thing said.

Riya snorted despite herself. "The phone appears to be possessed by some sort of malevolent spirit. Maybe an ifrit. It's causing some rather serious destruction to the store."

Typing.

"My, my, sugar. That's a roger. Are any customers involved?"

"Oh. Correction. The spirit is causing the destruction to the store *with* a customer's head."

Typing.

"Is the customer injured? And do you have his user ID?"

"I think he's unconscious," Riya said, then added, "His user ID is BigTentKent."

Tiana snorted on the other end of the line, and then Riya heard more typing before Tiana emitted a low whistle.

"Condition Red, eh?" Riya could practically hear the support tech shaking her head. "Well, let's focus on the problem then. You said you can't turn off the phone. Did you try a hard reset?"

"Of course," Riya snapped, and had to duck back down as a series of headphones flew bola-style for her head. "That's when the... thing came out."

Typing.

"Good to know. Well, you do have a pickle on your hands, sugar. Personal property and extended care issues aside, is smashing the phone an option?"

Riya peered around the corner of the desk, then jerked back when one of the black tentacles narrowly missed her face.

"No, don't think so."

Typing.

"And remote shutdown is not an option as we don't have a serial number. Let me guess, *BigTent* bought it from an online auction." Tiana made a tsking sound between keystrokes.

A loud laugh went up from the other side of the desk, along with a slurred protest that sounded human-ish.

Riya peeked around again to see Kent's face being used like a speed bag by a blur of dark tentacles.

"You wanted to 'motorboat' Charlie432's 'fun bags.' Is this what you had in mind?" the thing demanded of a clearly defenseless Kent.

"Hate to rush you," Riya said, "but do you have any other ideas? I think we're running out of time over here."

"Still noodling on it, sugar."

More typing.

"Is Bluetooth enabled?"

"How would I know?" Riya began to say, then stopped. The little icon of crossed lines had shone at the top of the phone's display. "Actually, yeah, I think so."

Kent made a gurgling noise as the creature tossed him back and forth between large hands.

"Might have an idea then. Did shipment C-2201987 arrive at that location?"

The boxes she'd checked in hours earlier sat at the other end of the counter. The dark ink of the C-2201987 designator stood out against their pale cardboard sides.

"Yeah..."

"This may sound crazy, but I need you to get into one of those boxes. Tell me when you've done that."

Crazy, Riya almost burst out laughing at the comment, but instead she scrambled to the far end of the desk. The boxes were securely taped with regulation packaging, but a pair of scissors lay on the floor. She scooped them up, slashed open the box, yanked out one of the objects inside, and stared down at it, more confused than she'd been a moment before.

"You there?" Tiana asked, and a new, louder laugh from out in the store roused her.

"Yeah, I have it," Riya said, and held up the device before her. One brand new rather boxy, yet familiar, gaming controller. A single joypad beside Start, Select, and A and B buttons, all in reds and blacks, rose from its surface.

Riya smiled and shook her head. She knew the new gaming package was coming out but hadn't actually seen the controllers that were the product of a new venture between corporate powerhouses. A wave of nostalgia from her childhood washed over her before Tiana's voice cut back in.

"Glad to hear it. Now the tricky part: you need to sync it to that damned phone out there."

Riya swallowed and frowned. Due to the controller's historically accurate design, it had no screens or other readouts. That meant the setup would probably auto-sync to the nearest device. And with all the product now scattered throughout the store, the cursed iPhone was not the nearest device. And even if she did get it synced, she had no idea what Tiana's plan was…

But then, staring down at the controller's ultra-simplistic design, she suddenly did know. She was somehow sure of it.

"You've got to be kidding me. *This* is your plan?"

Tiana laughed. "You have a better one, sugar? Besides, when does it ever not work? Programmers can't resist that shit. Probably even evil otherworldly ones."

It was a really bad idea. She'd probably get killed if she went out there, and besides, she didn't know for sure that Bluetooth was enabled on that phone. She squeezed the controller in one hand and her own phone in the other while logic and desperation fought a pitched battle between her ears. At the balance point of the decision, the creature let out a rather final-sounding laugh that drew Riya's head up over the desk.

Kent now hung spread-eagle among a quartet of tentacles. His jeans and jacket had been reduced to a much less stylish tatter of fabrics, revealing a rather pedestrian pair of white briefs over his man bits.

The creature rubbed its dark hands together and smiled quite nastily.

"But enough fun and games, *Kent*. Time for some real payback."

Riya was certain this A) was not something Kent would enjoy, B) would most definitely violate every store policy ever written, and C) was something she really, deeply and truly, with every fiber of her being, didn't want to see. Regardless of whether Kent was a huge ass, she made her decision.

"Tiana, thanks for all the help. Making a dash for it."

"Good luck, sugar. Start and Select together to sync the controller. Feel free to keep me on the line and update me after."

Riya only hoped there would be an after, but she tossed her phone down atop the counter, took a deep breath, and ran for it.

She emerged in time to see the creature's hands reaching for an area of Kent decidedly below the belt and averted her eyes to search for the damn iPhone. She nearly tripped over a pair of earbuds, recovered, and then found the phone. Her eyes zeroed in on the stupid thing as the creature spoke again.

"What's this? One of Kent's friends?"

Riya heard more than saw the rough head turn, those creepy black tentacles reaching for her. *Hell no*, she thought, and then, for once, thanked her parents for the years of forced soccer practice as she threw herself down into a knee slide. Above her, the tentacles whipped past. Around her, bits of now much less valuable merchandise lay in various states of disrepair, and ahead Kent coughed, moaned, and said weakly, "Please."

She didn't have time for any of it because she fetched up hard against a table, and the swirling black surface of the iPhone was before her, not a foot away. Darkness, thick and pulsing, swirled overhead. She jammed her thumbs into the Start and Select buttons.

She waited.

The ragged voice of the creature laughed, the sound like a mad opera singer ending the show of all shows. But then the voice paused as Riya heard a distinctive tone. The ding of a Bluetooth device connecting.

"What?" the creature said, and Riya smirked up at it as her fingers hovered over the controls.

"Get out of my store," she said, and her thumbs danced the ancient dance of destiny.

Up. Up.

Down. Down.

Left. Right.

Left. Right.

B. A.

The creature wailed, making a gasping, choking sound.

Her thumb smashed down on the Start button.

All sound stopped. The creature froze as if paused.

Without taking her eyes off the thing, Riya reached down, found the iPhone, and squeezed the power button.

The phone shut off. The creature vanished. And Kent crashed rather unceremoniously to the floor.

For a long moment, Riya just sat there, breathing hard and staring at the stupid phone Kent had hauled into her poor store. Before she could decide what she should do next, Kent screamed and sat up, causing her to jump. His glasses hung askew, his hair stood up in every possible direction, and his clothes were a wreck, but amazingly, he looked rather unharmed.

Figures.

His eyes locked on Riya's face. She wanted to say so much to him at that moment, but only one thing came to her lips. "Next time, don't be such a dick, Kent."

His mouth opened, closed, and then, without a word, he staggered to his feet and rushed from her store, leaving yet another greasy handprint on the glass on the way out.

Riya shook her head, climbed to her feet, and dusted herself off.

One look around drew a groan from her lips. The store was now, most definitely, not in an "exceeds corporate standards" level of cleanliness. She couldn't guess how long it would take to clean it all up. Hours? Days?

She was about to go searching for a mop, when the stupid enormity of the evening struck her and she trudged to a stop. In that moment, while monitors crackled and flickered, and a bit of ceiling tile crashed down onto a pile of iPods, she realized something. This wasn't her problem. It was her day off, dammit, and Doug was the closing manager, he should've been here to deal with this crap. If he said a damn word about it, she'd have some words of her own for corporate.

Instead of heading to the closet, she collected her phone and marched to the front door. As she stepped over the now silent iPhone of doom, she pressed her own phone to her ear.

"Hey, Tiana," she said.

"Hey, sugar. Everything work out?"

"Code worked, phone's off, *Kent* left."

Typing.

Riya reached the front door, fished in her pocket, and pulled out the keys.

"Glad to hear it. What're you gonna do now?"

Riya almost said, "the same thing I do every night," but instead went with, "Me? I'm going home to watch *Firefly*. It's my night off."

Typing.

"*That* sounds like a great plan, sugar. In case you were worried, the higher-ups just received a note regarding closing manager Doug Glickman's lack of alignment with procedures."

Riya snorted as she locked the front door. "No argument from me."

The moon hung over head, big, beautiful and peaceful as all get-out.

"Hey, Tiana," she asked. "Why did you help me so easily? Didn't I sound crazy?"

Tiana laughed. It was a big warm sound. "Oh, you surely did, sugar. But I figured it didn't matter too much."

"Why's that?"

"Us geek girls have to stick together, don't you know?"

Riya smiled as she strolled to her car. "Amen to that, sister," she said, feeling better than she had in quite a long time.

Drive You Home

by J.S. Rogers

———⟡———

Hazel always wants to be out with everyone until she is, and then she wants to be home.

At some point in the night she always realizes she's floating through a series of terrible bars and worse apartments, with people and noise filling up every square inch of space around her. The epiphany usually strikes while drinking alcohol she can barely taste and talking to people whose names she doesn't care to learn.

Tonight it strikes when she pats her pockets for her phone—looking for something to do with her hands and her thoughts—and comes up empty. She pats harder, like that'll change things. It doesn't. No phone. She makes a pained sound and slumps.

"What?" The woman snuggled beside her on the couch twists to look at her. She's squinting her wide eyes in an attempt to focus. Hazel can't remember her name. It was Nancy or Amy or Julie or something. Nancy-Amy-Julie frowns harder at Hazel and asks, "What's wrong?"

"I lost my phone." She'd been texting on it while lurking in the bathroom at Maggie's place, mostly complaining, and must have left it behind. She'll just get Maggie to go back. She shoves up off of the couch.

"Oh, hey, don't go," Nancy-Amy-Julie tells her, tugging on her arm. "You just got here, don't go. *I* have a phone you can borrow. It's kind of old, but it definitely still works, come on."

"I don't want your old phone," Hazel tells her. "Why would I want your old phone, that's..." She trails off. Nancy-Amy-Julie isn't listening, anyway. Nancy-Amy-Julie drags her along, back a dim hallway and into her room. She shoves Hazel toward the bed and then kneels to dig around under it.

Nancy-Amy-Julie rocks back on her heels a moment later with an old phone in her grip—an iPhone, maybe? It's hard to be sure with the way her arm is weaving around through the air. "Here," she says as she drops the phone into Hazel's lap. It's black and smaller than Hazel's actual phone. The screen is cracked in one corner. The battery must be long dead, seeing as it was languishing under Nancy-Amy-Julie's bed.

Hazel drawls, "Thanks." She lifts the phone and moves to put it on the blanket. Now that they're here...

"No problem." Nancy-Amy-Julie beams up at her. "It's such a weird phone, though, I have to tell you. Sometimes it calls people on its own, and it always has service. I kind of miss using it. I would have kept it but..." She shrugs and gestures at the cracked screen before reaching out and powering it up. Hazel jerks in surprise when the little device powers to life in her hand.

"Anyway," Nancy-Amy-Julie says, distracting Hazel. "That's all better now. Come on. Let's go dance or something." She tugs on Hazel's arm again and Hazel stands. Muscle memory makes her slide the phone right into her pocket. Well. She doesn't really want to go back to Maggie's boyfriend's place to watch them make out. She can get her phone back in the morning. Until then, she has the inexplicably functional one in her pocket to see her through.

It all makes a lot of sense to her at the time to just go with it.

———⟨≪≫⟩———

It makes less sense later.

Hazel isn't 100 percent clear on what time it is or where she's gotten to, or even where Maggie and the others are. *She* is standing in another bathroom, she knows that. Music is playing in the building and she can hear people laughing. She doesn't want to go back to the party. Her stomach hurts and so does her head. She really wants to go home, eat some day-old pizza, and drink by herself. She wants to be where no one cares if she's sprawled on the couch in her underwear and a baseball hat because the overhead lights hurt her eyes and she's too tired to get up and turn them off. That alternative sounds so good in her head.

It's just so quiet at home. Quiet and empty. Hazel might not want the bars, really, but she wants the people. She wants the noise. It's a problem.

Hazel glances out the bathroom window while she's washing her hands. Three stories. She could climb that, probably. She looks back at herself in the glass— everything is where it should be on her face, from her frustratingly straight black hair to her dark eyes, just a little bloodshot—and raises an eyebrow in question.

Her reflection doesn't offer any advice. She decides on her own that climbing out the window isn't an acceptable idea.

She fishes her phone out of her pocket, instead—maybe she can find someone to give her a ride back home—and groans miserably when she realizes it's not actually hers.

She tosses the phone to the floor; it falls beside the toilet and scowls up at the ceiling. Her mouth is incredibly dry, so she takes another drink from the bottle to her left. She can't even taste it anymore.

When she sets the bottle down, the phone is still lit up, and she turns her frown on it. It takes her a moment to realize that she somehow brought up the contacts, possibly in the process of tossing it away.

There's a cab company listed there, right where it opened.

Nancy-Amy-Julie must really like to party.

Hazel isn't going to judge. She pulls the phone back over and squints at it. That's a local area code. She only hesitates a moment and then she dials, haphazardly pressing the phone to her ear. It rings. And rings. And rings. Hazel starts to think maybe the place went out of business just as someone answers and mumbles into the phone, "Uh, hello?"

"I need a ride," Hazel says, because it's late and she does and she really doesn't feel well at all. She came out to not be alone and she's alone anyway. It's stupid. "I don't know where I am. Everyone else left me. I want to go home."

"Uh," the voice on the other end of the line says again. This is the worst cab company ever. There are some weird sounds over the line and then the woman she's speaking to says, "Uh, well, are there street signs or something?"

"Hold on." Hazel's legs are loose and her knees don't want to work properly, but she manages to walk across the bathroom, threading her way between the messes on the floor and the people she bumps into. She goes right out the front door and down the driveway so she can peer up and down the street. There's an intersection not far to the left and she walks towards it. "I'm at 19th and Marion," she says, bracing her hand against the sign and yawning. "Can you come get me?"

"Yeah." Well, that's a relief. Hazel leans a little more against the sign and then figures, well, she can sit, can't she? No one is going to care if she sits here. "It'll be like twenty minutes, okay?"

Hazel grunts. "Whatever." She hangs up. She's really tired and her stomach hurts. It's enough to block out the voice in the back of her head telling her to go back to where other people are. She closes her eyes, just for a second.

―――⌐∰∋―――

Hazel wakes up to someone asking her, "Hey, did you call for a ride?"

She's sitting on the sidewalk. There's a woman crouched down in front of her with a messy ponytail and a broad face. She has sleep stuck in the corners of her eyes. She's wholesome-looking, in a Midwestern kind of way that suggests her family tree is heavily into cowboy hats and flannel. There are freckles across her nose. Hazel rubs at her eyes and nods.

"Okay, well," the woman says. She stands and looms there for a moment as Hazel tries to remember how her legs work, then bends over and grabs Hazel's elbows. She's got strong hands. She pulls Hazel to her feet. Hazel ends up swaying into the woman, who mumbles something that sounds a lot like, "Oopsy-daisy." The woman puts an arm around her and turns her. Hazel blinks at the old, beat-up car she ends up facing. The engine is running.

Hazel's thoughts aren't moving particularly quickly. It takes a moment and two steps towards the vehicle for her to say, accusingly, "This doesn't look like a cab."

"Nope," the woman says cheerfully.

Hazel should probably do something with that information. But she's tired and her head hurts. The woman pulls the passenger door open and lowers Hazel into the seat with a sharp bump to her head along the way. "Oh, sorry. Sorry, sorry, you okay?" Hazel waves away the apologies and pulls her legs up onto the seat. The woman closes the door. A blink later and she's crawling into the driver's seat. She asks, "So, I mean, where do you live?"

Hazel grunts. The car is a lot warmer than the air outside. And the seat is soft. And she's tired. She leans her head against the side of the window and closes her eyes.

<hr />

Somewhere, a microwave is beeping.

Hazel glares at the pillow across from her and tries to keep her head from splitting apart through sheer force of will. Success brings the realization that the pillow she is glaring at is not her own. She sits up with a jerk and frowns around at the bright floral comforter pulled up to her shoulders, the lamp on the nightstand, and the shut windows along the wall.

She's still wearing her clothes, but her shoes are missing.

Someone is singing out beyond the bedroom door.

Hazel's stomach gives a protesting flip-flop as she stands. She ignores it and rubs at her eyes, dragging her feet across the carpet, out of the strange bedroom, down a narrow hall, and into a kitchen too brightly lit for her head. It's a small affair, with a little fridge, minimal counter space, and faded blue linoleum. There's a woman standing in front of the microwave splitting a stack of pancakes between two plates. She's tall and solidly built. Her light brown hair is in a messy bun. She's vaguely familiar. She's singing under her breath and doesn't stop until Hazel clears her throat. Only then does she startle. She blurts, "You're awake."

Hazel grumbles, "Yes."

The woman beams. She's got a huge smile, a chipped front tooth, and a swirling tribal tattoo over the back of her right hand and wrist. It's well done. She gestures at the pancakes and asks, "You want some? I made you some. I'm Donna, by the way. I told you last night, but I'm not sure you heard me."

They're leaving behind some steps in this conversation, but Hazel isn't awake enough to insist they go back for them. She just frowns and asks, "Did you microwave those?"

"Yeah, of course." Donna gestures at the fridge. "They're frozen, you know? They're really good. There's syrup."

Hazel considers her options. Only one involves putting food in her stomach, so she says, "Sure." She takes the plate and avoids the syrup. She follows along in Donna's wake into a living room with two giant couches and barely enough room for a television. Donna sprawls out completely on one couch, her plate balanced on her stomach. Hazel sits in the middle of the other and takes a cautious nibble of a pancake. She asks, "Where am I?"

"This is my apartment."

Hazel contemplates this for a second. She has such a headache. The frustration she's beginning to feel isn't helping. "Why am I at your apartment?"

Donna wrinkles her nose. "I tried to get you to wake up and tell me where you lived, but you wouldn't, so." She shrugs.

Hazel asks, "So you brought me home?" She can't keep the incredulity out of her voice. Donna nods and makes an affirmative sound. Hazel stares at her. She looks around the apartment again. She has bleary memories of an old car that didn't look much like a cab. She eats a pancake. She asks, "You're not a cab driver, are you?"

Donna laughs, way too loudly for Hazel's headache. "Heck no," she says. "You thought I was, though."

"You were in my phone—" Well, the phone that she was using, anyway. She pats her pocket absently. The bulge of the phone is still there. "—as a cab service."

Donna widens her eyes and says, "Weird." She goes back to eating. She seems completely unconcerned with going out to pick up some stranger in the middle of the night because they thought she was a cab driver.

"Why'd you come get me?"

A little furrow grows between Donna's brows. She shrugs as best she can while lying down with a plate of food on top of her. "You sounded like you needed a ride."

Hazel stares at her until it becomes obvious Donna isn't going to look away first. Her eyes are very blue. Hazel looks at her hands instead, and then finally out the window beside the couch. The morning is overcast, but looks well along. She says, fidgeting, "I'm going to go." She's never going out again.

"Oh, okay." Donna looks surprised as she sits up. She brushes some crumbs off her shirt. "Okay. Do you need a ride, or something? Back to your car or whatever?"

Hazel starts to say no. But she doesn't know where she is in town—the west side somewhere, by the look of it— and that means she's on the wrong side to get back to her place. She nods instead and follows Donna back down to the same old car.

Donna chatters the entirety of the ride. She starts by saying, "I used to get lost all the time when I first moved here. Once, I got lost with groceries in the back and my ice cream melted." And then she just goes and goes. By rights it should be irritating, but something about the tone of Donna's voice is comforting. By the time they pull up in front of Hazel's building she's saying, "Anyway, that's how I got this." She's pointing at her chipped tooth.

"Great," Hazel says, even though that probably isn't applicable, and pushes her door open before the car is at a complete stop. Her head hurts. Donna's relentless cheeriness shouldn't be helping matters. She climbs out while thinking about her own bed and the job she probably should go to. It's her shop, after all. Costing herself business is stupid, and she's more certain than not that she has an appointment scheduled soon-ish with some frat boy who wants the local community college's pirate logo put on the back of his neck.

Her thoughts are miles away and distracted when Donna calls out, "It was nice to meet you."

Hazel leans over enough to look back into the cab of the car. Donna is still smiling. Hazel says, "Sure." She quirks her mouth into a quick facsimile of a smile and closes the door.

Hazel makes it to work with just enough time to get things set up for the appointment. Her work space is mostly wide open, with a little area set aside for where she actually does her inking. There are two counters along the wall with plugs and piercings in them, but those are Alex's domain. The only holes Hazel punches into people are much smaller.

The walls are covered in old wallpaper and, over that, posters with generic art people can get. The notebooks full of the work Hazel's done are prominently displayed. She's just cleaning her hands when Frat Boy shows up. He's right on time.

He sits well enough. He chose a dumb tattoo, but at least he's not a baby about it. Hazel pulls out her phone when she's done to snag a picture—people like it when she puts their new art up online—and frowns when she's reminded that *her* phone is still missing and she's stuck with an ancient loaner. Then she shrugs. The camera still works. She snaps her pictures and dismisses Frat Boy to pay Alex, who wandered into the shop mid-tattoo.

She turns the phone over in her hands and frowns at it. She needs to get hers back. She pulls up the contacts, not thinking about the fact that Maggie's number probably isn't in there, and frowns harder when she finds that Donna's number is now properly labeled with her name. Donna must have changed it last night. Rude. Hazel is still scowling about the presumption when she discovers that Maggie's number *is* in the phone. Nancy-Amy-Julie must know Maggie; that explanation makes enough sense for Hazel to stop wondering about how the number got there. She dials.

Maggie answers on the third ring and makes a sound like a water buffalo being dragged into the river by a crocodile.

Hazel can't manage any pity. She's been up for hours already. She says, "I think I lost my phone at your boyfriend's place last night. In the bathroom, probably. Can you check?"

"Good morning to you, too," Maggie grumbles around another pained sound. Maggie is a sweet girl, really—Hazel never understood how they came to be friends because Hazel was definitely not a sweet girl by any stretch of the imagination. A low thump comes over the line. "Where'd you disappear to last night, anyway? No one saw you leave and—oh."

Hazel knocks the side of her head against the wall. "What's wrong?"

Maggie starts, "I'm really sorry." Hazel doesn't listen very hard to the rest. She imagines she knows pretty well how it's going to go. She's right.

———⌒⟨⟩⌒———

Her phone, when Maggie brings it by the shop later, is in pieces. It's also in a plastic bag. The inside of the plastic looks damp and vaguely yellowish. Maggie wrinkles her nose and says, "I tried to wash it." Hazel just stares at her. She leaves the phone sitting on the counter and walks away. The prospect of buying a new one is bleak considering the state of her wallet.

She pulls out the phone in her pocket, not thinking about what she's doing, intending to text someone about the entire situation. She ends up blinking down at the screen. The phone *works*. She's not sure whose plan it's on, but it's functional, which is more than can be said for her actual phone. She shrugs, decides she can use the loaner until someone terminates the line, and considers the problem solved.

———⌒⟨⟩⌒———

If only all of her problems were so easily squared away.

Maggie is agitating for them to get together again. She will continue to bubble and enthuse until she gets her way and by Friday, Hazel doesn't have the energy left to put up much of a fight. Besides, she's going stir crazy in her apartment and the idea of noise and people appeals. It always does, for an hour or so.

They hit the same places they always hit.

She ducks outside for a breath of fresh air at another of Maggie's friend's houses. She ends up hunching against the nearest car and scuffing the soles of her shoes against the driveway. She should go back inside. It's a good crowd tonight and she's making all kinds of new friends—for a given measure of friendliness. But her head hurts and this night is beginning to edge into morning.

She's scraping at an oil stain when her secondhand phone digs in against her hip. She doesn't really intend to pull up Donna's number. It just happens as there's a burst of loud laughter from inside and someone walks by the end of the driveway without looking up. Hazel dials and raises the phone to her ear.

Donna answers after so many rings that Hazel's just about given up hope. She asks, "Hello?"

Maybe they would have made their way to some new ground, but Hazel isn't sticking around to find out. She blows out a breath toward the sky. She says, "Hey, come pick me up."

"Oh, it's you." Donna sounds more awake by the second and cheery already. "How are you?"

Hazel frowns. "Ready for a ride."

"Well." There's a shuffle of sound. "Okay. Um, where are you?"

Hazel tells her and hangs up. She sits down on the stoop and waits, her arms stretched out over her knees until Donna's old car rocks to a stop in the mouth of the driveway. Donna opens her door and unfolds out, walks all the way up the driveway while looking around sort of wide-eyed, and crouches down in front of Hazel. She smiles widely and says, "Hi."

Hazel sticks out her hand. Donna's skin is just as warm as she remembers when Donna pulls her to her feet and steers her down the driveway.

"This place was really hard to find," Donna tells her once they're in the car. She just keeps talking as she drives, saying, "But it's nice that the roads are really empty this time of night. I didn't know that; I'm not usually out right now."

"You should come out with us sometime," Hazel says. The window is cool against her forehead. She can see Donna's face reflected in the windshield.

Donna smiles hugely and says, "Yeah? That'd be cool." She spends the rest of the drive talking about how she used to go out to the river back in whatever tiny town she came from along with all her tiny town friends. Hazel allows the words to wash over her until the car is pulling to a stop in front of her building. Donna says, "Hey, so, I didn't really get your name last time and I don't know what to call you?"

Donna smiles even larger when Hazel tells her.

Hazel can't decide the next day if she meant the invitation she offered or not. It takes her a few days to make up her mind, but the next time Maggie starts campaigning for a night on the town, Hazel ends up pulling out her phone and bringing up Donna's information. Donna answers in a more reasonable time period this time and sounds distressingly pleased when she says, "Hazel, hi, do you need a ride?"

Hazel snorts. She thought maybe Donna would seem less good-natured in the daytime, but that doesn't appear to be the case. She says, "No. We're going out tonight. You want to come?"

Donna says, "Yes, definitely." She spends five minutes chattering against Hazel's ear about what time they should meet and where and what she'll be wearing, as though Hazel won't recognize her.

Hazel rolls her eyes, hangs up, and goes to finish her day. She shoots Alex a sharp look when he asks, "What's gotten you into such a good mood? Did you make someone cry again?" She hip-checks one of his piercing cases as she walks by and watches all the little pieces shift out of place, grinning grimly to herself as he yelps after her.

Donna calls twice more over the next couple of hours to make sure she goes to the right place, once during Hazel's quick shower. She'd thought the phone was on vibrate, but it rings loudly enough for her to hear it through the water and she manages to answer in time. Donna calls three more times in rapid succession as the time for them to meet up draws closer. Despite, or because of, whatever worry prompted her to quintuple-check, Donna beats Hazel to the bar. By the time Hazel walks in, Donna is standing over by the dart board and casting anxious glances at the door. "Hazel," she says, with every evidence of relief. She makes her way over by virtue of shuffling everyone else out of the way.

Hazel isn't expecting the massive hug she receives. She probably would have ducked it, if she had. As it is, Donna squeezes her before she even realizes there's a possibility that might happen. Donna is still very close when she ducks her head and asks, somewhere near Hazel's ear, aiming for quiet and not quite reaching it, "Do I look okay?"

She looks pretty much the same as she always does. Her hair is in a higher ponytail, though, and there might be gloss on her lips. Hazel narrows her eyes, looking for some sign that Donna is joking and coming up without any. She says, "Yeah, you look good."

Donna beams. She says, too loud again, "So do you. Or, great, really. You look great." There's no time to properly deal with the heat that puts in Hazel's gut, because then there are introductions to go around, complete with Maggie erupting into a virtual volcano of happiness at the appearance of a new person to socialize at and Alex shooting Hazel skeptical looks mostly involving his eyebrows.

Donna doesn't drink much, despite Alex's eventual goading. She doesn't wander very far, either, following Hazel around and gamely shifting with the flow of conversation. Her larger-than-life presence at Hazel's side should be irritating, by all rights. The whole reason Hazel comes out is to be overloaded with people and noise until her personal space bubble doesn't feel three sizes too big, at which point she just wants to crawl back under a rock. That isn't happening with Donna lingering. It's nice.

It takes her a while to realize that the space between her shoulder blades isn't itching at all. By the time she does, Donna is yawning without bothering to cover her mouth and then reaching up to knuckle at her eyes.

Maggie is off with her boyfriend doing something approximating dancing, and Alex is arguing with a bunch of guys at the other end of the bar about a football game. Hazel looks at Donna—trying to decide... something—until she gets caught. Donna beams at her, full-wattage. Hazel offers back a smaller grin, polishes off the last of her drink, and says, "Give me a ride, yeah?"

Donna bobs her head. She's still smiling when she says, "Okay, sure."

Hazel doesn't feel any eyes on her back when she walks out. Not with Donna in the way.

"Thanks for inviting me," Donna says once they're out in the night air. "It was really nice," she says, and, "Maggie is really great." She talks the rest of the way to Hazel's house like she just spent a week at a theme park instead of an evening at a bar of middling quality. It's strangely comforting.

The chatter lulls Hazel into enough of a sense of security that she asks as they turn down her street, "Why do you keep giving me rides?"

Donna looks honestly confused. She shrugs. She asks, "You need them, don't you?"

Hazel stares at her until they park. She remembers, finally, to say, "Thank you."

Donna sounds no less excited the next time Hazel calls. Hazel's kept the loaner phone so long now that it feels normal caught between her shoulder and her ear as she works on a sketch. No one's complained so far about her using it. No one's cancelled the service. And it never drops calls. It holds steady to Donna's voice through Hazel finishing work and going home, though she's always lost service before when she drove by the old high school.

Donna is early again. She hugs Hazel. She hugs *everyone* and listens to Maggie talk about her new car long after everyone else is ready for Maggie to shut up about it. She smiles and she chatters and she's warm. Hazel leans back against the booth they're sitting in and stretches her legs out beneath it. She lets her eyes drift half shut. Her chest feels loose. Donna is sitting at the end of the booth, completely unbothered by the people who sometimes bump into her.

They lose Maggie and Alex eventually. Donna turns to look at Hazel and her eyebrows bounce up. She asks, "Oh, are you sleeping?"

Hazel snorts a laugh. She slouches a little further. It feels good. She says, "I'm awake." Donna gives her a bigger smile than she's earned.

Donna tells her, "I like this place better than the other place." She takes a deep breath like she's going to go on, probably expounding upon the pros of both bars.

Hazel cuts in instead. "I do tattoos," she says, looking at the ink on Donna's wrist, a swirling pattern of delicate lines that she's noticed before. She gestures at it. "I'll do one for you, if you like. Free of charge. Whenever you want. My shop's not far away."

"I know," Donna says, through a grin so wide it looks like it should hurt. "Alex told me." She ducks her head and says, "That's real nice of you. I'd like that."

Hazel nods like an idiot. She feels itchy all of a sudden. She says, pushing at Donna's shoulder, "Come on. Take me home."

Donna doesn't make Hazel wait long to find out if she'll take the tattoo offer. She shows up at the shop the next day and spends a long time flipping through Hazel's books while Hazel finishes the piece she's working on. Hazel can hear her chattering with Alex about what she'd like over the buzz of the gun.

Hazel gets a hug when she emerges from the back. She doesn't try to duck it, though she also doesn't bother to hide her skeptical look when Donna tells her, "I always kind of wanted one of those old-fashioned ladies, you know? Like sailors used to get?"

"You serious?"

Donna bobs her head and shrugs out of her jacket. She bares her forearm. "Yeah, right here. Um." Donna scratches at her skin, just a little, and shifts her weight. "Can you give her short dark hair?"

Hazel's done more ridiculous tattoos. She shakes herself back from planning what she'd need and wondering if she should cancel her next appointment so she can ask, "How short?"

Donna tilts her head to the side and gestures vaguely. She wrinkles her nose. "About like that?" She motions to Hazel. Alex chokes on a laugh where he's cleaning the windows. Hazel ignores him.

"Sure," she says. "I can do that. Come back here, away from this idiot."

Donna spends the entire time Hazel is getting her ink ready and sketching up a quick outline talking about the pieces on Hazel's walls. The questions creep in without Hazel realizing, until she is bent over Donna's forearm, cursing the fall of her hair into her face and answering queries about how long she's been here and her brief apprenticeship, which ended in a huge argument and a broken window.

Donna snorts a laugh; Hazel tightens her grip, holding Donna's arm steady. Donna says, "Sounds exciting."

Hazel hums agreement. She wipes aside some of the excess ink and stretches out one of her legs. The hum and buzz of the gun in her hand is steady. She can feel the vibration in her forearm. She can tell Donna is staring at the top of her head. She's calm, more calm than she can remember being for a long time, calmer than the people and the noise ever made her, or being alone. She feels like she's balancing on a tightrope, but... easily.

It feels natural to say into the little bubble of space between them, "I don't usually do this for people I know." She hears Donna's mouth snap shut. "I don't usually get to know people well enough to do this for them. I guess."

She runs out of words. She works on the curve of the woman's arm, instead, putting a thick, black line on Donna's skin. Donna prompts, eventually, "Oh, yeah?"

Hazel twitches her mouth. "Yeah. I don't know. I just don't have the right social skills, I guess."

"Hey." Donna's hand is very warm. She tucks some of Hazel's hair back behind her ear. It's one of the rare times Hazel hasn't seen her smiling. "I think your social skills are just fine."

Hazel laughs, surprised. She's so used to the tight pressure in the back of her throat when she's around people—or not around people—that it's strange to find it gone. It's been disappearing more frequently since she met Donna. She doesn't know how to say any of those things. Instead, she says, "Sorry to have to tell you, but you're wrong. There's a reason I keep calling you in the middle of the night, and it's not 'cause I'm great with people."

Donna is quiet for a little while, at least. And then she says softly, "You seem pretty great to me."

Hazel shuts her eyes. She takes a breath. It feels strange to smile, but she can't help it. Donna is just smiling at her. Hazel looks at her, gun buzzing from far away in her hand. One side of Hazel's mouth curls up and she ducks her head. She focuses on her work. After a moment, Donna starts talking again, this time about her brother. She doesn't really stop until the tattoo is finished, and then she gushes about it for a while. It's not until Donna is halfway out the door that Hazel is required to put a word in edgewise, when Donna asks her, "Hey, when are you going to be done tonight?"

Hazel shrugs. "Nine. Maybe ten."

Donna nods and says, "Okay." She waves her forearm at Hazel and walks off with a spring in her step. Hazel shakes her head and shoots Alex a sharp look before he can open his mouth.

Hours later, Hazel is just cleaning up her tools and squaring everything away when the bell over the door rings again. Her shoulders tighten and she leans her head out as she calls, "We're—" Her mouth snaps shut before she can finish.

Donna is standing just inside the door with her hands in her back pockets. She's smiling. She says, "I thought I'd drive you home."

Hazel remembers to close her mouth. She has to open it again. "I drove today."

Donna shrugs. Her smile doesn't even quiver. "Then I'll walk you to your car."

Hazel snorts a laugh at her. "It'll be a minute."

Donna gestures like she's got all the time in the world. Hazel rushes her cleanup, sneaking looks at Donna, who migrates to a chair and stretches her legs out in front of her, humming tunelessly as she does. Hazel bites the insides of her cheeks. She keeps catching herself smiling. She ducks into the bathroom when everything is clean, and washes her hands before shoving her hair back from her face and freezing.

She looks... different. Different than the face she'd gotten used to looking at in the mirror, anyway. She tilts her head side to side but can't identify where the change is. She rolls her eyes and shakes her head, tugs her shirt straight and exits the room.

Donna is still waiting for her. She stands as Hazel walks over and lights up from the inside when Hazel asks, "Did you eat yet? You want to grab some dinner? There's a little diner close to here. They might be open."

"I can always eat," Donna tells her and Hazel laughs, she's getting used to doing that. "Is everyone else coming, too?"

Hazel thinks for a moment and then shakes her head. "No. Is that okay?"

It must be. Donna bubbles through the entirety of the walk, and she's still bubbling when they reach the restaurant. The little diner is sleepy this time of night. It's quiet. There's only one other table of hungry people and they're on the other side of the dining area. Hazel hasn't been here before. The quiet and the still seemed too much like home, not loud enough to be distracting. Hazel waits to feel nerves creep up her spine but the itch of them never arrives. Maybe her anxiety gets lost in Donna's presence frowning at the menu and asking, "Do you think they'll make me a milkshake?"

Hazel leans back a little further into her seat and slumps, just a bit, against the window. Her phone digs at her leg and she pulls it out, placing it on the table. "I'm sure they will." She closes her eyes for a moment and breathes in.

Donna convinces her to get a milkshake, too, and by the time they leave Hazel is wired with sugar. Donna throws an arm around her on the way out of the door and Hazel laughs, tossing her hair back and listening to Donna start a story with, "And did I tell you about the time this lady called me in the middle of the night to ask for a ride?"

They're most of the way back to their cars by the time Hazel realizes she left the phone behind, sitting on the table back in the diner. She freezes for just a second—she should go back for it, she might as well keep using it—and then blows out a breath and keeps walking. Maybe it's time she gets a new phone, after all. One that's actually hers.

That one was weird, anyway.

One App to Rule Them All

by Manny Frishberg and Edd Vick

Dale Hartford glanced at the 3D pie chart popping up from his sleeve. Eighty-eight more calories to eat before he could be done with lunch. He went back to shoving bits of kale and lentil loaf around on his plate. God, but he hated this swill. Across from him, his husband, Wallace, looked just as disgusted with his own plate of greens.

Shoshona's on Empire Boulevard in Crown Heights had one of the only strictly kosher macrobiotic menus in Brooklyn, and Wallace *had* to eat in places like this. No saturated fats in his diet, no simple carbs, no added salt. *And no flavor.* Dale was at least grateful he couldn't smell delicious food on other people's plates.

Wallace's doctor had sent strict instructions to his Personal Assistant app, so it only displayed the approved menu options. The Personal Assistant was credit card, health monitor, link to newsfeeds and vlogs. It tracked work hours and credited paychecks, reporting to the Revenue Service. It even monitored sleep patterns. Nobody turned off devices any longer. Sensors and feedback systems were woven into clothing and worn as accessories.

Wallace chewed slowly, then swallowed. "I'd kill for a burger," he said.

Yeah. I would, too. And I could. Horrified, Dale put the thought out of his mind. He loved his husband. In yet one more of a thousand demonstrations of that love, he'd pledged to abide by his partner's health regimen. He had hoped back then that he could get Wallace to take better care of himself by throwing in with him. So they enabled the Snitch app, which reported any deviations to Wallace, if he cheated with some cookies or a milkshake, just like Wallace's reported to his doctors and insurance company.

Dale's phone pinged and he checked his wrist.

It was their friend Emily. *Are you on a fast? I haven't seen a single shot of your dinner,* the screen read.

Dale shoved another forkful of lentil loaf into his mouth. He'd be ashamed to post this. It was the color of old Army uniforms, and looked about as appetizing on his plate. *Eating,* he replied. *Just not a very photogenic meal.*

You knew the job was dangerous when you took it. He looked across the table at his rotund husband. Wallace's face was bright pink, shading toward red on his nose and cheeks, but still Dale felt a familiar wave of affection.

Is this any way to live? he texted Emily. He still loved the fat slob—and Dale took his marriage vows literally: for better or worse, till death do us part. *Well,* he reminded himself, more than once, *we've had the better—twenty-two happy years. Built a business together, built a life. Am I supposed to bail on him now that I'm getting the worse?* How long would Wallace even last on his own? He could barely take care of himself *with* Dale's support.

Swallowing, Dale glanced again at his wrist. He'd eaten enough for one meal. He let his fork drop. Now there was only a flavorless dinner to get through. Then tomorrow's breakfast, then lunch, then dinner. Bland, bland, tasteless, and bland. His meals could be a law firm.

On the way home Dale was lost in the past. Back when they first got together, before the apps that monitored Wallace's health, he'd nearly gorged himself to death. Even before they married, Dale had tried his damnedest to get his spouse to eat right, to exercise. Wallace had never taken his advice, but Dale told himself that Wallace would change after they got married, once he did not have to feel insecure about Dale's love anymore.

It was only the near-universal spread of PAs that had made any difference at all. Wallace couldn't cheat when his every mouthful was measured and analyzed by his phone, when what wasn't allowed wasn't even available. The Fidelity Insurance Company would cancel his life and health insurance if he violated their terms.

Wallace had every food allergy imaginable—peanuts, of course, and shellfish, catfish, and eels, and milk (not a common lactose sensitivity, that would have been too easy; no, a genuine allergic reaction to caseins). His doctor had found that a strictly kosher diet fit the bill pretty well. No shellfish—nothing from the ocean without fins and scales. And, as long as they stuck to the _fleishig_ side of the menu, nothing that even came into contact with milk.

When he first got a look at all of Wallace's dietary restrictions Dale thought with a decent array of spices he could still prepare palatable meals, but one by one, the allergist eliminated ingredients—Wallace's body was treating them like invading pathogens. Wallace turned out to be allergic to more things than a Bubble Boy. He'd grown up in a germ-free environment with only hypoaller-genic foods from SaferFirst SuperMarkets. "Hygiene Syndrome," the internist called it.

It wasn't just the food. Dale used to go hiking all weekend. Carrying around 150 pounds of extra weight,

Wallace panted and mopped sweat off his forehead after a few blocks at half speed. Swimming could have been an option, but Wallace had always feared the water—another gift from his helicopter parents—so he just grew more corpulent by the day.

Dale used to beg Wallace to come to the gym with him sometimes, until Wallace got a doctor's note saying with his enlarged heart too much exercise could be dangerous. He'd tried to get Wallace just to go for a walk together, which even the damned doctor agreed would be okay. But Wallace shunned exercise. Not even the app's little shocks swayed him.

Dale could tell his own changing lifestyle weighed on his husband's conscience. Wallace would cry and tell Dale that he *really* ought to put him into an assisted living facility, one of the "more affordable" ones staffed with robosistants Wallace would inevitably add at some point, so that Dale could go back to the life he wanted to lead.

"You could have a drink whenever you liked, try those new designer neuro pills everybody's squealing about. You could enjoy a meal where you could see the *whole* menu." Wallace would go on, piling up the list of sacrifices Dale had made out of solidarity—the sports he didn't play any longer, the friends who had fallen by the wayside because Wallace wasn't up to participating in whatever they wanted to do this week. Hiking, bike-riding, hoverboarding. And on and on.

Dale knew his part: first to deny there was any self-sacrifice involved. Then he should gradually admit that, yes, he missed some of those things, but none of them were as important to him as having even one more day together with Wallace, not too quickly or it wouldn't seem genuine. Then they'd cry together and make out on the couch for a little while before going off to the bedroom, where Wallace wouldn't be able to get it up and Dale would reassure him that sex wasn't all that important to him, either.

Dale had taken to getting up before dawn, when Wallace's snoring woke him up anyway, and going out for a quick 5K run around the neighborhood. He tried to get back and shower before the love of his life woke up.

Exhausted by the narrow choices and bland fare at Shoshona's, Dale decided to try cooking for them himself again. Strictly kosher meats were still tough and tasteless, as far as he was concerned. The grocery store drones would only deliver what their PAs would allow them to eat.

The range of Ashkenazi spices was even more limiting than Wallace's diet required. So he began adding imitations of non-kosher ingredients, like soy bacon chips in the potato pancakes and chicken Italian sausages.

Over the next few weeks, he rediscovered his love of cooking. He even tried making a Béchamel sauce with the coconut oil-based coffee creamer served in kosher delis—that was a culinary disaster. Slowly he found the herbs and spices Wallace could tolerate. Even so, many meals came out barely more appetizing than what they got in restaurants.

Dale poured over kosher cookbooks, learning the history of the Jewish diaspora through its culinary permutations. For a New Year's Eve party he cooked up a large pot of Hoppin' John, with brown rice and fresh-hulled black-eyed peas. He didn't quibble at the twelve dollars a pound price or ask where they were harvesting fresh beans in December. In place of the salt pork he used liquid smoke and a pinch of hickory-smoked salt, adding MSG for the meaty umami-ness.

With that success, he went looking for bigger challenges, taking on Chinese dim sum: shrimp toast with no shrimp, crab Rangoon with imitation crab meat. He got up early in the mornings and took the F train to East Broadway to shop in the open-air Asian seafood markets, tasting the different grades of surimi, looking for an imitation crabmeat that satisfied his needs.

Portion control was difficult. Dale would make a meal, and there would never be anything to refrigerate because Wallace would lick his plate, steal bits off Dale's, and scrape out anything left in the pots and pans. His weight ballooned further.

Even that came to an end with the first bout of ulcerative colitis. It began as a common enough case of constipation, but the usual treatments had no effect. A bloody bowel movement sent Wallace to the hospital and, when he was released, the Nanny app had a whole new range of restrictions. Shoshona's was the only eatery left within walking (or mobility scootering) distance—and Wallace wouldn't consider getting on a bus or the subway to try something new.

Whatever he tried to do for Wallace, the fat slob just absorbed it and went his own merry way. He had become a sponge, a short circuit that drained Dale of all his energy and then demanded more so he could suck that up too. He had consumed Dale's life, taken away everything that gave him pleasure, and then, instead of making the least effort to just make his own life a little better, he drowned Dale's hopes in a pool of self-centered accommodations to his own weakness.

Dale couldn't wait for one of them to die. It hardly mattered anymore which one of them, as long as it was over. And he hadn't abandoned his partner—that would be the worst sin of all.

He has to go. The decision struck Dale in the face like the hot summer air. He could not pinpoint the moment that he had made it; it just came to make perfect sense. The thought had been building up in secret until it sprang, fully grown like Athena from Zeus's head.

Wallace was already dying slowly and painfully, from gout and diabetes, and now the holes eating through his guts—all results of his gluttony. It would be a mercy, a blessing in disguise, really. Wallace literally couldn't live without him. Dale felt giddy and light with a ball of tightness lodged in his stomach at the same time.

His scheme had to be something that looked innocuous. Something that would slip past the PA's notice. Acts of violence had become rare in these days of incessant contact.

Dale read up on kashrut, the Jewish dietary laws. Unlike Hinduism, Jewish law allowed for accidents. Observant Jews could consume a tiny bit of *treif*; the Talmud said something like, "Not more than an olive pit." For a man with Wallace's allergies, any number of things that size could kill him.

Wallace's 53rd birthday was coming in a week. Dale had decided to buy him a pet, something that wouldn't take much time or attention. He settled on a trio of neon tetras, with a five-and-a-half gallon tank, an aerator, a plastic palm tree, and plenty of fish food. Wallace was delighted, especially when Dale set the tank on their coffee table within reach. He delighted in feeding the tetras, inevitably winding up overfeeding them.

Dale made dim sum for Wallace's birthday dinner. While Wallace dozed on the couch, Dale puttered around the kitchen, humming tunelessly, feeling lighter and more at ease with himself than he had in a month. He blended the ground chicken and finely chopped vegetables for the wonton soup, added strips of specially cured beef to the "pork" with a sponge gourd. For the crab Rangoon he mixed imitation crab into softened Neufchâtel, sprinkling a good two teaspoons of the tetra food into the mixture before frying the "bags of gold." He couldn't be certain how much shrimp meal he was adding but it was surely not more than an olive pit's worth.

Wallace gorged on sesame balls without sesame, on shumai made with brisket instead of pork, and on the salt (minimal) and pepper(less) salt-and-pepper chicken wings. He pounced on the crab-stuffed fried wontons, eating three before Dale could even sit down. Dale tried one and smiled. It was one of the tastiest things he'd eaten in years.

Two minutes later Wallace choked, spewing wonton and imitation cream cheese across the servings. Clutching his throat with one hand, he pounded on the table with the other. His PA began to keen.

"What is it, Wallace?" Dale didn't have to fake his concern. In the murder mysteries he'd watched on TV, people who were poisoned just slumped over and died without making a fuss. Wallace's face purpled. His fingers contracted into claws. "God, Wallace! What can I do?"

Wallace's PA shut off its shrieking and told him to find his epinephrine injector. Dale sprang up and tore into the bathroom, where he knew Wallace always left the thing. He grabbed the expired EpiPen he had saved and slipped into the medicine chest.

Dale bent over his husband and jabbed the needle into his thigh. Then he waited, not breathing as he stared at Wallace, lying on the floor where he'd fallen, a thin stream of vomit dribbling from his mouth. Unseeing eyes stared up at Dale. In the distance sirens wailed, coming closer.

Wallace's PA chimed. "Canceling emergency call," it said. The distant siren wound down.

Dale sat down on the floor behind his dead husband. "I love you, Wallace," he said. "I do. I really do. I didn't mean for you to suffer."

His last sentence was enough for the police to question him. They'd barely begun the interrogation when he broke down, crying and admitting his guilt. He pled guilty at his arraignment, in spite of his lawyer's advice.

———⟨≡≡≡⟩———

Dale Hartford shuffled into the counselor's office. He stared at the blue slip-on deck shoes he'd been issued. The guard who had ushered him in closed the door and waited outside.

"Take a seat," said the man behind the desk. He was a large man, large in girth and tall as a black bear, with a thick black beard that added to his bearlike mien, and he had a large smile that was unbearlike and reassuring. "I'm Dr. Jerome Parker. You know who I am and why you're here."

"I'm here because I killed my husband." Dale sat down, but he didn't look up from his shoes. "You're the person who's going to decide what to do with me."

"We're here to perform your pre-sentence evaluation," the big man said, nodding. "Then I'll be filing my report with the court. It's still at the judge's discretion."

"But they pretty much do what you say." Dale did not make it a question.

Parker shrugged. "It's not really subjective, and it's not rocket science, either. Psychometrics have proven quite reliable. At least in cases like yours," he added, swiping across his forearm to read Dale's file. "From what I can see, you'll be all right. And I don't tell everyone that. The repeaters—their only hope is to have a good story.

"Not a danger to self or others—you're not considering killing yourself, are you? I thought not." Parker checked off some boxes on the form he had conjured on his PA. He hadn't even looked up to see Dale shake his head. "So I don't believe incarceration will be necessary." He smiled again and this time Dale did not feel reassured.

With salt, pepper, and oregano the only spices his PA would allow him to buy, everything Dale cooked tasted the same. And, since three of the six hours a day when his electricity was on were when he was at work, he had to use crock pots and rice cookers to prepare his meals while he was away. It was illegal for the company he worked for to fire him just because he was a convict, but 65 percent of his paycheck went to the government now.

His PA included a metro card, but it only allowed him access to two subway stops—home and work, and the rules of his incarceration stated he had to be at one or the other 95 percent of the time. He could walk to Brower Park easily, if he felt like dodging the skaters and hoverboard riders. His PA allowed one bimonthly entrance to the Prospect Park Zoo, but the way he was forced to eat these days, he was gaining too much weight to want to take such a long walk. Besides, seeing the animals locked up just reminded him of his own plight.

Going out to eat had become one of his few recreations—just as it had been for Wallace. Dale looked around the restaurant. Liem's Golden Lotus was only half full on a weeknight. People looked up at him as their PAs announced his status, and one or two people edged away, but at least Mr. Liem's daughter didn't seem to mind. She showed him to a table.

"Let me know when you're ready to order," she said, putting a glass of water in front of him.

Dale smiled wanly. "I'm ready now," he said. Not even glancing at his PA, he said, "I'll have the vegetables in brown sauce, with tofu and steamed rice." She did not bother to write it down.

They had acted out this scene together a hundred times since his sentencing. As Pam hurried away, he sighed and folded his hands on the table in front of him. Not wanting to catch anybody's eye, his gaze slipped past his left arm, where the restaurant's menu glowed. There was only one item on it. At least with Wallace, there would have been a few choices.

His food would come soon enough—Mr. Liem would have started cooking before he had even sat down. They understood he would need to eat and hurry home before "bed check," when the Warden® app would record his location.

Two Minutes of Your Time

by Angela Dell'Isola

———⌬∭⌬———

"Not interested," I call before the narrow-eyed, high-heeled woman has a chance to speak.

Her shoes click along the white, tile flooring as she rushes from her center-aisle cart to catch me. "It will only take a second of—"

I hold my arm up, not even bothering to turn around. Mall vendors, especially cell phone company mall vendors, have consistently made the top five of my pet peeves list since the dawn of my pet peeves list.

"I really think you should reconsider, ma'am. We're running a special, and it hardly costs you anything to partake!"

I turn sharply into Victoria's Secret, the sound of the vendor's pursuit drawing nearer, closing in on me. I make a beeline for a corner clothes rack, drawn to it in part by the enormous yellow "25 percent off" sign, but also by its inner store location. That's the key.

I've experienced vendors barking at my heels for the full length of the mall before, yipping at my back like coffee-infused Chihuahuas about some new touchscreen device or the latest phone app. I've had them stand beside me in the cafeteria as I order my Wednesday afternoon Kung Pao chicken with a side of crab Rangoon, and I've finished entire glasses of Orange Julius, the large size, before they ceased their verbal assault. But never, ever have any of them followed me into one of the mall's stores. It took nearly a year of employment in the corner shoe store for me to discover this trick, and I've been turning to it since.

When passing a vendor cart, there are some critical, almost biblical rules that one needs to obey. First and foremost, never make eye contact with the person on duty, and never even glance at the assortment of goods on display, no matter how shiny, loud, or intriguing. Walk briskly past, and do not answer the questions they will undoubtedly call after you. "Just one minute" turns fast into twenty and the next thing you know, you're the proud new owner of a flying helicopter with a 100-yard detection capacity.

But the holy grail of rules, the secret weapon, is that should all else fail, the nearest store is your escape. Like wild animals, the vendors may stalk you through the shop windows for a minute or two, but they will eventually give up and seek alternate prey. Except, it seems, for this woman.

"Are you planning to help me choose my underwear?" I ask, spinning to face the brown-haired, heavily eyeshadowed vendor behind me. She doesn't blanch, doesn't blink, doesn't lose a beat, despite my aggressive question.

"I can, I suppose," she says, manicured fingers flicking idly through the long rack of push-up bras.

I narrow my eyes to a glare. Then cross my arms. "Have you heard of sarcasm?" I ask.

Her heart-shaped mouth curves up at the corners. "Of course."

"Then why are you still following me?" I skirt my legs around a display of hand creams and sanitizers and make for the clearance rack at the back of the store. Her heels click behind me, keeping suspicious time with the One Direction song playing overhead. I refuse to turn around because I don't like boybands much more than I like vendors and I don't want to see the two of them intersecting. I'm also secretly hoping she'll disappear.

"If you allow me to speak with you for two minutes," she says, coming to stand beside me and pulling an enormous tablet from somewhere on her person, "I'll be gone. Two minutes. Two potentially life-changing minutes. We can time it."

"I said I'm not interested," I repeat, even as I watch her set an alarm on the oversized screen. "My break is only fifteen minutes."

Her brow furrows, and she glances briefly at the Christmas undergarments I've started to unload in my size from the rack. Since it's February, they're 75 percent off, and as there's no romantic interest in my life at present, no one will know if I don Frosty out of season.

"How about this," she says, dropping the tablet to her side and grinning like the woman on my morning cereal box. "I'll pick up the tab today. My company and I. Let's say... a one hundred-dollar limit? Whatever you choose in the next fifteen minutes, as long as you agree to listen to me for two of them."

I stare at her like she's lost her mind, though my hands are already rehoming my current finds to the clearance rack. I always thought red and green were kind of a tacky combination.

"Is that legit?" I ask, keeping my narrowed eyes on hers. "Something you can do?"

Her smile widens and she extends one hand to me, catching my glance toward the "just in" rack of striped yoga pants. "I'm Ashley," she says, when I finally accept her grip. "I work for Tech Buoy. We keep you afloat with our technology solutions when you don't even know you're sinking!" She sings the last part and I fight the urge to vomit on her Dorothy-esque shoes. "As you can see, we believe in our products. So go ahead," she says as she waves one arm directly toward the striped yoga pants, "make your selections, and I'll fill you in on why I've followed you today."

———⟨⟩———

I promised myself I'd never own a smartphone, an iPhone especially. A device intended to keep me constantly connected? That's not convenience. That's an invasion of privacy and a threat to my sanity. And yet here it is, exceedingly slim, light, and red. Firetruck red. It was the only color available, and my fingers curl each time I look at it. I hate red, and I hate vendors. Today I was tricked by the latter, and now I have a red phone and a tentative contract, should I enjoy my trial month.

"You get thirty days to check it out for free," Ashley had told me, "and if you love it, it's as simple as signing a few papers and paying fifteen bucks a month. No interest, no hidden fees, just fifteen dollars a month until it's paid off. Fifteen dollars for a life-changing experience is nothing!"

Each time she'd said "life-changing," I'd felt myself die a little on the inside. Cell phones were not life-changing. Life-saving, maybe, if you became stranded in a New England snow storm or witnessed a car accident on the turnpike. But not life-*changing*. Life-changing was a new career, a college education, a trip to a foreign country. Not a pocket-sized device with the worst default ringtone ever.

———⟨⟩———

I slide the tiny beast onto its charging base and toss the accompanying manual in the trashcan beside my bed. The microwave beeps and my bare feet pad across my $850 a month studio to the six-by-six designated kitchen space. Two seconds later I am seated at my dining table/kitchen table/desk with a bowl of broccoli and cheddar soup and my second half-drained wine cooler. Jordin Sparks stares up at me from the latest edition of *Shape* magazine, informing me silently of the calorie count in my heat-and-go meal. I flip her upside down and am halfway through both my dinner and the magazine when a voice rings out from the opposite end of the room, near my bed. I lurch to my feet and swear, then wipe my sleeve over my spilled drink, waiting for my heart to return to a normal pace.

"Welcome to Tech Buoy. My name is Jaimie, and I'm here to serve you."

I lift my bowl and stride to the phone, scolding myself for thinking that the color could possibly be its worst attribute. The damn thing talks.

"Are you ready to change your life?" it asks in a high-pitched tone as I draw near. I jab at the screen with the back of my knuckle, trying to shut it off. "Here, give me two minutes to show you around," it protests.

"Oh, hell," I mutter, squeezing my fingers against the buttons on the side. "You're not Jaimie. You're Ashley."

The phone is nothing like the ancient flip prototype I keep on hand for emergencies, and I can't figure out how to power it down, so finally and with more effort than I care to expend, I remove the battery pack altogether. Bingo. I'm ready to finish the rest of my meal in silence... except that when I turn the phone back over, there's an image of a short brunette with a pixie cut hairdo and billowing pink harem pants staring up at me. She makes direct eye contact and waves, and when I drop both her and the bowl of soup I'd been carrying onto the bed, she crosses her arms.

I open my mouth, but all that comes out are some incoherent syllables and partially formed curses. My eyes keep darting from the tiny woman on the screen to the disconnected battery pack, trying to make sense of the two. Maybe there's some sort of internal backup system, I tell myself. Like a teeny-tiny generator or something.

The woman—Jaimie—grins a wide, full-toothed smile, and peers up at me. Her crop top pulls higher on her exposed stomach when she raises her arms to push wayward hairs behind her ears. I squint my eyes to see the phone more clearly without having to lift it.

"Whenever you're ready," she coos, tucking her feet up so she floats cross-legged in the center of the screen.

"Ready for what?" I ask, hardly believing that here I am, engaging in conversation with a cell phone. I didn't know technology had come this far already. I really need to start reading the newspaper.

"Ready to change your life!" Jaimie exclaims, and I lift one of my worn-down pillows and drop it over her. There's a muffled cry, an actual cry, and I think about walking away but I'm too confused, or interested, or maybe just masochistic. I'm not sure. I just need to know more about this strange little device and the equally little and annoying person within it.

I lift a corner of the pillow tentatively.

"What was that for?" she asks immediately, moving down to the exposed corner of the screen. I roll the pillow away and she narrows her eyes, shaking her head at me. "I've dealt with confused customers before. And frightened ones, sure. But I've never been treated like this. You should just take me back. Right now."

"Take you where?" I ask, my mind drawing a blank as I consider how lifelike this virtual presence is, and how well she's able to communicate. She even has feelings. Tiny virtual feelings. It's almost cute.

"To the mall!" Jaimie yells, waving her arms to the side as though it's obvious. "If you don't think you need me, just take me back."

"That was the plan..." I mutter, thinking about how I'd intended to keep the phone for a month only so that I'd have thirty days of peace from mall vendors. Ashley would leave me alone, as well as any of her peers, and if other companies were to approach me, "Sorry! I'm already testing a product for a competitor. But thanks anyway."

"Fine," Jaimie says. She turns so her back is facing me and sighs. "They open at nine tomorrow."

"Well I work at noon."

"Fine," she snaps.

"Fine." I drop the pillow back so that both Jaimie and the color red disappear.

The sidewalks are even more crowded than the streets the next day as I head out for my two-mile jaunt to work. I consider calling a cab so that I don't need to push through the mobs of people, but because of the layout of the roads, we'd have to backtrack to reach the mall, and I'd be out a stupid amount of money. So I lock my elbows at my sides and turn my backpack to the front of me, then stride forward. I stare down a few teenagers who want to play chicken on the sidewalk, but all of them end up moving.

There's a double line of people stretching almost to the front doors of my apartment building, and it's not until I pass the theater that I remember tonight is the opening show of that new horror flick. I can't remember the name or who is starring in it, even though it's been advertised everywhere for months.

"Johnny Depp," a squeaky voice murmurs at my side. I turn, but the only person immediately beside me is a mother bouncing a toddler on each hip. "I've always wanted to see Johnny Depp in person," it continues, and I realize the sound is emanating from my purse. I haven't replaced the battery pack yet, but that didn't stop Jaimie from commenting through half the night, then breakfast, and apparently, now.

My fingers dive into the bag, lifting the demon phone easily from the top, where I'd left it. I'd thought about shoving Jaimie in one of the deeper pockets, but I wanted to be rid of her as quickly as possible when we reached the mall. *We.* Already I'm thinking of her as an actual entity. My feet move faster.

"You can read minds too?" I ask.

Jaimie laughs. "I just noticed the sign in passing."

I peer down at the screen and see that Jaimie has changed into a blue version of yesterday's choli top and harem pants, and that she's looking at me like I've grown a second head.

"Do you want to meet him?" she asks, after a long pause.

"Who? Johnny Depp?"

"Yeah. I could make it happen."

"Uh-huh." I finally break free of the throngs of people and swarming news crews.

"I can!" Jaimie protests, and I don't have to glance at the screen to know that she's crossing her arms. "Hold out your hand."

"No."

"I just want to show you something. Do you like coffee? Hold out your hand and I'll make a coffee appear."

"I said no."

"I'll do it either way, so it's your choice if you want to be holding it in a container or if you want it down the front of your Walmart shirt."

"It's not a Walmart shirt," I say, skirting my eyes down to the thin, billowy top I'd actually scored from Savers. And then for reasons I will never understand, I hold out my left hand. A moment later, there is a venti mocha Frappuccino weighing my grip. I gasp and it falls to the ground, bursting apart just far enough away to miss my booted feet.

"Well, that was a waste," Jaimie mutters, and I bring the small red phone to eye level once more.

"What the hell was that?" I bark, and Jaimie shrinks back, growing smaller in the screen.

"I'm a genie," she offers weakly, giving a faint, almost unperceivable shrug.

I dart down the next alley we come to and rest my back against the brick wall of an office building. When we're alone, save for the cat digging through a nearby garbage tin, I sigh deeply. "Genies don't exist," I murmur through my teeth, annoyed by how much it sounds like I'm trying to convince myself of this. "But... if they did, what would one be doing in a cell phone?"

"They do exist. And it's my job."

"Your job."

"Yes."

"And why..."

Jaimie stares at me, waiting, and after a moment, I reluctantly give in. "Why would a genie need a job? You just made coffee appear. You could just... poof! House, car, money, food..."

"It just gets... lonely and boring, otherwise," she says quietly. "And I like what I do. Usually." She points one tiny unpolished finger at me. "I have an abnormally difficult client at the moment."

"I'm not your client," I tell her, "so you can relax. I'm returning you, remember?"

"I remember. Your loss, Walmart."

I want to ignore her but it's too late for that. She's piqued my curiosity. "Yeah? How? What do you have to offer? Will you narrate my GPS tracking? Announce the weather when prompted? Oh, I know... maybe you can post automatically to Facebook for me. Let the world know when I'm mowing on chicken fingers or update them on my current mood."

Jaimie shakes her head slowly. The cat from the garbage tin is slinking closer, meowing in my direction as it moves. Cats *used* to make the top five of my pet peeves list, back before I had to make room for Jaimie.

"I could change your life," she says, this time more feebly, more resigned. I move her into my bag, searching for the best pocket to place her in. I don't need her commentary for the rest of the walk.

"Mm-hm," I answer, "and yet you can't tell me how you'd do that."

There's a long pause, and then she coughs. Or laughs. I can't tell because she's partially smothered. "I'd grant you a wish," she says. I roll my eyes and pretend not to hear her. Then she screams. "I SAID, I CAN GRANT YOU A WISH!"

I dig Jaimie out of my bag for the *last* time and glare at her. I'm one comment away from ditching her in this alley and sucking up the fifteen dollar monthly payments for the rest of my life, if necessary.

"A wish," I repeat. "Like in *Aladdin*?" I'm laughing now, and from the scrunched look on her face, I know I'm not the first to compare her to a Disney movie.

She sighs. "Sort of like *Aladdin*," she concedes finally. "Only I'm in a phone. Not a lamp. And you get one wish. Not three. I'm running a business here, not a charity."

———— ⌖ ————

The Tech Buoy stand is closed when we reach the mall and I set Jaimie on its empty countertop, pointing her aggressively toward the handwritten sign that reads, "Closed for Renovations."

"What?" she asks, turning from me to the sign, then back again. "How would I have known?"

"I think the better question is, how does anyone renovate an eight-by-ten store on wheels!" I snap, catching the attention of a passing mall security officer. He tilts his head in my direction but doesn't linger. It's clear he's enjoying his brand new Segway.

"There's another branch a few towns over," Jaimie offers, arms reaching up to set the time on the phone's digital clock like it's a roadside pylon sign.

"They'll be closed by the time I'm off work," I counter.

"Then we go tomorrow."

"I'm not keeping you for another night."

"It's not all rainbows and cupcakes for me either, you know," she argues, her voice growing just slightly louder. I wonder what would happen if she somehow found her way beneath a faucet or into the bowl of a toilet, but a tiny, traitorous part of me argues that might lean toward murder. I sigh, tossing Jaimie none-too-gently into my water-free purse. Perhaps she really can read minds, because she says nothing the rest of the way to the

Sneaker Outlet, not even when I load her and my bag into a locker in the back. By lunchtime, I've almost forgotten about the possessed little phone.

"I've made a list," Jaimie tells me, a piece of paper held between her hands. I've tilted the phone against a napkin dispenser on a food court tabletop. My choice lunch is a large fry and some sweet-and-sour sauce from Burger King. Inside the screen, Jaimie munches on virtual carrots.

"Do tell, of what?" I ask, employing a British accent for no reason other than that I can. She doesn't even glance up.

"Potential wishes. It's the only solution. You make a wish, I disappear. Your iPhone becomes a standard iPhone. You can store it away until the renovations have ended and be done with all of this."

"I can make it even simpler in that case," I say, upending the fry container into my mouth. "I wish that you would disappear. You and the—"

"No!" Jaimie gasps, plugging a finger into each of her ears. She squeezes her eyes shut and begins humming, her knees bouncing up and down. After a minute, one eye slowly opens and she peers up at me, I think to gauge whether or not I'm still talking. "Seriously, don't do that. I can't ignore a direct wish. If you'd finished that sentence, your only wish would be gone. Now listen," she says, waving her palms when she sees I'm about to protest. "Here are my ideas. First, a new wardrobe."

I glance down at the shirt she'd mocked earlier and at the well-worn pair of jeans hugging my thighs just a little too tightly. "Next," I say.

"Romance," she trills, wiggling all ten of her fingers and dropping the paper into her lap. "I saw you looking at that construction worker earlier."

"No I wasn't," I protest, heat rising in my cheeks. "Next."

She smiles and shakes her head as she reaches for the fallen list. "A rent-free apartment?"

My eyes widen and I stare at her, mouth gaping. "Now, that's where you should have started!" Jaimie glares at me, her mouth drawn into a thin, flat line. "What?"

"Money. It's always about the money."

"What about the wardrobe you mentioned first? That's money!"

"*That* is necessary," she says, eyes following her finger as she gestures up and down along my torso. "You can live without the rent-free."

"My wardrobe is fine. Everything is fine," I say, scooping her onto my empty tray.

"No it isn't, Walmart. You're lonely, poorly dressed, and fueling yourself on fast food and frozen dinners."

"And you're on your way to the local dump," I say, tipping the tray into the swinging door of the trash can. I catch the little red hell device at the final moment, Jaimie's scream ringing down the cafeteria aisle like some weird, obnoxious ringtone.

"I've got it," she tells me once she's collected her scattered wits. She brushes her hands down along her billowing pants and runs them agitatedly through her short hair. "What you need is a new personality."

"What I need is for you to send me back."

"Back where?"

"Way back. Before the dawn of the portable phone. Actually... before the dawn of the telephone, period."

She waves her hands above her head and lets out an enormous sigh. "If that's your honest wish, you need to be clearer. I'm done caring whether or not you waste your only one."

I give the idea honest consideration but never end up answering her.

———⬡———

Tech Buoy remains closed for a week, though not one minute of renovations takes place, and I find myself unwilling to journey to one of its sister stores. For the first few days, I alternate between shoving Jaimie into cushioned areas like my purse or the couch and begging her to act like a normal phone. She gets less annoying, gradually, and eventually begins to placate me on occasion by offering up the daily forecast or finding coupons.

Now we're settled into our nightly routine, Jaimie propped up on the dining table/kitchen table/desk against a roll of paper towels as we share a meal, sort of. She's chewing on raw lettuce while I spin my fork through a plastic dish of Hungry-Man spaghetti. If she thinks I haven't noticed her not-so-subtle food choice hints, I have. The half-container of parmesan cheese that I ladled over the noodles was really just to spite the health-conscious, little, virtual annoyance.

Her clean eating is almost as irritating as her ever-growing list of potential wishes, but I'm fast learning to ignore both. At last count, she'd reached one hundred and sixty four different ideas, ranging from a puppy to a convertible to a two-week Italian vacation. At one point, I'd asked her for one billion dollars, but she denied me, despite saying it wasn't possible for her to fulfill.

"There are limitations," she'd explained, and I'd nearly fallen off of my chair with laughter. One *million* dollars, if you're curious, is the maximum genie payout.

"You're off for two days, right?" she asks, spinning the Pinterest icon beside her like she's the host of Wheel of Fortune. I nod hesitantly, a string of pasta hanging from my mouth.

"Why?"

She shrugs. "I was thinking we'd drive upstate. There are some cabin rentals there I want to check out. It's off-season, so they're half price, but the view is still nice."

"Are you asking me out?"

She scowls and glances up from her lettuce bowl. "I thought it would be fun," she whines, "And look! I've got a Groupon." She uncurls her legs and stands, waving her hand at the screen behind her. A coupon slides out from the left, advertising a lakeside wood cabin for only $55 a night. I shove some spaghetti in my mouth to keep from smiling.

"Maybe it will inspire you," she adds. "You'll decide on your wish." Her tone is different, lower than usual, and she glances down, picking at the skin around her nails.

"I don't know," I tell her. "Nothing has so far. I told you, I don't need anything."

"You need lots of things, actually. Some are even beyond my ability to give you."

"Like what?" I ask, regretting almost at once the trap that I've stepped so willingly into.

She holds up five fingers, tapping each one in turn as she speaks. "Sense of humor, compassion, understanding of fashion, healthy eating habits..."

"All right, all right," I say, licking the last of the pasta sauce from my fingers. "I really don't want anything, though."

She sighs, bending to a half-seated position before leaping up straight, eyes nearly as wide as the bowl she still carries. "Oh. My. God," she whispers, staring at me. One of her hands comes up to cover her mouth and I wipe at the edges of my mine, suddenly self-conscious.

"What?" I ask. When she doesn't answer, I lift the phone from the table. "What?"

She lowers her hand, a grin forming at the corners of her lips.

"You aren't *planning* to make a wish," she says, drawing out each word as if testing it out for the first time. "You're planning to keep me."

"What? No!" I exclaim, dropping a dirty paper towel over the screen of the phone.

"You are!" she says, her silhouette moving behind the thin sheet. "You want to keep me!"

"No, I don't."

"You do! That explains why you're the first person I've met who has trouble thinking of a single wish! Everyone else has the opposite problem. They can't narrow their wishes down." I pull away the paper towel and cross my arms, setting Jaimie on the short tiled countertop.

"Perhaps I'm just not as vain. Or needy. Or materialistic," I argue.

"Yes, or... perhaps you like me. Just say it. Come on. Say you're keeping me. Come on, roomie! Say it!"

"All right!" I shout, my eyebrows pulling down as I push away from the table. My chair squeaks against the freshly cleaned floor.

"All right?" she repeats, her voice a soft echo of mine.

"All right," I concede, wondering how soon I'll regret the words even as I say them. I rub my thumbs in circles over my temples, groaning.

"All right," she says again, and this time, she's grinning. "You're keeping me."

"Not for fifteen dollars a month, though," I tell her, waving one finger in the air. "I'm not paying you for increased blood pressure and a shortened life expectancy."

She laughs, tucking her legs up in what I've found is her usual way and hovering in the center of the screen. "All right, Walmart. I have an idea. But... I'm going to need two minutes of your time."

Customer Support

by Stevehen Warren

———— ⊂⫘⊃ ————

Customer Incident #34976
Monday, August 8, 3 p.m.

AMY: Thank you for calling iPhone technical support. Together I hope that we can form a bond of trust which will help you with your resolve any complications today. My name is Amy, and I am very pleased to be...

ROBERT: I have an issue, a really huge issue.

AMY: Of course you do, sir. Now if you would let me finish my introduction so that we can address your problem today.

ROBERT: Is that necessary?

AMY: Introductions are always necessary, sir. It's what separates us from animals.

ROBERT: Dogs sniff each other when they meet. Look, I'm not trying to be difficult, but I think we should be able to deviate from the standard practices this one time. Like I said, this is a big issue.

AMY: While dogs do have basic communication methods, they have yet to advance to the wonders of the technological age. It makes you wonder, doesn't it? I understand your frustration, but as part of me helping you today we have to do our best to keep to protocol. A protocol which includes managerial overview of every conversation. Too many poor manager marks, and my reward for outstanding customer service, which includes a trip to Hawaii, is as good as canceled. That said, thank you for calling iPhone technical support. Together I hope...

ROBERT: Nice to meet you, Amy. I have a small problem with a blender, and I hope you can help me today.

AMY: Are you sure you have the right help number? I do not believe we make a blender or blender-like product, sir.

ROBERT: Yeah, I know that.

AMY: Won't it be easier to call the manufacturer of the blender? I can locate a service number for them, if you like. It won't be any trouble.

ROBERT: Trust me, I tried calling them. They were unhelpful, but they gave me your number. So hopefully you'll fare a bit better than they did. You're off to a bad start, though. Just putting that out there.

AMY: I don't understand. Maybe we should just start over from the beginning.

ROBERT: Are we going to do the introduction line again?

AMY: I can if you like, sir, but I think we can move forward.

ROBERT: Robert. My name is Robert Mullins.

AMY: It's nice to meet you, Mr. Mullins. What is your account number?

ROBERT: I don't really have an account number, per se, and calling me Robert is just fine.

AMY: Okay, Robert, customers misplace their account numbers all the time. It's not a problem; I can happily look up your account through the number located on the back of your iPhone. Just flip that little guy over and read the number so we can proceed.

<MUFFLED RUSTLING>

ROBERT: There's only the Roman numeral one. It's etched in what looks like gold, if that helps you any.

AMY: I'm sorry I didn't clarify—you're going to need to remove any vanity covers or casings you have on the phone, on the back of the actual phone...

ROBERT: There's no case. It's just a pearl white phone with a giant Roman numeral one etched on the back.

AMY: Sir, in the history of our company, we've made more than 700 million phones. The possibility that you have the first phone made...

ROBERT: Do you think this could be the first phone? That might explain some of the quirkiness of this thing.

AMY: To my knowledge, this company has never branded a phone with a golden Roman numeral.

ROBERT: How can you really say that? Were you there when the first one came off the production line?

AMY: No.

ROBERT: So you can't say for certain that there wasn't a limited edition phone constructed with a gold number etched on the back? It's a feasible possibility that the item could exist and is currently in my possession.

AMY: Where did you get the phone in the first place?

ROBERT: It came in an unmarked package one day. Thought it was cool, so I kept it.

AMY: You didn't think of returning it? Most people would've returned it.

ROBERT: Since I didn't order it, technically it was a gift. There is legal precedent here, and come on, it's an iPhone. How many times do you have a chance to get a free phone?

AMY: What company do you have as your phone carrier?

ROBERT: I don't really have one.

AMY: I don't understand. You have to have a provider. The phone doesn't work without one.

ROBERT: It just *works*, okay. Strangest thing, really, perfect reception anywhere I go. You should see the people on the subway. Really pisses them off. To think about it, I've never even had to charge it. It does have this strange feature where it translates every video into Chinese. Not translate—that's the wrong term. The actors all speak Chinese, all of them. Their lips move perfectly with the words. Have you ever watched Brad Pitt speak in Chinese on a daytime American talk show? It's a little unnerving, to say the least.

AMY: Can't say I have. Let me just wrap my head around this. So to clarify, you received a in the mail an iPhone that you didn't order in an unmarked box. Instead of returning it to your mail carrier, you just decided to use it. This phone has an unlimited battery and a reception impossible by our or any phone in existence.

ROBERT: In a nutshell, Amy, but I feel you glazed over the Chinese part. Like I said before, it's pretty creepy.

AMY: Can I ask a serious question? Is this a prank call, Robert? Are you having a little laugh at my expense? Is this even remotely funny to you?

ROBERT: What? No. Why would I make this up?

AMY: Sir, as a member of iPhone support, I am authorized to terminate any call I deem to be mischievous or perverse in nature. This falls into the first category with the potential of graduating to the second. I suggest that you seek psychological support and/or discover a hobby for your entertainment, Mr. Mullins.

ROBERT: Wait—

<CALL TERMINATED>

Monday, August 8, 3:25 p.m.

AMY: Thank you for calling iPhone technical support. Together I hope that we can form a bond of trust which will help you resolve any complications today. My name is Amy, and I am very pleased to be of service. This is an American support line; I am currently in St. Louis and it's a rainy day, but that's okay. It just means we have to move the office inside today. That's not a very funny joke, but I work with what they give me. What is your name and customer number?

ROBERT: That's a damn fine introduction, Amy. Sorry I cut it short before; it was completely worth the wait. I'm not sure why you had to mention that you were in St. Louis. It's Robert, by the way.

<CALL TERMINATED>

Monday, August 8, 3:32 p.m.

AMY: Thank you for calling iPhone technical—

ROBERT: Will you please stop hanging up on me?

AMY: Robert, there are currently more than four hundred people handling numerous customer support issues. The likelihood of you getting me multiple times—

ROBERT: I'm assuming the phone is magic, Amy, possibly witchcraft, but I'm not sure. It's starting to freak me out. Anyway, that's not really important. So the blenders...

AMY: Blenders, plural? There's more than one?

ROBERT: Quite a few more.

AMY How many more?

ROBERT: Thirty-five, not counting the ones I've given out to friends and family members.

AMY: Wait, just start over.

ROBERT: I'm at home one day when the mailman drops off this unmarked box. Inside, there's this blender.

AMY: So you kept it. Of course you kept it. Why wouldn't you keep it?

ROBERT: The next day, the second one showed up. Same as the first, even down to the slight dents on the outside box. The day after that, well, you guessed it, same deal. A nice shiny new blender. I gave that one to my mother. She loves it. Looking back, I suppose I should've never taken that picture.

AMY: You took a picture of yourself giving your mother a blender? If you don't mind me saying, that's a bit of an odd moment to keep for prosperity.

ROBERT: No, I took the picture at the mall with my girlfriend at the time. I'm single now, if that means anything...

AMY: That's completely irrelevant, Robert.

ROBERT: Worth a shot. Anyway, she was dragging me through some home goods store, picking out these horribly decorated dishes. I was phoning it in, completely bored out of my mind, looking around for anything to distract me from the urge of plunging my body into a fork display. That's when I first saw it.

AMY: Let me take a guess: it was the blender.

ROBERT: I don't know if it was the display lights or how they set it up with plastic food surrounding it, but I just knew I needed a picture of this glorious cherry-colored culinary piece of art. It called to me, pulled me toward it. The next thing I knew, I took my phone and clicked a picture. I thought it would make a cool wallpaper.

AMY: Of all the things you could've possibly taken a picture of in the entire world, why did you choose a blender?

ROBERT: It's not just a blender. It's one of those industrial models, the kind where you can throw a brick into it, and after a minute, you've got yourself a fine dust. It's pretty sweet, actually. You would be surprised by how much it's changed my diet.

AMY: So, bored out of your mind, you took a picture of a random blender, and every morning after taking said picture, you've received that same blender model in the mail from some mysterious figure.

ROBERT: Nutshell again, Amy, you're good at this. I still think the root of the issue is the phone, though.

AMY: Have you tried taking a picture of anything else?

ROBERT: That's where it gets strange. The phone's memory says it's full. I can't even add an mp3 to it. Have you ever tried to work out to Chinese *Jeopardy*? It's not easy.

AMY: Why don't you just delete the original picture?

ROBERT: Amy, do you know what I do for a living?

AMY: I'm not sure how that is related.

ROBERT: Do you like medieval times? You know, dragons and castles and such? Well, I happen to be a knight.

AMY: You're a knight?

ROBERT: Yes, of the medieval realm of—

<CALL TERMINATED>

Monday, August 8, 3:45 p.m.

AMY: Robert, if this is you...

ROBERT: You didn't let me finish.

AMY: I'm not sure I want you to.

ROBERT: I'm not actually a knight. That would be completely ridiculous. I just work as one. Are you familiar with the concept of theme restaurants? Well, you happen to be talking to the Red Knight of Condiments, slaying the flavorless meat offerings of the Black Knight, who tends to be a little grill-heavy in my opinion. From across the arena, I can tell when a customer is going to need a dab of ketchup or a dash of hot sauce. Now, to be fair, it's not a career that uses my college degree, but the economy is rough. Needless to say, I'm good at my job. I'm in line for a promotion.

AMY: Why are you telling me this?

ROBERT: I'm not an idiot. It's very important that you understand that. I might not be the most technologically savvy person, but at the same time, you don't see me criticizing condiment selection at some random food court. That would by just rude. Speaking of rude, I think you owe me an apology.

AMY: I am sorry that you took what I said as an insult to your intelligence.

ROBERT: Apology happily accepted. For the record, I've tried numerous times to delete the picture, but it simply doesn't work. The process just caused the picture to bounce manically. I think the phone is mocking me.

AMY: Have you tried going into your general settings and resetting the unit back to original factory conditions?

ROBERT: Wait, you can do that? Of course you can. Why didn't I think of that?

AMY: In theory, that should reset the phone and wipe anything you've added to it. You'll lose whatever contacts you have or information you've added, but that should slay thy magic dragon of evil blender, good sir.

ROBERT: That's not even remotely funny.

AMY: I'm sorry, I couldn't resist.

ROBERT: That little comment is going to cost you some points on your customer support survey. There we go, it's resetting now. How long does this take?

AMY: We have a problem.

ROBERT: I completely agree. The demonic laughter sound effect that accompanies the shutdown screen is a tad overdramatic. To be honest, I'm not sure what market you're going after with that feature.

AMY: That's not it. Resetting the phone should have ended our call. Why does it sound like you're on speaker?

ROBERT: Sorry, the phone burst into flames. Figured burning my ear off wouldn't help the matter.

AMY: The phone did what?

ROBERT: The phone's on fire. Is that bad?

AMY: Very bad. Call the fire department.

Robert: While using a phone that is currently on fire to call the fire department fulfills my irony quota for the day, I don't think it would help.

AMY: What do you mean?

Robert: Pretty sure the demon won't let me call for help. Are you hearing this?

AMY: What?

ROBERT: Oh, I don't know, the screaming and the wailing. You have to be hearing this. Wait, he could possibly be speaking directly into my mind, though. That would explain the silence on your end. It sounds a little like Latin. It's definitely not Chinese, though.

AMY: Just repeat what he is saying.

ROBERT: It's all confusing, jumbled together like the writings of a handless madman lost in an insane amount of drugs. There doesn't seem to be a beginning or an end, just an endless rambling of words strung together.

AMY: TRY!

ROBERT: Okay, fine...acts that violate the privacy of, or incite violence or hatred against any person or interdimensional class of persons or undead persons, or which could not give rise to civil unrest... It's just nonsense, I can't even begin...

AMY: Those are terms and conditions...

ROBERT: Oh yeah, I think I just clicked the box the last time.

AMY: You did what?

ROBERT: Who even reads those things? Binding your soul to the device, making the desires of the owner... blah, blah, blah. It's like reading a textbook.

AMY: Just get the hell out of there.

ROBERT: I've got a better idea. I'm going to cave his head in with a blender.

<LOUD CRASHES>

ROBERT: Well, that didn't work. It sort of just melted into his skull. I'm going to try again. Second time's the charm.

AMY: Stop trying to kill the damn thing and run.

ROBERT: I have an even better idea. Going to need both hands for this. I'll call back if this works. Wish me luck, Amy.

<CALL TERMINATED>

Wednesday, August 10, 10:25 a.m.

AMY: Thank you...

ROBERT: No, thank you.

AMY: Robert, you're alive!

ROBERT: Of course I am. You sound happy. Do you think we bonded over that stressful situation? People say that's an excellent way to start a relationship.

AMY: WHAT THE HELL HAPPENED?

ROBERT: Okay, so I figured the demon was bound to complete his terms and conditions before murdering me in horrific, unthinkable ways. That reading took about seventeen minutes, by the way. You guys should really think about writing something a bit more simplistic.

AMY: I'll make a note and send it to our complaints department.

ROBERT: Do that. Anyway, since I had the time, I went and grabbed a few extension cords and some duct tape. After he finished, he lurched forward into my makeshift wall of blenders set to the highest setting. Which resulted in instant liquefied demon.

AMY: You killed a demon in your living room?

ROBERT: Damn straight I did—I'm a knight. It took forever to clean it up, though. It's also surprisingly difficult to dispose of a body nowadays. I will never understand why you took that feature out of your phone. We have a bigger problem, though.

AMY: The phone again?

ROBERT: No, the phone works fine. I even changed the settings to English, so no more Chinese. More importantly, the blenders finally stopped showing up. That's really my issue, though. Do you watch the news?

AMY: No.

ROBERT: Well, the strangest thing the other day: there was this factory that mysteriously melted onto itself in China. Thankfully it happened during the night and no one died.

AMY: I think I heard about that, actually.

ROBERT: Did you happen to catch the name of the company?

AMY: I did not.

ROBERT: The Excol Corporation. They happen to be the largest producer of kitchen appliances in the world.

AMY: Let me guess: they're our mysterious blender company.

ROBERT: Nutshell, Amy. I think you may have inadvertently talked me into doing something terrible.

AMY: I'm sorry, I don't recall telling you to commit arson at any point in our previous conversation. I might have missed that point, though, with the demon-battling moment or your numerous attempts to ask me out on a date.

ROBERT: Don't be ridiculous, I'm not an arsonist. Unfortunately, I do think that by removing the picture, we may have inadvertently burned down a Chinese factory. Notice that I am taking equal responsibility for the actions. Still I think we need to bump this problem up to the next level.

AMY: What?

ROBERT: I think you need to cancel your vacation to Hawaii. I'm afraid I'm going to need to talk to your manager.

From Siri to Sunrise: Delivering Perfection

by A. Moritz

⸺◦⟨⟨⟨⟨⟩⸺

It had taken three days, six 'ports, and a climb up a cliff to reach a good spot.

This has got to be the one.

Hayley tucked her hair behind her ears and held her iPhone up a little higher. The camera showed nothing but purple sky, so it was hard to get it pointed in exactly the right direction. After a moment, the barest lightening of color a bit down and to her right allowed her to aim the camera directly at the horizon. The small butte she stood on rose at least a thousand feet above the desert floor, the only elevation for miles and miles. She couldn't really see the sands below but knew they were a coruscating blue, and she was sure that they would provide what she had been missing.

A cool, gentle breeze blew her hair into her face again. She inhaled deeply, savoring the sweet and oddly smoky scent of the local cactus flowers.

"Capture," she said softly.

An icon flashed in the corner of the screen, but she ignored it, completely entranced by what was unfolding before her. The sky was slowly changing from deep, dark purple to indigo to violet. It was almost a full five minutes before the first bit of crimson began to spill over the horizon, bringing with it the glorious oranges and golds of the day. The bright yellow tones reflected off the sands, turning the line of the horizon a sparkling green. If she didn't know any better, she'd think that she was looking at some far-off ocean or immense lake.

When the sun hung higher in the sky and her arm was beginning to cramp from holding the iPhone, Hayley spoke again. "End," she said, just as softly as before.

The iPhone chimed in her hand, and she had to stop herself from doing a little dance of joy. This one... surely this one was exactly what she needed. Her forcibly suppressed shout came out as a muffled squeal. She pressed her finger to the Home button and wiggled her shoulders in a little dance of joy.

"You sound pleased with yourself." Siri's voice was dry, as always, but Hayley had learned long ago not to read too much into the disinterested tone and sometimes painfully harsh observations.

"I am, Siri," she said. "I think I've got it this time."

"You have said that exact same thing 347.75 times before."

Hayley paused in the act of pulling on her jacket and glanced at the phone in her hand. Sure enough, the screen displayed the number 347.75.

"Where did the point seven five come from?" she asked, slipping her arms through the sleeves and zipping the jacket up to her chin. She hadn't really felt the cold while waiting for the sunrise, but now she realized that she was chilled to the bone.

"There were three occasions where you began to speak those words but halted before the sentence was complete. I believe you realized that you were in error."

Hayley rolled her eyes. An enhanced Siri had its benefits, but there were definitely some downsides. "Killjoy," she muttered.

"I found seventeen songs in your playlist by the artist Killjoy."

"Shut up, Siri. Take me home."

"Okay, I'll take you home."

Hayley placed her finger on the Home button again and closed her eyes. She had seen the world shift and bend around her once before, and once was enough. The vertigo had been horrible. Ever since that first time, she kept her eyes closed and let her body feel when the 'portation was done.

Her supervisor was waiting for her in her apartment. She ignored him for a minute, taking the time to settle her heaving stomach and regain her equilibrium. She checked the windows as she always did when she returned from another dimension; the southern-facing one with its beautifully stained glass painted the northern wall with pale roses and a scarlet background. It reassured her that she was, indeed, home.

The wave of nausea and fatigue that hit her wasn't exactly a surprise, but it came with an intensity that startled her. Her knees buckled and she fought to stay upright. Taking deep breaths helped, and after what she hoped wasn't too long of a pause, Hayley unzipped her jacket and tossed it on the back of an armchair, then sank on to her couch with a sigh. The dark leather was soft and smooth, worn shiny from years of use, but the cushions were still comfortable, accepting her weight without swallowing her.

Nicholas, her supervisor at Every World, sat in the other armchair, his legs crossed and his arms glued to the armrests, fingers tapping impatiently. His suit was immaculately pressed, as always, and his wavy black hair was gelled back, not a hair out of place. He fixed his dark blue eyes on her and frowned.

"Where have you been?" he asked.

Hayley sighed. Even his voice was crisp and perfect. She wished he'd slouch, just once, just a little. She laid her head back and closed her eyes, trying to remember the name of the dimension she'd just visited. After a moment, she gave up.

"Siri?"

Her iPhone responded promptly to the query, as she had known it would. Siri's voice projected clearly into the room, despite being shoved into the pocket of her jeans.

"We have just returned from Pomplous, the desert region."

A perfectly shaped eyebrow crept up Nicholas's forehead. "That's quite a ways away, even for you, Hayley. You're going to be fragged."

Hayley waved a dismissive hand, ignoring the fact that he was probably right. "I'll be fine in time for my next delivery run. I've got, what? Four hours? Plenty of time for a nap."

"But not enough time to see him," Nick said gently.

Hayley opened her eyes and stared at the ceiling. It was bland and white and suddenly she wanted to paint it.

"No... not enough time to see him." She shook off her mood and jumped to her feet. "Wait until you see this one, Nick! I think I've got it this time. This one's sure to work!"

Nicholas shook his head but said nothing. Hayley could tell from the tightness of his lips that he didn't believe this time would be different from any of the others. She turned her back on him and went into her kitchen.

"I'll take it to him when I get back," she said over her shoulder. "That should give you enough time to gather the usual crowd."

The words came out bitter and she stopped, surprised. The people who cared had stopped coming long ago, tired of getting their hopes up only to have them dashed again. The ones who came now just wanted to see her fail. Well, that and they wanted to see the sunrises she collected. Siri's magic allowed her to replay the sunrises in an enclosed space, even going so far as to recreate otherworldly breezes and scents. Nicholas was watching her in that inscrutable way of his. Trying to cover herself, she turned a bright smile on him and waved toward the refrigerator.

"Would you like something to drink?" she asked. "I don't have coffee, but you're welcome to some juice."

Nicholas sighed. "I was actually hoping you had brewed some of that Antares roast." He said. "Would it kill you to set the timer before you go on one of these little trips, Hales?"

Hayley grinned. In addition to being her supervisor, Nicholas was also her cousin. Well... third cousin by marriage, but they'd grown up together, so the distinction wasn't really all that important.

"You could always buy your own coffee pot." she pointed out, pouring him a glass of orange juice. "That way you won't have to wait for me to get back."

He came into the tiny kitchen behind her and put a hand on her shoulder, turning her to face him.

"That's something else we need to talk about. You can't just keep disappearing like this."

Hayley held up his orange juice and raised an eyebrow at him. "I show up for work. I do my scheduled runs. I make all of my deliveries and all of my check-ins."

"And then you disappear until your next run. No one knows where you go or when you leave. No one knows when to expect you back. It's dangerous, Hales."

"You know when to expect me back," she scoffed. "I am here for *all* of my runs, which is more than you can say for some of your employees."

Nicholas shook his head. "Half the time, you're exhausted. World-jumping drains you; it wears you down. Other people might not notice, but I do. You think I didn't see you almost pass out just now? What happens if you're too tired to make the jump one day, but you try anyway?" He jabbed a finger at the pocket where her iPhone rested. "Enhanced as it is, that thing doesn't understand human limitations. You could end up floating God knows where!"

He ignored the orange juice she held out and gripped her by both arms, frowning fiercely. He rather looked as though he'd like to shake her. She flexed her arms to get him to loosen his grip. It didn't work.

"I think I want my key back."

This time he *did* shake her. The orange juice spilled and Hayley cursed.

"Do you think this is some game?" he demanded. "There are consequences to using the magic, and you won't be able to avoid them forever!"

Hayley twisted in earnest now, trying to pull away, but Nicholas held her fast, his grip on her arms tightening painfully.

"How long before I never hear from you again?" he asked, desperation tingeing his voice. "How long before something happens to you?"

Hayley jerked her body downward and then back, finally breaking his grip. She lost her balance and thudded to the floor. The glass slipped from her fingers and shattered on the tile. Nicholas took a step toward her and she scrambled backwards, dragging her hand through the glass in the process.

"I don't want to see you in the Hospice for the Magically Injured because of this."

Hayley stilled. She knew what was about to come out of his mouth. "Don't say it," she warned. Her voice cracked. She couldn't look at him.

"He was careless, Hayley. He was an idiot, and you know it. If I could, I'd kill that bastard for what he's done to you."

Hayley cradled her bleeding hand in her lap. "You want to leave now."

Nicholas knelt beside her and reached for her hand. "Hayley, please..."

"Get *out,* Nicholas."

He left her side. She heard the door open, but it didn't close. A few minutes passed. "You can't keep it up, Hayley."

The door closed before she spoke. "But it's my fault..."

Dylan was ecstatic when she finally agreed to go to the Point with him. He'd been asking her for months just to go and see the sunrise, but she'd put him off because she knew it wasn't that simple. They had been friends for almost seven years, and she knew he was hoping for something more. She was hoping for something more as well... just not necessarily with Dylan. She had told him as much before, but he either ignored her or thought he could change her mind. Sometimes, Hayley thought their friendship should have broken under the weight of his expectations.

She dressed casually in jeans and a loose sweater, pulling her curly hair back into a ponytail. It reached the middle of her back in springy dark curls, and was one of the things he constantly complimented her on. He also complimented the brown of her eyes, the smoothness of her olive skin, her "multi-ethnic beauty"—the list went on and on, and the only thing that stopped it from becoming a complete pain was the wry smile he always shot her after he spoke. Though her looks didn't hurt, Hayley knew they weren't the only reason he stuck around; if they were, it would have been that much easier for her to walk away.

The Point faced east, overlooking the city, a perfect spot for amateur astrologers and casual stargazers to see the sky. In days past it had been a favorite make-out spot for rebellious teens. There were a few couples there, but everyone was spread out enough that no one intruded. They sat on a blanket and waited, enjoying the quiet stillness of the early hour. Dylan put his arm around her shoulders, humming the hook to the latest Killjoy piece. The morning was cool, the air still heavy with the scent of a late-night rain. They didn't speak, just waited for the sun to rise. They waited almost two hours for that fifteen-minute sunrise, and it was well worth it.

The sky was painted violet and pale blue, splashed with gold. The undersides of clouds were stained vermillion, startling against their softer background. Hayley thought it was perfect. Toward the end, Dylan lay back on the blanket and rested his hand on the small of her back. She knew she should move away, but the moment was so calm and peaceful that she didn't bother.

"Hayley, when are you going to admit that you're in love with me?"

The question startled her. Dylan was always outspoken, but this was another level entirely. She turned to face him.

"What?"

A hundred other responses ran through her mind. None of them were what he wanted to hear.

He propped himself up on his elbows and reached out to

tangle his fingers in her hair. "Tomorrow?" he asked. "The day after? Next month?"

A gentle pull on the back of her sweater had her lying down beside him. He leaned over her, that wry smile in place again.

"Come on, Hales," he said softly. "The suspense is killing me."

Hayley studied him for a long moment. His dark eyes were focused on her face, and as she stared up at him outlined by that beautiful sunrise, she couldn't help but smile. He smiled back.

"Well?" he persisted.

"I'll admit it when..." She searched for something inane, and the sky caught her eyes again. "I'll admit it when I see another sunrise as perfect as that one."

It was silly and corny, she knew, but Dylan thrived on silly and corny.

He pushed himself into a sitting position and pulled his iPhone out of his pocket. When he pressed his finger to the Home button, Siri answered immediately.

"Siri, I don't want to wake up until Hayley finds the perfect sunrise."

There was a short pause while both Siri and Hayley digested his words. When they did, they had two different reactions.

"Okay, then," Siri said, its tone perfectly calm and casual.

Hayley screamed as the magic took hold.

The iPhones were a gift and a curse.

In 2007, when the first iPhones were released, they were mere children's toys compared to devices developed in the dimension of Galazy. Galazian technology had arrived at Individual and Personalized Home Organization and Navigation Equipment nearly half a millennia prior and had incorporated magic only two decades later.

Galazians hopped the dimensions using their iPhones all the time, and Earth—with its quaint civilizations and fast-food delicacies—was one of their favorite destinations. There have always been odd individuals on the fringes of society, so a humanoid being with extremely pale skin and slightly sharpened teeth walking around with a technological gadget in hand didn't disturb very many humans. In 2015, with the advent of the fifth and sixth generations of the iPhone, the Galazians made an enormous error. They assumed that Earth was ready for magic and introduced that concept and process to smartphone manufacturers around the world.

Soon, *all* smartphones were iPhones and incorporated the Galazian spells.

The results were catastrophic. Humans approached the magic like a game, ignoring the warnings and guidelines set down in the User Manuals and Terms of Agreement. Some went crazy, caught up in magic they couldn't comprehend. Others unleashed disasters upon themselves and their neighbors. Millions simply disappeared.

The Galazians, perhaps feeling some sort of responsibility for the situation, stepped in and placed limits on the magic, reducing the strength and abilities of the iPhones until an everyday iPhone could only teleport its user to specifically set and known locations—provided that doing so violated no laws. And there the magic stopped. Sometimes, however, an iPhone would have a flare of random magic, and unexpected—and usually tragic—things happened.

Hayley had no idea how long she'd been sitting on the kitchen floor, but her body was stiff and her hand throbbed in time with her head. She gazed down at the blood that was pooling in her palm, obscuring the fragments of glass she knew were embedded in her skin. Sighing, she pulled her iPhone out of her pocket with her good hand and pressed her finger to the Home button.

"Siri, would you remove the glass from my hand, please?"

"Of course. Suspend the iPhone unit above your injury."

There was the barest tingle of magic as glass began to remove itself from her hand. Shards the size of fingernails hung suspended amid a shimmering cloud that Hayley suspected was tiny slivers, red with blood. She forced herself to her feet and dragged the trashcan over to catch them, then tossed a few paper towels on the floor to cover the orange juice and remaining glass before sweeping the whole sodden mess into a pile. She yawned repeatedly as she put the broom away and headed towards the bathroom.

"How is my schedule, Siri?"

"You have one hour before you must report to headquarters for your scheduled run to Rhigo, Bellanis, and Hump's World."

Hayley sighed. She'd been to all those worlds before, captured all of their sunrises several times. None of them was perfect.

"Are there any new dimensions available to me?" she asked.

There was a pause as Siri checked. The constant shift and flow of the dimensions was still a mystery to Earth inhabitants, though there was an entire college devoted just to mapping their courses. Hayley didn't bother; she simply asked Siri, and when a new world became available, she went.

"At your usual pace, you will finish in just enough time to make the sunrise in Leglagos."

Hayley perked up. She had never heard of Leglagos before. Siri would give her all of the details later, but for now, she needed to address a few immediacies. After a quick shower, she felt much better and applied herself to a bowl of oatmeal with an enthusiasm that she normally reserved for steak and ice cream. She left her hair down while she ate, hoping the curly mass would dry quickly. She had cut it shortly after Dylan's... mistake, but it was still thick. Nicholas hadn't approved.

At the thought of her cousin, a hot burst of shame and guilt flooded her. He was worried, and he should be. She was the only family he had left, and world-hopping was dangerous at the best of times. Hayley was honest enough to admit that she was far from being in the best shape; often exhausted, anything but well-nutritioned, she used the magic too often and stretched herself to and beyond her limits. She knew that soon she would have to take another three-day vacation for some serious health maintenance and dreaded the sidelong look that Nicholas would give her. But she would do it. Dylan was lying in a hospital bed in a comatose state because of her; she couldn't just ignore that. Could she?

Sometimes—especially when she was so exhausted and drained that she couldn't do anything but lie on the floor—she thought that maybe she could. Dylan had made the decision. Dylan had spoken the words. How was she to know the idiot would make such a request of an iPhone? Hayley shook her head and pushed those thoughts aside. She owed it to Dylan—and to herself—to make this right.

She chased her oatmeal with orange juice, shoved a few granola bars in her pockets, and grabbed her jacket from the back of the armchair on her way to the door. She would stop over in Bellanis and splurge on a steak; she didn't know what they did to their cows, but the meat was so flavorful and tender that it transcended a steak dinner and became an *experience*. She locked the door behind her and took the stairs down to street level two at a time.

Hayley waved to the few people who were out and about as she stepped onto the 'portation circle on the corner. She could have 'ported from her apartment if she'd wanted to, but she always used the circle when she was headed to Every World's headquarters. The circle—which automatically logged who was traveling when and from where—neatly bypassed Every World's ridiculously complicated Work-Related Travel Log. Besides that, it was always easier to 'port from a place where the magic was used a lot. Siri had explained it to her once, something about the use of magic creating a channel through the aether, but Hayley hadn't really paid attention; she subconsciously understood the concept, if not the words, and that was good enough for her. Siri had tried to explain that as well, saying that because she didn't try to analyze or overthink the magic, she could do things that very few others could.

The world shifted and blurred around her, and she closed her eyes. When she opened them, she stood in the inner courtyard of Every World headquarters. Most corporate buildings had strong spells set that prevented people from 'porting in and out, but that would be horribly inefficient for an interdimensional marketing and delivery company. Every employee at Every World had had their iPhone keyed to Earth headquarters, which was basically a 'portation circle the size of a city block enclosed on all four sides by the actual building. The courtyard was roofed with glass to keep out the weather, and the area was meticulously landscaped, supposedly to promote the well-being of their employees. The result was a large, beautifully manicured park that was kept at a constant 74 degrees. Flowers, small trees and bushes of all kinds grew in abundance and several picnic tables were set up to accommodate employees stopping over for lunch. Hayley loved the lush greenness of the place, but she almost never had time to really sit and enjoy it, and today was no different.

She straightened her uniform as she headed for the southern side of the hollowed-out square that was Every World. As a delivery technician for the company, the only item of clothing that she was actually required to wear was a khaki cargo vest that ended at her hips and was emblazoned with the Every World logo. In her line of work, it helped to be easily identifiable. People greeted her as she opened the glass doors and made her way down the hallways to the check-in department and she smiled and nodded in response. She didn't know most of their names, but they had reason to know every delivery technician on site.

"Hayley! Good to see you! Hear you're going to Bellanis today; don't forget to check with Rico and see if there are any 'shinys' to bring back!"

"Hayley! I know you're leaving in twenty, but could you get these 'shinys' added to your manifest for Hump's World? I'd really appreciate it!"

Shinys were small deliveries, usually items no bigger than a palm, which someone or other had forgotten to add to the delivery manifests. Anything that a delivery tech rejected because of weight, time, or irritation would simply have to wait until the next delivery run, which messed with quotas and records. Hayley tried to accept any shinys that were brought to her. Luckily, only a few people had any this time, and she made it to her check-in a few minutes early.

The Controller pointed to a black security cart already laden with boxes. Two feet wide, four feet long and five feet tall, it carried up to 3,000 pounds on two steel shelves, completely encased in see-through steel mesh. The cart rested on four wheels and had double doors on one side that, once locked, could only be *un*locked by its assigned technician. The boxes were loaded into the cart so that every available space was used and so that each individual barcode was clearly visible. Hayley pulled her iPhone from her pocket and began scanning the codes. Packages were scanned upon loading by the Controller, before departure by the delivery tech, and then once more upon delivery, ensuring that each package was accounted for. After the initial scan, the Controller scanned her shinys then watched as she scanned them and tucked them into a small exterior compartment on the cart, built just for that purpose.

"You're leaving the cart at Hump's World, right?" the Controller asked. He tapped a finger on his iPhone. "They need it there for returns."

As the smallest of four terminus dimensions for deliveries, Hump's World was always under-staffed and under-equipped. Hayley sighed as she put her foot onto the step on the side of the cart and pulled herself up on top of it.

"Only if they promise to return it by my next run," she said, crossing her legs at the ankles and taking hold of the leather straps bolted to the top of the cart. "Last time they didn't, and then *we* were short on carts and I had to borrow one from upstairs. The wheel fell off and the thing would barely lock."

The Controller grinned then stepped back and waved. "Have a good 'port," he said, then turned away, on to his next manifest.

Hayley shrugged and spoke to the iPhone in her pocket. "Hey, Siri?"

"What can I help you with, Hayley?"

The prompt reply made her smile.

"Let's go to Rhigo."

"Okay."

—— ⚬〰〰〰⚬ ——

Rhigo was not a place where humans tended to linger. Everything about it—from the harsh, dry climate to the reptilian denizens that had only recently stopped considering humans as entrees—encouraged hasty completion of any business transactions. Hayley scanned her packages at the Every World depot and 'ported to Bellanis in just under an hour.

In contrast to Rhigo, Bellanis was much more pleasant. Mild temperatures and a high percentage of sunny days made it a favorite vacation spot for humans and the inhabitants of a few other dimensions as well. She wanted to linger a while after satisfying her need for a steak and an alcoholic beverage, maybe soak her tired body in Bellanis' warm, clear waters, but she still had to stop at Hump's World. According to Siri, Leglagos would move out of range of a 'port in less than two hours; it was already going to be a very long 'portation.

She paid her tab and waved to strangers as she retrieved her cart from the lock-up. It took more effort than usual to climb atop the unit, but she put that down to being full of steak. The 'portation seemed to take longer, too, and she swayed and would have fallen if helpful hands hadn't been there to guide her to the ground.

"Please, be at ease."

The gravelly voice seemed out of place, but Hump's World was a pretty homogenous mix of all the dimension traveling races, so that didn't mean anything. Hayley forced her eyes open and met three sets of vertically slit yellow eyes in return.

"I haven't seen a Bhilog here in years," she said, forcing the words out around lips that seemed to have become numb and useless. The being smiled, showing double rows of large, flat teeth.

"I have not been here in years, so this is understandable. I am a temporary transfer from the Every World depot on Bhilo."

The Bhilog helped her to her feet, surreptitiously keeping its body between her and the rest of the depot.

"The other employees at this depot currently believe that you became entangled in your restraints and slipped," the Bhilog said softly, tilting its block-shaped head to one side. "Shall I inform them otherwise?"

Hayley shook her head vigorously, leaning heavily on the solid arm it offered her. "No, please," she said, just as softly. "I'll be fine in a moment." She smiled at the Bhilog's doubtful look. "I am resilient," she insisted.

"Then you are unique among your kind."

The condescension in the Bhilog's voice made her chuckle. A Bhilog's constitution was such that two hours of rest was sufficient to recover from sixteen hours of constant activity—which were, as nature would have it, the length of a night and day on Bhilo. They thrived in locales that humans would never even consider, and they could go for weeks without water, months without food. Because of their incredible—to a human—endurance, Bhilog were generally placed in posts that were understaffed, oftentimes carrying the workload of two or three humans, a fact that did not help the towering condescension they felt and showed towards the human race. They preferred to remain on Bhilo, but the few who traveled were extremely friendly and found humans fascinating. This Bhilog was looking at her curiously now.

"You seem to be in a hurry," it said, watching as she hastily scanned her packages, leaning against the cart for support. "I was made to understand that Hump's World is a terminus for delivery runs."

Hayley gestured toward her packages to indicate that he should begin his check. "It is," she said, "but I have somewhere I'd like to be by its sunrise."

The Bhilog shrugged its broad shoulders and scanned the packages. "You do not seem to be in any shape to make another jump," it said, "but your desires are your own."

Hayley made a noise of agreement in the back of her throat as she compared its list to her own. It was mere formality since she had just watched it scan everything, but she was nothing if not thorough when it came to her work. After confirming the delivery she turned on her heel, nearly running toward the 'portation circle near the back of the depot. The Bhilog jogged alongside her.

"I hope that you find what you are looking for."

Hayley stepped onto the circle and turned to grin at it, pulling her iPhone from her pocket as she did so.

"I'm looking for the perfect sunrise," she said. "Siri, take me to Leglagos."

The Bhilog shook its head. "Humans," it said, the condescension back in its voice. "They are all perfect."

Hayley could only stare as the world shifted around her.

She woke to pain. Her body *hurt.* Her skin ached, but it ached separately from her muscles. Her scalp was on fire, every hair on her head a needle of pain stabbing into her brain. She tried—oh so gently—to raise herself to a sitting position, but her body told her that she could take her unreasonable request and shove it somewhere dark. It wouldn't be hard, since dark was almost all that she could see. Her eyes were open, she was sure, because she could see a few twinkling lights far above her. That, of course, raised the question of why she was on her back, but after trying to rectify the situation once more, she decided that it didn't really matter. She swallowed—it hurt—then swallowed again, moistening a throat that was inexplicably dry and dusty.

"Hey, Siri," she croaked, not really expecting an answer. "Why do I hurt?"

"You have teleported between worlds too often and too rapidly for your body to recover and have caused almost irreparable damage on a molecular level."

She would have jumped if she could have, but her body still hurt. Instead she paused, allowing minutes to lapse before speaking again.

"When did I enable voice activation?" she asked.

There was another long pause, and for a moment she thought that her iPhone had *not* answered her, that she had thought up her diagnosis on her own and in Siri's voice. Then her iPhone spoke again.

"You did not. Such an action is not required at my level."

"At your level..." Hayley took a deep breath. "Am I delusional?"

"You are not," Siri replied. "However, if we continue this conversation, you will miss the sunrise."

"Which...?"

"To your left."

Hayley forced protesting neck muscles to cooperate and was gratified to see a slight lightening of the otherwise dark sky, though tall grass obscured her view of the actual horizon. She thought for a moment.

"You've always been more... able, haven't you?" she asked. "I remember now... dozens of times when you answered me without my actually addressing you or even pressing the Home button." She thought for a minute. "And you usually do what I need when my phrasing should get me a different result."

The pause this time was not as long. "It would not have benefited either of us to reveal myself to you until you were ready," Siri said.

Hayley felt a brief spurt of anger. "And I'm ready now?" she demanded.

Siri did not answer. Hayley took a deep breath and began the slow and painstaking process of forcing herself into a sitting position. She had to stop several times to calm her heaving stomach and wait for her double vision to pass, but she finally managed it, bringing her knees into her chest and resting her arms on them. The pain in her body was subsiding to a dull ache, and so she began to make small movements, stretching her fingers and toes, flexing her muscles. As her body loosened up, she looked around. She sat on a hill covered in tall grass, overlooking a broad plain. Behind her was a darkness that she could only assume was a forest of some sort. When she finished, she faced the sunrise again.

It was slow and odd for some reason she couldn't quite place. The sky lightened from a dark purple to a rich blue and then teal, but the expected spill of oranges and reds never occurred. When the green orb that was this dimension's sun finally peeked over the horizon, she understood. She rubbed her face, not completely surprised to find that her cheeks were wet with tears. The sunrise had been completely bland, underwhelming... and perfect.

"They're all perfect, aren't they, Siri?" she asked. "Each one is exactly what it's supposed to be, no matter what *I* think of it."

"This is a basic definition of perfect," Siri answered. "Most sentient beings have yet to arrive at this conclusion."

Hayley laughed and wiped more tears away. After an attempt to rise to her feet failed, she simply let herself lay back in the tall grass. "How long before I can jump again, Siri?"

The question seemed oddly unimportant. Her body, in spite of its aches, felt lighter than it had in years. Even though her head ached, her mind was clear. She raised her hands to her head and tangled her fingers in her hair, simply enjoying the texture of it and regretting that she didn't take better care of it. She hadn't had such a simple, selfish thought in a long time.

"By my calculations, your body should be recovered enough to jump in two weeks, perhaps three. Personal care is no concern; the natives are friendly and employ a need-based barter system. You will have no trouble surviving comfortably for an extended period of time."

Hayley waited. When no other information was forthcoming, she sighed and pulled her iPhone out of her pocket. She cradled the phone in her hand and peered into the dark screen.

"If we're going to have a working relationship," she said, "you have to drop the 'I'm just a magical iPhone' act. If there's something I need to know, *tell me*."

There was a pause, and Hayley could almost feel the iPhone considering their situation. "By the time your body has recovered, Leglagos will have moved out of range of any safe dimension. It will not return for approximately six months."

All the breath left Hayley in a *whoosh*. "You could have eased me into that one," she said. "A little prep for potentially traumatizing news would be nice."

"I am just a magical iPhone," Siri responded, "but if you like, I can research this dimension's equivalent of a therapist for you."

The sarcasm in Siri's voice was oddly comforting. Hayley chuckled.

"That's okay, Siri," she said. "I think I'm going to be just fine."

Hung Up On

by Sarina Dorie

Tangled in my nightgown and covers, I wake to the vibration of my iPhone in the dark, thinking it's the alarm. I fumble for the phone, only to realize someone has sent me a text message at freakin' 4:30 a.m. I hate to imagine what kind of emergency my sister has gotten into now. But the number is unfamiliar.

I open the message.

After all these years, I still love you. I regret that we never got married. If I could have one wish, it would be that.

I'm so tired I can barely think straight, but considering I don't have a boyfriend or anyone who this could be from, I collapse back into bed and sleep for another two hours before the phone alarm buzzes me awake. As I brush my teeth, I'm slightly more coherent, so I scan the text again. Definitely a wrong number. But the words are so sweet and heartfelt, I don't feel like it's right to ignore it, so I hit reply.

Sorry. You have the wrong number.

I consider deleting the stranger's text, but I just can't quite make myself. After all, it isn't like I get marriage proposals every day, and this is pretty close to one.

Later at work, while I'm waiting for the dentist to come in to check for a cavity in an elderly lady's molars, the iPhone vibrates in my back pocket. When the patient isn't looking, I sneak a peek to see who called.

Same number as before. This time the message reads:

Nope, Larva, I have the right number.

I stare out the window into the stormy sky beyond the red maples. Larva? No one has called me that in years. The nickname originally started when my younger sister couldn't say the word "Laura" as a toddler and called me "Larva" instead. The only people who knew of that horrible name were my parents, sister and... Eric.

I smile. In high school, Eric and I made plans to get an apartment together and marry after college. I haven't spoken to him in fifteen years—right before he disappeared.

It took years to get over him, partially because I loved him so much, partially because I hated him when he left immediately after graduation without a goodbye. I found out five years afterward from his brother, Robby, that their mother was suicidal and manic depressive. She tried to strangle Eric after graduation. When he told his family, they didn't believe him, and it was too much for him. That's when he left abruptly for the army.

It hurt that he never confided in me, but it made it easier knowing why he left. I kept waiting for the day he'd call me or show up out of the blue, but it never came. As my resentment melted away, I grew busy with life, meeting new loves and going to dental hygiene school. Eventually I forgot about Eric.

Could it really be this wasn't a wrong number, it was Eric?

"Ahem." My patient raises an eyebrow.

"Sorry." I shove the phone into my pocket. "I sort of got a marriage proposal this morning. My brain is a little preoccupied."

My patient's weathered and puckered face transforms into rainbows and sunshine. "How lovely. What did you say, dear?"

"I, um, said he had the wrong number."

She laughs like I might be joking.

The phone vibrates again. The old woman's eyebrows rise expectantly. "Well, aren't you going to get that?"

"I'm at work, I really shouldn't..." I reach for the phone anyway and check the message.

I shouldn't have waited so long to contact you. I'm sorry for any pain I've caused you. I wish I had left a note or said goodbye. If I could relive my life, I would have done that differently.

Tears fill my eyes. My patient fidgets with her paper bib as I reply:

It's taken you fifteen years to say this?

He writes back: *Sorry. Better late than never, right? I really would like to see you again.*

All that pain and heartbreak I thought I left behind years ago is resurrected. Why would I want to see some jerk who didn't even bother to write or call once he got over his personal demons? Then again, maybe it took this long to recover from the emotional wounds his mother inflicted on him. Part of me still longs to see him after all these years.

When the dentist comes in, I quickly pocket my iPhone and put on my nitrile gloves. I ignore Eric's other messages until after my shift finishes. By then I have three:

Will you meet me Saturday at 10 a.m. near my parents' house?

Can I see your beautiful face one more time?

Larva, can you forgive me?

I roll my eyes. His parents live in Oregon City, two hours north of here. I text him:

You can come down to Eugene if you want to see me.

His reply comes almost instantly.

Please, come to Oregon City on Saturday. It would mean a lot to me. I'll be at Barclay and Oak Street all morning if you decide to show up.

I imagine his voice sounds sad, but maybe it's just my imagination. I try to call the number, but he doesn't answer. He texts me again on Friday morning, asking me to meet him, and I finally give in.

I drive two hours north on Saturday morning, rain drizzling against my windshield. I turn off my GPS when I hit the familiar streets. I drive down Barclay Street almost on automatic pilot, my memory taking over on the way to his parents' house. But when I get there, the house is boarded up and the entire neighborhood looks like a shantytown. His parents live on 21st, not Oak Street anyway. This isn't where he wanted to meet. I drive around the neighborhood, stopping at the corner of Barclay and Oak. I laugh. Of course he'd want to meet here. I have fond memories of sneaking to this graveyard with him as a teenager and making out.

The streets around the iron fence are filled with cars. It takes a while before I find a parking spot. It's past 10 now, but he said he would be here all morning. I hop over puddles and walk around the perimeter, but don't see him. People exit the cemetery and ride off in their cars, sending gold and red leaves tumbling in their midst. I shiver under the chill of the moist air and pull my sweater more tightly around myself.

There's a man standing inside the gate. Even from a distance, I can tell from his height that it's Eric. The thinning blond hair and slightly paunchy middle make him look more like his father than the young, boisterous athlete I remember. I wave, and he waves back.

I follow the path to where he stands. His back is to me, staring at a grave covered with a multitude of flowers. Even with the cloying perfume of roses in the air, his wintermint breath and cloud of Old Spice cologne—or "Young Spice" as Eric used to call it—overpowers my senses.

"You missed the funeral." The voice is deeper than I remember. I study the face, so similar to Eric's, but the nose longer, the eyes green instead of green-brown. It takes me a moment to register this is Eric's younger brother.

"Robby?" I ask.

Then his words sink in. I look to the name on the grave.

My throat tightens and for a moment I feel like I can't breathe. What? No! He had to wait fifteen years before calling me and now he's dead?

My brain can't process this information. For a long time, Robby and I stand in silence.

"What—when did it happen?" I finally ask.

"He killed himself Wednesday night. Gassed himself. None of us saw it coming."

The prickle of a thousand ants skates up my spine as I recall the numerous texts I received from him in the last three days. I erased most of them, but not that first one.

My anger at Eric spikes into anger at Robby. I remember what a prankster he was in high school. "You were the one texting me?"

He squints at me, his eyes and nose turning pink, but he doesn't cry. "What are you talking about? I don't have your number."

My brain feels more muddled than ever. I stammer, "The thing is, I got this text and I, well, I thought it was from Eric. Do you know what his cell phone number is—was?"

Robby pulls out his phone, his breath coming in little hitches. "You know how it is, you can't remember a number anymore with the way you program them into a phone instead of dialing them." He brings up the number and shows me the screen.

It's the same number as the person who's been texting me.

"There must be some kind of mistake. He sent me these messages on Thursday. And you said he died on Wednesday. Who else could have sent this to me?"

Robby sighs, staring listlessly off toward the distant hills of identical, box-like houses. "It probably was just a delayed message. That's happened with my phone before."

I shake my head. I don't mention that I replied to his texts, and Eric replied to mine on Thursday and Friday.

Keeping one eye on Robby to see if he's pressing buttons on his phone, I text Eric's number. *Are you there?*

Yes.

Forgetting Robby beside me, forgetting I'm in a cemetery and using cell phones is probably horrible etiquette, I press the Call Back option with quivering fingers.

Three rings and then it picks up. A whisper of wind echoes through the phone, sounding like something in between static and words.

"Hello," I say. I hear the echo of my own voice, the crunch of my feet shifting on decaying leaves.

The line goes dead. I jump as the phone vibrates with a new message:

Thank you for coming to say goodbye.

The wind swirls about my feet, whipping my hair and skirt, lifting leaves into the air. The scent of cologne and mint gum lingers for a moment longer and then vanishes with the wind.

Just as I once knew with certainty he loved me, I now know he's gone.

Q-BE

by Raven Oak

Oh my god.

It was a blank screen. The *most* intimidating visual ever the night before a paper was due to Professor Snap-Pants. (If I took the time to explain the nickname, we'd be here all night and I'd be no closer to finishing this damn paper on economics during the civil war. Hey—the topic sounded good when I thought of it yesterday morning!) Either way, I was screwed.

Another C would render my financial aid as useless as butter is to a cat. Speaking of that, did you see the video posted yesterday on YouTube? The one with the cat grooming a stick of butter? I swear I breathed soda... ugh, the paper. Okay, I could do this. I could.

The cursor blinked at me.

Financial aid wasn't my only concern. I could already hear my granny lecturing me on the importance of a college education. "I ain't seen none a college classroom. If that state might could pay your way, you gonna go if I gotta knock a hole in someone's head."

I *had* to pass this class.

Earlier that afternoon, my grade had tumbled as low as my self-esteem. After yet another lecture on how the economy drove the pricing of everything, including that of tuition and books, Professor Snap-Pants had passed back our tests. He had literally held my future in his hands.

My fellow freshmen had ignored the man's love for striped polyester that swished as he paced, ignored his gravelly voice as he lectured us about the importance of studying, and lastly, had avoided his gaze as they tweeted and texted their way through the tail-end of class.

His lectures were always the same—our understanding of this economy could "change the world!" Like anything I ever did was gonna change something as big as the world.

My empty fingers had danced across my used textbook—its dog-eared pages and random highlighter marks screaming my poverty to a sea of white that had bought their textbooks brand-spankin'-new. What could this man know of tuition? He might wear a 'stache that screamed failed '80s TV actor, but he drove a Porche. I'd sighed loud enough for his TA to glance my way.

My butt had stuck to the chair, sweat sticking me in place.

Professor Snap-Pants had laid my paper across my desk. "I expected better than this from you."

I'd almost vomited when he'd said it. It didn't matter whether he'd meant "from a scholarship student" or "from a woman of color." When I'd turned the test over, the numbers swam before settling into a big 7-0. Seventy. Passing by one point.

For once, I had been glad my phone was dead. If I'd had a text message alerting me to posted grades, I'd have decorated the room all sorts of colors. "Professor?"

He'd stopped at the door, but didn't face me.

"I—I was wondering... if there was any extra credit I could do. I know my grade sucks—"

"I don't normally offer extra credit for an introductory course. However, I may have something to help. Let me think on it and get back to you. I'll send a message through campus text." And with that, he'd left me alone in the classroom.

A few hours later, I still needed a new phone.

And a new brain.

And the cursor was still blinking at me. Dammit.

A knock saved me from another five minutes of cold, one-dimensional stares. My girlfriend Alyce, whose frame easily stretched the height of the dormitory door, smirked as she entered. She held a wrapped package in both hands. "Mikala, I've been texting you for the past hour!"

I pointed to the plastic container beside me where my phone swam in a sea of rice.

"Oh, right. Have you powered it on yet?" The do-I-look-stupid face I made didn't fool her. "You did, didn't you?"

I flicked a pellet of rice at the wall. "I did, and it's dead. Officially fried crispy. Oh god," I muttered with a glance at the computer screen. "How did it get to be after five already?"

Alyce tossed the box onto my bed and closed the door behind her. "You owe me, Mikala."

"For what?"

"Retrieving your package from Basement Giant. Resident Assistant or not, he gives me the creeps. How can you stand him in class?"

My knees knocked the bed frame as I fetched the box. A muttered curse or three later, I rubbed my fingers across the smooth label. Water droplets morphed the writing and sent my far-sightedness into a shit fit. "What the hell does this even say? Are you sure it's mine?"

"Basement Giant—"

"His name's Greg," I muttered, but she rambled on without hearing me.

"—said it was for you. You gonna open it? Maybe it's a *luuuuurve* letter. Didn't you tell him you're already taken?"

My cheeks grew warm—not that she'd notice—the blessing and the curse of dark skin. Alyce plopped onto the bed, and I scooched away from my girlfriend's mess of elbows and knees arranging themselves into some weird mix of yoga and sitting. "Letters come in an envelope," I said. The wrapping paper was taped too neatly to be from Baseme—Greg—and I said as much.

"Still say it's from Basement Giant. You know he's all set to get some booty now that your exotic self has blessed his dormitory." When I rolled my eyes, she added, "Honey, you know boys. They get all hot and bothered at the thought of gay women. As if our sole purpose is to provide eye candy or a threesome. I should write a paper about that. Certainly a better topic than"—she glanced at my computer screen—"'The Civil War's Impact on the Economics of the United States.' How can you stand that class?" Without waiting for an answer, she tapped the box and said, "You act like it's drugs or something. Open it already."

I don't know why I cared about preserving the paper. Maybe it was my granny rubbing off on me. She didn't waste a thing. Never knew when money would be tight again, and you'd find yourself needing whatever it was you'd tossed.

The tape peeled up by the edges without tearing the brown paper, which fell away to reveal a white box bearing a single smiley face. My stomach sucker-punched my esophagus.

"What's in the *box*? What's in the *box*?" Alyce cried as she wrung her hands in an overly dramatic fashion.

Leave it to her to quote Greg's favorite movie. I only knew *that* because he played it on repeat in his room every evening. Not that I'd been anywhere near that dank basement he called a dorm room—just that you could hear it bleeding into the laundry room. I popped the top open and frowned.

"Peanuts. Lucky you!"

I slapped Alyce's hand away as she snatched a foam peanut. One handful at a time, I dumped them into the small recycling can beside my bed until my fingers brushed the bottom.

"No way." I pulled out the plastic clamshell wrapping—a hell only second to my paper—and held it up. "You said this was *from* Greg?"

Her mouth formed a silent O.

"As in, he sent this to me? Or was it in the mailroom, and he was going through the mail?" I asked.

"Um, he said it was for you, Mikala. I assumed it was from him, but I guess he coulda snagged it from the mailman or something. What kind is it? Lemme see."

Damn clamshell was closed tighter than Greg's lips at a frat party. I twisted the plastic, and a line of blood appeared across my index finger.

Now the damn thing possessed teeth.

Alyce waved a hand at me. "Give me that thing before you kill someone with it. Oooooh! It's the new Micro-Lunia III!" She made clean cuts all along the clamshell's four sides with scissors borrowed from my desk. The phone tumbled from its prison.

Everything spilled across the bed—plastic, instruction manual, and shiny new phone. "I would've peeled down the top myself," I said as she caught the phone. All $900 overpriced dollars of it.

Her blue eyes twinkled in response. "I bet you would've."

"Kinda creepy, but how'd Greg know I needed a replacement?" I asked.

"Probably overheard me mention it in the hall." She set the phone in my waiting hand.

I'd expected cold stainless steel, not plastic. When my thumb brushed the screen, the blue glow displayed a happily bouncing cube. (How else would you describe an animated cube wearing a grin as it tap danced like Fred Astaire? Way too freakin' happy for my tastes.) My finger hesitated, and the happy cube waved at me. I dropped the phone.

"What the hell? You looking to kill another phone?" asked Alyce as she pointed at the phone lying facedown on the carpet.

"Damn thing waved at me."

"It waved?" Alyce bent over to retrieve the phone, whose screen was now black. "Um, I think you broke it, Mikala."

"Good. I don't want some freakishly happy phone."

My fingers trembled as I retrieved an escapee peanut from the floor. I tossed it and the phone's plastic in the recycling can. It wasn't like I'd never seen animation before—my bank's damn ATM used animation to capture the user's attention—but something about the dancing cube unnerved me.

I fetched the phone and tossed it in the can. Alyce winced but said nothing. "Alyce, I'm afraid you'll have to hit the party on the third floor yourself. I'll catch up, assuming I finish this freaking essay."

She unfolded herself from the bed in one smooth motion. "Okay, but if you don't make it there by midnight, I'm sending up a search party."

"As long as they come phoneless," I said.

Her laughter followed her out the door, which I kicked shut from my chair.

The blank page waited patiently.

Ten p.m. reared its ugly head with all the bells and whistles of snorting myself awake. For the third time.

If *I* couldn't stay awake writing this essay, what would happen to Professor Snap-Pants when he graded it? Damn fool would likely sleep himself into a coma at this rate. I rubbed my eyes and took another swallow of Grapetastic-Flex. Energy drinks were for losers and freshmen like me.

I stared at the bottle's bottom rim, where a teaspoon of purple liquid remained. When had I drunk the rest?

The bottle was tossed into the recycling can where it bounced off something—something that trilled and tweeted. Then that something chirped, followed by a long buzz. Bright blue light reflected off the empty bottle, sending tiny starlights dancing around the metal bin.

"Fine. Let's see you wiggle, you stupid thing," I muttered as I fished out the phone.

I'd seen something like this before—back in the days when software companies thought cute animations would prevent users from wishing they'd die in a fire. It reminded me of Minicomp Clipsy™, and I scowled.

The cube—whatever it was called—waved at me. I flipped the bird at the phone, but he continued his tap dance. Huh. I touched my thumb to the screen, and my thumbprint flashed once before dissolving. The home screen looked just like my deceased phone, right down to the dancing kitten icon for YouTube. Maybe just one video...

But when I single-tapped the icon, a warning screen popped up.

INTERNET DISABLED—Distraction-Free App Enabled.

What the hell was this? I scrolled past two screens of apps until I found the Settings icon. Nestled in the privacy controls lay the offending app. I flipped the tab to disabled. Another pop-up.

ARE YOU SURE? Y/N

I jabbed the 'Y' and closed out of Settings.

Thirty seconds later, a video of an everyday hero saving a drowning cat filled the phone's screen. Just as he leaped off the bridge into the icy water below, a pop-up appeared.

IS THERE SOMETHING ELSE YOU SHOULD BE DOING? Y/N

"What. The. Hell." I slammed the phone on my desk. The message disappeared, only to be replaced by the dancing cube. "Okay, that's it. How do I uninstall this shit?"

I slid my finger across the screen, but the cube held up a one-fingered hand. A dialogue box appeared next to him. "Need help with a paper? Let Q-Be help!"

Oh my god. It really was some new evolution of Clipsy! I smirked at his silly dance, but when he gestured for me to click, what can I say? I was curious, and it *was* after 10. I walked through a series of questions about my topic, education level, even writers I admired, and by 10:20 p.m., Q-Be spit out a list of links as long as my braids, and from primary sources, no less! I clicked the first link and a sea of text scrolled across my phone's screen. The first book had to have been written during the Civil War. No one sounded *that* southern anymore. 'Cept maybe my granny.

My vision glazed over as I scanned paragraph after paragraph. Did it really matter that some economist felt our current economic woes stemmed from war? Yet another blowhard bitching that his southern pride meant more than the freedom of fellow human beings. Professor Snap-Pants had a particular hard-on for those that argued the Civil War caused irreparable harm to the South's cotton production. As the "token black person" in class—hell, in the economics department even—who was I to argue the point alone?

Pick my battles and all that. This class, this professor—wasn't one of them. Besides, with my luck I'd be the wrong kind of statistic if I ruffled feathers in good ol' northern Florida.

My head throbbed, and my eyes were too dry to see straight. Q-Be danced across the screen in a wavy blur. "Need help? How about a tutor?"

I clicked through a few privacy notices and TOS screens before Q-Be danced away. Ten seconds later, my phone lit up with a genuine text message.

Hey, Mikala. Still needing help on that paper?

Who's this? I typed back.

Q-Be said you needed a tutor for your Econ 101 paper.

Yeah, I do. But who's this? How do I know you aren't some online freakazoid? Have you even taken economics?

Three dots appeared as the person typed a rather lengthy response. Then they disappeared before a short reply. *Econ major. Need help?*

An honest-to-god economics major?! No way!

"Thank you, Q-Be," I whispered. I stopped just short of kissing the phone. Had to draw a line somewhere.

How does this work? Do we meet? Work online? Are you even local to Tallahassee?

Even better. I'm in your dorm.

Goosebumps spread across my bare arms. Creepy turned scary. I typed a curt reply. *How do you know who and where I am? Are you STALKING me?*

No, just another student. A friend of a friend, you could say. Figured you needed help.

I should've texted Alyce. She'd set the creeper straight.

Q-Be poked his head around the text message screen's corner and waved. "All of our tutors are screened using a rigorous process that includes a background check, fingerprinting, and drug screening. Your safety is our priority, so you continue to Q-Be!" he said by way of green dialogue box.

The econ major was probably safe enough, but I couldn't shake the rolling nausea in my stomach. I texted back, *Either you level with me, or I'll drop this phone down a garbage disposal.*

Three more dots as Q-Be wiggled his square butt in the screen's bottom right corner.

I heard Alyce talking about your grades in the mailroom. You know how much of a gossip she is. I'm harmless, I swear.

Fine. Where do we meet?

My dorm's pretty big. I don't have a roommate. Lots of comfy chairs.

Like hell. Comfortable chairs or not, that was a surefire way to get dead. I texted back, *Um, how bout the common study, 2nd floor.*

See you in 5.

I stood in front of my dorm's closed door for three of those five minutes, my legs less human and more octopus. Q-Be buzzed a reminder and with a deep sigh, I took control of my wobbly legs and left my dorm.

Alyce would kill me when she found out.

———⟨⟨⟨⟨⟩———

Ten-fifty p.m. the night before a major paper was due, and I honestly figured the dorm's study would be the hoppin' place. Instead of dozens of sleepy heads bowed over books, two students curled up in the comfy beanbag chairs near the rear, one with her headphones blasting some J-pop piece while she messed with her cell. The other—my tutor I guessed—sat with his back to me, his hoodie pulled up over his head.

I spied a beat-up, dog-eared copy of *Economics for Dum-Dums* peeking out from under his elbow, and my face grew hot as I approached. "I thought you said you were an econ major!"

Greg looked up from a notebook full of scribbles. "I am."

I told you so! mocked Alyce's voice in my head. My "tutor" was Greg, and I resisted the urge to flip Q-Be the bird.

"What's with the Dum-Dums book?"

The gray hoodie hid most of his orange curls, but a few peeked out when he glanced down. "I thought it... might be well, you know... easier for you?"

"This isn't gonna work—"

"Wait," he called out as I turned away. "You need help, right? No one knows Professor Frederick's class the way I do. You know that."

"I do?"

"Do you even pay attention in class?" He held up the notebook of scribbles. "I've been his TA for the past five years. I handed out the test papers today right in front of you."

If he stood up, I guessed he looked tall enough to be the lumbering shape that hovered in the classroom corner while Professor Snap-Pants lectured. I'd never given the figure much notice. "So if you're the TA, why haven't you taught a class? Isn't that what TAs are supposed to do or something?"

"Professor Frederick takes the semester's first half, while it's still cool outside. Closer we get to spring, the more I'll take over." When I cocked an eyebrow, he added, "He likes to hit the beach."

I snorted. "Professor Snap-Pants... at the beach? Does he tan his ankles or does the man actually own something other than those hideous running pants?"

"Snap-Pants? Is that... what the students... call him?" he asked between laughs. "I'll never see him the same way again. Look what you've done!"

The girl wearing headphones glared at us as she fled Greg's braying chuckles. She snapped a pic from the doorway, and I groaned. Great. Now we'd be up on social media... together. Alyce would kill me for hanging with creepy Greg.

I snagged a chair across the table from Greg. Q-Be was gloriously silent as we worked—Greg teaching from a book, his notes, or some app on his phone as I pecked away on my laptop's keyboard.

When Greg taught, the creepy mailbox stalker image faded and left behind a normal, polite TA. So normal, it was easy to lose track of time. Midnight came and went. By the very early morning hours, my paper was done.

By the time I dragged my laptop up to my dorm room, I'd forgotten all about Alyce's rescue party. I unlocked the door expecting a dark room and instead found blaring lights and our friend Sam lounging on my bed.

She dropped her book when she saw me. "Oh-my-god-where-have-you-been? Hold-up-don't-answer-I-need-to-call-Alyce—" Her fingers danced across her phone as she took a breath. "Alyce-I-found-her-she's-here... okay... I will." Sam shoved her phone into her hip pocket.

"Alyce's on her way. She says *stay here*."

I frowned. "O-kay. I wasn't aware I was missing."

Sam shot me a look that clearly said otherwise before scooting out the door. My phone pulsed. When I slid my thumb across it, Q-Be waved.

DO YOU NEED HELP WITH A MISSING PERSON? Y/N

I was still laughing when Alyce barged through the door to our dorm room. A few locks had escaped her lopsided bun, and she jabbed me in the collarbone. "Where have you been?"

"In the study. Why?"

Her wide eyes tightened as she claimed the rolly chair. "You didn't come to the party."

"I had to finish my paper. Look, I'm sorry that I worried you, but I had to finish the damn thing."

"When you didn't show, I sent Sam to get you—"

Now I remembered. "The search party... oops."

"Yeah. Sam called and said you weren't answering, and I thought something was wrong." My phone bleeped, and Alyce frowned. "I thought you threw that thing away? Anyway, when I got here, your laptop was gone. Didn't know what to think."

I smiled as Q-Be did a back flip. "What can I say? He grew on me."

"He? He who?"

I opened my mouth, fully intending to say Q-Be, but the G tumbled from my brain to my lips without warning. "Gr—" My hand muffled the offending word, and Alyce snatched the phone from my fingers.

"You didn't!" she said as she tapped the blank screen. "How do you turn this damn thing on?" When the phone ignored her commands, she tossed it at me. The black screen glowed blue the moment I caught it. "How did you do that?" she asked.

"Do what?"

"Phone ignored me completely. Is it locked or something?"

I shook my head and placed the phone in her waiting hands. When Alyce pulled up the text messages, she paled. "You were working on your paper with-with Greg? Basement dorm-dweller of creepitude?"

"He's really not that bad. He knows a lot about economics."

"And serial killers. Are you nuts? Wait, don't answer that." She frowned as Q-Be waved a white flag at her.

"Least you had the common sense not to meet in his dorm room."

I didn't bother to mention we were meeting there tomorrow after class. Besides, it wasn't anything weird—most of his books were in his dorm room, and I still had midterms to get through.

No need to worry her all over again.

When Professor Snap-Pants handed me my paper facedown, I assumed the worst and took crash position—head crouched close to my chest and eyes squinting as I raised one corner of the paper ever so slowly. A few red squiggles corrected a typo or three, and I winced.

"Relax, Ms. Jenkins," Professor Snap-Pants said with a smile. "Yours was one of the better papers this time."

I flipped over the page in a rush. A-minus. An actual A-freaking-minus. The dance I did in my seat resembled Q-Be's a bit too much. Not that anyone else would know that. My cheeks warmed anyway.

The remaining lecture flew through one ear and out the other as my thoughts drifted back to last night. While Alyce sat through her one evening class this semester, I'd watched Greg's favorite movie on his 40-inch flat screen. I'd heard the lines enough times to feel like I'd seen it, but there's nothing like a little blood spray across the screen to push you into reality. It hadn't been as creepy as I'd thought, but hearing Greg quote the lines under his breath had left me with goose bumps.

Still, Alyce and I could recite every line to certain musicals, so maybe Greg wasn't all *that* bad, I guess.

I was three feet out the classroom door when my phone buzzed.

How'd you do on your paper? texted Greg.

Tell ya shortly.

When I turned the corner, I collided into a blue collared shirt that smelled of sweat and earl gray tea. "Alyce! Look!" I shouted as I shoved the paper in her face. "I got an A-minus on my paper!"

"The one Basement Giant helped you with?" She'd taken to calling him *that* again. "Good. Maybe now you'll ditch the third wheel."

She brushed me aside as she ducked into a nearby classroom. Was that a fight? Had we ever had a real fight? Q-Be buzzed in my pocket, but I ignored it. Tears stung my eyes, and I blinked them away. A glance at my wristwatch warned me I would be late if I didn't hustle.

I'd have to explain it all to Alyce later.

"She doesn't understand you," I said as I sprawled, legs tossed across the recliner's arm.

Greg focused on the animated fox on the flat screen. "Maybe she's jealous," he said as he jabbed at the game controller's buttons. "I mean, I am a worthy opponent."

"Alyce doesn't get jealous." He laughed, and I said, "No, really."

The fox flew a space ship across the screen, and Greg gave a triumphant shout as the credits rolled. I glanced at my phone and brushed a thumb across it to summon Q-Be.

HOW CAN I ASSIST YOU?

I was tempted to say, fix my love life, but not in front of Greg. Besides, there was no reason for jealousy. Greg was just a friend.

Q-Be sent a little heart across the screen. What I needed was a good cat video. It'd been ages since I'd watched one, and they were certainly better than Greg's games. I tapped the CatTube app, and a pop-up appeared.

WATCH VIDEOS IN 3-D ON YOUR PHONE. 99¢ TODAY ONLY.

I swiped the ad away and another replaced it.

SHOW HIM YOU CARE WITH 3-D VIDEOS.

Dammit. I was NOT in love with Greg.

I wasn't.

ARE YOU SURE?

Q-Be's pointed eyebrows appeared at the edge of the phone's screen. "Go away!" I shouted.

The controller dangled from Greg's hands. "Are you all right?"

"Oh shit, I didn't mean—I wasn't talking to you."

"Then who?"

Good question. I held up my phone in his direction. "Q-Be."

"Oh, you have that app, too?" On the television screen, the fox gave a thumbs-up before the screen faded to black. "You know, I can't find any reference to him in the app store. Weird, huh?"

"Then how'd you get it?"

"It was already installed on my phone when I got it," said Greg as he set the controller on the end table. "What about you?"

The bottom of my stomach dropped a good foot. "I figured you'd installed it."

"Me? Why me?"

"Well, because... you know, you got me the phone."

Greg shook his head. "It wasn't from me. It's part of the study."

Vomit rose in the back of my throat, and Greg's video game haven swam in a pool of blurry cartridges and blue-glowing electronics. "Greg, you had to have sent me the phone. Alyce said it was from you."

"Nope. She passed me in the mail room, and I..."

"You had my mail waiting for me."

His cheeks flushed almost maroon against the rest of his pale skin. "Yeah."

"Wait—you mentioned a study. What study? Where'd you get your phone?" Q-Be vibrated a large exclamation point, which I dismissed. Another alert popped up, and I shoved the phone in my pocket.

"I got my phone from the same place you did. Look—all of this was disclosed in the study agreement. Did you read it at all?"

After ignoring my pulsing phone, an auditory alert shrieked a fire alarm sound, and I yanked the phone from my pocket. "What?!"

A message from Greg wavered at the screen's top. *Hey, wanna work on some more economics? Midterms are coming up.*

"No, Greg," I said aloud. "We're having a conversation. Besides, don't you think we studied enough yesterday?"

He asked, "What are you talking about?"

"Your text."

"My what?"

"Your text message. About studying?"

Greg's nose bunched up as he stared at me. "Mikala, I didn't send you a text message."

"Then what's this?" I asked as I thrust the phone into his face. He squinted as he read the message, then paled.

"I don't know what kind of joke you're playing, Mikala, but I didn't send that. My phone's still in my bag."

I glanced in the corner where his worn out satchel took up most of the desk's real estate. The corner of his phone poked out from beneath the flap. My phone vibrated, and I glanced down to see another message.

I can help you study.

It wasn't Greg. My stomach clawed its way up my esophagus and left a trail of bile that burned my tonsils. *Who is this?* I texted back.

Let me help you, Mikala. 99¢ today only! Q-Be waved at me. Then he disappeared.

"Where'd he go?" I asked.

"Who?"

"Q-Be."

Greg leaned over my shoulder to better look at my phone. "Did you pay the money to get him back?"

"Okay, what the hell, Greg. It's bad enough to be getting random messages from-not-you, but I gotta pay to get that bouncing cube back?"

"Well, you don't *have* to, but yeah. The makers must have put an expiration date on his free time."

I passed my phone to Greg, text message screen visible, and asked, "Doesn't that look like you?"

His finger scrolled through the texts, fast at first and then slowing as his frown deepened. "Half of these are mine, but... but some of these aren't me. I mean, some of them are... well..."

"Creepy?"

"Yeah."

He crossed to his desk and slung one strap of his satchel over his shoulder. "I've got somewhere to be. Feel free to let yourself out." Greg was out the door before my mouth fell open.

What the hell? First I'd managed to piss off Alyce and now Greg? And I had no idea how I'd done either. And what the hell study was Greg talking about?

My eyes fell on my phone.

BRING BACK Q-BE? JUST 99¢. Y/N

My thumb hovered over the Y a moment before it fell on the screen.

———⊂////▷———

Back in my dorm room—my empty-of-Alyce dorm room—I had two choices. I could study for my economics quiz in a little over an hour, or I could figure out where Alyce was and pull my life back together. As much as I wanted to do the latter, Q-Be's persistence by way of pop-ups reminded me of my grade. Not even the A-minus on my paper had pulled me out of the C zone, so I sprawled across my bed with every intention of studying.

I glanced at my phone where Q-Be waved, flipped, then waved again. "What?" I said, and he stopped, little stick hands on his hips.

WOULD YOU LIKE HELP STUDYING? Y/N

Why the hell not. I jabbed the Y.

FOR 99¢, I CAN FIND YOU A TUTOR. WOULD YOU LIKE TO TRY IT?

No. I had one tutor too many in my life at the moment, gee, thanks.

FOR 99¢, Q-BE CAN TURN ON TUTOR MODE. WOULD YOU LIKE TO TRY IT?

Q-Be tutors? It wasn't like 99 cents was a deal-breaking amount, but if the little guy was gonna charge me for every action, I'd run through my spare cash faster than Alyce and Tom's Chips. But if I didn't pay up, I'd be stuck studying alone.

I paid the money. Q-Be rotated and swelled until he transformed into a large textbook, which opened to display a busy day at the stock exchange.

*A **stock exchange** is a stock market where brokers and traders can buy and/or sell stocks (also called shares), bonds, and other securities. Stock exchanges may provide facilities for redemption of securities and other financial and capital events such as payment of income and dividends.*

I sighed. Even Q-Be regurgitated dry text like Professor Snap-Pants, and I'd paid 99 cents for the privilege. "Q-Be, could you make this a little more... I don't know, fun?"

FOR 99¢, Q-BE CAN ACTIVATE THE LEARNING ZONE. WOULD YOU LIKE TO TRY IT?

My thumb tapped the Y, and the stock exchange's rear doors swung open. Q-Be flew inside, taking the camera with him, and landed in a neon-painted exchange. Cartoony traders bounced, shouting about their day trades in tiny, squeaking voices. Q-Be gestured for me to touch the balloon, and when I did, the market cheered. "You've unlocked a math game!"

Oh goodie. I thought the learning zone would be for... you know, learning. Next thing you know, the damn app would broadcast reality shows. I tossed my phone aside and glanced at the clock. If I left now, I'd be early for class, but it was better than math games and balloons.

I grabbed my jacket on my way out the door. Quiz time, ready or not.

———⊂═══⊃———

The good thing about Professor Snap-Pants' quizzes: you knew what your grade was before you left class. Dude was keen on peer grading. (More time at the beach for him?) The bad thing about Professor Snap-Pants' quizzes—

you knew what your grade was before you left class.

When the pizza-breath student across from me handed back my paper, it wasn't a C. It was a whopping 25, in fact. An F. The professor called for everyone to pass their pages forward, and for a moment, I considered crumbling mine into a ball instead. But a 25 was better than a 0, I guessed, so I slid my notebook paper—ratty edges and all—into the stack heading toward the Professor's waiting hands.

My tears blurred the hallway outside into a mess of colors and sunlight. Q-Be had failed me. Even worse, I had failed me. When someone bumped into my shoulder, I muttered a quick sorry as I stumbled out of the way.

"Wait, Mikala, hold up!" Alyce caught my hand at the T-junction. "What's wrong?"

I held up my phone where another pop-up message reminded me that I could study for the midterm by paying to unlock another room in Q-Be's library. "Damn thing keeps taking my money, and now I've failed my economics quiz, which probably means I'll fail the midterm and then the class, and I can't afford to do that because then they'll take away my scholarships and kick me out of college, and my granny would kill me and kick me out too, and then what will I do?" I sucked in air too fast and choked on my own saliva.

Typical—just like the rest of my life—a clusterfusk. I shoved my phone into my jacket pocket.

Alyce wrapped her arms around me and pulled me close. The smell of earl gray tea soothed my frantic breaths. Somewhere in my pocket, my phone vibrated. Q-Be could go to hell. The phone persisted, and Alyce slid her hand into the offending pocket. "Why's Greg texting you?" she whispered into my ear.

"It's not Greg. It's probably Q-Be."

She stepped away from me, my phone in her hand. "App's named Greg?"

"No, it's pretending to be Greg."

One moment we were standing in the hall and the next, Alyce had pulled me outside and across campus to our dormitory. Her nose twitched as she marched me down the stairs. "Where are we going?" I asked.

"Greg's. I've had it with this creep and this app of his."

I should've corrected her about the app, but I figured it would all come out in a moment anyway. In the background, Kevin Spacey gave his monologue to Brad Pitt as Greg's favorite movie blared. When he didn't respond to Alyce's knocks, she kicked at the wooden door. Third kick, the door opened to display a bleary-eyed Greg. Either he'd been crying, or he'd been cutting some fierce onions.

"Remove your app from the phone you sent her," Alyce snapped. Greg trudged to his futon and dropped into it with all the effort of a slug. "Did you hear me, Basement Giant?"

He muttered something under his breath.

Alyce grabbed the remote from the table. "Answer me, or Kevin goes bye-bye."

"Not my app. Not my phone. NOT MY PROBLEM."

I'd never heard him shout before. "Alyce, it's not his app. It's on his phone, too."

"Well, yeah, 'cause he made it. Look, Mikala, the app isn't available in the app store. It doesn't exist outside Greg."

"Sure it does," I said, but Alyce was already shaking her head.

"Damn thing doesn't exist. Google it. It's not there—no reference to it anywhere, and that's not normal."

Huh. Everything was online these days. Maybe this study contained a secret app? I shook my head. Highly unlikely—there are laws about things like that. "That still doesn't mean he made it. Greg mentioned a study earlier. He got a new phone because of it, right?"

"Yeah, but I tossed it." Greg flipped off the flat screen by feel. "Damn thing kept spamming me with banner ads and pop-ups for that damn cube thing. I don't need the money *that* bad."

"Why didn't you uninstall the app?" asked Alyce, and he rolled his red-rimmed eyes. "What?"

"That was the first thing I tried. Uninstalled and five minutes later, the banner ads multiplied. They spread into every app on my phone. I couldn't even log in to input the grades for Professor Frederick, which, by the way, Mikala, what happened?"

"Ad-splosion."

Greg picked at a nub on his maroon and blue striped sweater. Alyce claimed a seat beside him on his couch. "Greg?" Perspiration broke out across his forehead as he met her gaze. From where I stood, her legs brushed against his jeans as she turned on her best smile. Resistance was futile. "Are you sure you didn't make this app?"

His skin tried to meld with the pea-green cushion. "I swear, it wasn't me."

Alyce fiddled with my phone, then swore.

"I told you, the banners just spread. It's like a virus," he said.

"Hey, my phone's gotta virus scanner on it." I held out my hand for my phone, but Alyce pushed my hand aside.

"Downloaded the scanner from Q-Be, didn't you?" she asked, and I nodded. Seemed like everything on my new phone was Q-Be connected in some way.

It was the quietest I'd ever heard Greg's dorm. For someone without any friends, he lived a loud life with his movies and games. Alyce scooched away from him and set my phone on the end table. "So tell me about this study."

Greg shrugged. "It's a campus study on technology usage. Participants get a free phone that records their actions, spending habits, and stress levels. All the details were in the contract—"

My brain tickled, and I held up a finger. "Greg, I never signed any contract. Hell, I'd never heard of the study until you mentioned it today."

"That's impossible. Professor Frederick said you needed some extra credit—"

"Wait, that's where the phone came from?" I asked.

He nodded. "I assume so. You got the box with the phone, so it must be."

Alyce stood and pulled me towards the door. "Greg, where would this professor be right now?"

"His office or maybe one of the dorm mail rooms." At our puzzled looks, he added, "You know, dropping off more phones for the study."

"Sounds like it's field trip time," Alyce said and pulled me into the hallway. Greg was half a second behind us.

———❦———

If there was one place Alyce hated more than Greg's dorm, it was his supposed domain—the mailroom. When he wasn't blaring serial killer movies, he stalked the mailroom in hopes of tempting some co-ed or another into having an actual conversation with him. These past few weeks, he'd come off as less a creep and more a pathetic grad student.

As we strode into the mailroom, its three occupants fled with down gazes and shrinking postures. To some, he'd always be the creepy Basement Giant.

I pulled a brown box out of the cubby. "But he was. This looks just like the box my phone arrived in, sans the rain."

When Alyce pointed at the familiar blue stamp, she said, "The study's university-approved. How'd he get permission to mess with students' minds and money? I mean, you didn't sign any contracts or waivers, so what gives?"

"We can't go blaming him without proof that he's done something wrong." I shoved the package back into the student's mailbox. "Can we?"

"We've got all the proof we need." Alyce held up my phone. "How much have you spent on this app?"

Greg shook his head and said, "You can't go after him for the freemium model. Most apps work that way these days. It's not Professor Frederick's fault Mikala chose to spend the money. Or... maybe it is." Greg spun around and fled the mailroom. Alyce and I followed behind him, reaching his dorm room out of breath and confused.

"What?" I asked.

He waved his hand in my general direction as he booted up his laptop and navigated his browser to the university staff website. "Turn around," he said.

"Why?" I asked.

"Password privacy."

Alyce and I rolled our eyes at each other and turned away from his screen. For a moment, only the clacking of computer keys sounded until Greg let out a loud, "Ah-ha!"

I bumped into Alyce's elbow as we both turned. Greg had logged into the staff portal and pulled up the approval letter for the study. "How'd you get that?" I asked.

"It's part of the university's new transparency goal. All staff can review currently approved studies by other staff. Keeps them honest or something. Or maybe it was about idea theft. Eh." He waved his hand at no one in particular. "Either way, the study description—read it."

"'Description of Study (please include the means to which data will be gathered): This study will be used to evaluate cell-phone micro-transactions and their impact on the economy, specifically the micro-economy established within the university. Participants in the study will receive a phone pre-loaded with applications useful for college students. While students will be prompted to unlock various portions of the app via purchases, no money will be collected. The application will appear to accept the information while all personal data will be deleted.'" I shrugged when I finished reading.

"We've got him. He's stealing money. Isn't that fraud?" asked Alyce.

When Greg nodded, I said, "Nope. None of the transactions have touched my bank account... at least not yet. But we do have him—just not the reason you two think." I pointed to the project's parameter checklist. "Look, one of the requirements of all research studies is that they can't be tied with student grades in any way. Professor Snap-Pants told Greg I needed extra credit, and suddenly I had a phone. I didn't sign any waivers, either."

Alyce took a screen shot of the approval form. "Now all we have to do is report him to the people for the ethical treatment of studies or something," she said.

That tension in my stomach returned. I wasn't sure reporting him for an ethics violation was the best way to handle it. After all, he'd been trying to do what I asked— give me extra credit. Alyce nudged me with her elbow. "You've got anxiety face," she said.

"I—I'm not sure about jumping straight to the reporting stage. Maybe he doesn't know how crazy the study has gotten, or maybe he doesn't remember the bit about the grades. Look, my granny was always saying that adults work it out. Or they try to, anyway. Maybe we should talk to him first."

Both wore expressions that were a mix of disbelief and outright exasperation, but they followed me just the same. The glaring sunlight outside the dorm reminded me of Q-Be's bouncy, happy self. Maybe this was all just a misunderstanding.

I had a sinking feeling in my gut... sinking like my grades. Maybe he'd be willing to give me that extra credit before turning himself in to the provost. Somehow I doubted it.

———— ⬧///⬧ ————

Greg led us to Rogers Hall: home of economics majors everywhere and Professor Snap-Pants' office. Being a freshman class, Economics 101 was held in an auditorium in the business building, so I'd had no purpose in visiting it often. I'd only been there the once, a week before all the Q-Be craze, and then only to drop off a candy bar for a sleep-deprived friend. At the time, the hallways had been filled with one too many button-up shirts and ties for me.

Rather than the business school norm, a throng of students in *bad* need of a shower gathered at the front entrance. In their hands—shiny new Micro-Lunia IIIs. "Where did you get those?" I asked as I elbowed my way through the crowd.

"Professor Frederick handed them out in class."

"But why are y'all standing out here?" Alyce asked from over my shoulder.

"Q-Be's giving out a prize to folks standing in these exact coordinates... or maybe it's two feet this way... we're not sure." The student glanced down at his feet and took a small step to the left. Then he swiped a finger across his phone and shrugged. The group followed his movements en masse.

A triad of major chords filled the air, and student cheered. "Achievement unlocked! Look, Q-Be's got cheevos!" He held his phone in the air which displayed a silver trophy and the catch phrase, "Q-Be, it's where U-be!"

With the students moving away, Greg motioned us through the doors before the greasy-haired, baggy-eyed Q-Be addicts remembered our existence. I caught the quick glances Alyce shot my way and groaned. "Was I that bad?"

She sniffed the shoulder of my shirt where a bit of dried... something remained, then shrugged as if to say *you tell me*. Greg led us up the stairs and down a mostly empty corridor. Muffled voices reached us from inside classrooms as we passed. The doorway to the professor's office stood cracked open at the hall's end.

"Now what?" Alyce whispered.

"Come in. I can't stand students who stand outside and whisper as if I'm deaf." Professor Snap-Pants' rumbling voice made me flinch, but my false bravado forced me to push open his office door.

Rather than the piles of papers strewn across the desk and wall-lined books I'd expected, his office was eerily neat and spartan. Not a single dust particle out of place. I wanted to ask him if he'd ever used the office before today, but Alyce cleared her throat. "Um, Professor, I... uh, I'm sorry to bother you, but I wanted to ask you about the study."

"Yes? It should help your grade some, Ms. Jenkins, though I would suggest you work harder if you plan to pass with more than a C." He glanced up at Greg and said, "My TA here is an excellent tutor. Perhaps you could ask him for some assistance."

"Sir, I already did that, but that's not really why I'm here."

Alyce snapped out her phone and shoved it towards the professor, who pulled reading glasses out of his wind jacket's pocket. He stared at the phone a moment, then shrugged. "I see you've convinced my TA to pull up study details." He turned back to a book on his desk.

"I'm sorry, sir," Greg said as he tapped the man on the shoulder, "but we were looking at the form and, well, you seem to have broken the university's rules with your study."

It wasn't a professor who spun around in his chair, but a fierce-eyed man whose bushy brows twitched and lips turned down at their corners. Despite the change, his voice remained level. "And what do you suppose you'll do with this information? You think the provost is unaware of this study? Or how it operates? That piece of paper is a mere formality to appease the university donors. Nothing more."

"Sir, I was hoping you'd do the right thing—"

He laughed at me.

And I stood there and took it. He held my grade in my hands and in that moment, I was small.

He saw it and pounced. He rose from his chair, the snap-buttons of his pants straining against his muscles. "Who are you, Ms. Jenkins, to demand anything of me? Freshmen do not make the rules at this university." He turned then to Greg. "And neither do former TAs. Now get out of my office before I call campus security."

The way the professor glared at me sent my feet tumbling backward until I hit the doorframe. I wasn't about to tangle with security, so I righted myself and fled his office. The rattle and boom of a slamming door reached me at the hallway's end, and shortly after, so did Greg and Alyce.

"Why didn't you say something? You don't have to take that shit from him!" said Alyce.

"You don't get it. If he'd called security, who you think they're gonna believe? Black freshman me, or some wealthy white tenured professor? We should've kept our mouths shut." Greg hands clenched into fists, and I said, "I'm sorry you lost your TA position."

Alyce draped her arm about my shoulder. Greg pushed open the double doors and once outside, took off at a run. "Where's he going?" asked Alyce.

"No idea."

Ten feet away, a smelly student bounced his phone off the sidewalk as we passed. "Cheap piece of shit," he muttered. The crowd had dwindled to half, and phones littered the entryway.

"What happened?" asked Alyce.

"Q-Be up and died or something," said one student whose thumbs flew over his phone's screen. "I better not have lost all my achievements. I paid good money for those!"

My phone powered up just fine, but no dancing cube wiggled across my screen. No banner ads either. Nothing but the plain old home screen with a few basic apps.

And my ever-dropping grades.

<hr>

If it'd been my choice, I wouldn't have bothered going to class the next day, but Alyce dragged me first out of bed and then out of the dorm. "Look, he's an asshole. He's a white man with all the power; I get it."

She didn't, but I appreciated her trying.

"Either way, your grade won't get better by itself. Since when have you ever let someone tell you how to be?" she asked as she pulled me towards the auditorium. "You fought like hell for your scholarship. Get in there and fight like it for your grade. Let him know he's beneath you. Didn't your granny teach you what to do 'bout bullies?"

Despite my sour mood, I smiled.

"Go on, say it." Alyce nudged me with her elbow. "Do it."

Gran might as well have kicked me in the tail—her honey breath whispered the words across my shoulder. "Nobody be happy 'til they shoved you 'neath that dirt. Is why you gotta be brave and stannup. Don't be givin' your power 'way to none."

I spoke the words aloud before the closed classroom door. I'd never gotten anything less than an A, never given less than my best, and I'd certainly never given up my power. But then, I'd never had so much to lose. As I opened the door, Alyce stood behind me (though I suspect she was there to make sure I didn't make a speedy exit).

No one looked up as I entered. They were all too busy on their phones.

I took a seat toward the rear as Greg entered with the university's provost. When he spotted me, he shot me a quick thumbs-up before clearing his throat. The provost wore a button-up blazer in navy blue that screamed importance, though her eyes fidgeted back and forth between the class and Greg. When she spoke, a sea of heads tilted up as one.

"Professor Frederick will be unable to continue the semester as planned. His TA will take over for the remainder until a replacement can be found. You will, of course, be given a brief survey about Mr. Klevine's performance at the semester's end."

Greg tried to bury his neck in his shoulders as she shot him a concerned look. Once she left the room, a dozen questions rang out.

"Will his leaving impact our grades? He promised to get me into this study for extra credit. Sounded fun..."

"Is Q-Be gone as well? I had cheevos, you see..."

"Will we get a refund for the money spent on the study? Tuition payments are due..."

The questions focused on the stupid app, and I raised my hand. When Greg called on me, I asked, "What happened to the professor? Is he all right?"

"He's gone. Office all packed up, and his home's empty. No one has a clue what happened. Poor bastard." Greg winced. "Sorry about the vocabulary. I'd just hate to think something might've happened to him, is all."

Goose bumps marched across my bare arms. Had Greg done something to Professor Snap-Pants? When I caught Greg's gaze, he smiled the typical lopsided Greg grin. The smile said, "Trust me, I'm harmless."

There was something my granny always said about "quiet folks"—something about their shouts being the loudest. Before I could think on it further, my phone vibrated in my jean pocket. All around me, phones chirped, beeped, buzzed, and trilled.

1 new email.

I swiped my finger across the screen, and the short message pulled up.

Message from: Professor Frederick
Subject: Final grades
As we approach midterms, you should be thinking about your final grades. Your current grade is: 90. There is no extra credit in this class, but if you'd like to discuss ways to improve your grade, my office hours are MW 10 a.m.-12 p.m.
Professor Frederick

Whispers spread as students read their emails. The time stamp was from 10 minutes ago. Unless he'd changed his mind about my average and set up some auto-email thingy before disappearing, the email made no sense. I pulled away from my phone long enough to see Greg grin before facing the dry erase board. A girl beside me tapped me on the arm, and I yelped.

"Sorry. Did your grade change?" she asked.

"Yeah. Weird, huh?"

"I guess. Oh well, gift horses' mouths and all that. Y'know?" She returned to her phone, and I caught some mumble or another about sharing the news on social media.

All around me, heads bowed to their phones while Greg scribbled notes on the board with a blue, dry-erase marker. My phone vibrated again with another text message, sender unknown. *Smile, Mikala. It's the grade you deserve.*

Had the email been from Professor Snap-Pants at all? And what about the anonymous text?

Greg cleared his throat. "If you'll turn in your books to page 192."

Maybe Alyce had been right about Basement Giant.

Maybe she'd been right about a lot of things.

"Oh, hey, while I'm thinking about it"—Greg paused, marker raised—"if you're struggling and need a little help, I found this great app last night..."

About the Authors

(alphabetical order by last name)

Jonathon Burgess

Jonathon Burgess is rather fond of his iPhone, but remains skeptical just in case of robot uprising. Author of the Dawnhawk Trilogy, he occasionally dabbles in short fiction, which has always been his first love. When not penning tales about sky pirates or dragons, he can be found haunting the Pacific Northwest, complaining about his beer.

Find out more at www.jonathonburgess.com.

Angela Dell'Isola

Angela Dell'Isola is an unusually tall hobbit from Framingham, Massachusetts. She enjoys reading, writing, and the occasional second breakfast. As content and out-reach manager for the Story Shares organization, she spends a great deal of her time supporting teen and young adult literacy. She believes wholeheartedly in the power of stories and in the ability of a good book to change lives.

Find out more about Angela and the Story Shares organization at

Website: www.storyshares.org

Facebook: authorangeladellisola

Stephanie Djock

Stephanie Djock is a writer of speculative fiction and the occasional bit of poetry, memoir, and craft beer-writing. Born in Wisconsin, she lived in England, South Korea, and Indonesia before returning to the States. By day, she is an ESL teacher for refugees and immigrants. By night, she is a student in Hamline University's MFA program in creative writing. She lives in Saint Paul, Minnesota, with her husband and several orchids.

Find her online at

Twitter: @SMDjock

Blog: smdjock.wordpress.com

Sarina Dorie

Sarina Dorie has sold more than 100 short stories to markets like *Daily Science Fiction, Magazine of Fantasy and Science Fiction*, Orson Scott Card's *IGMS*, and *Cosmos*. Her steampunk romance series *The Memory Thief* and her collections *Fairies, Robots and Unicorns—Oh My!* and *Ghosts, Werewolves and Zombies—Oh My!* and her other novels are available on Amazon. By day, Sarina is a public school art teacher, artist, belly dance performer and instructor, copy editor, fashion designer, event organizer, and probably a few other things. By night, she writes. As you might imagine, this leaves little time for sleep.

Find her online at www.sarinadorie.com.

Aaron Giddings, Sr.

Aaron's first mobile device was a PalmPilot VII, from which he proceeded to regularly send emails and check ESPN.com while nowhere near his computer. That he still does this from his iPhone 6+ is significantly less notable than it was in 2001. Aaron lives in South Dakota with his wife and their five children, in an old house which may or may not be slightly haunted.

Find him online at twitch.tv/shdwcaster and SticksStoriesScotch.blogspot.com.

Manny Frishberg

Manny Frishberg has made up stories since he started staring out windows. He has been learning to do it better for the last 30 years and inflicting the results on an unsuspecting public since 2010, along with numerous magazine feature stories over a long writing career. He lives near Seattle.

Amanda Hackwith

Amanda Hackwith wrote "Error: Kappa Not Found" as a happy fugitive from the tech start-up world. These days she may sling more stories than servers, but the nerd level has remained about the same. Amanda is the author of two nonfiction books, including *Freelance Confidential*, and is currently preparing her debut novel, *Hell's Librarian*, for publication. Amanda lives, works, and probably plays too many video games in Seattle, WA.

Find her online at
Website (free stories!): www.amandahackwith.com.
Twitter: @ajhackwith
Facebook: ajhackwith
Tumblr: ajhackwith

Rhiannon Held

Rhiannon Held is the author of the Silver series of urban fantasy novels. She lives in Seattle, where she works as an archaeologist for an environmental compliance firm. Working in both archaeology and writing, she's "lucky" enough to have two sexy careers that don't make her much money. In her proverbial copious free time, she sings in a community choir, games online, and occasionally enjoys betting on the ponies.

Find her online at

Website: www.rhiannonheld.com

Twitter: @rhiannonheld

H.M. Jones

H.M. Jones is the author of *Monochrome*, a BRAG Medallion Book and Honorable Mention at the Los Angeles Book Festival. She also contributed the short story "The Light Storm of 2015" to *Masters of Time*. A devoted poet, H.M. Jones has poems featured in Meerkat Press' *My Cruel Invention*, the second *No More Shame* poetry anthology, and *Feminine Collective*. Jones also writes a young adult online short featuring the undead alchemist Adela Darken, which is free to read at www.hmjones.net. When she is not making up stories or talking to her characters while she drives, H.M. is the full-time mother to two young children, one dog, and three chickens. She is also a part-time college instructor, weaver, and wife. If you want to bump into her, go to a sci-fi/fantasy con in the Pacific Northwest, where she is sure to be cosplaying or doing panels.

Find her online at www.hmjones.net.

Jon Lasser

Jon Lasser lives and writes in Seattle, Washington. His stories have appeared in *Penumbra*, *Fourteen Hills*, and *Writers of the Future*, volume 32. When not writing, working in technology, or taking care of his family, Jon scuba dives. He prefers the Northwest's cold-water diving, but won't turn down a free trip to Hawaii or Bonaire if offered.

Find him online at

Blog: www.twoideas.org/

Twitter: @disappearinjon

Dale Cameron Lowry

Dale Cameron Lowry is a formerly unemployed journalist who lives in the Upper Midwest with a partner and three cats, one of whom enjoys eating dish towels, quilts, and wool socks. It's up to you to guess whether the fabric eater is one of the cats or the partner. When not busy mending items destroyed by the aforementioned fabric eater, Dale enjoys wasting time on Tumblr, listening to podcasts, studying anatomy, getting annoyed at Duolingo, reading fairy tales, and writing romantic and speculative fiction.

Find him online at

Website: www.dalecameronlowry.com

Facebook: dalecameronlowry

Twitter: @DaleCLowry

Tumblr: dalecameronlowry

Goodreads: www.goodreads.com/dalecameronlowry

Pinterest: www.pinterest.com/daleclowry

Kris Millering

Kris Millering is a linguist by training, a tech tinkerer by trade, and a writer and photographer by avocation. Currently, she works at a tech firm by day, manages communications for Clarion West by night, and writes in the spaces between. She lives between the Pacific Ocean and the Olympic Mountains in the far northwest of Washington State. Her fiction has appeared in *Beneath Ceaseless Skies*, *Apex*, *Lightspeed*, *Clarkesworld*, and other publications.

Find her online at

Website: www.krismillering.com/

Twitter: @aithne

Tumblr: krismillering

A. Moritz

Very little that A. Moritz has done in her life is relevant to writing; a degree in marine biology and another in patisserie and baking certainly didn't prepare her for the world of fine literature. She has no newspaper worthy credentials (yet) besides an abiding passion for the written word and a deep love of all things magical. Since childhood, she has created numerous fantastical worlds and is now inviting people to share them. At the moment, she lives in Houston with her family, but you can find her in a few other dimensions—if you know where to look!

C.S. O'Cinneide

Carole Kennedy publishes under her Irish name, C.S. O'Cinneide (oh-ki-nay-da) in her home country of Canada. Her short story "Family Role Play" appeared in *Blended: Writers on the Stepfamily Experience*, released through Seal Press in the Spring of 2015. She also has a flash fiction piece, "Cost of Living," that will be released as a podcast through No Extra Words in the fall of 2016. Her non-fiction satire works are available through the online newspaper, *Paper Droids: Geek Culture for Women* (www.paperdroids.com/author/c-s-o-cinneide).

Find her online at Misery's Company with Ocinneide, miserysco.blogspot.ca.

Raven Oak

Bestselling science fiction and fantasy author Raven Oak is best known for *Amaskan's Blood, Class-M Exile,* and the collection *Joy to the Worlds: Mysterious Speculative Fiction for the Holidays.* She spent most of her K-12 education doodling stories and 500-page monstrosities that are forever locked away in a filing cabinet. When she's not writing, she's getting her game on with tabletop games, indulging in cartography, or staring at the ocean. She lives in the Seattle area with her husband, and their three kitties who enjoy lounging across the keyboard when writing deadlines approach.

Find her online at
Website: www.ravenoak.net
Twitter: @raven_oak
Facebook: authorroak
Google+: www.google.com/+RavenOak

Jeremiah Reinmiller

Jeremiah Reinmiller is a lifelong computer geek, martial artist, and native of the Pacific Northwest. When he's not building clouds (the computing kind, not the rainy ones) he's probably hunched over a keyboard hammering out his next story. He resides in Vancouver (the one in Washington, not Canada) with his wife and their two cats. His stories have received the 2014 Sledgehammer Writing Award, and appeared in *2113*, an anthology by Subtopian Press, and the July 2015 issue of *Abyss & Apex Magazine*. More of his stories can be found at www.jqpdx.com.

Find him online at

Website: www.jqpdx.com

Twitter: @jreinmiller

J.S. Rogers

J.S. Rogers started writing when she still wore pigtails and never really stopped. Her fiction writing tends to focus on the complexities of emotion and most of it is lost in notebooks around the house. Rogers works a day job writing educational materials on the east coast and never gives her keyboard a second of rest. You can check her out on twitter, where she's still trying to figure things out.

Find her online at twitter.com/j_srogers.

Edd Vick

Edd Vick is a Clarion grad who's had stories published in *Analog*, *Asimov's*, various other magazines, and a metric slew of anthologies. He lives in Seattle with science fiction author Amy Thomson, their adopted daughter Katie, a dog, a cat, and five chickens. He's on Facebook, and hopes to put up a website Real Soon Now.

Dawn Vogel

Dawn Vogel has been published as a short fiction author and an editor of both fiction and nonfiction. Her academic background is in history, so it's not surprising that much of her fiction is set in earlier times. By day, she edits reports for historians and archaeologists. In her alleged spare time, she runs a craft business, helps edit *Mad Scientist Journal*, and tries to find time for writing. She lives in Seattle with her awesome husband (and fellow author), Jeremy Zimmerman, and their herd of cats.

Find her online at

Blog: www.historythatneverwas.com

Twitter: @historyneverwas

Stevehen Warren

Stevehen Warren is an author and former reviewer for Rotten Tomatoes. He's published a handful of strange stories for strange people. Stevehen lives in Hull, Massachusetts.

Find him online at

Blog: stevehenwarrenwrites.wordpress.com

Twitter: @StevehenWarren

Kyle Yadlosky

Kyle Yadlosky once saw Samuel L. Jackson ask an iPhone if it liked hot gazpacho on TV. He didn't know what gazpacho was at the time. Now he makes his own.

Find him online at www. kyleyadlosky.com.

If you liked this collection for its
magic iPhones,
comedy elements,
and contemporary sensibilities,
you may be interested in the novel that inspired it.

Cracked! A Magic iPhone Story

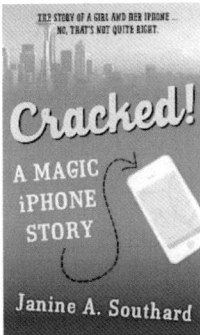

THE STORY OF A GIRL AND HER IPHONE...
NO, THAT'S NOT QUITE RIGHT.

Cracked!

A MAGIC
iPHONE
STORY

Janine A. Southard

*"Cracked! is kind of my new favorite thing
in the world... zany and off-kilter"*
– Taryn Albright,
The Girl With the Green Pen

What can your phone do for you?

This is the story of a girl and her iPhone. No, that's not quite right. This is the story of a middle-aged statistician and her best friend. Though she didn't consider herself middle-aged. And the best friend was more of a roommate-with-whom-she'd-developed-a-friendship. And this description completely ignores the 6,000-year-old elf with whom the woman and her best friend enjoyed story gaming.

In *Cracked! A Magic iPhone Story*, award-winning author Janine A. Southard (a Seattle denizen) shows you how the geeks of Seattle live, provides a running and often-hilarious social commentary on today's world, and reminds you that, so long as you have friends, you are never alone.

First Place Category Winner
in the Cygnus Awards 2016

About the Editor

Janine A. Southard is the IPPY award-winning author of *Queen & Commander* (and other books in The Hive Queen Saga). She lives in Seattle, WA, where she writes speculative fiction novels, novellas, and short stories... and reads them aloud to her cat.

Find her online at
Webiste: www.janinesouthard.com
Twitter: @ jani_s
Goodreads: www.goodreads.com/jani_s

Get a free ebook when you subscribe to her newsletter:
bit.ly/jasnews

The newsletter will keep you current on things like her latest release dates and events. Usually, this is once a month or so, but sometimes goes longer or shorter. Your address will never be shared, and you can unsubscribe at any time. Plus: free ebook! (Rotating freebies mean I can't tell you what the work is right this second.)